Operation Redemption

George!
Thanks for your support!
I'm honored to share
this with you -

Paul R. Hevesy

ISBN 978-1-68517-688-4 (paperback)
ISBN 978-1-68517-689-1 (digital)

Christian Faith Publishing
832 Park Avenue
Meadville, PA 16335
www.christianfaithpublishing.com

Printed in the United States of America

For the One who redeems us all.

For He will command His angels concerning
you to guard you in all your ways.

—Psalm 91:11 (NIV)

PART 1

The Warriors

CHAPTER 1

Isabella

She was nervous. Isabella knew that for sure. The obvious signs were there. The trembling hands. The constant pacing. The solemn look. But there was something else that Isabella noticed, something deeper which led her to begin to understand why the Creator had sent her.

The woman she was sent to protect was scared. Scared as if she had seen something she was not supposed to see, and that something was bringing her to the brink of a breakdown.

Isabella had seen this kind of fear before in a human being, but more often than not, it was influenced by a fallen or a horde of fallens. Other humans would say they looked as if they had seen a ghost.

Isabella knew better. In those circumstances, Isabella knew a fallen had revealed themselves to a human, intending to frighten them into submission. But this, Isabella surmised, was not that. Although the human she was sent to protect exhibited the kind of fear common to those who had been exposed to a fallen, she didn't exhibit the resignation that always befell humans exposed to a fallen.

She was equal parts scared and equal parts resolved. Ready for whatever came next. Ready to complete her mission.

*****

In that moment Isabella recalled when Gabriel had chosen her for this mission. As usual Gabriel, who typically communicated mission details from the Creator to the angels, had told her only what she needed to knows. That, in fact, the human she was to protect was soon to face a life-and-death choice, and she needed comfort. That was the mission. To bring comfort to a woman in a king's palace.

The only problem was that Isabella is pure, raw strength. A warrior angel like no other. If it needed to be broken, Isabella broke it. If it needed eliminated, Isabella was the one. Sharp. Strong. Ruthless.

Striking dark-green eyes, sharp and strong facial features, long straight bright-platinum hair, and a subtle dovish smile gave her the look of a warrior without overdoing it. Standing slightly less than seven feet tall in human measurement, what she lacked in size, she made up for in strength, speed, agility, and fearlessness unmatched in the ranks of warrior angels.

She once encountered a gaggle of fallens during her mission to ensure Joseph's safe passage to Egypt. The unsuspecting fallens were traveling with the caravan that bought Joseph, and none of them realized the magnitude of the transaction nor did they see the sheer force of Isabella descending upon them until it was far too late. The stories of that surprise attack are legendary.

She did let one survive, if only to tell the terrifying tale of what took place that day. That particular fallen would never fly again or see for that matter, but Isabella made sure he could still hear.

It was the hearing part that was so important to Isabella. She wanted that particular fallen to hear the terrifying sounds of his demonic comrades being annihilated for the rest of his days. All of which made this mission of comfort so confusing. She was created to wreak havoc on fallens.

After a long silence, Isabella asked, "Sir?"

"What is it, Isabella?"

"The Creator created me to be a warrior. A fighter. A destroyer. Are you sure I'm up for this mission of a comforter?"

"Not up to it?"

"Yes, sir! Whatever the Creator needs of me, I will do wholeheartedly. It's just I'm not sure what kind of comforter I will be."

"I understand. No need to worry, Isabella. You are uniquely qualified for this mission. The Creator would not have chosen you otherwise. Your mission is to comfort. But be ready for anything." Gabriel flashed a quick smile and an even quicker nod and turned to leave the briefing room. Leaving Isabella wondering aloud what he could possibly mean.

"Okay?" she asked quizzically more to herself than anyone.

"Be ready to leave within the hour, Isabella," instructed Gabriel.

"Yes, sir," she said as she watched Gabriel disappear, now with more questions than answers.

"A comforter?" Sam, a fellow warrior angel and close friend, laughed as he watched Isabella pack her gear. "You better leave your sword then and maybe replace it with a box of tissues."

"Very funny. The Creator always knows best, but I do seem to be an odd choice for sure," Isabella surmised as she was coming to grips with the reality of her mission.

"When do you leave?" asked Sam.

"Within the hour," replied Isabella.

"Wow. It must be serious. We usually get more time to prepare," Sam said.

"I'm ready for anything. Especially since Gabriel hinted more would be asked of me," recalled Isabella.

"More?" Sam asked.

"I don't know. I just got a feeling the way he asked me to be prepared for anything. I mean, he knows better than anyone that if I even sense a hint of a fallen close to the human I am sent to protect, I am wired for action, right?" Isabella was looking for some sort of validation from her friend.

He gave her none. "The Creator's plans are perfect. He chose you. So follow His instructions, no matter what. That's always the first, best, and last rule," Sam said without a hint of lecture. Just a reminder for a friend from a friend.

And Isabella took it that way too. She simply nodded, put the last of her gear in her pack, lifted it over her shoulder, and moved toward the door.

"Bella?" Sam said.

"What?" she replied.

"Godspeed, friend," Sam said with a whisper and a genuine smile.

"Thanks," Isabella said, knowing he meant it. He always did. And with that, she was gone.

*****

Entering the earthly realm was always dangerous. Something Isabella, along with most of the other angelic warriors, liked to do under the cover of nightfall.

Of course, the Creator's warrior angels were always ready to fight, but timing and the element of surprise always helped the cause and reduced casualties. It was not a fear thing to be sure. Simply a tactical advantage thing.

So when Isabella was asked by Gabriel to leave within the hour, she knew that meant a daylight entry into the earthly realm. Which meant risk. Which meant Isabella needed to be ready for anything. She wondered if that was all Gabriel meant by what he said. Or was it something more? Plus, she was entering into a region firmly controlled by fallens.

Persia was ruled by Rusalmeh, and his region was notorious for enslaving human hearts and wreaking havoc on living beings throughout the region.

If I'm going to Persia, I want to be able to fight, she thought to herself, remembering some epic battles she was a part of in Persia over past millennia.

In what was a surprising turn of events, Isabella's daylight arrival was uneventful. It was as if the fallens designated for lookout duty were pulled away suddenly or were preparing for a yet-to-be-initiated battle. She didn't think too much about it as she was just happy to arrive without any fanfare, especially since this was not a warrior mission.

She arrived at a designated grove of trees a short distance from the palace. Her instructions were to arrive and hold a defensive position long enough to determine if she attracted any attention on the way in. As she waited, she noticed a significant amount of human activity heading in the direction of the palace. The same palace within which the human she had been sent to comfort resided. The human activity continued to build, and then she saw them.

A massive horde of fallens moving in and out of the crowds of people, doing their part, whipping them into an angry frenzy. *But angry about what?*

With an eye toward the crowds and the fallens among them, Isabella decided to move out in the opposite direction. Moving against the flow of humanity and fallens, she was doing everything she could to make her arrival at the palace fully undetected.

And she did. An accomplishment with which she was both happy and perplexed. She wondered about the significance of all the angry human activity and how that might impact her mission. She shook off those thoughts and stayed focused.

She entered the palace and found the woman just as Gabriel said she would. And she was strikingly beautiful. Her back was to the door through which Isabella entered, so she couldn't see her face. But her long black hair, strong shoulders, and feminine figure were breathtaking. She sat quietly in a lounge chair, facing an open window overlooking a massive palace courtyard.

The mass of humanity along with a horde of fallens Isabella had seen when she arrived was not visible from this room, but they could be heard in the distance.

Clearly, the beautiful human woman, sitting and facing the window, could hear their approach. She stood quickly and quietly while calling to her attendants. She was asking for water and privacy. They quickly and dutifully provided both.

Now it was just her and Isabella. That's when Isabella noticed the combination of fear and resolve in the face of the woman. Isabella had perched herself in the corner of the window out of which the woman was looking.

The woman approached the window fully unaware of Isabella's presence. She peered intently past the courtyard and toward the massive gates on the opposite side.

Isabella followed her gaze and could make out a single human figure in the dark distance on the outside of the gate. She wondered who that might be but quickly remembered her mission of comfort. It must remain her first priority.

As the woman continued to stare into the distance, Isabella took the opportunity to study the woman up close. She wore a long white dress along with gold jewelry around her wrists and neck with her black hair shimmering in the soft light of the room. Mere inches from her, Isabella studied her facial features and asked the Creator to send comfort for the woman and wisdom to herself. The only thing she could think to do was sing.

Isabella loved to sing, especially in praise to the Creator. All angelic warriors did. It's what they were made to do. To sing praises to the Creator for all eternity.

For this night, Isabella began to sing softly, her voice carrying throughout the room. She sang a sweet melody of love and adoration to the Creator. Her words speaking lovingly of His provision, protection, mercy, comfort, and love. All of which, Isabella surmised, were exactly what this young woman needed that night.

Isabella did not think the woman could hear her singing, and Isabella was under strict orders to not reveal herself to the woman. But in some way, in a spiritual way, Isabella could tell she was finding comfort. Her eyes closed gently, and her demeanor calmed. She stood motionless now in front of the window, eyes closed, arms crossed at her wrists behind her back, as Isabella continued to sing softly and sweetly of the Creator's love. This continued for a long time, a time Isabella remembered as a special time of connection and comfort for both of them.

Eventually, an attendant entered the room again and said, "Queen Esther, it is time."

"Queen?" Isabella said to herself. "I've been asked to comfort a queen? A queen whose kingdom is in Rusalmeh's region?" she again asked rhetorical questions of herself.

"Fine. Thank you," Queen Ester replied, this time with clear resolve. With her hands still clasped behind her back, the queen began to leave the room.

Isabella quickly and closely followed.

*****

They exited the room and walked through a massive hallway and down two flights of stairs into the massive courtyard. They crossed the courtyard from east to west, the sound of the human mob and fallen horde now very close, sounding more menacing and angrier than before.

The queen and her attendants paid the crowd no mind and continued their journey into what Isabella could only described as the palace of a king.

Just then, one of the attendants spoke up, "King Xerxes is in his chamber, Queen Esther."

"Thank you. Please send word to my father if I do not return. Tell him I completed my mission and my life is, as it has always been, in God's hands."

"We will," they all replied seemingly simultaneously, all with tears in their eyes.

"And thank you to all of you who have attended to my needs so well. You have served the king well, and you have been wonderful friends to me," Esther said, her voice trailing off into a whisper.

No one spoke for a long moment. The only sound was the angry mob drawing closer.

Esther spoke with urgency and a sense of calm that Isabella would long remember as a moment in which the Creator's gift to Esther was fully revealed. She was created for this moment, no doubt. But what was this moment?

The queen entered the chamber of the king with an angry mob descending on the palace.

Isn't the queen always welcome in the king's chambers? Isabella thought. *What's different this time?*

As she was thinking this, Esther took her first step toward the king's chamber and toward her destiny. Isabella followed. She expected to find fallens in and around the king's chamber as was usually the case. Many human rulers, in fact, would freely surrender their integrity and freedom for the greed, lust, hatred, and pride that always accompanied the fallens.

But this king was different. The fallens were outside the palace gates, not within them, which was very unusual. Although she knew her mission was comfort, she kept her hand firmly on her sword currently sheathed on her left side. She would be ready for anything. Isabella followed Esther closely, a step behind her and to her right. Isabella's left hand was on Esther's right shoulder, designed to bring her comfort and a peace only known in the heavenly realm.

Esther stopped. And so, it seemed, did the world around them. A very long silence. Esther holding her breath. Then as if starting the world up again, the king nodded, extended his scepter, and requested her to come forward in his presence.

Isabella later learned that was the most important moment in Esther's life. King Xerxes had earlier decreed that anyone who attempted to enter the presence of the king without his permission would be put to death unless he gave them permission by extending his gold scepter toward them.

Because of her extensive warrior training and her built-in warrior mindset bestowed upon her by her Creator, Isabella was constantly on the lookout through the expansive king's chambers. She still was not comfortable with the idea that there were no fallens, so she kept a sharp eye out for them. Left hand on Esther's shoulder as they proceeded slowly toward the king, her right hand on her sword.

Esther made her request of which the king happily granted. A dinner party later that night. The king and a special guest.

Esther quickly departed the king's chambers with Isabella directly behind. The queen had passed the first big test, and while she appeared relieved, she was still very urgent as she spoke quickly and quietly to her attendants who were thrilled to see her. They happily followed her instructions and got to work preparing the feast.

Isabella followed Esther back to her chambers. As soon as she was there, Esther fell to her knees, sobbing, her head bowed low in prayer. Isabella also dropped to her knees and wrapped her arms around Esther as she cried and prayed. Isabella wished she knew more of the circumstances at that moment, but she also knew enough.

Esther had succeeded in her approach to the king, and the Creator's plan of redemption was underway.

Later that night, as the king's court gathered for the feast, Isabella saw, for the first time, fallens within the palace gates.

And who she saw left her frozen with fear.

*****

Rusalmeh.

Right there in the presence of the king, the queen, their attendants, and a special guest of the king.

The guest's name was Haman. It's clear this man Haman and the king were friends. As he walked into the banquet hall for a feast prepared by Queen Esther and her attendants, Haman was accompanied by the most powerful fallen in Persia. Rusalmeh was as ruthless as he was sinister with hatred, pride, and lust emanating from him like an early morning mist off the water's surface.

Along with Rusalmeh was an additional fallen. At once, Isabella recognized the other fallen as Javva. While he appeared to be Rusalmeh's lackey, the fact that he was there with Rusalmeh meant the Persian prince had big plans for him.

Isabella stayed close to Esther, her hand on Esther's shoulder, the other on her sword still in its sheath. Ready. Isabella could see the hatred transferred from Rusalmeh to Haman, his eyes showing the decay his spirit was, at that moment, undertaking. Isabella never took her eyes off Rusalmeh and his lackey as she moved about the great banquet hall, never leaving Esther's side. She kept reminding herself about her mission of comfort.

"The Creator's plan is perfect," she kept saying to herself, all the while desiring desperately to force the issue with the disgusting fallens in her presence.

Plus, Rusalmeh was smug. From the moment he entered the room with his human, he displayed a smile that Isabella could only describe as if he knew something Isabella didn't. He too kept his gaze at all times on Isabella as they both moved around the room. Isabella knew even she would not be able to overpower Rusalmeh, but she figured she wouldn't have to. If it came to it, Rusalmeh would not engage her. He would simply summon his horde to attack her. This she could handle if needed, or at least that's what she told herself. Part of her didn't want to find out while the rest of her wanted to fight. And fight now.

The banquet ended without incident and with a simple request by Queen Esther for another banquet the next day. Same time. Same guests.

As Isabella followed the queen out of the banquet hall, Rusalmeh spoke directly to Isabella, "What do you think you are doing here? Don't you know I own this region?" His voice raspy with hate and contempt.

"You own nothing. You are here because the Creator allows you to be here. It's like your lackey there, Javva. He's your lackey in the same way you are the Creator's." Isabella couldn't wipe the smile off her face as she turned to look at Rusalmeh as she left the room.

Rusalmeh said nothing in response although Isabella was quite sure it wouldn't be the last she saw him before her mission was complete.

Back in the queen's chambers, Esther and her attendants spent time together as if they were long-lost friends. As Isabella listened to their conversation, she was struck at how much love and care the queen showed to her attendants and how much they adored her. The queen seemed more at ease this night, although she could tell her heart was still heavy. Isabella knew her ability to provide comfort was still necessary in the hours ahead.

The crowd outside the palace gates had dispersed with the horde of fallens. Isabella wanted to so much to explore outside the gates in the hopes of getting a better sense of what was going on and, more importantly, a better sense of why Rusalmeh was there. But she stayed on mission, the mission to comfort the queen as crazy as that sounded to her.

Here was Rusalmeh, a key asset in the fallen hierarchy, and she couldn't do a thing about it. As she was thinking these thoughts, she noticed the queen, once again on her knees, praying to the Creator for wisdom and protection.

She quickly moved to embrace the queen and join her in asking the Creator for comfort as well. They prayed together for a long period before the queen rose and prepared to sleep.

Isabella wouldn't. She would keep watch throughout the night as she expected Rusalmeh to conduct some counterintelligence of his own that night. It didn't take long. Within the hour, Javva appeared outside the queen's window.

Isabella was standing at the end of the queen's bed, which turned out to be the perfect position to catch a 360-degree view of the room, including all the windows.

"Watch yourself, demon," Isabella commanded with steely resolve.

"Ah, Isabella. So nice to see you," rasped Javva, his voice dripping with hate and sarcasm. "The prince and I were surprised to see you tonight. Have you lost your will to fight?" he teased.

"Not my mission. At least not yet," the warrior replied.

Javva began to take a step into the room where Esther was sleeping.

"No!" Isabella said without a hint of hesitation.

"Okay. Okay," Javva replied, quickly retreating back to the window. He wanted no part of what Isabella could offer. He knew that for sure.

"Why are you here, worm?" asked Isabella, more of a command than a question.

"Who is this woman?" he asked.

"She's the queen."

"Of course. But who is she? Why is she so important the Creator would send you?" wondered Javva, more to himself than to anyone.

"She has the king in the palm of her hand. That's for sure. He'll do anything she asks," mused the angelic warrior.

"Oh well. It doesn't really matter, I guess," replied Javva, this time with a whisper and a sly smile revealing his rancid teeth.

"Oh?" asked Isabella, now genuinely curious.

"Oh no. No. No. No. That's for me to know and you to find out, presumably once it's too late," Javva said as he turned to leave.

For a moment, Isabella wondered urgently about what Javva just said but quickly reminded herself that Javva was a poser, and the Creator was firmly in command.

After a moment and before Javva flew back into the darkness, she asked, "Do you have any regrets?"

Javva stopped and turned back to face Isabella. "Regrets?" He wheezed.

"We worshipped for millennia together. Your love for the Creator was unmistakable, and He gave you such an amazing voice to sing," Isabella replied as she remembered all the times she and Javva worshipped the Creator together.

"No regrets," Javva lied. "I realized it was Lucifer I was singing for and worshipping, not the Creator. So when he led the rebellion, I was all in. Still am," Javva said without a hint of hesitation. He had convinced himself of this long ago so as to not show even a hint of doubt. Even though he regretted his decision bitterly, he would never reveal such regret to an angel. Never.

"I don't believe you. Look at you. Millenia separated from the Creator and His love has turned you into…" Her voice trailed off.

Isabella and Javva were close friends over millennia in the heavenly realm. They spent endless moments worshipping the Creator together. They had a connection that spanned eternity, and Isabella's emotion got the best of her as she remembered her friend, now a symbol of hate and destruction, heaving and wheezing before her.

"Don't worry about me, Bella. I'll annihilate you if I need to, and I won't regret it for a second."

"Time to go, worm. And don't look back. You will not want to see me coming for you. I promise you that."

Javva said nothing because there was nothing to say. He knew Isabella was right, and he knew he didn't stand a chance in a one-on-one battle with her. He would soon find out how right he was.

Isabella kept watch over the queen throughout the night without further incident. No fallens approached after Javva's departure, and all remained quiet throughout the night. Isabella sang songs of the Creator's deliverance, hope, comfort, and love over the queen as she slept doing what she could to bring comfort to her troubled spirit.

The morning was filled with furious activity as the queen and her attendants prepared another banquet for King Xerxes and Rusalmeh's slave Haman. Isabella loathed the idea of being in the same vicinity as Rusalmeh and his lackey Javva again, but she knew her comfort mission was still engaged.

Little did she know how quickly that would change.

*****

"Today is the day God delivers my people from annihilation," Esther spoke quickly and urgently to her attendants. "No mistakes please. And be sure to bring the best wine to King Xerxes and his guests as soon as they arrive," she instructed.

They all nodded in understanding and agreement.

Just then, the king's attendants announced his arrival. Isabella noticed the king was in high spirits and was clearly smitten with the queen's beauty and elegance. He would do anything for her, it seemed.

The queen greeted the king with humility and honor. Isabella stayed close but, this time, felt no need for a hand of comfort to be upon Esther. Isabella noticed the confidence building in the queen. A woman in total command of the situation. A woman fulfilling her destiny. But Isabella stayed close, knowing Rusalmeh was close at hand.

As per the usual, Isabella could smell fallens before she could see them. This moment in the great banquet hall was no different.

Spending millennia apart from the Creator did weird things to celestial beings. The void left by the Creator's love is quickly filled with hatred, lust, greed, gluttony, envy, and pride, leaving celestial beings void of light and engulfed in an unimaginable foul stench emanating from them like a dense fog.

His slave Haman entered first, and Isabella noticed something strikingly different about him from the night before. Gone was the arrogance and pride of a man in total control. Instead, Isabella saw a human dejected, humble, and scared.

Soon after, Rusalmeh and Javva entered the room. The same haughty look from Rusalmeh as he made sure to make eye contact and keep it with Isabella as he made his way across the room with his slave. Javva, on the other hand, was less able to hide his emotions. He looked scared too. Something had happened to them since the night before, and it completely changed their demeanor.

With everyone seated, Rusalmeh and his slave Haman were on one side of the banquet table, the queen and Isabella on the other. Each celestial being staring at each other as the humans conversed. Only the Creator knew what would come next, and it was at that moment that Isabella recalled the slight smile and nod from Gabriel as he said, "Your mission is to comfort. But be ready for anything."

It was the "be ready for anything" that quickened Isabella's spirit in that moment, and for the first time on this mission, she began to realize why she was chosen for this time and place. So she smiled. And Rusalmeh noticed.

Just then, the king asked, "Queen Esther, what is your petition?"

The queen answered, "Spare my people. This is my request."

The king looked confused.

Esther continued, "My people have been sold to be destroyed, killed, and annihilated."

The king stood as visible anger overtook his face as he shouted, "Who is he? The man who dared to do such a thing?"

"This vile Haman!" screamed Esther as she stood from her lounged position, pointing across the table at the man whose head was now bowed low. Her passion for her people revealing itself as the rising sun broke the horizon. Blazing and magnificent.

In the moment of the queen rising to her feet, as if in slow motion, Rusalmeh reached for his sword as he leapt forward with great force across the table in a direct attack on Isabella. The tables had turned quickly, and Rusalmeh sought an advantage in a fight he knew would ensue.

Isabella was ready. Anticipating such a move, Isabella had quietly removed her sword from her sheath and stood ready to defend the queen at any costs. After all, she was made for this.

Even though she was ready, Rusalmeh was a senior leader for Lucifer for a reason. So fast. So strong. He struck Isabella on the forearm, his blade bouncing off her armor as she barely was able to react in a defensive posture.

As the demon regrouped, Isabella leapt back, leaving Esther's side for the first time her mission began. As she leapt, she also spun a way from Rusalmeh, who was now standing above her, feet firm on the surface of the giant banquet table.

Rusalmeh, in a defensive stance, eyes on Isabella who was now ten feet away regaining her footing. "Javva!" Rusalmeh screamed. "Attack the queen and create doubt and fear now!"

Javva was frozen. Isabella was terrifying. She was so strong to be sure. Javva knew that just by looking at her. But Javva had never seen such quickness and agility before. From any being, let alone Isabella. They had known each other for millennia, but Javva had never seen Isabella fight. And he wanted nothing to do with her. He wanted no part of that fight. His glimpse of her in that one moment of initial battle with Rusalmeh destroyed any will Javva had to fight. Her pure white clothing moved in perfect sequence to her movements with such grace to Javva it seemed like he was dreaming.

"Javva! Now!" Rusalmeh screamed again.

In the moment, Isabella took one step toward the prince before leaping with sword extended. She did so with such force that Rusalmeh took a slight step back, giving Isabella all she needed as she slashed the outside part of his upper right arm. Rusalmeh cursed Isabella wickedly as he screamed in pain. This action spun the demon around as Javva finally made his move toward Esther.

By this time, the king had left his seat at the banquet table and was moving to the palace balcony, clearly enraged by what Esther had just revealed.

Using a backflip motion, showcasing his own unique set of agility skills, Rusalmeh landed back where he had first launched his attack on Isabella. This motion surprised Isabella as she knew

Rusalmeh as one who never retreated from a fight, but she quickly realized the reason for his perceived retreat. Rusalmeh was heading toward the king at the same time Javva was moving toward Esther.

She was at a moment of indecision. Which battle should she fight? Keep Rusalmeh, who surely was going to try to influence the king's next decision, away from the king or stop Javva from influencing Esther.

Even though Esther was her primary mission, Isabella recognized her mission had changed instantly from one of comfort to one of confrontation, and she knew exactly what she needed to do next.

In one fluid motion as if planned from before the beginning of time, Isabella leapt toward Javva, cutting off his path to Esther. She was on Javva instantly, taking him fully by surprise, sliding across the palace floor, bending low, and grabbing his right leg by the ankle. She grabbed him with such force he immediately lost his balance, his head slamming hard against the palace floor as his legs replaced the space his head occupied less than a second before. She came to a sliding stop and, without hesitation, threw the hapless demon with every ounce of strength she had directly at the feet of Rusalmeh.

Rusalmeh, moving away from the action and quickly upon the king, did not notice his lackey flying through the air directly toward him. As Javva, helpless and unable to change his trajectory, crashed awkwardly in the back of Rusalmeh's legs, the two landed severely, falling over each other as they slid helplessly across the floor.

As soon as she had released Javva from her grip sending him hurdling through the air toward Rusalmeh, she herself raced to stand between the king and Rusalmeh to ensure protection against any evil influence.

Isabella had determined that Esther's job was complete, and the Creator had given her the courage needed to speak up for the Hebrews, the Creator's chosen.

Now it was up to the king to set things right. And Isabella knew instinctively he was to be protected from the evil influence of Rusalmeh. She also knew she could not hold off Rusalmeh for very long on her own. She knew he wouldn't be outmaneuvered again.

She took her one chance and succeeded. Rusalmeh wouldn't allow that again.

The king exited the banquet hall onto the palace balcony, and Isabella took position in the doorway to the balcony, sword drawn, feet firm, and spirit ready. She would defend with her life against any evil influence Rusalmeh might try to inflict on the king who now held the fate of the Creator's chosen people in his hands.

Javva was groggy, both from his head smacking the floor hard as Isabella flung him across the room as well as from Rusalmeh who, in his anger, smacked Javva's head against the floor a second time.

Rusalmeh stood, his arm bleeding, his rage building. "Not too bad," he sneered as he reached from his weapon that had fallen from his grip as he crashed to the floor only moments before.

"You should pick better lackeys," replied Isabella. "Ones that obey better and don't make a fool of you."

"You seem quite confident for being severely outnumbered," Rusalmeh jeered with a smile.

No sooner had those words left his wretched lips that Isabella heard the fallen horde she had seen the night before. And they were approaching fast.

Protect the king. The fate of the Creator's people hangs in the balance, Isabella told herself.

Just then, Rusalmeh lunged at her, his sword blazing as a perfect representation of his current mood.

Isabella lunged toward him a split second later in response, her sword meeting his in an epic clash of warrior strength. The momentum of which spun both warriors away from each other, giving Rusalmeh a clear path to the king on the balcony. As he raced toward the king, Isabella began to realize she had lost control of the situation as Javva had recovered enough to swiftly moved toward Esther and the fallen slave Haman.

The king's guards were in the banquet hall, but none was moving toward Haman or Esther since, Isabella quickly surmised, the king had not given command to do so.

Esther remained in danger, especially if Javva was able to influence Haman to inflict harm on Esther in a fruitless attempt to save himself. Of course, that would be reckless and would surely mean sudden and immediate death, but the fallens were desperate and had no regard for human life. Human life to them was only a means to an end. Disregarded as necessary.

All these thoughts and calculations were running through her mind at a furious pace. She was working so hard to process what was unfolding to form her next decision that she didn't realize who had just arrived. Her first hint that help had arrived was Rusalmeh's sword whirling past her and crashing hard into the banquet table.

And then from the balcony into the great banquet hall, a new warrior arrived—Sam. Ferocious light surrounded him as he stepped into the room and nodded with a huge smile to Isabella. His arrival startled Javva so aggressively that the demon retreated quickly from his pursuit of Esther and his slave Haman, his hollow eyes transfixed on Sam.

"You," hissed Rusalmeh as he collected himself and rose once again to his feet. "What's so special about this woman that He sends two of His most powerful warriors?" he screamed as he motioned behind him toward Esther, who was now lounging in her chair, oblivious to the spiritual battle raging around her.

"It's time for you to go," Sam said, smiling. "You've lost."

"Have I?" Rusalmeh said as he looked past Sam to acknowledge the first of the fallen horde arriving on the balcony. "I'm not sure I'd be smiling so much based on the circumstances."

Sam turned to face the oncoming horde as Isabella arrived to join him. They joined together back-to-back, Sam facing the balcony door, smiling, while Isabella faced the room, ready to take on all comers.

Just then, the king emerged from the balcony with an urgent rendering of his verdict. "Seize the traitor Haman and put him to death!" cried the king.

"The only invitation for you and your horde is being carried away, Rusalmeh," Sam said, smiling and pointing with his sword toward Haman, his head completely covered, being dragged out of the great banquet hall by the king's guards.

"You can stay and fight, but for what purpose?" asked Isabella. "Your human slave will be dead before dawn, and you and your minions will have no authority here."

Rusalmeh weighed his options. He knew they were right. A fight now without a human slave to carry out his evil was, in fact, pointless. He didn't need to lose half of his horde or more to angelic warriors, like Isabella and Sam. "We were close. And we'll be better next time. We'll find a better slave from which to annihilate the Creator's chosen and wipe that smile off your face," Rusalmeh hissed to Sam as he motioned to his horde to stand down.

"Go!" Sam demanded.

Rusalmeh hesitated. Javva and the rest of the horde awaiting their next instructions.

"Now!" screamed Sam, his smile gone for the first time since arriving, shaking the heavenly realm with his booming voice, massive frame, and bright-topaz eyes that burned with the brightness of the surface of the sun.

Rusalmeh nodded to his horde and took flight, Javva and the horde following closely behind. The battle was over. The Creator's mission complete.

"Thank you," Isabella said as she put her sword away.

"For what? You clearly had this well under control," Sam said with his trademark smile.

"Not quite. It turned so quickly from a comfort mission I felt like I was a half step behind from the beginning," explained Isabella, trying to not make it sound like she was making excuses.

"No need to explain. I was glad to help. Gabriel mentioned you might need an extra hand, what with Rusalmeh and the approaching horde."

"Yeah, it was going to get ugly pretty quick. I mean I would have taken a lot of them with me, but I'm glad you arrived when you did. That's for sure."

"It's not over yet," Sam said.

"No?"

"No. The Creator's chosen will need our support as they defend against attacks all over the country."

"Attacks? The queen just exposed Rusalmeh's plot through Haman, right? Isn't it over?" asked Isabella.

"Not yet. Haman had manipulated the king to put out a decree all across his kingdom to annihilate the Creator's chosen people at an appointed time. It's why you saw the horde of fallens last night and again today. They have been sent to foment hate and anger against the Hebrews. People everywhere are preparing to kill all of them. I expect the king to issue a decree protecting them, sending his royal forces to join the fight and to allow the Hebrews to defend themselves. Destroying Haman's plot was the first most important step. But there is more work to do. Plus, you'll get to demonstrate some of the power the Creator gave you to use," Sam concluded with a smile as he headed for the balcony.

He didn't notice the much-bigger smile that spread across Isabella's face as the realization of the Creator's full plan for this mission dawned.

As she headed to the balcony following after Sam, grinning from ear to ear, she couldn't wait to complete the second phase of the Creator's mission. She was sent to comfort. But to most of the Creator's missions, there was more than was visible at first. At the perfect time, she was also sent to right some wrongs and leave a mark in the fallen world that would never be forgotten.

"Thank you," she whispered as she descended into the darkness.

Ready for war.

CHAPTER 2

Petros

"Whatever the Creator needs," Petros said, mustering up as much confidence as he could in those four words.

"He'll be safe now that he is part of the Egypt king's family," Sebastian replied. Sebastian was referring to a young baby boy named Moses.

They were on a mission in Egypt. The Creator's chosen people had been slaves there for hundreds of human years. Although they didn't know it, the baby they had been sent to protect would fulfill the Creator's plan for escape.

The mission to protect the baby had succeeded, so Sebastian along with several other warriors were heading back to the heavenly realm.

The Creator had determined Petros was the most equipped to stay behind and protect the young boy as he grew. Petros wasn't so sure.

Sebastian continued, "Plus, his mother is nursing him and caring for him on behalf of the king's daughter. He's safe now. No need for me to be here too."

"I understand. I'm not entirely comfortable being surrounded by so many fallens," Petros said, more to himself than anyone.

"Listen, Pete, they will not touch the child out of fear," reminded Sebastian.

"Fear?"

"That's right. Egyptian Pharaohs are notoriously superstitious, and while the fallens exploit that superstition, they also don't want the Pharaoh turning soft and letting the Israelites go if bad things start happening to his family. And keeping the Creator's chosen people enslaved is Lucifer's main priority. Now and always."

"Rules of engagement, sir?" Petros asked. A standard protocol question for any warrior on any mission.

"Defend yourself and the child as needed. I expect the fallens here to leave you be. If needed, don't hesitate to call for backup. You'll get the support you need."

*****

Many years had passed since Sebastian left him to protect the child in Egypt surrounded by a horde of fallens larger than he had ever seen.

The words from Sebastian kept ringing in his mind: "But if needed, don't hesitate to call for backup. You'll get the support you need."

Angelic warriors, like Petros, don't count time. But for Petros, the mission seemed like an eternity as he sat watching the shepherd from a distance.

The shepherd used to be a prince living in luxury in the Pharaoh's palace. The only excitement since battling the fallens who were trying to drown him after his mother put him in a river basket was when he killed the Egyptian and buried him in the sand.

And Petros almost missed it. So many years of waiting, watching, and wondering about the purpose of the mission. Like most warriors at one point during at least one mission in their existence in service to the Creator, Petros wondered if he had done something wrong to deserve what seemed to be such a pointless mission. Racking his mind trying to remember past missions and failures that might have led to such a punishment became a sort of pastime for the angelic warrior. The inevitable "Why me?" often asked was not an exclusive to humans. Angels would, at times, ask it as well. Especially during long missions behind enemy lines in the earthly realm, separated from the Creator.

Because the human he had stayed behind to protect was part of Pharaoh's palace and ultimately his family, Petros had grown accustomed to being surrounded by fallens endlessly sneering at him but never engaging. Always threatening but never attacking. Moses, just as with all of Pharaoh's family, was protected.

The Pharaoh had given his soul to Rusalmeh, the demonic prince of the region, in exchange for power long ago. The power Pharaoh craved came with a price. A price only much later would prove to be costlier than the Pharaoh could have ever dreamed. The price to be paid in exchange for power was the continued enslavement of God's chosen people. The Hebrews.

As long as Pharaoh kept the Hebrews enslaved, Rusalmeh explained to a young Pharaoh in a dream one night that his power and his family would be protected. The next morning, the Pharaoh took the deal and assigned slave masters over the entire Hebrew population. And Rusalmeh's horde descended upon the entire land of Egypt.

As part of the arrangement, the fallen horde assigned to Pharaoh were under strict orders to protect the Pharaoh and his family and to allow no harm to come to them physically. Of course, the horde, as they always do, tortured Pharaoh and his family in other ways. From hellish nightmares to emotional, mental, and relational pain, Pharaoh and all his family lived in a constant state of torture. And like so many, Pharaoh never connected selling his soul to his family's endless emotional and relational turmoil. All of Pharaoh's family, except Moses.

The fallens knew better not to engage Petros in an attempt to inflict the same emotional and relationship pain and torture on Moses. It's not that they feared they could not overcome Petros. They knew their horde was certainly large enough to overwhelm even a magnificent angelic warrior like Petros. It's that they knew they would ultimately face the wrath of Rusalmeh. And no one wanted that. It was Rusalmeh's agreement with the most powerful human in the ancient world, and no one wanted to interfere with such an arrangement.

And so Petros protected Moses and watched him grow in the lap of Pharaoh's luxury with little else to do than pray over Moses and the young children who grew with Moses. Petros felt compassion for those young Egyptian children who were innocent in Pharaoh's deal with the devil. So he prayed for them too.

And Moses grew strong in stature and in mind. He had become a man. All the while protected as part of the king of Egypt's family. Until one day he wasn't.

That's the day Petros almost missed it. So much time had passed with little to do except to pray. And then suddenly, in an instant, the world changed.

The Creator had clearly put the Hebrews on Moses's heart from an early age as he was constantly inquiring about the Hebrew people, their history, and their work. As he grew older, Petros would travel with him to visit the slavery fields. They were always accompanied by a group of fallens charged with keeping an eye on Moses and his protector at all times.

The scene of the slavery and agony of his people hung on them like a dense fog, and Moses grew angrier with every visit. Moses would always find some with whom he could speak and would always bring extra food to give out to those who were in need of it most. He became very good at avoiding the attention of the legion of slave masters, or at least he thought he did.

It was, in fact, Petros putting in the work of distracting the slave masters and generally confusing the small of group of fallens sent as spies. It was the only small action Petros had seen in so long he relished the opportunity to confuse the fallens and the Hebrew masters. It was easy really. Each of the slave masters had a dozen or more fallens surrounding each of them, influencing them incessantly with hatred toward the Hebrew people. So Petros figured out all he needed to do was distract the fallens assigned to the slave masters, and in so doing, the slave masters would be distracted.

Many of the fallens assigned to the slave masters had not seen an angelic warrior for hundreds of years as the darkness of the Hebrew plight descended further into the void. So when these fallens spotted Petros, he became their singular focus. And because the fallens had become so intertwined with the spirit of their slave masters that when they shifted their focus to Petros, so did the slave masters.

So Petros would move with such speed and with such force the fallens would barely see his form before he was gone again, often leaving a welt or deep bruise on the head of one of the unsuspecting fallens. And it was fun.

It was during these times that Moses would hand out food and supplies to beleaguered Hebrew slaves. This went on for some time as Moses began to visit more and more often, becoming popular among the Hebrew slaves as word would spread fast any time Moses and Petros would be seen approaching.

Until the day. The day Petros almost missed it.

At six feet tall in human measurement, Petros was smaller than most angelic warriors. His height disadvantage, so called, often was his greatest strength as most fallens would expect easy victory when going up against Petros. This day was no different.

The fallens surrounding Moses, Petros, and the Hebrew slaves that day found out quickly that Petros's speed and strength more than compensated for any perceived height disadvantages. He was so fast. And agile. His ability to outmaneuver the enemy, especially when they made the first offensive move, was legendary.

Petros was busy distracting the fallens as he usually did on Moses's visits, but this time, Moses spotted a slave master beating one of the Hebrew slaves. Beating him and beating him and beating him.

On the edge of his peripheral vision, Petros spotted the scene unfolding quickly. In a fit of rage, Moses descended on the Egyptian with such force the first blow likely doomed the man. But Moses kept at it as he delivered blow after devastating blow. The Egyptian man was dead, and the Hebrew slaves stood, slack-jawed in disbelief. And in a way, so did Moses. As did the fallens. But not for long. The truce had been broken.

Rusalmeh would understand any retaliation the fallens would bring upon Moses because of what he had done. So it wasn't long before the fallens assigned to the slave masters as well as those assigned to spying on Moses and Petros began to realize what had just happened and what that meant for them.

The truce was over. Moses was fair game. Pent-up frustration and anger from years of being unable to lay a hand on Moses began to seep out as the fallens gathered together as they began to converge on Moses's location.

Petros realized he had to act fast to keep Moses free from harm. With dark curly hair that hung at his shoulders, dark-emerald eyes, and an olive complexion, the Creator made Petros in part to represent those humans in the earthly realm who were often underestimated or overlooked. It was at this moment that he made the most of what the Creator had given him as he landed with such impact next to Moses that the fallen horde converging on Moses's position fell back. So much so they began to second-guess exactly who this angelic warrior was and if they should engage.

Petros didn't let any of them make a decision before descending upon their position, sword drawn, carving through the horde with such force and precision that more than half of the horde lost the will to fight that day. Petros always brought more than expected, and this moment was not different. By the time Moses had buried the body of the Egyptian in the sand and began to make his way back to the palace, Petros had left the stunned horde of fallens bloodied, bruised, and gnashing in his wake.

They would soon regroup. The word would go out about the broken agreement, and a new plan of attack from the fallens would be formed.

Petros remembered the words of Sebastian so long ago before leaving him. "If needed, don't hesitate to call for backup. You'll get the support you need," Petros wondered out loud to himself as he accompanied Moses back to the palace. "Is now the time to call for backup? Not yet," he told himself. "The Creator gave me the skills to handle this," he told himself. Doing his best to believe it.

That night was chaotic. The entire fallen horde in and around the king's palace was in an absolute uproar. Word of Moses's deadly action had spread throughout the demon horde, and they were furious. But no change in the rules of engagement had arrived from

Rusalmeh, primarily because the king had not found out about the Egyptian murder at the hands of Moses. And as a result, Moses was still an accepted part of the king's family and, as such, remained off-limits to the fallens. Such a circumstance made Moses and, by proxy, Petros the most hated among the fallens. They jeered, hissed, and wheezed at Petros all night as Petros stood guard over Moses as he slept. The fallens screamed insults of hatred so vitriolic and sinful that no human in the king's palace slept without haunting nightmares brought about by the fallen horde's demonic emotional presence throughout the night.

The very next day, whether out of spite or curiosity or both, Moses set out to visit the Hebrew slaves.

Petros pleaded with the Creator to turn Moses back, but Moses persisted, and so did Petros. Right by his side, unsure of what awaited them both. Petros had been created to be the rock of consistency and determination, and if ever a time called for both, it was now.

Moses was not greeted as he usually was by the Hebrew slaves. Word clearly had spread about the murder of the Egyptian at the hands of Moses, and instead of praise and celebration, he was treated as if he did not exist. All of them avoided eye contact, and no one engaged in any conversation.

No Hebrew slave took the food he brought to offer them that day. Petros noticed they all had fear in their eyes. Instead of feeling protected by Moses, they all feared him and his presence. Out of fear of retaliation from their Egyptian masters, no one wanted to be seen talking with Moses once word of the murder became known.

So they shunned him that day, and Moses grew increasingly agitated and angry over it.

He would soon realize his life had changed forever.

*****

Warrior angels had no concept of human time per se. Even in the earthly realm bound by earthly realm rules, time was not a concept to which angels were held.

But Petros knew, even without the concept of time hardwired into his mind, that he had been on this mission a long time. A very long time. Moses had barely escaped Egypt after the murder of the slave master. And now he and Petros were in the middle of nowhere. For a long time. *What did I do to deserve this assignment?* he wondered, clearly feeling sorry for himself. In human time, it had been forty years since he and Moses barely escaped from Egypt.

Now Moses was a shepherd. Tending sheep and cattle of all kinds. A nomad. A man without a country. From the richest palace in the known world to a hellscape of sand, dirt, and desolation.

Petros knew he served at the pleasure of the Creator. And the Creator's plans were perfect. He knew this in his mind, but it didn't mean he didn't question if maybe the Creator forgot he was here. Just thinking about the possibility made him smile. "Of course not. I'm right where the Creator wants me to be. But it does feel like some sort of punishment."

"Hey, buddy," a voice came like thunder from behind him as he sat watching Moses in the distance as he had thousands of times before.

Petros froze. No one, except an archangel or a fallen prince, could sneak up on him like that without him noticing. He slowly turned, hopeful for the best but planning for the worst as he slowly reached to clasp his sword that was slung across his back.

"At ease, warrior," a friendly voice said. Gabriel.

"Come on, sir. Not cool," Petros said with a smile.

"What?" Gabriel asked with an exaggerated innocent smile slowly spreading across his face.

"Couldn't you have given me a 'Do not be afraid' or something like you give to the humans when you arrive?" Petros asked. Only half joking.

"I'm here on another assignment, and I thought I'd drop in for a minute," Gabriel replied.

"Assignment? Out here?"

Gabriel nodded in affirmation.

"Brother, there is nothing our here but dirt, goats, sheep, and a dude that has been on the run for forty years."

"Exactly," Gabriel said with a big smile. His bright-blue eyes were blazing with delight.

Petros looked thoroughly confused as he cocked his head and raised his eyebrows, looking directly at Gabriel.

"What better place than for Him to make an appearance."

Petros's dark-emerald eyes grew wide with pure excitement as he whispered, "The Creator?"

"Gotta go!" Gabriel whispered as he gave Petros a wink and was gone.

As Moses encountered the Creator that day while the bush burned, Petros soaked it all in. A warrior angel's spirit is always connected to the Creator as the source of everything they are. Their strength, their wisdom, their courage, their kindness. Everything. And even in the earthly realm, they stay connected, but it's not the same as being in the heavenly realm. Not even close.

That day when the Creator arrived to speak with Moses was exactly what Petros needed after decades in the earthly realm. It's precisely what makes the Creator and His plans so incredibly complex and wonderfully amazing. While the Creator was laying out His plans for rescuing His people from slavery in Egypt to a nomadic shepherd living in the desert, He was also refueling Petros and preparing him for the incredible battle that was soon to come. Just being in the presence of the Creator that day gave Petros renewed strength and determination to protect Moses as he faced the deepest, darkest evil the world had ever known.

And he was ready. It was his time.

*****

"What are you doing back here?" Rusalmeh said, spitting the words out through his raspy voice.

"After all this time since I last saw you and that's the hello I get?" Petros replied sarcastically. His face expressionless.

"I'm not sure I'd be so confident, fool!" one of Rusalmeh's lackeys shouted with all the hate he could generate.

"Enough," Rusalmeh replied, holding his wretched, mangled hand in the air, motioning for silence from the horde that had lined up behind him. Death and destruction throbbing through the horde like the rhythmic beat of a drum.

"No one remembers my VIP here?" Petros asked, motioning to Moses who was standing before the Egyptian king.

"Oh, but we do. And we remember the agreement he broke," Rusalmeh said matter-of-factly. He continued, "A debt must be paid for the destruction you caused that day."

"Just relax. Before you get too far ahead of yourself on this one, you should probably know I just had a chat with Gabriel," Petros said with a smile.

Rusalmeh said nothing. Petros, however, knew he got the prince's attention. Everyone, especially Rusalmeh, in the spirit realm knew a visit from Gabriel in the earthly realm, especially one that went undetected by the demonic scourge, meant serious business.

"You're bluffing," Rusalmeh spit the words at him.

"Am I?" Petros said, realizing that the news of Gabriel's involvement was more than enough to give Rusalmeh a pause. He decided in that moment to keep the fact of the Creator's direct communication with Moses to himself. It would be the information he would use at a different time for a different purpose.

The two warriors stared at each other from across the enormous throne room of the Pharaoh that stood between them. Each sizing the other up.

Petros knew he could never defeat the demonic horde that virtually surrounded him should they choose to attack in that moment. But he also knew that if the Creator was directly involved with Moses and his brother, there was likely a level of backup in the form of legions of angel warriors, the likes of which Rusalmeh would have never seen.

On the other hand, Rusalmeh knew Petros was no real threat, and he wanted desperately to avenge the beatings his hordes took that day when Petros broke their agreement. But he also knew that if Petros was not bluffing and, in fact, the Creator was orchestrating the men standing before his slave, the Egyptian king, there was literally nothing he could do to stop them.

So both men waited for the other to make the first move. No one did.

The meeting between the humans ended with anger and threats as Rusalmeh and his horde watched Petros and the two humans walk away without further incident.

The demonic prince, however, couldn't shake the news of Gabriel's involvement. If it was true, he couldn't help but wonder if his crowning achievement as a prince of darkness and the centuries-long oppression of the Creator's chosen people at the hands of the Egyptians was soon coming to an end.

Author's Note: The story of Petros's battles and the miracles he experienced as the protector of Moses during the exodus from Egypt is worthy of its own book. Suffice it to say, Rusalmeh never forgot the significance of Petros's work to fulfill the Creator's plan to free the Hebrew people from the hands of the Egyptians. It would occur to Rusalmeh hundreds of years later, when he encountered Petros again in the middle of yet another rescue attempt, that he should have put everything he had into annihilating Petros that day in the Pharaoh's palace.

And because he didn't, the history of the world would be changed forever.

CHAPTER 3

Sebastian

The mission had come from the Creator through Gabriel. The missions always came through Gabriel. Which was fine for Sebastian and all the warrior angels really. They loved the Creator with all their being, and they would do anything to fulfill the missions He gave them, but the Creator was an all-consuming fire. So overwhelmingly awesome. So terrifyingly powerful. So wonderfully dangerous. The warrior angels were always so honored to be chosen by the Creator while equally delighted that Gabriel was the one who communicated the details.

"Your mission is to protect a young shepherd. The youngest of eight from the household of his father, Jesse the farmer."

"Where?"

"Bethlehem."

"Rusalmeh's region again."

"Yes, there's a reason Lucifer put his best warrior in charge of this region."

"What's that?"

"Jerusalem," Gabriel answered without hesitation.

"The holy city of the Creator's chosen," Sebastian said, more to himself than anyone.

"That's right. Lucifer studies the Creator's words more than anyone. Lucifer's hatred of the Creator doesn't blind him from studying the prophesies and making his plans accordingly. He knows the

Creator's plan for redemption has the city of Jerusalem at the heart of it."

"So he put Rusalmeh in the charge of the region of the earthly realm that encompasses Jerusalem in an attempt to disrupt the Creator's plans?" asked Sebastian.

"You got it. So don't mess this one up. The Creator's plans for the young shepherd boy are quite special," Gabriel said with a very serious tone.

"Copy that, sir. When?"

"As soon as you have your gear together."

"Fallens in the area?"

"Minimal. They are around, of course, but they have no use for a farmer's youngest son in a dusty town like Bethlehem. Your biggest challenge will be the wild animals," Gabriel said, still serious but this time with wry smile.

"Copy that. I'll be ready."

As expected, the arrival was uneventful. Sebastian arrived at the farm just after sunrise and caught a glimpse of the entire family as they were finishing their morning meal and heading out to tend to their farm.

The father, Jesse, was giving instructions with most only half listening as if he had given the same instructions the same way at the same time every day for many years.

There he was. The youngest. The smallest. The least among them. Sebastian spotted the confidence right away. He sought the affections of his father and hung on his every word, but when he didn't get it, he remained unfazed. Something Sebastian took note of right away. That and the fact Eliab, the boy's oldest brother, looked to be the one destined for greatness.

"Strange," Sebastian mumbled to himself as he began to follow the young shepherd out past the entrance gate surrounded by the flock of sheep the boy was now driving into the fields for the day.

For being so young, the boy was in total command of his flock. It was impressive to watch. He took his job seriously, and Sebastian could tell the boy wanted to please his father with a job well done. Up early and back late. Day after day after day.

Gabriel was right. The only threat to the young shepherd were wild animals looking to feast on his sheep. And the shepherd boy was having none of it.

Sebastian still likes to tell the story of the lion. It happened so fast. The part that often gets left out of the story he tells is how his lack of attention almost kept him from intervening. The lion came out of nowhere, but the young shepherd was fearless and determined. Sebastian remembered the lion, a sheep dangling from its mouth, trotting away with her new prize. Not a care in the world. Sebastian expected this. They were out in the earthly realm wilderness after all. What he didn't expect was that the young shepherd, the human subject he was specifically sent to protect, went on a dead sprint pursuing the lion.

"What is he doing?" Sebastian whispered to himself. And he set out to intervene if needed. The last thing he wanted was to have to tell Gabriel his mission failed because a lion killed the boy he was sent to protect. The very wild beasts Gabriel had warned him about.

Sebastian arrived right at the point in which the lion and the shepherd converged. He was expecting to simply ensure the animal would not harm the boy, when out of nowhere the shepherd caught up to the animal, rapping its back hard with his staff, stunning the beast for a moment. The sheep in its mouth was now free as the lion turned his attention to the young man. And the boy was ready.

To Sebastian's utter amazement, the boy had already pulled his knife and was ready to fight. *Fearless* was the first word that came to Sebastian's mind. For a split second, Sebastian froze. Everything was happening so fast, and this shepherd was so audaciously brave he wasn't sure how he could help without killing the lion himself, which he was not authorized to do on this mission. So he did the only thing he knew to do in that moment. As the lion crouched in order to pounce on the boy, Sebastian revealed himself for a split second, catching the lion's attention. His intention was to frighten the animal and chase her away. The lion froze, taking her gaze off the boy. Bad move.

With fire in his eyes, the boy took extreme advantage of the distraction, jumping on the lion's back, plunging his knife into the back of her neck, killing her instantly. Incredible. It was at that moment that Sebastian began to rethink exactly why he was sent and what kinds of plans the Creator had for this young shepherd from Bethlehem. If he had the courage to risk his life for one sheep, for what must he be destined? This was no ordinary shepherd. And as always, Sebastian marveled at the Creator's plans, and even though he wasn't privy to them, he trusted them wholeheartedly.

The days passed as Sebastian watched over the young shepherd and his flock. The boy was turning into a man, and he remained fearless as ever.

There was one day that a bear found out the same thing about this special young man the lion did. Basically, don't mess with his sheep, or you will most certainly die. Sebastian wondered, more than once, why he cared so much for those sheep.

Many days passed. The boy grew stronger and more fearless. If Sebastian hadn't seen the transformation himself, he wouldn't have believed it possible. But it was.

Then one cloudless night as the boy slept and Sebastian let his mind wander, Gabriel appeared. Sebastian had been flying solo on this mission for a long stretch without any angelic interaction of any kind, so Gabriel's sudden arrival more than startled the giant warrior. Standing close to eight feet tall with a jaw set like stone, dark-blue eyes like bright sapphires, and short dark hair, Sebastian was an imposing figure. But when Gabriel showed up unannounced, even a warrior with the size and experience of Sebastian would get startled.

"Hey, Seb," Gabriel whispered with a smile.

"Gabe," Sebastian whispered back while staring straight ahead, not wanting to give the archangel the satisfaction of scaring him half to death.

"Did I frighten you?"

"Nope."

"I don't believe you."

"Believe what you want. I'm on a mission. Always ready. Never scared."

Silence for a long moment. Then smiles from both. First from Sebastian and then an even bigger one from Gabriel. The two friends embraced.

"To what do I owe this pleasure of a visit from the mighty Gabriel himself?"

"Your boy here is about to get some big news."

"More sheep? Maybe a move up to cattle?" Sebastian was joking.

And Gabriel knew it, so he acted like he didn't even hear it. "The Creator is anointing him king of Israel."

"King?"

"Yes. A prophet will be arriving soon with a message."

"Does the enemy have any idea?"

"Negative. No one is expecting the next king of Israel to be a shepherd from a farm in Bethlehem." Silence as both warriors pondered the moment. "Oh, and be ready to fight. The Creator says he's making some changes, and you may be called upon."

"Copy that." Sebastian's smile returned. A warrior is a warrior is a warrior. And Sebastian was a warrior.

"What's next after…" Sebastian's voice trailed off as he realized in that moment that Gabriel was gone. "Huh?" he said out loud to himself. "King of the Creator's chosen?" He looked at the boy as he slept once again, marveling at the complexity of it all.

It wasn't too many days after Gabriel's visit that a servant boy from his father's farm came running, calling out to the young shepherd, informing him of his father's command to come home immediately.

"For what?" the young shepherd asked.

"I really don't know. Your father just said to tell you to come quickly."

The young shepherd packed his gear and gathered his sheep and headed for home. Sebastian, his silent and invisible guardian, tagging along with him.

The scene moved quickly as the young shepherd corralled his sheep into their pen and headed for the small crowd of his brothers and his father gathered around a very old man.

Sebastian didn't recognize the old man either, but he did notice his guardian. The angel warrior accompanying the old man smiled as he and Sebastian locked eyes. It was always a pleasant surprise to encounter a fellow warrior, both on different missions, intersecting with each other. The two quickly embraced as the humans spoke.

"Jarden, my friend."

"Sebastian! How's your mission?"

"The truth? It's been quite boring, but today's a big day."

"I see that. A king is among us, eh?"

"Aye. Who's the old man?"

"A prophet. Samuel. The first king he anointed hasn't worked out so well. So he's back for round two."

"Well, the Creator created a special one here," Sebastian said. "He's an incredible athlete and an absolutely fearless warrior."

"What's his name?"

"David."

"Well, he's about to become King David. Watch this," Jarden said as he nodded toward the prophet. "But his brothers don't think much of him, do they?"

Both warriors could clearly see the disappointment in the young shepherd's older brothers as the prophet anointed him in the presence of his brothers and his father. It was clear to both Jarden and Sebastian that no one there that day understood the deep meaning of that moment. But it wouldn't be long before all would see just how powerfully anointed the soon-to-be king had been.

Nothing much changed after that moment. Jarden moved on while Sebastian stayed with David who once again returned to the fields with his sheep, dutifully carrying out his shepherding responsibilities as his father asked.

It wasn't long before the soon-to-be king was on the move. And things got weird.

*****

The king of Israel wanted young David to come and play his harp for the king in his palace. What Sebastian saw there was nothing he expected, especially on this mission. As he entered the king's chambers directly behind and to the right of young David, he knew he wasn't the only spirit being in the chambers that night.

In the spirit world, there is no way he could have been missed. Sebastian commanded a presence in the spirit realm wherever he was. This time was no different. The eyes he felt on him were not human. He knew that right away. The smell of sulfur and hatred was a dead giveaway that evil was inhabiting the same earthly realm in that moment.

The spirit now occupying the same space as Sebastian glanced his way, her eyes piercing and hard. But the glance lasted only a moment as Sebastian quickly realized he and the soon-to-be king were interrupting something.

Suddenly, the words Gabriel spoke not that long ago quickened in his mind: "Oh, and be ready to fight."

"Indeed," Sebastian whispered to himself.

Indeed. The fallen was actively tormenting the king. She was hulking over the king who was slumped over on a lounge chair, causing him great distress. Her complexion was dull gray in the chamber light, her head bald, and her dead eyes dark red. Sebastian knew right away why she had come. To torment. To inflict suffering and anguish. And she was an expert at it. Sebastian had seen fallens torment humans for millennia, and he knew the signs of agony and affliction such torment could render. Her long, sinewy, and gnarled fingers complete with long, black, sharp fingernails were wrapped tightly around the man's skull as she leaned over him, whispering daggers of torment and pain into his surrendered mind. She was concentrating heavily on the king as she stood over him, hissing in his ear the fear, hatred, and self-loathing to which all humans in the earthly realm were so easily susceptible.

But why? Sebastian wondered to himself. He knew she could only be there if the Creator allowed it. And why would the Creator allow it? The first king of His chosen people would certainly be a target for Lucifer and his army. So why was there no protection for this king? Why wasn't one of his fellow angelic warriors protecting the king? Why was this fallen so easily able to torment such an important human leader? These questions were racing through his mind, when the fallen tormenting the king hissed angrily into the king's ear one last word of torment.

And then, as if she could wait no longer, she fixed her eyes on Sebastian and stood staring straight at the angelic warrior standing now in the same room. A crooked, evil smile slowly spreading across her distorted face. "I was wondering," she hissed.

"Wondering?" Sebastian replied immediately.

"When one of you would come."

"How did you get here?"

"I was invited."

"Invited? By who?"

"By this pathetic, worthless king you see weeping before me. Begging me to stop," the demon hissed and spit the words in a transparent attempt to antagonize the angel warrior now before her.

Sebastian said nothing. It wasn't the time. It soon would, but not now. Not yet.

She continued, "But I never stop."

By this time, young David had set up his instrument after receiving instructions from the king's attendants. Sebastian took notice of the poise and presence David had, even as the king agonized in pain and misery. It's like the young man knew just what to do. So did Sebastian. As soon as David began to play his harp, Sebastian took a step out from behind him and toward the massive demon in front of him. Drawing his massive sword as he stepped.

The demon didn't move. Her red eyes blazing with fury and pride. Sebastian was definitely stronger. That was for sure. But as she made her first move away from the king, plotting toward him, Sebastian was surprised at how she moved. So fluid. Like water. All spirits had a fluidlike characteristic about them, even in the earthly realm. But hers was different. Better. Advanced. Like something he had never seen before. Her eyes burned red, her grayish complexion now translucent as she moved effortlessly away from the king. Her long fingers now clenched into fists, and her contorted face seized as if frozen in terror with a total focus on Sebastian. She was ready to fight. And then she was gone.

David continued to play, and the music began to soothe the troubled king as he now lay prostrate on his bed. With his tormentor gone, he began to relax.

Sebastian knew this was only temporary. Her torment now gone. But she wasn't. Sebastian was sure of that. No fallen left a scene without a fight. Not ever. And as he processed what was happening and what might come next, he understood this fallen would not leave the presence of a human king without a fight. But where was she? He didn't see her at first. He smelled her. The smell of sulfur was unmistakable.

"Why don't you give up now?" she hissed, whispering directly into his ear. Her black teeth giving off a foul stench to which angelic warriors never grew accustomed.

Sebastian froze. How did she get directly behind him without him knowing? Where had she gone? How was she moving in and out of his vision? These questions were racking through his mind as he plotted his next move.

"It's not in my nature," he said calmly as David continued to play.

"I hate music. When I'm done with you, I'm turning my attention to your boy," she growled low and hateful, her face contorting and her red eyes narrowing.

"If I were you, I'd take on one task at a time," the angel warrior said, his voice deep and calm.

Sebastian hadn't seen her do it, but she had drawn her sword, and she was pressing it against the base of his thick neck. His time had come. "What was your plan with the king?"

"Torture. Of course."

"Why him?"

"Why not him? He's as good as any. Plus, your Creator let me in."

Silence as Sebastian absorbed the accusation like a punch to his neck. Would the Creator allow that? If not, why would she bring Him into it? Most fallens he knew didn't like to speak of the Creator under any circumstances. So why did she?

"Maybe He wanted us to meet," Sebastian replied as he clenched his right fist, set his feet straight on the ground, and prepared to turn the tables on the demon.

"Maybe..." But she didn't finish. She couldn't.

Her face exploded as Sebastian landed a crushing blow. His fist had come from below his waist to over his left shoulder, landing a massive blow directly to the center of the fallen's face. As soon as he landed the blow, he twisted down and away from the tip of the demon's sword, knowing the thrust of her sword would likely be her immediate reaction to his decisive action.

She stumbled badly, eyes clenched and face contorted. But she didn't stay that way for long. In fact, she vanished again.

Sebastian decided this time to not be a stationary target and decided to fly. Sebastian realized he needed to move in ways that made him as much of an elusive target as his enemy. But he also added an additional movement. As he flew in jagged, hectic movements, he kept his sword close to his body, both hands clenched tightly together on the handle. And he swung his massive sword in short, choppy motions. Back and forth. Back and forth. Lightning fast like a whip. As he moved, he kept an eye on young David, now fully into his music, the king mesmerized, his eyes drooping.

Sleep was coming, and Sebastian could tell it was the kind of sleep for which the king had been waiting many days. As long as he could keep the king's demon occupied like he was, the king was going to get the relief he needed.

Young David didn't know it, but he and his invisible warrior angel were working together.

He didn't see her at first. It didn't matter. His sword landed a slicing blow as she reappeared directly in front of him. He guessed she was trying to anticipate where he was going to be, and she was right. Mostly. What she didn't factor in was the tip of the sword from the angelic warrior which sliced directly across her upper torso, soliciting the kind of demonic scream reserved for nightmares. And not just human nightmares. Sebastian would remember that one for a while.

She had disappeared again, but the massive angel kept moving. And swinging. She was hurt. Badly. Sebastian knew he landed more than a glancing blow but couldn't know for sure how much damage he had inflicted until he could see her. She didn't give him the chance. She was gone.

He kept moving as David played, but he knew almost immediately that she had left. It was as if a dense fog had lifted. The king's chamber was cleared of the evil spirit the Creator had allowed Lucifer to send.

With the threat eliminated, at least for now, Sebastian's mind once again attempted to seek answers for why a fallen so easily infiltrated the king's chamber.

David continued to play, but more softly now as the king had drifted into a deep sleep. The torment over for the night. Then without any word from the king or his attendants, David stopped playing and began to gather his things to leave. His confidence and self-awareness, even in the presence of a king, surprised Sebastian. It was just one more piece of evidence Sebastian filed away, confirming how special this young man was. It was becoming clearer moment by moment that the Creator had created David for purposes well beyond what even David could likely dream.

As they left the king's palace together, they both took a quick glance behind as if in unison, catching a final glimpse of the sleeping king.

Deep down, Sebastian knew he would be back. The demon he had defeated that night would be back, and she wouldn't make the same mistake again. He knew that for sure.

What he didn't know was that he would need to be prepared for the fight of his life.

*****

It wasn't long before young David and Sebastian were back in the king's palace. It turned out that David and his music was the only thing that gave the king relief from the evil spirit when she came around.

Sebastian knew the truth but was happy to oblige and support the young king-to-be in any way he could. That was always the mission of all angel warriors. To fulfill the Creator's plans. And to take no credit for doing so. Plus, Sebastian, also like all angel warriors, loved a good fight. With each opportunity to fight a fallen came the opportunity to right the wrong of their choice to reject the Creator and go their own way.

Sebastian knew the king's demon of torment had returned. He was not surprised. He also knew she was not going to be as easy to defeat this time. He was going to have to be ready for war, and the last thing he wanted to have to do was call in reinforcements. He'd never live that down. But most importantly, Sebastian knew instinctively that should he be overcome by this demon, her first act of malice would be toward the very human he was sent to protect. The Creator's chosen one.

These thoughts crossed his mind as they approached the king's palace, this time for good since the king had requested David to take up permanent residence at the king's palace. Sebastian knew why the request had come. Everyone did. David's leadership abilities were endless. Confident with a servant's heart. Humble but never prideful. Strong, handsome, artistic, and deeply thoughtful. The king and most, if not all, of his attendants wanted David around. Things were just better when he was.

Of course, something none of them knew and would never know was Sebastian's role in bringing peace to the troubled king. Everyone, including the king, attributed the tormenting relief to David and his music. It was Sebastian that preoccupied the king's tormentor and ultimately sent her away permanently.

David received all the credit for the relief Sebastian was able to ultimately bring, and that was just fine with him. That was his mission now. To prepare the way in every way possible for the Creator's chosen king. But little did he know that he was in for the fight of his existence.

It had been more than a few days since David and, by default, Sebastian were in the presence of the king. By the looks of it, the king's tormentor had returned with a vengeance. Sebastian surmised she would reenter the scene as soon as he left with David, and he was not wrong. By the looks of it, she had been tormenting the king since they left a few nights before.

By the time they arrived back in the king's chambers, she was well into weaving her tapestry of torment and enjoying every moment. The king was beyond distraught.

"You?" she hissed. Her sinewy arms and legs wrapped around the king in a wicked, evil embrace. Her face pressed up against his as she screamed a relentless string of hatred and obscenities.

"Did you miss me?" Sebastian asked. It was the kind of sarcastic question that would have normally solicited a smirk, but he knew this was no time for joking. He had to be ready.

She didn't answer. She just stared at him. A look of fury and hatred emanating from her.

The king looked pale, weak, and on the verge of slipping into a catatonic state. David began to play. The music was soft at first, but he played so beautifully, so effortlessly the volume level was of no consequence. Everyone in the chamber leaned in and listened intently. Mesmerized. Everyone except the demon.

She let out a sinister, grotesque scream at the sound of David's music that Sebastian wondered if other fallens in the surrounding area had heard. If they did and came rushing to her aid, he might very well lose this battle. He knew he had to act fast just in case.

"Who are you?" Sebastian asked calmly.

The demon was still wrapped tightly around the king, not willing to relinquish her control over him. She loved the control she possessed over the human she had been sent to torment. All fallens did. "Sha," she hissed. She continued, "I'm the spirit of hope." A wicked smile spread across her face.

Sebastian said nothing.

"After only a short time with me, my slaves *hope* for the sweet relief of death." She continued, "A death that never comes. At least not from me. Death isn't my department. That's your Creator's."

Sebastian knew she was trying to provoke him. To make a move or a mistake. Or both. Fallens always try to provoke a fight from angelic warriors by speaking of the Creator in derogatory terms. He stayed calm.

He finally spoke after a long silence, "He's your Creator too."

"Shut up!" she screamed, veins emerging from her neck and her slick bald head like dozens of vipers emerging, each from their nest.

"He created us both. But only you thought you were better."

Sha said nothing. There was nothing to say, and they both knew it. Her decision to follow Lucifer had sealed her fate. She knew it. They all did.

Sebastian always figured that was one of the secondary reasons fallens were such hateful, terrible beings. They knew they were doomed. They knew they made a mistake, but it's a door that closed through which they could never pass again.

"Don't worry about it," Sebastian said, this time with a smirk. "Our Creator is in total control. In fact, you aren't even here without His permission."

Sha was now loosening her grip on the king. Her legs and arms unwrapping themselves from around the legs and upper torso of the king. "Permission?"

"That's right."

Sha said nothing as she slithered away from the king, readying herself for another battle with her angelic foe. "I only take orders from one master," she said, spitting the words at him, her body like water as she moved toward him.

"And your master takes orders from the Creator," Sebastian said, this time whispering in his own attempt to get her to make a move out of anger in order to gain an advantage.

David continued to play. He really was an incredible artist, Sebastian thought, his eyes fixed on the water-like fallen moving toward him. But then he decided to glance at the king who was now resting, exhausted. The demon must have been relentless, Sebastian thought.

Sebastian looked back from his glance at David and then the king, only to lose sight of Sha. She was gone. A bolt of panic tore through his mind as he recalled how easily she approached him from behind after moving in and out of the spiritual realm. His first instinct was to keep looking for her. But then his mind was screaming at him, *Move!*

But it was in that split second of hesitation that Sha took advantage of him as she reemerged on his right side, delivering a massive blow to the side of his head with her fist. The blow knocked Sebastian clean off his feet and sent him and his massive sword skidding across the king's marbled chamber floor. The blow was so hard and so direct Sebastian knew instinctively he was in serious trouble, especially if he couldn't collect himself enough to get back on his feet. His ears were ringing and his head pounding, and he couldn't get his eyesight to focus. As he tried to regain his bearing, he couldn't see Sha. She was gone. Again.

As David played and the king slept, a spiritual battle was beginning to rage all around the humans in the king's chamber. Sebastian would later recall the oddity of such a fierce, intense struggle happening only one dimension removed from the humans and just how oblivious they all were to what was raging all around them.

Sebastian was up on one knee now, trying desperately to anticipate the demon's next move. He was in no position to stop it or avoid it, but perhaps he could anticipate it enough to minimize the damage. He failed.

Sha waited until the very last moment as Sebastian stood up, first his right leg and then his left. As soon as his unsteadied left leg made contact with the floor, Sha reemerged, this time flying so fast and so low she took the massive warrior out at the knees.

He landed hard. First on his back and then his head as it whiplashed against the cold marble floor of the king's chamber. Even though they were spiritual beings, when they were in the earthly realm, they and their bodies played by earthly realm rules. Rules like gravity. And pain.

The music had suddenly stopped. And for a split second, Sebastian thought that perhaps the humans had seen or heard of the battle raging around them. Or was it that his ears were ringing so loudly from Sha's first blow that he simply couldn't hear the music? It was neither.

David had noticed the deep sleep that had overtaken the king and decided to stop playing for a bit.

Sha had disappeared again. Sebastian was hurt. And he was losing. The demon's ability to move in and out of the spiritual dimension without detection was a distinct advantage and something wholly unfamiliar to Sebastian. He knew his victory in their first battle was far too easy, and he had anticipated a much more aggressive foe the next time around. But he knew now that if he didn't do something quickly, he was going to be in serious risk of having to surrender this ground and the king to the enemy.

"Creator," Sebastian whispered, "I could use Your strength and Your wisdom right now. Please." He need not say any more. He knew the Creator was in charge, and He knew His will would always be accomplished. Whether he failed or succeeded in his mission. So saying the prayer was more for him than for the Creator. Prayer in difficult times didn't just calm the Creator's human creation; it also helped calm His spiritual creation just the same.

As he finished his whispered prayer, he suddenly realized he couldn't move his legs. He began to feel an enormous amount of pressure on them. The more he struggled to free them, the more pressure he felt. There he was, the great Sebastian, a massive angelic warrior lying flat on his back, ears ringing, eyesight in a fog. And now he couldn't move his legs. And without the movement of his legs, he couldn't get up. And he had to get up.

And then it dawned on him. Sha was doing to him what she had just been doing to the king. Starting with his legs, she began wrapping her massive snakelike body around him. She had played it perfectly so far, Sebastian thought to himself.

Even in moments of terror and panic like this one, he always had a way of thinking critically about the situation. Understanding the important aspects of how a situation came to be always seemed to helped him chart his next series of moves. This situation was no different. If Sha was able to wrap herself around his legs, his torso, and his arms, he would be completely helpless to stop her. He needed something to change the momentum, but without his sword, he had limited options. He decided in that moment to wait. As big as Sha was, she was slightly taller but much slenderer than Sebastian. And Sebastian was wide. Like the Creator chiseled him out of a massive block of granite, nothing about Sebastian was slight or slender. So even though the fallen's grip was suffocatingly tight, rendering Sebastian's legs motionless, he noticed it was taking all her strength and, most importantly, all her limbs to keep him paralyzed. Which meant she was leaving her head and neck completely exposed as she slithered herself around his massive frame. So he waited, thinking at some point she was going to realize her mistake and make an adjustment. She didn't. So he waited. He just needed her close enough to slip his arm around her neck and put her to sleep. She continued to tighten and slither. And then, as if she realized her mistake, she vanished.

Sebastian's legs pushed out wildly as the pressure he was putting against the demon as she constricted his legs and torso was instantly gone. Sebastian scrambled to his feet and quickly sought to locate his sword which, in his mind, felt like he had been without for days even though it had only been a few moments. He spotted it just as young David began to play again.

The music was beautiful, Sebastian thought as he started to fly toward his sword. He didn't make it. Sha had anticipated his move toward his sword as his first instinct after regaining his feet, and she was right. But instead of hitting him or knocking his feet out from under him as she reentered the earthly realm, she slipped herself around his upper torso and neck. She did this by attacking him from behind. So by the time he could tell what was happening, he was already entangled in her snakelike physique. She was made for this kind of maneuver, her slick snakelike frame combined with her strong, sinewy arms and legs.

Sebastian kept his feet as his massive legs were able to keep the rest of his body vertical as the demon worked relentlessly to get him down. Sebastian could see things in slow motion now, as any panic that he might have felt at the beginning of this battle was now a distant memory. He was ready for what came next. He had seen all of Sha's moves now, and while the disappearing act was interesting, the reality was that she needed to be present and visible in order to take him down. She had to face him and defeat him up close and personal. And that's where the battle began to turn.

Sebastian shuffled his feet into an athletic, offensive stance with one foot in front of the other. He then shifted his weight ever so slightly onto his back foot and then waited. Sha was an incredibly sleek and agile fallen. She moved like water. She moved in and out of the spiritual realm with incredible speed and unpredictability, but they both knew the one thing about the spiritual realm that always wins any war across all millennia. Power.

Sebastian had it. She didn't. Sure, every once in a while, a skirmish is won with the element of surprise or a fancy new skill or weapon. But if the element of surprise or a new weapon or skill didn't take out the opponent quickly and the battle lingered, then power began to take over. This battle was no different.

He waited. He wanted her to put all her strength, all her energy, all her attention, and all her focus on squeezing him out. And she was. And he was in serious anguish as she squeezed harder and harder. Still, he waited. He figured he had one opportunity to take her down. And the tighter she constricted, the harder it was going to be for her to release and disappear. If he was right, then he would use the split second of time to put her down once and for all. He didn't need permission to deliver a fatal blow. All warriors were given rules of engagement before every mission. While some rules changed from mission to mission, there were a handful that did not. One such rule allowed for angel warriors to never hesitate to eliminate a fallen from the battlefield when the life of a human or angel was in danger. This rule was in place to ensure angels engaged in battle never had to worry about making the wrong decision about using lethal force on a fallen. If your life or the life of a human is in danger, eliminate the threat. No questions would be asked. Every warrior knew and lived by this rule, and they all knew the Creator had their back.

Sebastian remembered this rule as Sha's grip on his upper body began to set in like concrete. His vision began to darken on the edges as the fallen began to wrap herself now around his neck. He stayed calm and waited for his moment. He could hear her grunting and striving as she constricted herself around him harder and harder. And harder.

David continued to play. Masterfully.

As his eyesight continued to fade and darkness on the edge of his vision continued to spread, he thought of how beautiful the music was. Something he could have heard while worshipping the Creator, he thought. And as that thought drifted lazily from his mind, the next one came screaming in to replace it with such force. Sebastian would later wonder if it was his thought or someone else's. Someone watching over him. From someone fully in charge.

One thing Sebastian had been doing since the moment Sha had wrapped herself so sinisterly around him was to slowly bend his knees. Each bend was so slight and her concentration so intense the demon never realized that Sebastian was slowly bending into a crouched position. A position that had anyone noticed, they would have recognized the massive angel, built seemingly out of granite with a dark complexion and blazing blue eyes, was ready to launch. With a final push knowing full well there were no other angelic warriors on their way to save him, Sebastian made his move. He closed his eyes and pushed up first and then back with every ounce of energy his eight-foot frame and massive bulk could offer. He knew he would likely knock himself out with the plan he had devised but was equally as confident the blow Sha would take would likely annihilate her existence. He was just too massive, and she was too exposed. Sebastian knew she would not have the time or the ability to protect herself from the blunt force trauma he was about to inflict on her. As he ascended up, he remembered later worrying about not getting enough lift and perhaps underestimating how much more weight Sha had added. He knew he needed to get maximum height before making his next and final move. As he reached the apex of his jump, it was clear to him Sha was still very much concentrating all her strength and focus on suffocating him and still had not realized they were on the move. It was only after he whipped himself backward that he noticed her grip begin to loosen, but by then, they both knew it was too late. She was wound too tightly to make any kind of meaningful counteraction or even slip into another dimension as she had been doing. She would have to face the full force of a massive angel coming down on her. The move took only a split second to happen. Up and then back with reckless abandon. But to Sebastian, the time from the apex of his jump to the landing on the chamber floor seemed to pass excruciatingly slow. It was only after he heard the distinctive smack of Sha's slick bald head off the marble that he knew the battle was over. That and a split second later, he felt the life go out of her as he felt her body go slack.

The taking of a life, any life, was a serious thing for any angelic warrior. Yes, they were created for battle, but they were also created with a passion for life and an innate passion to protect it.

Sha's life ended on the floor of the king's chamber while young David played a beautiful melody designed for the king. Sebastian couldn't help but wonder if the Creator planned it that way. Planned it so Sha, one of His creations, would have a song played for her damned spirit as it ceased to exist for the rest of eternity. He couldn't be sure of that. There was so much about the Creator that he and all the angelic creation didn't know. But he knew the Creator's love had no boundaries. He knew the Creator's love was endless. He knew the Creator loved unconditionally, and he would not have been surprised in the least if the Creator ensured a song played for Sha in her final moments even though she had rejected Him and His love completely. His Creator, Sebastian knew, is the definition of love, the depths of which are endless.

With her body limp and her miserable existence gone, Sebastian was able to move his arms, slowly at first, out from under her constricted grip. First his right arm and then his left as he used one to peel off the demon to free the other.

The battle was over. Sebastian had defeated the wicked demon sent to terrify the king.

But had she not been sent and her torment of the king not have taken place, then there would have been no reason for the young shepherd to visit the king. As Sebastian looked down on the lifeless body of the twice-fallen angel, once out of heaven and now out of all space and time, he marveled at how the Creator works all things together. Like a master craftsman or artist, weaving a tapestry of a seemingly infinite number of possibilities into His plan.

As he turned his attention from Sha, he realized his part in the Creator's plan was just that. A part. But he also knew he was perfectly placed here, at this time for a specific purpose. He didn't know what lay ahead, but as he turned his attention to the young future king he had been sent to protect, he realized the Creator's plan was quickly coming together. With the threat to the king now eliminated, Sebastian didn't want other fallens descending on this area and potentially endangering the king any further.

So as David began to pack up his gear for the night, Sebastian made a split decision. He decided to leave David behind, only for a short time. Time enough for him to scoop up Sha's lifeless body and move her far from the king's palace and far from the scene of their battle. He left her body a great distance from the king's palace in an area he knew was regularly patrolled by Rusalmeh's fallens in that region. They would find her soon enough, and they would know quickly who she was and who she had been sent to torment. Finding her lifeless body an impossibly far distance from where she was supposed to be would send the message Sebastian wanted to send: "You lost. Don't retaliate."

Sebastian knew Rusalmeh would want to. Retaliate, that is. But he also knew Rusalmeh as a master manipulator and one who was willing to play the long game. He would retaliate, Sebastian knew that for sure, but it would be of a time and place no one would expect.

*****

Many days went by after the battle with Sha, and as David stayed in the king's service, Sebastian soon realized Rusalmeh ceded the victory to him and would wait for a time of his choosing to retaliate. Plus, Sebastian figured, Sha had no doubt reported the weakness of the Israelite king, and Rusalmeh likely determined he was not worth the risk of more annihilated fallens.

So when the king led his army to war and sent David back home, Sebastian wondered if his mission was complete. He knew oftentimes missions from the Creator were started for a seemingly obvious purpose, only for the mission to end abruptly in a battle, like the one he endured with the water-like serpent demon. But no new orders came. No word from Gabriel. No one to relieve him of his post. Only him and young David back home tending his father's sheep.

Sebastian was just beginning to prepare himself to endure for a long uneventful stretch as he watched over David when something went terribly wrong. David had come back from the fields with his sheep, and after securing them, he quickly turned in for the night. Running sheep all day every day was not an easy life. But David never complained, but he never missed a chance to sleep either.

That evening, as Sebastian sat relaxing on a small granite outcropping just to the north of the family home watching the last remnants of sunlight giving way to darkness, he was startled to see the silhouette of a massive being flying fast and low. At first, he didn't believe his eyes, wondering to himself if he was just imagining it. But as it drew closer, he realized that the being not only was heading straight for him but was not friendly.

Perhaps I'll get to fight again on this mission after all, he said to himself as he stood to face the being flying toward him, right hand on his sword still in its sheath.

As the mysterious being continued to fly directly toward him, the final vestiges of light gave way to complete darkness. Sebastian quickly reached for his night vision as he was reminded again of the need to play by the rules of the earthly realm. As soon as he positioned and activated his night vision, his soul shuttered. "No," he whispered as he suddenly recognized the massive being coming toward him and what it meant.

For a brief moment, he questioned whether he had made a mistake. He quickly began replaying in his mind every memory he could recall of his mission from when he first arrived to his battles with Sha to now. He was desperately trying to reconcile his experience on this mission so far and connect it to what was happening now in this moment.

The prince of darkness for a massive region encompassing most of the known world. Rusalmeh, a fallen outranked only by Lucifer himself, was now descending on his position, and he had a decision to make. Flee or fight?

If Rusalmeh came to fight, Sebastian was a seasoned warrior who could handle his own against anyone, including Rusalmeh. But he knew if Rusalmeh intended to fight, then he didn't come alone. He wasn't going to risk losing a battle or worse to an angel warrior. But it was clear no horde was in tow.

Sebastian continued to scan the dark horizon behind the fallen prince in an attempt to identify a trailing horde. He found none. If he fled, he would be ceding ground to one of the most powerful fallens in the earthly realm, potentially leaving David and his family completely exposed. He didn't hesitate. He was created to fight. To fight for truth. For justice. For all the Creator holds most dear.

So he stood his ground. As he watched the demon softly descend in the moonless night, he knew his decision to stay was the right one. His mission was to protect and defend the future king of Israel. Nothing was going to stop him.

His first indication, however, that this visit was not what he expected was how Rusalmeh approached. His wings back, arms out, and no weapons in sight. As he landed, he did so with clear intention of creating enough space between him and his foe to indicate no ill intent. Sebastian remained motionless as his distrust of fallens and their intentions regardless of their appearance had always been high. Every warrior angel knew the rules when encountering fallens. Namely, there are not rules. So he didn't move. He didn't speak. He was in no hurry. Besides, he figured, *I'm not the one that likely flew a great distance. Let him speak first.*

The two enemies sized each other up as the sounds of night echoed all around them.

Finally, without a hint of malice or sarcasm, the dark prince spoke, "Sebastian. So good to see you."

Knowing that everything this demon, along with all the others, spoke was a lie, Sebastian said nothing. He simply nodded in his direction.

"What, I come all this way for a visit and I don't get so much as a hello?"

There was the sarcasm Sebastian had come to expect. Finally, Sebastian addressed the demon in front of him, "That didn't take long."

"Oh? What's that supposed to mean?" the fallen hissed, no longer able to mask his hatred for the Creator's messenger standing before him.

"It doesn't matter. Why are you here?" Sebastian said, essentially barking the words back at him.

"Calm down, Sebastian," Rusalmeh said softly. "I mean you no harm tonight."

"I won't ask you again," Sebastian retorted, not wanting to give credence to the lies being spoken. "Why are you here?"

"Or what?" Rusalmeh sneered.

"Or we'll quickly see how battle-tested you are without a horde of your best fallens here to defend you." Sebastian's voice was low and firm, his lips barely moving to form the words he was shooting like daggers.

Rusalmeh ceded the point. Both spirits stared at each other and said nothing for a long moment.

Finally, Rusalmeh spoke, "Assuming you were the one who annihilated Sha."

"Why do you assume it was me?"

"You are the only one active in my region, and my slaves claim they saw you coming and going from the king's palace on at least two occasions."

Sebastian said nothing for a bit. Then he said, "Maybe she tripped and fell. It happens time to time."

"Don't patronize me, Sebastian," Rusalmeh whispered begrudgingly, giving him the respect he had earned in battle. He continued, "She was one of my best warriors, and you are one of the few spirits able to take her on and take her down."

Sebastian said nothing. Partly, he was basking in the soft glow of respect being shown him by the highest-ranking fallen in all the known earthly realm and mostly because he was calculating what he should and should not reveal. Sebastian was as shrewd a negotiator as he was a warrior. He knew just how much to reveal and when. It was a skill the Creator intentionally instilled in him and one he honed over millennia fighting fallens in the earthly realm.

"What I can't figure out is why you are here in this place," Rusalmeh said as he looked around, waving his arms back and forth.

Surprising even himself, Sebastian decided to speak up, his blue eyes sharp like daggers in the dark night, "I don't know."

Rusalmeh pressed, "Of course, you know. You just don't want to tell me."

Sebastian said nothing.

"I get it," the demon prince finally said after more than a bit, "but I intend to find out why one of your Creator's strongest warriors is here, in the middle of nowhere, protecting a farm."

"His ways," Sebastian whispered with a smile.

"I know. I don't want to hear it," Rusalmeh said, spitting the words as he held up his dark mangled hand.

Sebastian's response was in reference to the universal truth that all spiritual beings knew to be true. The Creator's ways were well above their own. They could never anticipate or ever know for sure of anything. The Creator and His plans were a mystery, even to those beings who existed in the same dimension.

Without another word, Rusalmeh took flight, immediately disappearing into the darkness of the moonless night.

Sebastian watched him through his night vision as he disappeared beyond the horizon, pondering the real reason for such a visit. One thing was for sure, Sebastian thought to himself, the fallens were going to start paying more attention to him and David than ever before. Rusalmeh would definitely send spies, if he hadn't already, he surmised. With the fallens' radar officially on his actions, he prayed the actions he took next would not derail the Creator's plans for the future king.

His prayer would be severely tested.

*****

As the sun again rose on Bethlehem, David's routine had changed. Normally, it was all about getting the sheep ready for a day in the fields. David was scrambling with his father shouting instructions to both his son and his servants.

Sebastian, who hadn't moved from the position he held during his encounter with Rusalmeh the night before, decided to investigate. David's brothers were off to war, and their father wanted to send them some supplies from home. So David was chosen as the one to deliver them.

The king and his army were nearly a three-day journey, and David's father was urgent to get him and his supplies on the way to his brothers as quickly as possible.

With Rusalmeh's radar up, Sebastian was on high alert as David set out with his brother's supplies headed for the front lines. Sebastian knew they would be watched by the fallen prince's spies, but he finally decided he really had no idea if they would mount any kind of attack. He figured that word of Sha's demise at his hand had reached every fallen horde in the region and likely beyond. It was unlikely any fallen or horde of fallens would try to take a run at him and risk annihilation, especially over a young shepherd from nowhere.

The journey was uneventful. David kept course and pushed hard during the days, often pushing well after darkness, sleeping a few hours, and was then on his way again before dawn.

They arrived at the field of battle early on the third day, and that's when the uneventful part of the journey changed dramatically. Sebastian could sense the fallens long before he could see them, but even then, his mind could not have imagined what his eyes made clear.

The Philistine army was wholly and completely invested with fallen hordes as far as his eyes could see. The stench of hatred, fear, pride, and death hung in the air like a dense fog. They were everywhere.

And eventually, as with all spirits existing within the spirit realm on earth, they spotted him. And word quickly spread throughout the hordes. Sebastian's dark complexion, blazing blue eyes, and massive frame cut a sharp path as he stayed close to David. He had quietly drawn his sword and made no attempt to hide it. If they decided to attack, he would be more than ready, but they didn't. They just watched him and sneered, making no attempt to create a conflict.

As David approached the king's tent, Sebastian noticed that the overall vibe he was getting from the hordes was one of confidence. Like they could not be defeated. As if even his massive presence meant nothing compared to their current standing in the situation.

As he contemplated the justification of such confidence, a booming voice echoed from within the enemy camp. A massive human emerged, sword in hand, taunting the king and his army. Sebastian had never seen such a massive human in all his missions in the earthly realm.

And then he saw it. A massive fallen. One of the few who appeared to be taller and wider than Sebastian. An imposing figure not to be ignored. "Well, this just got very interesting," he whispered to himself. He knew who it was without hesitation. The massive fallen's name was Ra.

Although they had never met, Sebastian remembered Petros talking of the biggest, most imposing fallen he had ever seen who had been one of the Egyptian Pharaoh's demons. He also remembered what Petros had emphasized about him. His massive bulk made him both overconfident and slow. Overconfident because he had yet to face anyone his size and slow because he really was an enormous fallen.

The cacophony of hackles, howls, slurs and slander from thousands of fallens throughout the enemy camp was deafening. At first, Ra didn't pick up on the source of all the racket. Sebastian thought he looked slightly confused. Then their eyes met. Sebastian had been sizing him up since he and David crested the valley overlooking the battlefield.

The overconfident one spoke first. "Are you the reinforcements?" Ra shouted, a greasy, rancid smile with his voice booming sending a hush across the hordes of fallens as if in unison.

All eyes were on Sebastian. He was the lone warrior in a sea of fallens with only the battlefield separating them. He said nothing. Just because a fallen asks you a question doesn't mean you have to answer. It was one of his rules. He just couldn't think of which one. It didn't matter, as he was in assessment mode and had been as soon as he realized the seriously dire situation into which he had just stumbled. He stayed calm, his eyes blazing and his brow furrowed as he began to assess all the possible battle scenarios. It was obvious to him that he was going to fight that day. The sheer number dictated that. Sebastian knew fallens to be primarily cautious, especially around an experienced warrior like him. But he also knew fallens gained confidence in the kind of overwhelming number that existed currently. Add to that Ra and his massive, albeit slow, presence and he concluded it was not a matter of if, only a matter of when.

Keeping an eye on David, who had entered the king's tent some time ago, Sebastian stood watch outside the king's tent.

"I don't like to be ignored!" Ra shouted again, this time the smile gone.

At this point, his slave, a human giant named Goliath, was also spewing slurs and hatred at the Israelite army, leading to a significant amount of cross talk. Additionally, the hordes began cackling and screaming again, creating an incredibly chaotic scene.

Without a word, Sebastian raised his left hand to his ear, singling his inability to hear the giant fallen. He could, of course, but he was more interested in agitating him. It worked.

Without hesitation, Ra stomped his foot and screamed, "I am Ra, and I will not be ignored!" The boom from his voice quieted the hordes as the human giant continued his onslaught. Ra continued, "You are not invited, and you are not welcome. So I suggest you start showing me respect, or I will force it on you."

Sebastian smiled. Which infuriated the demon even more. The hatred, pride, and violence that spewed from his mouth was intelligible and, even Sebastian had to admit to himself, quite terrifying.

At that moment, David stepped out of the king's tent, following what Sebastian thought was a dispute between David and the king's men. Sebastian noticed something he had seen more than once from the future king. A look of confidence, a look of inevitable victory. Inconceivably, David was walking toward the battlefield.

Sebastian would later recall the sheer bizarreness of the moment. A human giant hurling racial slurs and all kinds of hatred at David as he approached while the biggest demon he had ever seen was spewing the same hatred upon him all with the thousands of fallens, adding to the deafening cacophony. Chaos.

But Sebastian, like the human teenager he had been sent to protect, remained calm, trusting his instincts and his experience. He was working all available scenarios through his mind as he planned his next move, one eye on David and the other on Ra.

And then he saw her. Just a flash at first out of the corner of his eye. It took it a second to register. But then he recognized her signature move. As was her tradition on every mission to earth, as she left the heavenly realm, she would draw her sword, signaling her readiness to fight. The flash of light he saw was hers as she removed it from its sheath while in flight. Isabella. One of the Creator's greatest fighting warriors.

The sight of Isabella entering the battle lifted Sebastian's spirit like few others could. At that moment, he knew together they had tipped the scales in their favor. This was a battle they could now win and likely have some fun winning it. So much speed. So much quickness. So much attitude. So little patience.

She was coming in so fast with what Sebastian would later describe as a bit of reckless abandon that he figured the Creator had removed from her all rules of engagement on this mission. He figured right. She timed her landing perfectly for maximum destruction, swinging her sword so aggressively she easily annihilated a dozen or more fallens just as she landed.

The next moment was a toxic mixture of gore, fear, hatred, anger, and cowardice as just as many fallens panicked in fear of Isabella's arrival as they did press to attack her. Those fallens who chose to attack instantly regretted it as she anticipated their arrival and moved with such quickness and agility that her sword could barely keep pace.

As Sebastian watched Isabella send hundreds of fallens into annihilation, he kept his eye on young David. He was, after all, his mission.

David was now facing the human giant Goliath alone on the battlefield—the rest of the king's army, including David's three older brothers, cowering in fear. "You are going to die today," David said calmly.

Sebastian smiled as he whispered to himself, "That's my boy." Sebastian had seen David's warrior mindset on this mission many times before. The future king was establishing his leadership before the entire army he would eventually lead.

And then it happened. It was subtle but significant. Just as Sebastian had taken the attention of Sha, the shape-shifting demon, away from her torment of the king, allowing David's music to soothe him, Isabella was able to take Ra's attention away from the human giant. When Sebastian arrived, he posed no immediate threat to Ra as his mission was one of defense, not offense. With Sebastian posing no threat to his human slave, Ra kept his guard up, protecting Goliath. But Isabella was a different story. She was wreaking massive destruction, and her actions demanded his attention. And just as he turned to face her, letting down his guard of protection over Goliath, young David struck. With Goliath's spiritual protection gone, David delivered a perfect, devastating shot from his sling. It all happened so quickly as if it were choreographed.

Maybe it was, Sebastian thought. *Maybe it was.*

As Ra's human slave landed with a thud, lifelessness in his eyes, all hell broke loose. Realizing he had been outmaneuvered, Ra sent out a scream that was the purest form of hatred and malice that Sebastian had ever heard in any realm. The fallens under his command scattered in panic as did the rest of the Philistine soldiers they had been sent to enslave.

Isabella had not stopped in her quest to annihilate as many fallens as she could that day as she continued to weave and spin, slicing effortlessly through hundreds of outmatched fallens. That was until Ra turned his full attention on her.

Just as Ra was accelerating toward her to engage her in battle, Sebastian noticed something else entirely. The Israelite army, having witnessed young David slaying Goliath, immediately began to pursue their enemy who, having witnessed their massive warrior killed, was now on the run. The battlefield in the human and spiritual realm was now total chaos.

Sebastian had a decision to make. He knew Isabella was going to be in serious trouble as Ra was angrily pursuing her, but he also knew his primary mission was for David's protection. Fortunately, the decision turned out to be an easy one. David did not join the pursuing army, and all fallens were scattering, paying David no attention. Additionally, Isabella had captured Ra's complete attention. David was safe.

As Sebastian rushed to fight alongside his friend, he saw her take the first of many massive blows from Ra. Isabella was so quick, but Ra's strength and ability to absorb blows due to his massive frame made for an epic battle. As the human armies battled around them and the cries and insults of the retreating fallens swirled mercilessly, Isabella and Ra were locked in an epic struggle. Sebastian arrived just in time to see Isabella land a massive blow to Ra's neck, turning him away from her and falling to one knee. Needing no invitation, Sebastian landed an equally sickening blow to Ra's exposed torso, sending the fallen giant to all fours. He didn't stay there long. In fact, his quickness and ability to recover surprised both angelic warriors now operating in sync with each other.

"Ra!" Sebastian bellowed, his sword in front of him, both his hands clasping the handle, ready to deliver another blow if necessary.

The massive beast said nothing.

Sebastian continued, his voice remaining urgent, "You have lost. You have no protection or backup. We are prepared to annihilate you." Sebastian wasn't sure why he gave such a warning, and it sounded strange even as he said it.

Isabella must have been wondering the same thing because as they made eye contact, her face made the universal sign for "What are you doing?"

Ra was silent for a bit and then bellowed, "This is none of your concern! This is between me and this nasty little bitch!" gesturing toward Isabella. He continued, "You have no standing here!"

"Doesn't work that way, Ra, and you know it. We stand together and fight as one, and we all know you may be able to take one of us down. But together, you have no chance at victory," Sebastian said, this time more calmly.

As if he heard nothing, Ra stepped forward, spun, and landed a blow to Isabella's forearm, her armor taking most of the blow as she barely had time to raise her arm to protect herself. Though not slicing her open, the blow was so massive it did knock her clean off her feet, landing on her back. Instantly, Ra pounced, landing most of his massive body on top of her. Isabella was in real trouble.

But that was the advantage of two against one. Sebastian knew his warning to Ra would mean nothing. He knew fallens had lost their ability to reason not long after complete absence from the Creator's love. They began to become beasts in the truest form. Out for blood. At all times. So as soon as Ra was making his first move on Isabella, Sebastian was moving to his right, sliding directly behind Ra, out of his peripheral vision. So by the time Ra had landed on Isabella, Sebastian was already well above the massive demon, having taken flight, intending for his next move to take the fight or the life out of him. Sebastian knew the time had come to try to end this fight Ra would not willingly retreat. It wasn't in his nature.

Ra began his assault on Isabella, delivering blow after blow with clenched fists. Isabella was doing her best to defend against them. She blocked some of the massive blows, but many of them landed and were doing serious damage.

As Sebastian began his descent, it was as if Ra had forgotten about him. Because he had. Ra's rage and fury toward the warrior angel who had helped ensure the demise of his giant slave was myopic. Singular. This extreme focus crowded out any thought in Ra's wretched mind of the other warrior angel present in that moment. It was a thought that would never arrive.

As Sebastian landed directly on top of the giant demon, he drove his sword straight through the top of his head. The incredibly violent action severed the fallen's grasp on existence and instantly sent him into his final annihilation. The battle was over.

Without hesitation, Sebastian leapt off his enemy in search for David. David, after all, *was* his mission. He spotted him almost immediately. Sebastian smiled as young David was now carrying around the severed head of Goliath, his slain enemy.

"Thanks for that," Isabella said weakly.

Sebastian quickly turned and knelt to help his fellow warrior to her feet. "How bad is it?" he asked.

"I'll survive," Isabella replied.

"You sure?"

"Yup. I'm good. These wounds will heal, but a lot of fallens aren't so lucky," Isabella said as she smiled broadly. She had lived one of her greatest moments as a warrior angel. All rules of engagement suspended. No restraint on the strength, speed, and power the Creator had given her. She would be just fine.

With a quick nod to his friend, Sebastian set out to protect young David as Isabella ascended once again back into the heavenly realm.

Little did both of them know in that moment that one day they would find themselves together again on a mission to save the world.

CHAPTER 4

Sam

"Abraham?" Sam asked, more to himself than anyone.

"That's right," Gabriel replied.

"Why do I know that name?"

Gabriel said nothing.

Then a broad smile spread across Sam's face as he finally recalled why that name sounded so familiar to him. "The old man and his wife who were promised a child even though they were ridiculously old!" Sam shouted as the memories came flooding back.

"That's right, Sam. One hundred years old in human years for Abraham. Ninety for his wife, Sarah."

"So cool. I remember being there that day when we told them about the Creator's promise of a child."

Gabriel said nothing.

Sam continued, "His wife laughed at us when we said it."

"Laughed?" Gabriel asked.

"Yeah, laughed. It didn't seem like a time to laugh, but I don't always get why humans do what they do when they do it."

"Precisely why the Creator created us. His angels."

Sam nodded in agreement, a smile still broad across his bright face.

"Well," Gabriel said, getting back to the mission at hand, "the Creator's promise has been fulfilled. The child has arrived."

Sam just smiled. The excitement and awe of the Creator always fulfilling His promise filled his spirit in that moment. It never ceased to amaze him.

"Your mission is to protect the child," Gabriel continued.

"Protect him?"

"Yes."

"From what?"

"You'll know. Just protect him no matter what from everything and everyone, okay?" Gabriel concluded.

"You got it, sir."

No one spoke for a long moment.

Then Gabriel gave one final command that created in Sam both a feeling of awe and fear. "The Creator is directly involved in this one, so don't be surprised if you receive direct communication from Him."

Sam's smile slowly receded from his face. For Sam and any of the other warrior angels, the thought that the Creator would speak directly to them while on mission in the earthly realm was daunting, to say the least. Of course, they worshipped the Creator and loved being in His presence at all times, but being spoken directly to while on a mission was a completely different thing. The pressure on Sam increased tenfold in that moment. He would be ready to complete his mission, but he couldn't mess this one up. He had to be perfect.

As these thoughts raced through Sam's mind, Gabriel put his hand on his shoulder and simply said, "Relax."

Now Gabriel was the one with the big smile.

*****

Quick-witted and always ready to poke fun at himself and others, everyone loved having Sam on their team. Except when he found himself alone on a mission. And on this particular mission, he was alone.

His arrival was uneventful. Gabriel said it would be. He followed the usual protocols. Arrival under the cover of darkness in the earthly realm. Full camouflage engaged. Stay hidden until able to fully assess enemy activity. Uneventful.

Abraham and his wife were as he remembered them. Sam had been one of their three angelic visitors a while ago.

One of the angels had told the man that his wife would give birth to a son. His wife laughed. The angels did not. That night, the man had pleaded with the Creator to save the town some of his relatives were in. The Creator finally agreed but called Sam off the mission while the other two proceeded on.

As Sam approached the encampment of the man and his family, he recalled Gabriel telling him that the town the man had pleaded to save had been destroyed. He smiled as he saw a young boy bound out of one of the tents, chasing one of the young goats wandering throughout the camp. "Another impossible promise fulfilled," Sam whispered to himself.

No one in the camp could see their new angelic visitor, and Sam was not authorized to reveal himself. Only the Creator could authorize that.

As Sam familiarized himself with the camp, its inhabitants, and especially the boy, he wondered why an angel of his skills would be needed in the middle of nowhere to watch after a small child. "Oh well, it should be fun," Sam said out loud to himself, not expecting anyone to respond.

Except someone did.

*****

"Is that why you are on this mission? For fun?"

Sam froze for two reasons. First, as the only spiritual being anywhere near his location, he was not expecting a response. And second, the voice who responded to him was unmistakable. The Creator. He was here. Talking directly to Sam. Sam instinctively took a knee in full reverence of the Creator once his mind fully registered what he had just heard.

"Please stand, Sam. You need to be ready to protect the boy," the Creator said, His voice now unmistakable to the angelic warrior.

Sam obeyed, rising to his feet, saying, "As you wish, my king."

Even in the earthly realm, the Creator was everywhere all the time. So Sam could hear Him speak but could not see Him. He didn't need to. He didn't want to. It was just too dangerous. He was happy to feel and hear him. That was more than enough.

The Creator continued, "I will be sending Abraham and his son, Isaac, on a journey."

Sam said nothing. There was nothing to say. The Creator of all things was talking directly to Sam in the earthly realm. He didn't want to miss a thing.

"I need you to ensure Abraham doesn't harm his son," the Creator instructed.

"As you wish," Sam replied softly.

"It will seem confusing for a time as I will be speaking directly with the man, but just ensure no harm is done to the child."

"Of course, my king," Sam replied.

Nothing was spoken for a long moment. Sam wasn't sure if the Creator was still there or if He expected him to speak.

As Sam lifted his head to look around, the Creator spoke again softly, "Sam?"

"Yes?"

"Be sure to smile, okay?" Before Sam could respond, the Creator added, "It's your thing."

And in that instant, He was gone.

*****

"Gabriel did say I might hear directly from the Creator but…" Sam said out loud to himself, not finishing his thought.

As he followed Abraham, his son, and two of his servants the next morning, he wondered what could possibly lie ahead that required the Creator to spend time preparing Sam.

Time in the presence of the Creator was something wonderful for an angel. In the heavenly realm, the opportunities to honor and worship the Creator were endless, and even those interactions were amazing. But to engage in conversation with the Creator in the earthly realm was something entirely different. Add to that to be working hand in hand with the Creator on a mission and Sam couldn't wipe the broad smile off his face as they began to climb the mountain.

Abraham took the lead, his son at his side and the two servants with the donkey trailed behind. Sam trailed them all, his head on a swivel, on the lookout for anything or anyone who might want to endanger the boy. There was none.

The journey continued for three days. Sam marveled at the stamina of the old man and the relationship he shared with his one and only son. As they walked and talked and laughed together, Sam could feel the love the man had for his son.

But something weighed heavily on the man. At first, Sam thought it was his old age and the fatigue inherent in a mountain climb. But he quickly realized it was something more. Abraham loved his son more than anything, and their bond was unmistakable. But the man was sad. Each night of the journey, the man would leave his tent and walk a distance from the camp, only to begin weeping bitterly.

Sam stayed close to the boy asleep in the tent but took note of the emotions of the father.

Each morning, they would awaken, share a meal, and continue the journey. The man not letting his son know of his sadness. The two enjoying each other's company. Theirs was a special bond.

A bond that Sam would soon find himself attempting desperately to save.

*****

Everything happened so fast. The Creator spoke again, this time directly to Abraham. Sam had stayed back at the camp that morning, keeping watch over the boy Isaac as Abraham spent time alone a distance from the camp. As he came back into the camp, he instructed his servants to stay behind and commanded his son to come with him.

Abraham, his son, and some firewood. Abraham was on a mission. On a mission of obedience. And so was Sam. To keep the boy safe.

Before Sam could make sense of it, the man was arranging the wood on a stone altar and binding his son with rope and placing him on top of the altar.

"Whoa, whoa, whoa!" Sam shouted, not realizing his human companions could not hear him. "Stop! What is going on here?" Sam shouted, again to no one but himself. It was a natural reaction to a rapidly deteriorating situation.

And then he saw it. An impossibly long blade. A knife. So many questions were racing through Sam's mind, until a singular thought broke through like a thunderclap. The boy!

In that moment, Sam flung himself instinctively on the boy, creating an invisible barrier between the man with the knife and the young boy. It was all he could think to do. He knew the Creator was the only one who could authorize a reveal of an angel to humans in the earthly realm, but in that moment, he panicked. His thought was to put himself between the man and the boy and, at the very last second, reveal himself and absorb the knife if need be. That way, the boy would be protected at all costs. That was his mission. Protect the child. Of course, such a move would create all kinds of complexities that would be nearly impossible to explain to human comprehension. Fortunately, for Sam, such complexities never materialized.

The Creator intervened a split second before Sam was ready to reveal himself. "Abraham!" the Creator's voice boomed.

"Here I am," the man cried, tears streaming down his face.

At less than inch away, Sam had a close-up view of the man's distorted face. He would remember seeing the relief crash over him like a wave.

The Creator explained the test and told him to not harm his son.

Now it was Sam's turn to spring into action.

At the same moment the Creator was speaking to Abraham, He was also speaking directly to Sam. "There's a ram just on the other side of the hill. Direct it to the man and his son." The Creator's words were sweet and peaceful.

It wasn't often that the Creator would communicate directly with His angel warriors. He usually left such communication up to Gabriel or one of His other archangels. But occasionally He would. And when He did, it was an amazing experience, even for a warrior angel like Sam who had spent countless millennia worshipping the Creator.

Without a moment of hesitation, Sam leapt away from the altar, away from the man and his child and toward the other side of the hill.

The man immediately took to cutting away the bindings from his still-terrified son.

And just as the Creator had said, there was a ram. Actually, there were three of them. All three were oblivious to the massive spiritual being flying low and fast toward them. Until they weren't.

As Sam flew over the three animals, he began to reveal himself. So by the time he landed behind them, he was fully visible to the animals. "Hey, guys!" Sam said, his voice booming in a way only the animals, not the humans could hear.

At first, the three rams did nothing. They were frozen in fear. This always happened. Every time. So Sam expected it. Anticipated it really. He had already picked the one he wanted to capture. No reason in particular. Just picked one. So he began to move toward them. That brought them out of their fear-frozen state, and they began to jump and scatter.

Sam's athleticism kicked in instantly. At seven feet tall in human measurement, Sam was as quick and agile as he was massive. It was a devastating combination when going up against fallens in battle, but it also came in handy during times like this. As the ram he had chosen began to bound away, Sam's quickness allowed him to anticipate and force the ram to move in the direction he had planned. In the moment, Sam smiled as he envisioned what the scene must have looked like to the human eye. An invisible massive warrior angel and a ram entangled in the most awkward of dances. All the humans would have seen was a ram bounding and running haphazardly toward the top of the hill.

And so it was. The animal grunting and snorting as a massive angel thwarted his every move of escape. The dance of sorts culminated, after a few terrifying seconds, into destiny. The ram's horns got caught aggressively by the thick bush Sam had forced the animal into. There was no way of escape. The animal the Creator had designed specifically for this purpose had fulfilled his duty.

Without delay, Abraham, who had been directed by the Creator, captured the ram and sacrificed it in place of his son. The mission was over. Abraham had passed the test. His son lived. The Creator's promise fulfilled.

Sam's brief mission and dance with the ram was now complete. As he left the earthly realm, all he could do was smile.

The smile of an angel.

CHAPTER 5

The Cleaner

Strong. Not necessarily in the physical sense, although he was that too. Strong in the emotional sense. In that he never flinched under times of incredible pressure. Magnis was often asked to perform his unique and exceptional skill during times of high stress and limited time.

Magnis worked alone. He always said he preferred it that way, and most of his fellow warriors agreed. His work was dirty work. The kind of work that rolls around in your conscious mind forever. The kind of work the Creator only gives to a select few warriors and for good reason. Magnis had been given such skills. He was made for it. Specifically designed for this work before the beginning of time. And he loved it. Not in some sort of sick or twisted way. He loved it because he knew it was his gift given specifically to him by his Creator. His gift from his Creator. This knowledge deep in his heart gave him the strength he needed during times of great stress and uncertainty.

Magnis was a cleaner. The one special angelic force called upon when an unfortunate situation needed to be cleaned. His first mission ever allowed him to display his gifts perfectly. Magnis was called to carry the angelic body of Abel's guardian who had fought mightily but lost to the demonic forces who had infiltrated the mind of Abel's brother, Cain. Cain and Abel were some of the first humans to exist in the earthly realm. And even though they were brothers, they took two very different paths. And it cost Abel his life.

The scene was terrifying. Abel's body lay lifeless with blood everywhere. Magnis described the blood as if it were screaming out for anyone to hear. An unrelenting scream. The eyes of the deceased human were still open, lifeless. As if replaying his final moments over and over again in his mind. Except he wasn't.

The influence over human behavior fallen angels, or fallens for short, possess in the earthly realm is significant. Under the right conditions with human hearts and minds surrendered to their depravity, fallens can lead humans to do unimaginable evil. This was one of those evils. In a fit of demon-induced rage, Cain had murdered his brother, Abel, in the earthly realm. In the adjacent dimension, the spirit realm, Abel's warrior angel warred against a horde of raging demons in an attempt to protect him. It failed. The horde of fallens overpowered the warrior angel and annihilated him. These fallen angels had been damned by the Creator to a miserable existence in the earthly realm, and their only delight came while destroying the Creator's most prized creation: humanity. So in nearly every human activity in the earthly realm, there is equal activity in the spirit realm as warrior angels war against fallen angels, also referred to as demons, in an effort to protect against destruction. Sometimes warrior angels are successful in thwarting demonic influence over humans and complete their mission to protect. And sometimes they fail. It's part of the curse of the earthly realm. It's not like the heavenly realm where everything is and has always been perfect. The earthly realm is unpredictable and dangerous, which is why Abel's warrior angel's effort to protect him was so utterly courageous.

Magnis wept at the sight of his Creator's unique and precious creation left cold and lifeless in the vast expanse. Magnis, as did all the other angels, knew the deep love and affection the Creator had for His earthly creation. And he knew this situation was heartbreaking for his Creator. It's why he was weeping, he supposed. Yes, the scene of destruction was incredibly sad, but he knew the deep sadness his Creator was feeling. And that thought, the thought of the Creator's deep sadness, led himself to weep.

Close by was the human's guardian warrior angel. The body of whom was lifeless as well. Magnis knew this angel well. They had worshipped the Creator together many times, and at that moment, Magnis recalled the sweet voice of his angelic friend, his body bearing the signs of an epic battle for good. He had fought so hard.

Evil had won that day, but Magnis had a job to do. Magnis's mission from the Creator was clear. Bury the human remains with dignity and return the lifeless angel to the heavenly realm. Do it swiftly and without aggression.

Gabriel's voice rang out in Magnis's mind, saying, "You will want to exact vengeance upon the fallens who caused this great destruction, but you cannot."

Magnis understood, and although he wept, he remained strong and set about his work with pace. It was his gift after all. To face incredibly heart-wrenching circumstances and see the mission through.

Angels are able to interact with the physical nature of the earthly realm, only in circumstances with which they have been given permission. Magnis had been given permission so he could both handle and bury the human remains. So he quickly dug the earth and created a hole deep and wide enough to cover the human remains. The earth was cold and damp, the likes of which he had never experienced.

As he laid the body of Abel to rest into the hole, his eye caught movement to his right. Unsure of what he saw, he unsheathed his sword while gently laying the human remains to the ground in one fluid, lightning-fast motion. The movement he saw was not demonic forces returning to the scene as he first had thought. They were instead the slight movements of what Magnis had thought was his deceased angelic friend. He rushed to his side, and while his wounds from the battle were grave, his friend was fighting for his life. Magnis took a sleeve of lotion from his pack and quickly began to address the angel's severest wounds.

It was at that moment that he heard the sound of a gaggle of fallens approaching from a distance. The grunts and howls of the fallens were unmistakably evil and dripping with violence. And by the looks of his wounded friend and the size of the approaching horde,

Magnis knew he must act quickly in order to avoid the same fate as his friend. To be overtaken by a horde of fallens would be a mission failure, and Magnis was determined to never let that happen.

He quickly returned to the human remains, covered the body, and shared a brief but sincere blessing. Then grabbing the rest of his gear, he resheathed his sword and returned to his wounded friend.

By now the horde had spotted Magnis's movements and quickened their pace. Their grunts and now screams were like piercing knives penetrating Magnis's spirit and quickening his resolve to escape this soon-to-be dire situation. He knew once he put the wounded warrior on his back, his ability to move and eventually fly would be slowed. He moved faster. It wasn't until he began slumping his friend over his right shoulder and then onto his back that he realized he was in serious trouble.

The horde was moving faster now, faster than he had ever seen. They were close enough for him to see their wretched teeth and bloodred eyes. Eyes that craved pain, destruction, hatred, and death.

He couldn't make it. He realized that now. Not with his friend slumped lifeless on his back. The realization that he had to leave his friend and fail the Creator's mission was gut-wrenching. But he had to make a decision. It was now or never. There was no way he could fight off a horde of fallens this size. No way.

But that's what he decided to do. He had no choice. If he was going to fail the mission, he was going to take out as many fallens as he could. They betrayed his Creator and nearly killed his friend. For that, they were going to pay dearly. As he set the lifeless body of his angelic friend down on the cold, damp surface of the earth, he once again drew his sword and took a defensive stance, his sword now parallel with his eyes, his right hand on top of his left. Ready. Willing.

But just as he was bracing for contact, he noticed something unbelievable. Almost simultaneously, the eyes of the fallens looked up and to the west. And as if in slow motion, their mouths gaped.

In the very next instant, Magnis saw him. Well, he saw the flash of him. Gabriel, sword drawn, eyes on fire, blazing through the earthly realm, landing with such force the horde of demons fell back in what Magnis would later describe as a beautiful moment of salvation and hope.

The horde of fallens was stunned. No sounds, just gaped mouths in a tangled mass.

Gabriel said nothing. He simply stood, a towering presence in his own right, and looked back at Magnis over his shoulder. A quick smile and nod before he turned back to eye the horde of fallens still working to untangle themselves from one another.

Magnis, needing nothing more than the nod from Gabriel, quickly sheathed his sword, grabbed the wounded angel, and simply said, "Ready."

"Excellent. Let's go," replied Gabriel with grin.

Magnis took flight, and Gabriel followed close behind, all the time keeping an eye on the fallens who knew better than to pursue. Taking on one angelic warrior was risky enough, but every fallen knew never to mess with Gabriel. Never.

They flew in silence for a few moments.

Magnis spoke first, "Thank you, sir."

"For what?"

"You saved me, sir."

"Me?" Gabriel said with wry smile. "Nah, you had the situation well in hand. The Creator just thought you may need a companion for the return trip."

"I failed my mission," Magnis said, his spirit crushed at the thought of disappointing the Creator.

"No, you didn't, Magnis. The circumstances changed. Therefore, the mission changed. You buried the human remains with dignity and secured the angelic remains. You completed the mission."

"Sir?"

"Yes?"

"The angel I was sent to recover. Well. He is..." Magnis's voice trailed off as he tried to figure out exactly how to say it to Gabriel as they approached the heavenly realm, slipping the bonds of the earthly realm.

"What?" asked Gabriel.

"He is alive."

*****

"Quickly!" Magnis shouted as he arrived back in the heavenly realm.

Gabriel had sent a message ahead that they were arriving with a severely injured warrior who would need immediate care upon arrival.

The team charged to care for him was ready and waiting when they arrived. Magnis set the angel gently down, and without delay, the team of angelic physicians went to work. The angel was severely wounded virtually everywhere.

As Magnis stepped back to make room for those tending to the angel, he could see deep scratches, bruises, scrapes, and bit wounds all over his face, hands, neck, torso, and head. A huge gash had opened up across his forehead as well. "I'm not sure he'll make it. Those wounds look terrible," Magnis said softly as Gabriel stood next to him, both of them watching the angelic physicians feverishly working to save his life.

"I've sent word to the Creator," Gabriel said.

"But the Creator already knows," Magnis replied.

"Yes. For sure. He knows everything. But I think He allows things to happen like this and allows us to suffer and work through them so that His perfect plans are administered. Both here and in the earthly realm."

"I wish I had gotten there sooner. Maybe if I had worked quickly…" Magnis's voice trailed off.

"No. You did your job. Did it well," Gabriel said. He continued, "The Creator designed the earthly realm for something entirely unique. Completely different than here."

"Different? How?" Magnis asked as he watched the wounded angel begin to show signs of life.

"Free will. Choice. It's unique because, like here, the Creator is in control of everything. But He allows humanity to make their own choices. And that brings with it all the consequences that come with the bad choices they make."

Magnis said nothing. There was nothing to say.

The archangel continued, "Add to that Lucifer and his hordes roaming the earthly realm, looking to steal, kill, and destroy and you have all the ingredients of what happened to our fellow angel here." Gabriel sighed as he watched the wounded angel open his eyes for the first time since arriving.

His wounds were still visible, but no longer life-threatening. He thanked the Creator in his spirit while he and Magnis shared a moment of silence together.

"I heard you were there," Magnis said after a long silence.

"There?" Gabriel asked with a side-eye glance at Magnis.

"At the first sin. The first bad human choice that started the whole thing. Is that true?"

"Yes," Gabriel confirmed. "The Creator was there too. It was amazing. They had no idea what they had with the Creator. One-on-one time with the Creator and His creation. And the Creator's love for them was so deep and so pure. I was so glad He let me be there with Him," Gabriel reminisced with an energy in his voice unfamiliar to Magnis.

"Why were you there with Him and the humans?" Magnis asked, genuinely curious and at least slightly surprised that his friend was sharing such details.

"The Creator knew Lucifer would be there. It was just a matter of time. And sure enough, he arrived just as expected."

"But he is one of the Creator's creations. Lucifer is no match for the Creator."

"Very true. No match at all, of course. But the Creator wanted me to look after both of the humans at that time. The free will that exists in the earthly realm brings with it a level of uncertainty in which the Creator wants us to actively participate on behalf of His new creation. I was fortunate to receive the first assignment in the earthly realm."

"Amazing," Magnis whispered.

"It really was. To see the Creator walking with His new creation, fellowshipping with them. It really was amazing. I had never seen the Creator demonstrate so much love. It was like it radiated from Him in a way I had never experienced."

"We've heard about what happened, but why did the Creator allow it?" Magnis wondered.

"I pleaded with Him to allow me to take on Lucifer because I could see what he was doing, and I was furious with rage. Lucifer had seen exactly what I had. The radiance of the Creator fellowshipping with His new creation. They became the perfect target for Lucifer. His hatred of the Creator perfectly demonstrated in the manifestation of the snake."

"I'll never understand it. Why the Creator allowed His creation to be deceived and ruin the fellowship He had," Magnis mused.

"I'm sure if there was another way He would have made it," Gabriel responded matter-of-factly.

"Another way?"

"Yes. A way in which His earthly realm creation could have the freedom to choose to love Him while keeping them from rejecting Him."

Magnis nodded.

"But I saw it firsthand. I saw the Creator love something so profoundly that He allowed them to reject Him. He later told me forcing someone to love you isn't love at all. That's how He views it. He loves His creation so deeply and desires their love so passionately that He would rather give them the freedom to choose than force them to comply."

"So He allowed Lucifer into the garden and told you to stand down?"

"Yes. And He and I watched it all happen."

"I'm not sure if I could have restrained myself. Just watching it happen. Lucifer tearing it all down," Magnis said, his eyes narrowing as he replayed the scene in his own mind.

"You do as the Creator says, Magnis. He knows everything, and His will is perfect," Gabriel reminded him.

Just as he was finishing the sentence, the wounded angel sat up on the table and began to look around. The angel looked around until his eyes met Magnis.

At this, Magnis stepped forward toward the table, again reaching toward his wounded brother. "You gave me a serious fright down there," Magnis said.

"What happened to Abel?" the wounded angel asked.

Magnis didn't reply. He just looked over his wounded brother and hoped the question would fade away. It didn't.

"Brother, what happened to Abel?" the angel asked again, this time with more urgency.

"He's gone. I was sent to clean the scene and give him a proper burial."

At this, the wounded angel dropped his head, swung his legs off the side of the table, and stood on his feet, unsteady at first. But he quickly recovered. Without another word, he began to walk on. Then he stopped. Looking back at Magnis with pain and disappointment emanating from his entire being, he simply said, "Thank you, brother." Then turning back around, he continued to walk on. Wholeheartedly dejected.

Magnis watched him go. He didn't know what to say.

"There's nothing to say, Magnis." The words came from behind him, Gabriel simply verbalizing what Magnis already knew. "He will need to work through it, and he will. In time," Gabriel said, putting his strong hand on Magnis's shoulder, bringing a sense of comfort and relief for them both.

"Anything I can do?" asked Magnis.

"Just continue to be a friend and brother to him," Gabriel responded.

"Yes, sir."

PART 2

The Mission

CHAPTER 1

Javva's Decision

It was faint as a whisper, but Javva had heard the sound before. The sound of a sword cutting the wind at speed. He would swear to it. Bent over, weak, and faint with exhaustion, he didn't want to hear what he thought he just heard. But you can't unhear something, not when your sole purpose for existence as a fallen is to hear and see things.

Javva hated his existence, hated humanity, hated nature and anything and everything made and loved by the Creator. Every once in a while, he would remember the days worshipping the Creator and basking in the glow of His glory, but he would never linger on the thought for too long because any thought of what could have been made him even more miserable. He knew he chose wrong when he sided with Lucifer, and even worse, he willingly allowed the reprogramming of his mind to take place as well. He knew he and the others were doomed, something they never talked about, but all just knew.

So there he was, days on end at his outpost, living out his fallen existence full of hate, full of pride, and full of misery listening for any disturbance, any possibility of enemy activity so he could report back to Rusalmeh, the lead demon, the prince of Persia. Javva's master. A report that would be met with disdain, mockery, and a demeaning tone. It always did. Every time he would report anything back to his master Rusalmeh, he wished that much more for the sweet release of annihilation that he was sure awaited him and the others who so brazenly betrayed the Creator.

But that sound. What could it have been? Was it enemy activity? Should he investigate? All these questions were rumbling through his mind like a series of thunderclaps in a dark thunderstorm when he first heard Rusalmeh's call to assemble.

"I can't believe Rusalmeh would do that," he whispered to himself. Javva forced himself to concentrate. The sound of Rusalmeh's call still ringing in his demonic brain.

There it is again. Or was is it?

"Now what?" he whispered to himself. His tiny demonic brain went to work weighing the punishment of not responding to Rusalmeh's call while he investigated what he thought he had heard. And comparing it, heeding Rusalmeh's call, not investigating what he thought he heard, only to later discover he allowed the enemy to enter his territory on his watch. Which one would result in a deeper, more painful punishment?

As he pondered that question, he saw it. A faint streak of light, for a split second, faint as a whisper, but definitely there.

"Forget Rusalmeh," he whispered to himself, his voice raspy and weak. "I make my own decisions."

With that, he rushed to investigate.

CHAPTER 2

The Creator's Plan

"Gabriel?"

"I'm here," the archangel said, kneeling before the Creator.

"It is time."

"Time?"

"For a baby to be born," the Creator spoke softly. He continued, "The life of this child is to be protected at all costs."

"Who is this child?" asked Gabriel.

"Your time of understanding will soon come. For now, you are to assemble your greatest team of angelic warriors. Not for their strength and might only but, first, for their stealth."

"Stealth?" Gabriel asked.

"Yes, their ability to operate undetected behind enemy lines while armed to protect humans is critical," the Creator answered.

"I understand," the archangel replied.

The Creator continued, "The enemy knows nothing of the significance of this child, and neither will your team. Not until the appropriate time. But the child's life is, as is all of humanity, surrounded by evil. And the life must be fully protected."

"When?"

"Soon. Assemble your team and await further instructions."

"What is the message to our chosen forces?" asked Gabriel, knowing his teams were always curious and ready to fight. The opportunity to pursue the enemy behind enemy lines in the earthly realm is the hope of every angelic warrior.

"To protect the child and to do so undetected by the fallens. That is all they need to know. For now, the less they know about the child, the better for them. They must only fight the fallens to defend the child's life and to otherwise protect one another."

"Where?" asked Gabriel, now understanding there were to be no more intrusive questions regarding the mission. He trusted the Creator wholeheartedly and knew he would be told everything he needed at just the right time.

"Nazareth."

CHAPTER 3

The Mistake

The room that night was crowded. It was always crowded on the nights the prince of Persia, Rusalmeh, was rumored to be furious. None of the fallens wanted to be there, but none of them dared avoid such a meeting out of fear of facing the prince's notorious wrath frequently poured out on any who missed his call to assemble.

Not long ago, a fallen named Javva missed the call from the prince and subsequently missed the mandatory assembly that particular night. Rusalmeh showed no emotion about the infraction that night, but that was about to change. Moments earlier the prince had summoned Javva to his chamber, which was not all that unusual as the prince often summoned fallens designated for lookout duty for various updates, discussions, and missions.

No doubt, Javva had forgotten about the infraction he committed days earlier as he nonchalantly and quite carelessly entered the prince's chamber. Only at that very moment did Javva realize the trouble he was in.

The prince had assembled two fallen warriors with him in the chamber. The warriors were not warriors in the common sense. The depth of their depravity and lack of any emotion was legendary among the fallens, and any interaction with them never ended well. They were like wild, untamed, rabid beasts with no regard for anyone or anything. They wore hatred and menace like a cloak, and their dead eyes made them appear soulless and condemned. As if they were the only fallens who had contemplated their fate, understood their hopelessness, and decided long ago to live the rest of their meager existence inflicting as much pain and suffering on anyone with whom they encountered for as long as possible. They emitted the depths of hatred of which even the average fallen was incapable of comprehending.

And there they were, a rare sighting indeed, like statues flanking the prince on the right and the left, heaving with rancid breath as if they had moved with reckless abandon from the deepest depths of hell when called upon by the prince.

The demon froze as he entered, knowing at that very moment that there was no way out. At the same moment, remembering his infraction from days before and realizing that, in fact, the prince had noticed his absence and, as a result, punishment would be coming. Because days had passed since his inadvertent insubordination, Javva had convinced himself, and other fallens who had inquired, that he was in the clear. *The prince had not noticed my absence*, he had told himself confidently. All those conversations and thoughts came crashing in as did the simultaneous realization of this current fate as he began to visibly tremble.

"Come," demanded the prince.

Javva hesitated.

"Now, Javva."

More hesitation as his body began to tremor in waves of terror.

"Now!" the prince screamed.

The scream was so loud, so piercing, and so full of putrid hate that it reached such a high octave that perhaps the human world could hear. So menacing that even the warriors at his side flinched at the sound that could only be described as something from the deepest part of hell itself.

Javva leaned forward, forcing himself with everything in his wretched soul screaming at him, "No! Don't! Get out!" All of which he knew were impossible for him now. His punishment was coming, and for that, he had only himself to blame.

As he moved toward the prince, his mind raced to that night in which he missed the call to assemble. He had heard something. He couldn't be sure, but it definitely was something. And as one of the prince's designated lookouts, Javva's sole purpose was to identify and locate any enemy activity in his designated territory. What he heard was like nothing he had ever heard before. So slight. So quiet. And only once. Nothing repeated. Which was why he had to investigate.

He had heard the enemy enter his realm before, and usually, they were looking for a fight. Usually, they entered with such urgency, with such force there was no way he could miss them. They usually moved so fast and with such purpose, like the Creator Himself gave them the order.

But this time was different. If it even was something. He couldn't be sure. At almost the exact same time he heard this slight noise, the unmistakable bellow from the prince went out. And his bellow to assemble drowned out the noise he thought he had just heard. This simultaneous event created even more uncertainty for Javva.

It would only be many years later as Javva reflected on the sheer enormity and power of the enemy's presence in his territory during this unique time in history that he realized the sound he heard and the prince's simultaneous bellow was likely perfectly planned by the Creator. Once again, the Creator had shown his total sovereignty over all things, including the fallens. Reminding Javva that despite his total focus on wreaking havoc against the Creator's angelic warriors in an attempt to thwart the Creator's plans, he, along with all the fallens, were simply being used by the Creator to fulfill His purpose. Such a realization burned like hot coals searing his demonic brain without relent.

But that night, he decided to ignore the prince's call to assemble and instead investigate the noise he had heard. He convinced himself the prince would want him to investigate. He figured any punishment he might receive for missing the call to assemble would represent only the fraction of the punishment he would receive should the enemy enter his territory undetected. So he pressed on into the night, fast and mean toward the sound he had heard. Knowing that ignoring the prince's call was something the prince would not easily forget and hoping with the entirety of his miserable, soulless life that he had made the right decision.

He hadn't.

CHAPTER 4

The Team Assembles

"I've gathered you here at this moment for the most important mission of your existence," Gabriel said, his voice calm, urgent.

"The mission, sir?" asked Sebastian.

"A child."

"What's special about this child?" asked Sam.

"I don't know," Gabriel responded.

No one spoke. For Gabriel the Archangel to not have a mission detail like that was telling. No one knew what to make of it.

"Look, the Creator made it clear the mission is secret, even to us," Gabriel said after a long awkward pause.

"At least we get to fight and kick the fallens around a bit," mused Isabella. She loved to mix it up with the fallens. She was created to be a strong and fearless warrior, and she knew it. She loved it actually.

"Actually, no, Isabella. That's not the mission," Gabriel announced sternly.

Isabella glanced at Gabriel, thinking, at least for a moment, that he was joking. He wasn't.

"You are to remain undetected until given further instruction. Your first and only priority is to protect the child. Our intelligence indicate there is no fallen activity in the area. But this is in the heart of Persian territory, and we all know what Rusalmeh is capable of."

"The worst," Sam grunted.

"You'll get the hang of it," said Gabriel.

"We'll be sitting ducks. Completely exposed in enemy territory with our hands tied behind our backs," complained Petros.

"The Creator assembled this team for just this purpose. He picked each of you. You'll be ready for anything but planning to encounter nothing. You are to protect the child and remain undetected. That's the mission."

"They will find us," said Sam. "No matter how quiet we are, we are in their territory. They will eventually find us."

"Then you fight," Gabriel shot back.

"Yes!" shouted Isabella.

"You fight by being undetected," Gabriel said, quietly staring directly at Isabella.

She said nothing.

Gabriel continued without looking at her, "Something of which I'm not entirely sure you are capable." He continued to the rest of the team, "That's the mission. Don't get found. And if you are found, fight. But only as necessary to protect the child while remaining undetected."

"Sounds easy enough," Sam said sarcastically.

Gabriel let it pass.

"When do we go, sir?" asked Sebastian, finally speaking up.

"Only the Creator knows. Just be ready."

"Do we at least know where we are headed?" Sam asked.

"Nazareth."

CHAPTER 5

The Team Prepares

"All right, everyone. Get your gear together and be ready to fly in one hour. The Creator's time is perfect, so when He's ready, we'll be ready," Sebastian said as he stepped into the team room.

"Will you be coming with us?" Isabella asked.

"No. The comms will be open, and I'll be monitoring your movements at all times," replied Gabriel.

"I wish we knew more going in," said Petros.

"I know it's not our place, but we usually have more to go on," Isabella added.

"And have to stay undetected. The worst," whispered Sam. As the one who took it upon himself to keep things light while on mission, staying undetected was going to be the hardest on him.

"Why are you whispering?" asked Isabella.

"Just testing out my stealth skills," replied Sam.

"You'll have to do better than that, bud," whispered Petros, in a whisper just slightly quieter than Sam's.

"Who do you think this baby is?" Sam asked, changing the subject.

"No idea," replied Petros. "But I remember watching Baby Moses, you know before he grew up, flew off the handle, killed the Egyptian, buried him in the sand, and fled the scene."

Isabella smiled and said, "I didn't know that. I heard the story about the basket in the river though. Did you have to stay undetected watching Baby Moses too?"

"No way," reminisced Petros. "Egypt was crawling with fallens, and the Egyptian king invited them in like they were family. Plus, the fallens were given free rein on the Israelites, so the Creator let us loose. When the baby was placed in the water, the fight was on."

"I have always wished I was there," said Isabella. "I heard the Creator cancelled all rules of engagement to protect the baby. True?" asked Isabella.

Petros nodded.

"The fallens hate water, right?" asked Sam.

"Sure do. But they had figured out Baby Moses was important to the Creator's plan, so they went all out. I mean all out."

"Sebastian, you were team lead on that mission too, right?" asked Isabella.

"Yes," Sebastian replied without making eye contact.

"It was Sebastian's idea to influence the daughter of the Egyptian king," said Petros. "Turned out to be a brilliant idea. He quietly reminded her of the majestic beauty of the Creator's sunrise at the river's edge at just the time the baby basket was floating by."

"She couldn't resist," Sebastian said quietly. "We had heard her talking to her servants about all the beautiful babies through the palace grounds."

"It worked beautifully and just in time," Petros recalled. "As much as the fallens hate water, they hate the Creator and His plans even more. So they were ferocious that day, trying to drown the baby boy. Plus, in the river, there are so many creatures to influence, so many forms of nature to weaponize against a helpless baby like that."

"Scary," Sam said.

"It was. It really was. But getting the baby into the hands of the king's daughter was brilliant. Literally brilliant," said Petros.

"How so?" asked Sam.

"You have to remember, the Egyptian king literally invited the fallens in, but our intelligence services had told us the king and his whole family were off-limits and, in fact, to be protected by the fallens," recalled Petros.

"What for?" pressed Sam.

"Not entirely sure. But because the Egyptian kings were notoriously superstitious, we think they were fearful of the king turning soft and letting the Israelites go if bad things started happening to his family," recalled Petros. "And keeping the Creator's chosen people enslaved was and will always be Lucifer's main priority."

"Okay, but I still don't get why ensuring the baby wound up with the king's daughter was so brilliant," stated Sam.

Petros hesitated, sighed, and then smiled. "Simple. We knew the family was off-limits, and once Baby Moses became part of the family, we knew he would be protected. So even though he was surrounded by fallens, he was not to be touched."

"That is brilliant," Sam said, gazing into the distance.

"The Creator is brilliant. He's the one who weaves all of this together for His purposes. Anything brilliant is from the Creator. Don't ever forget that," Sebastian said this while looking at all of them, one by one, making sure they met his gaze.

"Copy that, sir," they all said in unison.

Sebastian left the room.

After a long silence, not surprisingly, it was Sam who spoke up with a smirk. "Hey, Isabella, do you even know what the word 'undetected' means?"

"I'm fairly confident you don't want to find out, so I would watch your back, my friend," Isabella shot back, herself with a smirk.

Isabella and Sam had been on several missions together as a team, and they enjoyed each other's company, even though they both liked to take shots at each other for good measure.

"Listen up," said Sebastian sternly as he stepped back into the room with a look of resolve in his bright eyes. "Tonight we fly."

CHAPTER 6

It Is Time

"All right, everyone, time for a final gear check," Sebastian said quietly with resolve in his eyes and a deadly serious way about him.

As he walked to another room, he asked Petros to lead the check with the team.

"You got it, sir," replied Petros eagerly. Starting with his own gear, Petros shouted, "Comms are a check! Weapons?"

"Check."

"Armor?"

"Check."

"Night vision?"

"Check."

"Camouflage?"

"Check."

"All ready, sir," said Petros in a loud whisper in Sebastian's direction in the other room. Sebastian was staring off into the distance, and at first, Petros thought Sebastian didn't hear him. So he stood up, began walking toward his commander in the other room, and began to repeat himself, saying, this time a little louder, "All set—"

"I heard you, Petros," said Sebastian quietly.

"Sir?"

"Is the team ready for this mission?" asked Sebastian, staring into the distance.

"Ready as always, sir," replied Petros. "Why?"

"This one is different. Feels different anyway. Not even Gabriel has been told any of the details of the mission. Why wouldn't the Creator tell him?" wondered Sebastian.

"The Creator's plans are perfect, and so is His timing," said Petros with as much faith as he could muster. But he still sounded like he was trying to convince himself as much as anyone.

"Of course. Always has been. Always will be," said Sebastian like a warrior who had never been deceived or let down or left behind on thousands of missions over millennia.

"But?" asked Petros.

"But what?"

"But why are you hesitating and staring vacantly into the distance?" pressed Petros.

"I don't know. Just feels different this time. Bigger. Gabriel senses it too," he said, turning to face Petros, resolve emanating from his face like waves of heat flowing off earth's horizon at sunrise. He continued, "To stay quiet and to not engage the enemy without a clear mission other than to stay hidden and protect a child? Seems impossible and a fool's errand, especially in Rusalmeh's region. Seems reckless and extremely dangerous…" Sebastian's voice trailed off, letting his words linger like the smoke of a newly extinguished flame.

"I'm not sure what to say, sir," said Petros sheepishly.

"Nothing to say, Petros. Thanks for listening. The Creator's plans are perfect, and we are to do His work. He tells us what we need to know when we need to know it," he whispered as he bent over to grab his own gear. "It's time to go."

CHAPTER 7

Javva Investigates

It was right here, he thought to himself.

"Right here." The combination of his whisper and his rasp made his voice sound more demonic than most. Javva had arrived at the spot he believed to be the most likely location of the enemy based on the trajectory of the flash he saw. He stopped. Looked hard in the darkness and slowly turned. He kept turning, listening, looking. Turning, listening, looking. Turning, listening, looking. Nothing.

He realized at that moment his decision to pursue potential enemy activity and ignore Rusalmeh's call to assemble was not just wrong but could prove fatal. So he kept searching. Searching for anything or anyone that might be there.

As time passed, the pressure in his mind mounted. He knew he must find something, some reason for ignoring Rusalmeh's call, but there was absolutely nothing to be found. He began to accept the fact that he chose wrong. That what he saw and heard was nothing at all and his decision to pursue would likely come back to haunt him.

As he turned to leave the grove he had so thoroughly searched, eight angelic eyes watched his every move. The angelic warrior team hidden within the thick foliage of the grove, camouflage still fully intact and ready for swift action in case of discovery, watched Javva with the intensity and stillness for which they all had trained for millennia. As the demon moved on, they all relaxed a bit, not realizing the worst was yet to come.

CHAPTER 8

Behind Enemy Lines

They could smell Javva before they ever saw him. A combination of fear, hate, and the unmistakable stench of a demonic being damned for eternity, scratching out the last moments of his meager existence against the backdrop of eternity. A stench best described as some form of organic feces and burnt camel hair.

Upon entry, they had flown in a V-shaped pattern low and wide. Their night vision was engaged along with a thin layer of camouflage designed to reflect the environment around them as they flew into the earthly realm's darkness.

Their only communication was nonverbal with strict orders from Gabriel and with emphatic agreement from Sebastian to stay off comms and to say nothing. Absolute quiet entering enemy territory was not the usual mode of entrance.

Especially for Isabella. She loved to make an entrance and did everything she could to attract fallens. A tactic that usually worked at least at first. It wasn't until the fallens would realize who it was that they would turn tail and seek escape as quickly as possible. Isabella was so fast, so powerful. One moment of hesitation by a fallen spelled certain doom when Isabella would come barreling into enemy territory. She loved to tell the story of being sent to enter a battle already underway in which a young shepherd named David was about to take on an entire army of enemy soldiers, starting with their human giant.

The word came down from the Creator through Gabriel. And He simply said, "Protect the boy and use all the gifts I have given you to do so."

Isabella knew exactly what that meant. Game on. The words had barely left Gabriel's lips and she was off.

The way she told it, the fallens were everywhere, all throughout the Philistine army as if they knew the importance of either the battle or the young boy or both. She tore through the fallens within the Philistine camp with such speed and force that most never saw her coming, and those who did would never forget the searing pain she caused them.

Her arrival on the scene created such a commotion the human giant's demon took notice. He was a massive, hulking beast, surely one of Rusalmeh's best most-equipped fallens. But he too made the mistake of underestimating Isabella's speed and power. After seeing Isabella's onslaught of so many fallens so quickly, the warrior demon made the split decision to leave his human slave named Goliath to take on Isabella, certainly never imagining for a moment the young boy would be any threat to his giant human slave.

It turned out the Creator only needed that slight distraction, that moment of unprotection to slay the human giant at the hands of the young future king of Israel.

Isabella told the story of that day always with an extra sparkle in her eyes because of the wide-open rules of engagement and all the pain she inflected on so many hundreds of fallens.

But it was always in her quieter moments when she would whisper in awe of the Creator's plans. So subtle yet so perfect. She would speak of how she thought she had been sent for her power and speed, but she was sent by the Creator at just the right moment in human time and space to be one thing and one thing only. A distraction. And that single act of distracting the fallen warrior away from his master allowed the future king David to land the fatal blow and change the course of human history forever.

These memories raced through Isabella's spirit as they raced toward Nazareth in absolute silence. Until it happened. So slight. So subtle.

As they prepared to land, Isabella drew her massive sword, more out of habit than anything else, causing a slight noise of wind friction across the massive blade and a fraction of light bouncing off the blade as she prepared to land.

Sam and Petros saw the scene play out, and while frustrated at the infraction, no one made mention of it. It wasn't until they all smelled Javva, that distinct smell of a fallen so close to their point of entry that they realized how critical the mistake Isabella had made.

No one made a move. To be detected and to have to take on a fallen mere seconds after landing in enemy territory could be a complete disaster.

As they landed, they instinctively folded their wings and hugged the cool, damp earth. Gabriel was a meticulous planner, and this mission was no different. He wanted no chances to be taken, and although no significant fallen activity had been detected for some time in the area, he insisted on a small olive grove a significant distance from the property for which they were sent to protect.

It was in this small olive grove surrounded by a dozen trees and tall wispy grass that they lay in complete silence as Javva approached. Their advantage was the element of surprise coupled with superior planning spotting Javva well before he noticed the disturbance created by Isabella and her sword. They all watched him as he quickly turned toward them, hesitated, and then raced in their direction.

All eyes were on Sebastian now. Everyone had the same thought. Would he make a battlefield decision to change course and charge the fallen, taking the attack to him since they still maintained the element of surprise? Or would he obey orders all the way through entry?

His stoic gaze making specific eye contact with each member of the team made his intentions clear. Stay the course. His simple gesture of his left wing partially covering his face was all the direction the team needed. Drop down and stay hidden.

By the time Javva showed up at their location, he clearly was unsure of himself. He was moving tentatively and seemed more than a little distracted. That and the sweat. He was sweating like crazy. Sweat was a fallen's natural reaction to stress, and based on the sweat pouring off Javva, he appeared to be on the verge of a complete breakdown. As he moved throughout the grove, around trees, and through the tall grass, he kept looking pensively behind him from where he had come. Stressed and distracted, the fallen missed several signs of enemy activity which, under normal circumstances, would have led to a violent confrontation.

But not this night. Java moved through the grove a second time, only to flee as if running to or from something else, leaving his stench wafting through the still night air like the sound of ocean waves crashing in the distance.

No one moved.

CHAPTER 9

The First Encounter

"Clear?" asked Sam with the slightest whisper.

All eyes were on Sebastian. It was his mission to lead, and everyone counted on his wisdom and experience. With a single hand motion, he told them to hold in place, keep night vision in place, and stay hidden. Sebastian had been in these situations before. Many times. Across enemy territory. And he knew one important fact of the fallens. Rarely, if ever, was there only one. If one saw the flash of Isabella's sword, then at least one other did as well. Isabella's mistake was costly. However, it could result in no harm, but they had to stay hidden. Stay hidden and wait.

As Sebastian was thinking these very thoughts, he heard him. Well, technically, he smelled the fallen before he heard him. That distinct smell of sulfur, feces, and death. It had only been a few minutes between visits from the curious fallens. The first one scoured the area and fled quite quickly. He seemed distracted or in a hurry or both.

This one, however, was much more methodical. As if he was on strict orders to not return unless he found something or someone. As the fallen approached the grove of trees in which the team was well hidden, his approach was cautious, and he didn't enter right away. He circled the grove twice as if planning out all his moves, not simply the next one or two.

From where Sebastian was hidden, he had clear view of half of the grove with the ability to stay hidden, swivel his head, and follow the demon the rest of the way. With a slight motion, he commanded his team to stay hidden and fully undetected. He was confident in his team, but this would be the true test of their mission. Stay undetected and fight only as a last resort. This demon was going to test the mission in its first hour behind enemy lines. Sebastian could sense it.

After the fallen had circled the grove twice, he made his entrance into the grove slowly, just east and slightly north of where Petros was hidden. They all were wearing a special camouflage covering their wings and heads that drastically reduced the natural shimmer and left only a dull, dark gray in the moonlight. A near-perfect representation of the trees and foliage around them. They were impossible to see, but they were not completely invisible. They weren't ghosts. They could easily be stumbled upon, and then what? Sebastian wasn't sure.

They had gone over and over the rules of engagement for what seemed like hundreds of times, and they all conducted scenario training on how to respond to as many different fallen encounter scenarios as possible. But testing out their training so early in the mission was close to a worst-case scenario. Alerting the enemy and their forces was the exact opposite of what the Creator intended. They had to stay undetected. For the sake of the humanity. For the sake of the mission. For the sake of the baby.

The fallen moved slowly. Painfully slow. He was checking every tree. Every bush. Every dark area in the grove. And he was meticulous. He was methodically covering every inch of the grove, and he was working his way toward Isabella, who had hunkered down behind a tree and wedged between the root system protruding from the ground and large bush.

By now, the entire team had picked up the fallen, and each warrior was watching and, by this time, smelling his every move. As he drew closer, checking ahead and behind, above and below, he suddenly stopped, as if he heard or saw something. They all watched as excruciatingly long moments passed. No one moved. Including the fallen. There he stood, as if frozen in time, until he wasn't as he started to move again, this time away from the group and toward the west edge of the grove. He moved as if he second-guessed his strategy and was starting over.

With the imminent threat from discovery now slightly averted, all warrior eyes turned to Sebastian. Through subtle hand motions, Sebastian reminded his team to stay hidden and to wait for his signal. No one was to move until he said so.

The fallen was now circling back west to east slowly, methodically drifting closer and closer to the team of angelic warriors.

They all watched him. No one was nervous. Quite the opposite. They were ready. They all had accepted this mission. Although they didn't know the stakes and wouldn't know for a long time, they knew the Creator was depending on them to stay hidden, undetected, and they were ready to do just that. No matter how much they wanted to rise up and annihilate this fallen among them, they all knew what a scene that would cause. No one wanted to jeopardize a mission from the Creator. They loved Him too much. So they waited. Patient and ready. All eyes from the fallen back to Sebastian. Back and forth. Back and forth. Closer and closer. And then it happened.

It was subtle at first. A slight step that kicked past Petros whose back was to the fallen. He was unable to completely fold up behind the bush under which he was hiding. His left ankle and foot were exposed, and although he was covered in camouflage, his leg created just enough of an obstruction to trip the fallen as he moved past. The action created a natural reaction from Petros, moving dead leaves and underbrush as he recoiled from the contact with the fallen creature.

From Sam's position, he could see everything unfold as if in slow motion. He was anticipating the encounter and Petros's subsequent reaction. So as soon as contact was made, he lunged straight up and out from his prostrate position, instantly enveloping the demon. The force and speed of Sam's movement left no reaction time for the doomed fallen. His left arm instinctively wrapped around the fallen's neck, hard against his slimy, wretched skin. He didn't want to give the creature any opportunity to make a noise or let out a cry, for fear of what might come next. They were the best of the best, but they all knew a full onslaught from Rusalmeh's forces would prove fatal. So he squeezed tighter. In a simultaneous movement as if choreographed, his right arm reached for his weapon, the sound of which made the fallen's blood run instantly cold.

"Stop!" a shouted whisper escaped through Sebastian's teeth. "Enough, Sam. Enough."

Sam's grip remained firmly in place around the fallen's neck, but he resheathed his weapon slowly but firmly. "Sir?" asked Sam.

Using that one word in the form of a question, Sam asked the most important questions that everyone on the mission in that moment were asking. "What now? What do we do with this fallen? What's our next move? Do we eliminate the threat? Do we keep him in captivity?" No one even entertained the thought of letting the demon go, knowing full well that their location, their number, and their identities had all been compromised by this one insignificant fallen.

Sebastian waited.

"Sir?" Sam asked again, this time more urgently as the fallen struggled for freedom from the vice grip of Sam's left arm.

"So sorry," Isabella blurted out. "I should have known better."

"You do know better," said Sebastian sternly. "This will be a short mission for you, Isabella, if you treat this like another chance to pile up fallens on your scorecard," Sebastian chastised. He continued, "This is a secret mission and must be treated as such at all times."

"Yes, sir. I understand. I'm sorry," Isabella replied, truly remorseful.

"Sir?" asked Sam, still firmly in control of the enemy combatant.

"Petros, set up comms and communicate with Gabriel our status. Do so with extreme caution and only speak what is necessary and then shut it back down."

"You got it."

Establishing a secure communication behind enemy lines from the earthly realm to the heavenly realm required several key steps. First, Petros created a false entry and exit point of the comms as it left the earthly realm. This was designed to ensure no fallen in this region detected the communication, eliminating any possibility of tracing back to their location. Second, disguising the communication as fallen activity was a specialty of Petros and critically important to this mission.

With superior technology, the Creator's warriors were able to disguise their communications behind enemy lines to appear as if they were fallens communicating with each other. Petros was able to do this by scrambling his voice and anyone speaking to sound like a fallen as it left the earthly realm and unscrambling the voice as it entered the heavenly realm. That way, in case any of their communications were intercepted, they would sound like the scrambled words of a fallen speaking, leaving little, if any, reason for alarm on behalf of a fallen who might have intercepted their communication.

As Petros was quickly establishing communications with the heavenly realm, Sebastian continued to provide direction to his team. "Isabella, establish a perimeter and stay concealed but ready for any follow-up action from the enemy. Move quickly."

Isabella was gone, and in her place was left the quiet stillness of the dark, deep night on earth. Silence fell on the scene like a dense fog.

Only after a very long moment, Sebastian spoke quietly, "Sam."

"Yes, sir."

"End it."

In an instant, Sam brought his right arm around the chin of the fallen's slimy face, being careful not to get bitten. And in one fluid motion, the warrior wretched the chin of the demon. He did so with such force that no sound escaped except for the slight grunt Sam made in taking the deadly action. The body of the fallen fell slack to the ground, emitting the kind of stench that would linger in both warrior's memory for a long time.

None of the other warriors saw the action Sam had taken, but they all knew its potential consequences.

Sebastian looked down at the slack, dark, lifeless form of the fallen and then back up at Sam as he dropped the severed head to the ground.

With a slight nod from Sebastian, Sam stepped away from the scene and took a knee to collect his thoughts and begin to calm his nerves. The adrenaline from the last several moments had yet to reach its peak as he worked to slow his breathing.

"You good?" asked Sebastian.

"Good, sir," Sam quickly replied.

"We had no choice, Sam."

"I know, sir. I know. What's next?"

"I'll request a cleaner immediately," Sebastian said as he looked for comms connectivity from Petros, who was on the edge of the trees at the moment, establishing a secure communication to the heavenly realm.

Just then, Petros spoke up through the comms device they all had as part of their equipment. "Secure comm established, sir," Petros whispered.

"On my way."

In a swift movement, Sebastian arrived at Petros's location. Before reaching for the comms device that Petros was holding out for him, he asked Isabella through their secure communications link if she was seeing any additional enemy activity. Time was of the essence now. It wouldn't be long before the fallen they had just annihilated would be missed.

"Nothing, sir," whispered Isabella a split second later.

"Hold your positions," commanded Sebastian with a firm calmness that kept everyone on the team focused and confident. He was a great leader, and they all loved him for his steadfastness and strong leadership under pressure. Grabbing the comms device from Petros, he said, "Sir?"

"Go." The voice of Gabriel was strong and fierce on the other end.

"One enemy fallen confronted and the threat eliminated." Sebastian paused, knowing the impact of the news and his next request. He continued after a long moment of silence, "Requesting a clean crew immediately."

"Who took the action?" Gabriel asked calmly.

"Sam."

"How is he?"

"No injuries and good to go."

"Okay. Any signs of additional enemy activity in the area?"

"No, sir. Not yet."

"Any concern your position has been compromised?"

"No, sir, but we will not be staying here much longer. We will support the arrival and departure of the cleaner, and then we will move out before dawn if possible."

"I'll send Magnis. He will arrive within the hour. Stay alert and lay low," Gabriel responded, fully in command of the situation.

"Thank you, sir," Sebastian said, equally in command of his situation.

Gabriel and Sebastian had been working missions together for the Creator that spanned millennia. They trusted each other explicitly, and both new time was of the essence here.

"And sir?" asked Sebastian.

"Yes?"

"We had no choice. I made the decision to eliminate the threat to save the mission. I hope you understand."

"I trust you, Sebastian. No need to explain yourself. The Creator chose you for this mission, and you have His complete trust. I know you will keep your mission to stay undetected and to protect the child and the family. We were ready for this."

"Thank you, sir."

"Magnis is on the way to clean the scene. Within the hour."

"Great."

"And Seb?"

"Sir?"

"Tell Sam I said try not to eliminate any more fallens, at least for the rest of tonight, okay?" Gabriel said with just the slightest of smiles.

"Will do, sir," Sebastian said with a smile. "Will do." Sebastian gathered the team quickly together to plan their next move.

Isabella spoke quickly, "I think that was Javva."

"Who?" asked Sam.

"The fallen. His name is Javva."

"The one Sam eliminated?" inquired Petros.

"No. No. The first one that came by. I knew him before the fall. I encountered him again as Rusalmeh's lackey in an annihilation plot years ago. I know it was him."

"What does it mean?" asked Sebastian, giving Isabella the opportunity to draw her own conclusions.

"Not quite sure, sir," Isabella continued. "The last time I saw him, he had failed Rusalmeh so miserably I didn't expect to ever see him again among the living."

"Well, if it was him, Rusalmeh has decided to keep him around for one reason or the other because we could not be more in the middle of Rusalmeh's region. He rules this entire landscape," Sam said as he looked around wearily.

"And the clock is ticking," whispered Petros. He continued, "Rusalmeh is going to be expecting a report, and when it doesn't arrive soon, all hell will break loose."

Sebastian nodded at Petros and said, "Sam, you stay behind and meet up with Magnis. He has the coordinates for this exact location. I will meet him first, give him my instructions, and then send him your way. Stay well hidden. I figure you'll have at least an hour before any suspicions are raised by the deceased fallen."

"Yes, sir."

"We'll meet at our second rendezvous point as planned. Everyone else, gear up and be ready to roll in two minutes. No time to waste. We have to get hidden before the sun," Sebastian commanded.

No one spoke for a long moment.

"Tomorrow we'll set up camp and prepare for the child's arrival," Sebastian said, looking into the distance at a small house and barn well into the distance.

"This must be one special child," Sam whispered to himself but loud enough the entire team heard.

Special indeed. This was the first encounter that would lead the entire team to question the Creator's mission to stay hidden.

It would be far from the last.

CHAPTER 10

Magnis Arrives on the Scene

"It's been a while," Magnis said with a short smile.

"Indeed, it has," replied Gabriel, acknowledging Magnis's smile with one of his own. Gabriel continued, "We have a warrior team deployed that needs your services. They encountered a fallen and eliminated the threat."

Magnis said nothing.

"You will need to clean the site, remove the fallen remains, and leave absolutely no trace of any angelic or fallen activity."

"Understood," Magnis replied.

"Your mission tonight is critical as their mission is to protect a human child and the family while staying completely undetected."

Magnis nodded with a mixture of understanding and excitement.

"With a fallen missing, Rusalmeh will turn that region upside down looking for him. So you'll need to deliver your best work and keep our team on the ground completely undetected," Gabriel instructed. He knew Magnis, and he knew he could trust his work completely.

"Yes, sir," whispered Magnis, a thousand thoughts racing through his head.

Gabriel continued, "Add to that the Creator's explicit instructions to stay hidden throughout the duration of the mission and we have a very challenging situation to solve. And to solve quickly." Gabriel was staring directly into Magnis's eyes as he spoke, looking for any indication that Magnis was not up to the challenge. He found none.

Magnis was staring right back at him with a steely resolve Gabriel knew no angel could fake or force. Magnis was ready. "Sir?" asked Magnis, surprising the leader of angels slightly.

"What is it?"

"Thank you," replied Magnis. "I'm grateful to serve the Creator in this manner today."

"You are welcome. You are to meet Sebastian at the rendezvous point, and he will take you in from there. Bring the fallen remains back with you to the heavenly realm. We will dispose of it properly upon your safe return," said Gabriel as he moved past Magnis.

After a brief moment, Magnis spoke as if to reassure his angelic leader, "I'm ready."

"I have no doubts. It's time to go. You'll need all the time you can get," Gabriel replied without looking back.

Magnis took flight while darkness still enveloped the earthly realm. Angelic forces, especially those looking to go undetected, found darkness to be the most effective time to arrive in the earthly realm. The fallens could see in the dark but, like humans, not as well as during the daylight. And the angelic forces always looked to exploit that advantage. So with his camouflage in place around his wings, torso, arms, legs, and head along with his night vision in place, Magnis took flight for the rendezvous point to meet Sebastian.

His arrival, unlike that of Sebastian's team not long before, was uneventful.

"Magnis?" Sebastian whispered as even he wasn't quite sure if he was seeing things.

"It's me, Seb," Magnis replied.

"Good to see you, my friend."

"Likewise."

"Thank you for coming so quickly. We are racing against time here."

"I understand."

"An hour has passed since we took the action against the fallen. They will be searching for him soon, and I expect Rusalmeh will leave no stone unturned."

Magnis nodded in affirmation.

"Sam is currently at the location of the incident, hidden and awaiting your arrival. The remains of the fallen are there as well. The remains are hidden but would be discovered quickly without the work you are about to do."

"Let's get to it. Dawn is arriving soon, and I want to be long gone before that happens," said Magnis.

"Okay. Sam is hidden in the grove of trees about a half a click south of our current position. He's expecting you."

"Can you let him know I am here?" Magnis whispered this, thinking to himself that the last thing he wanted to do was surprise Sam who was likely on high alert with angelic adrenaline still coursing through him.

"Negative. We are radio silent due to the evening's events. You'll find him hidden on the south end of the grove. Just don't sneak up on him. He doesn't like that."

"I'm gathering that maybe I'll ask the fallen I'm here to recover how that worked out," Magnis whispered with a smile.

"Time to go."

"For sure."

"Magnis?"

"Yeah, Seb?"

"I'm glad you are here."

"Me too, brother. Me too."

And with that, Magnis flew fast and low, night vision still in place. And with no fallens in sight, he arrived at the grove quickly and quietly.

He entered at the south end of the grove, eyes open for fallens and for Sam. The situation was tense. Time was of the essence, and until he made contact with Sam and was able to assess how much cleaning needed to be done, he remained intense and on edge.

"Sam!" Magnis whispered with a force that kept his voice low but would allow Sam to hear him clearly. Silence. "Sam!" he whispered again as he moved south to north through the grove. Still silence.

A few more steps and then he stopped and listened. Total darkness. He saw no movement. Nothing out of the ordinary as he scanned the landscape for Sam. Knowing he would be hidden and on high alert kept Magnis very tense. He didn't want to surprise Sam. He had seen Sam's explosive quickness and had no interest on being on the business end of that. He knew that for sure. He moved on. One slow step at a time.

And then he stopped cold. A feeling of panic passed through his body like a bolt of lightning. His eyes were locked in what he would later describe as a terrifying blend of the urge to fight for while simultaneously running for his life. While the earthly realm remained silent at that moment, Magnis's spirit within him was screaming for deliverance from this moment. For his eyes had locked in on another set of eyes in the darkness. Eyes, hidden deep within a tall bush, that were set, immovable. Silent. Focused. A combination of ice and steel.

After what seemed like an eternity, Magnis spoke in a low whisper, "Sam?" Silence. "Sam?"

One second, five seconds, fifteen seconds of silence. And then like the relief that came from the dawn following an endless night, a wide smile emerged deep within the bush.

"I had you going there, didn't I?" Sam said, his grin getting wider by the second as he exited from the bush, reaching for Magnis for a brief but heartfelt embrace. Being behind enemy lines was stressful, dangerous work, so encountering a friendly face during those times was always a welcome event.

Magnis relaxed, saying, "Hah! Hardly, my friend. You're going to have to do better than that if you want to scare me. Besides, what's there to be afraid of?"

"I'm pretty sure that was likely the thought going through his mind, right before his world went as black as his soul," Sam whispered as he pointed with his chin to the left of where Magnis was standing, revealing to Magnis the cleanup work that lay ahead.

There, covered by think underbrush, was the hulking body of a fallen, headless. Lifeless.

"Sheesh, Sam. Where's his head?" Magnis asked, a bit taken aback by the swift violence for a such scene.

"There," Sam whispered, his chin indicating its location just beyond the body, itself covered in underbrush as well.

"Well, you left no doubt. That's for sure. Do you recognize him?"

"It's always so hard to tell after so long separated from the Creator. The distortions make so many of them mostly unrecognizable. If I had to guess, I'd guess it was Rafar," Sam said.

"Rafar? The musician?"

"That's my guess. Just a guess."

"Well, we'll get a positive ID back home for what it's worth."

"Not worth much at this point. He sealed this fate long ago when he followed the rest of them in rebellion," Sam said with more compassion than even he expected.

"Did you know him back when?"

"Not well, but I remember his music. I remember it being breathtakingly amazing."

"Yeah, until it wasn't," Magnis said, his eyes completing the final assessments of the scene as his mind raced to put the plan together.

"Yeah. Until it wasn't," repeated Sam. "It happened so fast. I attacked him before he knew what he stumbled upon. The moment he stepped on Petros, it was over for him. We knew we couldn't let him go since he would expose our position and ruin the mission before it started. So Sebastian gave the word. And I left no doubt."

"I'd say, brother. I'd say."

"So what's next?" Sam asked, still whispering. "I want to get out of here. I've been a sitting duck for an hour until you got here."

"Let me get to work," Magnis replied as he dropped his pack and grabbed a bag designed to carry the remains of the decapitated fallen.

"Copy that," said Sam with more than a hint of disgust as he watched over the scene.

Magnis worked quickly as he scooped up the head first and placed it into the bag. "Can I get a hand please?" he asked in a hurry, hunched over, grabbing the upper torso of the fallen corpse.

"I'd rather not," shot back Sam, this time with real disgust.

"We're sitting ducks here. Just grab his feet. It will take two seconds," Magnis scolded.

"All right. Fine," whispered Sam, not liking any of it but knowing it had to be done.

The two picked up the corpse, lifted it, and placed it into the body bag. Just as they did, they heard the sound well in the distance of an approaching horde of fallens. The sound was unmistakable. Like a dreadful combination of wheezing and hate. Unmistakable.

Sam swung his head around to see if he could get a glimpse and gauge distance with his night vision still in place. "We have two minutes," he whispered. "Maybe less."

"Plenty of time."

"Seriously?"

"No, just trying to keep it light. Zip the bag. Quick. Leave it open at the top."

"Got it." Sam did as instructed.

Meanwhile, Magnis went to work, cleaning scene of any debris, mucus, and particles left behind by the fallen. He scooped up what he could find and quickly put it on top of the bag and then zipped it up the rest of the way. In one motion, he grabbed his gear pack and the now full body bag and slung them both over his shoulder. "Let's get out of here," Magnis said as the sound of the horde drew closer.

Moving to the west out of the grove, the two warriors embraced quickly.

And just before they went their separate ways, Sam said, "Say hey to Gabe for me."

"You know only Sebastian can call him that, right?" Magnis replied, turning away to prepare for flight.

"I know," Sam said with a wink as he too turned to take flight to meet up with Sebastian at the rendezvous point they determined ahead of time.

In an instant, they were gone. Vanished to the wind as the horde of fallens began to arrive at the grove. The fallens would know nothing of what took place there, nor would they find any trace of their now-deceased comrade. They would search the grove and eventually expand the search in all directions as Rusalmeh grew more and more agitated at the mysterious disappearance of one of his soulless beings.

It wouldn't be until many years later that Rusalmeh would realize the significance of this moonless night. A night that began one of the greatest missions the Creator had ever assembled. The protection of a human child who would soon usher in the greatest gift the world would ever know.

CHAPTER 11

Rusalmeh Confronts Javva

With his mind racing, Javva moved slowly toward Rusalmeh's throne. It was more like a perch than a throne as Rusalmeh used it to tower over anyone in his presence. As Javva approached, he felt himself getting smaller and smaller. To be called on an individual basis to go one on one or, in this case, three on one—counting the hulking beasts flanking the prince on both sides—usually meant significant pain to follow. Javva knew that, but he knew he had no way out either. Both were true at this moment.

"Do you know why I have summoned you here, demon?" Rusalmeh spewed with each word dripping with more filth and sulfur as the one before it.

"Yes," replied Javva head down, voice low.

"Is that right? Tell me, Javva, why are you here?" the prince asked mockingly.

"I missed your summons two nights ago," Javva said with an unmistakable hesitation. If his punishment was coming, surely it was coming soon, he thought to himself.

The prince smiled. And then let out a slight chuckle, looking at each of the beasts hulking beside him. It was then that the prince let out a howl of laughter, the likes of which Javva had never heard. He stopped laughing abruptly and jumped off his perch as if lunging at Javva, stopping an inch from his face.

There they were an inch apart, each dripping with the stench that resulted from their separation from the Creator and subsisting in the earthly realm devoid of life-giving connection to the Creator.

"Do you really think I would summon your miserable existence over a missed summons two nights ago?"

Javva could think of countless times demons had faced the prince's wrath and punishment for missing a summons but was beginning to think he had gotten the purpose of this meeting all wrong.

"You are here, Javva"—demonic spit from Rusalmeh's putrid mouth landing like sharp needles all over Javva's face—"because you saw something the other night that you believed was enough to investigate. And I brought you here to hear it for myself. From you."

But I hadn't found anything. I had searched and searched hard. I found nothing. Plus, how did Rusalmeh know? Who had told him? Who else was there? All these thoughts and questions raced through Javva's mind as he searched for the next words. Words that could determine his fate like never before in his now-miserable existence.

"Sire, I thought I saw something. I investigated. I didn't find anything. There was no one there. Perhaps I only thought I heard something. I determined it was nothing, sire," replied Javva, suddenly feeling exhausted with a sinking feeling he was repeating himself and sounding desperate.

"Nothing?" whispered the prince.

"Yes, sire. Nothing. I swear."

"Then how do you explain what brought these two here?" He glanced behind him at the two versions of hell hulking behind him.

"Sire?" asked Javva, confused.

"Someone entered our territory two nights ago, and what you saw and heard was definitely something. I'm so confident I requested these two be sent to ensure whatever it was has no chance of survival." He motioned behind him.

"But I looked, sire. There was no one. No sign of enemy activity," objected Javva.

"How dare you question me!" howled Rusalmeh, getting closer to Javva's face, which seemed impossible to Javva at the time.

"Please, sire. I'm not questioning you. I just don't understand what I am missing," he whispered, evading the prince's burning gaze. "Was there another report of enemy activity at the same time?"

"In fact, there was. And at least that demon had the wits about him to tell of what he saw," rasped Rusalmeh. "An eager one named Rafar happened to be in your territory two nights ago, saw what you saw, and witnessed you take off with haste and decided to follow you, but not before reporting to me of his plans. You see, Rafar understood my authority, unlike you." His voice now steady and calm. "And he obeyed my summons as his first priority but requested my permission to pursue as a being, unlike you, who respected my authority. I agreed and asked him to follow you closely but not too closely. I wanted to see if you, in your miserable existence, would find anything that night," finished the prince, his voice trailing off.

After a long pause, Javva spoke, "I'm sorry, sire. I found nothing," his head bowed low.

"I know, you miserable being!" screamed the prince. "Why must you repeat yourself? How dumb do you think I am?" asked Rusalmeh rhetorically. He continued, "I'm not surprised. You have always been worthless to me and our cause," basically spitting the words back at him.

"May I ask a question, sire?" Javva sheepishly asked.

"What?" Rusalmeh said, annoyance in his voice.

"Did Rafar find anything that night?" Javva's voice was barely audible, and he was expecting Rafar to enter the room at just the right time.

But he didn't. No one did.

Rusalmeh now turned away from Javva, facing his perch, moving slowly toward it, shaking his head. "Nothing," the prince finally responded after a long pause, climbing back up onto his perch.

Seeing perhaps a glimmer of hope in an otherwise-hopeless situation, Javva stepped forward, eager to make amends. "Perhaps, sire," started Javva, "perhaps Rafar and I can compare notes. Perhaps together we can retrace our steps and find some piece of evidence together that we otherwise missed on our own." His voice was now rising with positivity of hope of escaping the punishment that only moments earlier was surely to come.

Unfortunately, Javva took Rusalmeh's silence as permission to continue to speak, so he found the courage to ask one question that he was sure would ensure his safe passage through this frightening encounter with Rusalmeh and his henchmen. He simply asked, "Sire, where is Rafar so that we may collaborate on this together?"

Silence.

"Sire?" asked Javva, his voice cracking.

More silence.

"Sire?" Barely an audible whisper.

"He's gone."

CHAPTER 12

Gone

"Gone?" Javva whispered to himself in disbelief.

"Gone," replied Rusalmeh, practically spitting the word out. "And I am holding you responsible for his disappearance."

"Me, sire?"

"Yes. You disobeyed a summons, explored a potential enemy infiltration on your own. And after failing to properly investigate, you failed to even report it. This failure costs us precious time. Now a fallen has disappeared, and now we are days behind!" The prince's voice rose with every word until his face was shrieking just an inch from Javva's wretched and disfigured face. "So bring me back something that gives me reason to not end your miserable existence and don't delay. Understood?"

Just then, one of Rusalmeh's slaves entered the chamber, head bowed low with a look of a fallen beaten down by endless slavery and bondage. "Excuse me, Prince Rusalmeh," the pathetic demon said.

"What is it?"

"All territory leaders have reported back, sire."

"And?"

"And there are no reports of any enemy activity anywhere in the region."

Rusalmeh stared deep into Javva's eyes as he spoke to his demon slave, never averting his fiery gaze from Javva as he asked, "Anything else?"

"Yes, sire," the demon replied. "No reported contact from the missing fallen from any of the territories."

Silence.

"That is all, slave." The prince seethed.

"You have failed me, Javva, and I will tolerate no more failure. Find the missing fallen. Your time is running out. For your sake, you better hope my patience doesn't run out first."

CHAPTER 13

Javva's Search

Javva had searched every square inch of that grove. He retraced every step he took that night, replaying over and over the sequence of events in his mind until he could no longer separate fact from fiction. He had seen a flash and heard something in a fast sequence. Or did he?

He was questioning himself and likely would have talked himself out of it had it not been for Rafar going missing the same night he saw the flash in the night sky. If enemy activity was in the area, they usually made themselves known and were looking for a fight. But this time, it was different. Quiet. Stealth. If it was anything at all.

Maybe Rafar met some other demise. Perhaps he stumbled upon another fallen or horde of fallens roaming the landscape, looking for blood. That had been known to happen as the evil raging inside every fallen over millennia being separated from the Creator took its toll and could lead to violence against other fallens. Maybe, but Rusalmeh would have heard about it. Someone in the region would have reported such activity.

Rafar was missing. Gone. And without a reason to leave and no other fallen activity in the area, the only logical explanation was enemy activity. Angels from the heavenly realm descending into Rusalmeh's territory. But for what? Why? It had been three days and nights since Rafar disappeared, but no enemy activity had been reported anywhere. If there were enemies here, they didn't want to be found. Javva knew that for sure.

He had been looking day and night, desperate to find something to take back to Rusalmeh before his miserable life ended in great pain and suffering at the hands of those two terrifying goons that Rusalmeh had summoned.

"Javva?" Slavot, the young demon, asked.

"What?" Javva seethed, the word leaving his lips like an exploding projectile.

Javva had been assigned a helper, Slavot, by Rusalmeh. Slavot was significantly more junior in the fallen ranks than Javva, and the mere assignment of such a junior officer was punishment enough for Javva. But he knew that was just a precursor of the punishment awaiting him if he didn't find out what happened to Rafar.

"May I suggest we search the human homes in the surrounding area?" asked Slavot.

"You can suggest all you want, but if there is any evidence to be found, it is in this grove. This is where whatever happened that night," hissed Javva, "well, happened."

"But, sir, if I may, we have been over every inch of this grove at least five times and have found nothing," Slavot replied, mustering all the confidence he could but still sounding like he was sniffling the words through his nasal passages.

"Enough. We will continue to search this grove," Javva said.

But just as he finished, someone caught his eye in the distance. A human walking between a home and a barn, a small light giving off a bright illumination against the backdrop of darkness.

"Let's go," said Javva, changing his mind quickly, knowing he was finding nothing. And at least a movement from a human was more likely to yield the clue he needed instead of the still, blackness of the grove.

Javva led the way with Slavot trailing quickly behind as they made their way to the homestead. They caught up to the woman with the light just as she was about to enter a small barn. What he failed to notice were the two warrior angels hidden in the tree line, watching his every move. Mere inches from her, they studied her closely. They were looking for any hint of enemy activity.

They had learned that any human who had recently encountered the enemy would typically exhibit both a sense of fear and a sense of awe that turned out to be unmistakable to the fallens. They had learned to identify such enemy activity by studying the human facial expressions up close.

Javva would often recall the first time he noticed this expression with the humans. Javva was part of the horde in Sodom that night, working the crowd into a slavish frenzy to attack the man who was harboring the two angels in his home. Javva remembered sneering and swearing at the angels as they approached, but neither he nor his fellow horde decided to attack. Even though Javva's horde vastly outnumbered the enemy, they knew the consequences of taking on two angelic warriors. And they were warriors. Impossibly tall and strong. And they seemed to move in and out of the demonic dimension in which they resided as if they could exist in both realms simultaneously.

Nevertheless, Javva and his horde protested and leveraged the depravity of the humans in Sodom to continue to build up a frenzy from within the crowd.

It wasn't until the human emerged from the home to address the crowd that Javva noticed the unique expression or aura that surrounded the man like an evening breeze. He had seen an angel. Two actually. Javva always remembered that look and used it to identify angelic activity in his area many times since.

He was recalling that look as he and Slavot approached the woman on the small homestead approaching the barn. "Did she have the expression as one who had seen an angel?" he asked himself as they approached.

There was none. Although she seemed content and was singing, she didn't have the "I just interacted with an angel" expression for which he was looking.

So they lingered a few more moments, followed her into the barn in case there was something to see there, but there was nothing. They followed her back into the home and no doubt searched the home for any potential clues. Then, after huddling together outside the back entrance of the home, they quickly moved on.

Javva was running out of options and running out of places to look.

Two warrior angels watched all this hidden in the tree line.

CHAPTER 14

The Home and the Humans

The homestead looked like so many Sam had seen before. A mixture of farm animals and a small plot of land for growing various food items for consumption and for sale.

A single light shown through a small window at the back of the house. No movement. The house was small, perhaps three, maybe four rooms, guessed Sam. Likely a small kitchen, a place to eat and socialize, and one or two sleeping rooms. There was a front entrance along with one on the back of the home, presumably to allow access to the barn just south of the single-story house.

The barn was a sturdy structure and likely housed some sheep, goats, and a donkey or two. Surrounding the homestead were three other homesteads that he could see far into the distance with a small dirt path likely connecting them all.

Sam was part of the advance team on this one. They were tasked with scouting the area, identifying any potential risks, and finding the best place to set up camp.

For Sam, this homestead reminded him of one long ago that had created a deep emotional bond to the humans who lived there. A man named Abraham and his wife Sarah. So kind and so loving toward each other. They wept together for a child for so long.

Sam and a team of warriors had been sent to watch over them, but not until they were well advanced in years. The Creator's instructions were simple: "Their prayers will be answered. Deliver the good news and be sure to stay around to ensure their safety and that of their newborn child."

Sam was part of the angelic group of three who arrived at Abraham and Sarah's homestead that day. Gabriel had told them of the Creator's plan that allowed them to be seen by human eyes, something that only the Creator could authorize, and they were thrilled. It was a wonderful opportunity for any angel to interact with God's most precious and sacred creation. Sam remembered it being a little daunting.

The humans were so fragile, every breath critical to survival. Add to that the rarity of human and angelic interaction and Sam couldn't help but be slightly terrified. He was part of the three that met with Abraham, but he didn't say anything. The Creator had given their group His authority to speak on his behalf regarding the arrival of their new son. Sam heard Sarah laugh as she listened from inside the tent. He remembered it as subtle but audible. Definitely a laugh.

For Sam, he never fully comprehended the unbelief of the humans. So many signs all around them of the Creator's love and affection for them. But it was easy for Sam to forget that he had seen the Creator, and he had been in His presence ever since he could remember and the humans had not, at least most of them.

That day, in the shade of that large tree talking with Abraham, listening to Sarah's laugh, and interacting with the Creator's creation reminded him of this night on the outskirts of Nazareth. There were no tents like there were with Abraham, but the scenery and the feel of this moment brought those memories back. The breeze through the trees and the smile of joy mixed with confusion combined with wonder that had swept over Abraham's face that day all reminded him of this moment in time. Again, behind enemy lines, on a mission from the Creator, this time protecting a human life waiting to be born.

As these memories and thoughts raced through his mind, it was a tap from Petros that quickly brought him back to present. Sam and Petros lay prostrate deep in the tall grass next to a large tree, partially concealed by the giant root system that jutted mightily out of the ground. They chose that tree as it positioned them directly east of the home, giving them a good view of any movement in and out of both the front and back doors along with a clear line of sight to the small barn. Sam was using the night vision scope that captured light from all around while giving the magnification necessary to see at great distances. Sam had seen movement in the dimly lit home, and as he handed the scope to Petros, he gestured to the back entrance as a small figure exited the back of the house toward the sheep pen and barn.

Petros dialed in the scope and caught a glimpse of a woman walking briskly in the night air, clearly on a mission. Petros motioned to Sam the universal "Let's go" sign, and they quickly stood and followed her movement toward the barn. They wanted to keep their distance for now as Sebastian wanted to make sure their movements after the incident the night of their arrival did not arouse any unnecessary enemy activity. Their job was to protect the family at this specific homestead and stay undetected.

Sebastian had repeated that so much it was at once comical and, at the very same time, maddening. As they followed the woman, they noticed her singing. Gentle and sweet, they couldn't make out the song, but they could tell it was heartfelt and the woman was in a way lost in her thoughts as she made her way to the barn.

She entered the barn, and with the cover the barn afforded the two angelic warriors, so did they. Barns in the earthly realm were something for which you could never prepare yourself as an angel. Your sense of smell worked just as well as your sense of sight and your sense of hearing. Angels possess all the senses as well. And, well, there was nothing quite like the smell of a barn in the earthly realm. This one was no different.

But as the woman approached a sheep, lighting her way with her lantern, it became clear that she was simply checking on a mother and her newborn lamb. Singing softly, she tended to the mother, made sure there was water enough for both, and carried on sweeping around the barn before heading back the way she came.

"Maybe that's the baby the Creator wants us to look after," whispered Sam, only half joking.

"Would you be up for it if it were?" asked Petros, without taking his eyes off the woman as she left.

They followed her out and made their way back to the relative cover of the tall grass and tree again.

Sam hadn't noticed, but Petros did. The sweetness of new life in the face of the woman tending to the sheep. Petros noticed the contentment of a soon-to-be mother before he noticed the beautiful baby bump that so innocently proclaimed the new life to come. There was their mission. Growing and building strength in the mother's womb. The majesty and wonder of the Creator's creation manifesting itself in the birth of new life.

The angels never tired of discussing the beauty of the birth of a new human baby in the earthly realm. They always marveled at the Creator's creativity, and knowing they would have the honor and privilege to protect this new life deepened Petros's resolve to ensure the success of their incredible mission.

The thought had barely drifted from his conscious mind when he saw it. Just a flash of a dark wing against the light of the lantern being carried by the woman. He didn't think much of it at first. It could have been anything really. But then he saw it again. And again. The fallens were clearly on the hunt, trying to make sense of the warrior angels' supposedly undetected arrival.

Of course, they had been detected. And Sam, with Sebastian's permission, had eliminated the threat. Magnis had arrived swiftly and swept the scene completely clean.

The team had moved that very night to a new, secure, nearly undetectable position. But a fallen wouldn't just disappear without raising a significant alarm. That's exactly what Petros was seeing that night. Fallens on the search for their missing. Looking for clues and for angelic activity in the area in an attempt to piece together what had happened.

Utilizing his night vision, he determined there were two fallens searching the homestead that night. One was following the woman as she entered the small home while the other searched the small barn and the surrounding property. Their mere presence disgusted Petros and Sam as they could smell the stench emanating from their miserable existence.

"Just had to pick a spot downwind, didn't you?" asked Sam, staring through his night vision without even a glance in Petros's direction, a wry smile across his face.

"Only place to be. They must be checking all the homesteads within a radius of our entry. The first fallen must have seen Isabella's sword upon entry while the second one followed him in."

"Yep. Only way to explain why they are crawling all over a place like this," surmised Sam.

"The good news is they appear thoroughly confused under the circumstances, and without the fallen that you eliminated to provide any further details, they likely are going to continue chasing shadows of angels that may or may not exist," Petros whispered without taking his eye off both fallens who had now huddled up outside the back door of the home.

"They look angry and frustrated," observed Sam.

"They always look that way. You would too if you were separated from the Creator's love for millennia," Petros said.

"What's next?" asked Sam.

"We wait. We stay concealed. We protect this home and everyone and everything in it. That's what's next." Petros was on mission and focused. Something Sam always respected about Petros. No one could focus on the mission quite like Petros.

Sam remembered a mission not long before this one in which Petros had stayed in a single location for what seemed like endless days and nights, keeping watch over a group of Hebrew children taken captive by the Babylonians. He followed at a distance for many days through searing heat. He never let those young boys out of his sight, later retelling of the rage that burned within him over the slavery inflicted on the Creator's chosen people. It was that focus that Petros demonstrated time and again that anyone who served with him came to admire. Petros stayed on mission no matter what. He never gave an inch.

Sam could see that passion in Petros that night as well. A passion for the safety of the child yet to be born. The protection of the Creator's most precious gift. The emergence of fallens surrounding this family only made Petros's resolve even stronger. It was as if Sam could literally see the resolve like a wave wash over the countenance of Petros's face as he waited patiently for the fallens to leave.

They finally did. To them, it clearly was just a homestead of no significance. Little did they know that they had descended on the epicenter of the Creator's mission.

Leave it to the Creator to begin to build the greatest rescue mission in all human history on an unassuming, nondescript countryside farm.

CHAPTER 15

The First Big Test

The fallen activity in the area had quieted down significantly as they came to realize their missing comrade was never going to be found.

This gave Sebastian and the mission team the opportunity to find a spot and build a camp. They had been moving every night for some time to make sure they left no trace and no opportunity to be detected. By staying in a different location every night, they kept any fallens looking for them completely off-balance.

They all noticed the woman was with child in a very visible way.

"Any guesses on how long?" asked Isabella.

"Not sure, but it can't be much longer," suggested Sam.

"The baby will be arriving soon," said Sebastian quietly.

The woman had not been seen outside the small home the last several days, so the team was relieved to see her moving around, albeit slowly, outside the home. She made her way to the barn and tended to the animals there while her husband repeatedly asked her to rest. She quietly reminded him something about being cooped up inside and wanting to get some fresh air.

The two continued to have a conversation in clear disagreement when Isabella spoke up again. "The way the Creator designed humans and the way they bring new life into existence is fascinating to me."

"Creating new life in a unique and amazing way for sure," responded Petros.

"Has anyone experienced a human life being born?" asked Sam.

"I have," responded Sebastian. The team was a bit taken back as Sebastian rarely offered up information like that. He was known for keeping his past missions to himself. "Abel," Sebastian said quietly.

No one said anything. They all knew of the pain and anguish that Sebastian had gone through being with Abel for so long, only to see his life ripped away at the hands of his brother. Adding to the pain was his own near-death experience, only to be saved by Magnis and Gabriel from a horde of fallens.

"It was amazing to experience. Eve's pain in childbirth but the joy of new human life all at the same time. I'll never forget the joy for Adam and Eve that night he was born."

"I was there to see Moses's birth," Petros said as he leaned against a tree, sharpening his sword. "There was so much joy and fear all mixed together. They were so worried about keeping the baby quiet at that time. The Pharaoh had instructed all Hebrew boys to be thrown into the river and drowned. So they kept Moses's birth quiet."

"For a long time, right?" asked Isabella.

"Yeah, for three months. And then they put him in a basket in the river, and all hell broke loose," said Petros.

"Let's get ready to move," Sebastian whispered, quieting the rest of the team with the seriousness of his demeanor.

"Looks like they are loading a donkey for a trip of some kind," Petros observed.

"While she's almost ready to give birth?" asked Sam.

"I was with her in the house this morning, and they were discussing making a trip to her cousin's to be with family for the birth," Isabella said, proud of the intel she had just provided.

"Why wouldn't they come to her?"

"The cousin lives in the hill country, but there is a trusted physician with more access to special care if needed apparently," replied Isabella. "But the husband is not thrilled with the idea, to say the least. He's worried the trip, especially into the hill country, will cause complications with the birth."

"Sir?" Sam asked with a worried look on his face as he addressed Sebastian.

"Yes?"

"Traveling will expose us to detection by the fallens. They have moved on from this place a few days after one of theirs went missing, but there is still activity in the area," Sam said.

"True, but we are trained for this. We knew there would be a possibility we wouldn't be able to hunker down in one spot for the duration of the mission," Sebastian replied, confidence in his voice and posture. "So let's get ready. Get your camouflage on and night vision. No swords this time, Isabella."

"Yeah, please, Isabella, no flashes of light to draw the attention of every fallen from here to the horizon, okay?" Sam said with no more than a wry smile.

"How about I..." Isabella's voice trailed off as she thought better of getting in a back-and-forth with Sam, even if it was in jest. This was serious business, and she had already jeopardized the mission once. So she decided to take Sam's jab and absorb it. For now.

"Isabella, take a position close to the man and woman and get a sense of the conversation and plans," instructed Sebastian.

"I'm on it."

"Everyone else, gear up and get ready to roll. They likely will be planning on an early morning departure, and we'll need to be ready to travel with them undetected." Sebastian was preparing his team for their first big test of the mission. Broad daylight, staying close enough to protect, but far enough to stay hidden as best they could.

Sebastian continued, "Petros, establish comms with Gabriel. I want to make sure he knows what is happening."

The next moment, Isabella was back. "Looks like they are planning on leaving in the morning. They plan to leave before sunrise. They expect the trip to take most of the day. They hope to arrive at their destination before nightfall."

"Got it," Sebastian said. "Good work. Thanks."

"Sir, comms established," Petros said.

"Okay. I'll take it here. Everyone, stay ready. Gabriel?"

"Yes, Seb."

"They are on the move in the morning. We'll be exposed, but we'll be ready. Any chance you can find out where they are going?"

"Sure thing. Did you get any indication of who they are visiting?" asked Gabriel.

"Affirmative. A cousin. They believe they can leave before dawn tomorrow and arrive before nightfall. They are preparing two donkeys tonight for the journey."

"Okay. I'll find out the most likely destination."

"Thanks. I'd like to send an advance team tonight to check it out, establish a perimeter, check for fallen activity, and scope out a good place to stay hidden for the next few days."

"Understood. Give me some time and I'll get back to you tonight."

"Thanks."

At that, Gabriel was gone.

They didn't want to stay on comms very long. Even though the communications were scrambled and made to appear as fallen cross talk, they didn't want to run the risk of unnecessarily alerting any fallen listening in to their conversation. So they always kept it short.

Sebastian returned to the camp to find the team geared up and ready just as he instructed. He spoke softly but resolutely, "Sam. Petros. You'll run scout for us tonight. Gabriel is identifying the most likely destination of our family based on the intelligence we have gathered. He will be reporting back in the next few hours. Once we know where they are going, you'll go ahead today and scope the location."

"Yes, sir," both warriors spoke in unison.

"I need you to identify any fallen activity or fortifications between here and there, and I'll need you to scope out a spot in which we can stay hidden but have eyes on our family at all times," Sebastian said with confidence and resolve.

He continued for the entire team of warrior angels to hear, "Should you be detected, do not engage. Initiate evasive maneuvers and then find the nearest spot to hide."

"I have to say, I really do hate the idea of running and hiding from fallens," Sam said without a hint of humor. He was serious.

"Comms protocol, sir?" asked Petros, ignoring Sam's comment and doing his part to stay focused.

"Silent. Nothing in or out. You'll be on your own out there. Especially if you are detected, there is no circumstance by which you get on comms and communicate. That's why it's critical to take your time, and don't get caught. Get to the destination. Set up a perimeter. Find a good place to stay hidden for the rest of the team. And then wait."

"Affirmative, sir," Sam said as he packed his gear.

Petros spoke up, "Sir, Gabriel has news."

"I'll take it," Sebastian said, reaching for the comms device. "Sir?"

"I've got the location. Best guess is they're heading to a cousin's house in the hill country," Gabriel said. He continued, "I'll send the coordinates through to Petros."

"Thank you."

"Who's the advance team?"

"Petros and Sam."

"Petros leaving his comms gear behind?"

"Affirmative."

"We cannot afford detection, especially via comms."

"Correct, they know the risks, sir. They understand they are on their own, and if detected, they must flee and hide. They've been instructed that under no circumstances are they to engage the enemy."

"Very well."

"Thanks again for the quick turnaround."

"Welcome. And, Seb? We can't afford any more mistakes, okay?"

"Check that, sir. We all understand."

Back with the team, Sebastian spoke clearly and confidently, "Gabriel is sending through the coordinates to your destination tonight."

"Just received from Gabriel, sir. We are ready," Petros said with as much confidence as he could muster, knowing this would be a big test.

Exposed and on the move in the earthly realm during daylight hours. Not easy. The reality of the mission began to sink in for the first time since they arrived.

"Leave the coordinates and your comms gear with Isabella," Sebastian instructed Petros. "She's your backup."

"Yes, sir."

"Sir?" Sam spoke after being quiet for a long bit.

"Sam?"

"What if we encounter fallens along the way?"

"Well, don't."

"Don't, sir?"

"That's right. Don't. We can't afford another interaction with the fallens, especially one that ends like the last one. Not so close to each other. If you believe you have been detected, use all evasive measures and do everything possible to disappear."

"Okay," Sam said hesitantly.

"Are you up for it, Sam?"

"Yes, sir. I'm ready."

"Okay then. You and Petros should get going."

Both Petros and Sam were geared up, ready to go.

Petros spoke to the team, "We'll be set up for you all tomorrow. We'll see you when you get there."

They all nodded in Petros's direction the affirmative, and with that, Petros and Sam took flight to the coordinates Gabriel had provided them. They were gone instantly. Their camouflage a near-perfect match to their surroundings.

"Get some rest, Isabella. I'll take first watch," Sebastian said.

Sebastian wanted first watch because he knew he wouldn't be able to rest. He knew the success or failure of the mission hung in the balance that night. His confidence in his team was high, but he also knew the extreme risks.

An all-out war, even if in self-defense, would ruin the mission and expose the plans of the Creator to the enemy. He asked the Creator for protection and safe passage for his warriors. He knew the Creator was listening.

And He was. Always.

CHAPTER 16

A Long Night

The air that night was crisp, cool, and breezy. Sam and Petros were presumably establishing a perimeter and preparing for their arrival the next day. Without comms, they had no way of knowing for sure.

Sebastian and Isabella watched with resolve and focus. They each knew what was at stake, and they had prayed for safe passage of Petros and Sam.

"Confirm you have your camouflage in place," reminded Sebastian. "The sunlight will reflect off the camouflage in a way that will allow us to blend into our surroundings, but any part of you not protected by the camouflage will be exposed."

Isabella appreciated the reminder. Her mistake on the night of their entry into the earthly realm was never far from her mind. She didn't think Sebastian's direct command was intended to remind her of her mistake, but even if it was, she deserved it.

Regardless, she would be ready.

CHAPTER 17

Reconnaissance

Dark. Cold. Quiet. As Sam and Petros set out on their reconnaissance mission, they both knew the severe dangers that could lie ahead. They were on a mission to scout out the route their family would take as well as the place they would be staying. Their mission was to ensure it was a safe place in which to stay.

Sam led the way. His seven-foot frame covered in camouflage provided an additional layer of protection for Petros who trailed close behind and slightly to his left. They stayed low to the ground to ensure they didn't cast a silhouette across the night sky. Outside of a few tree groves here and there and a scattering of a few small homes and structures, the coverage by which to stay hidden was scarce. So they moved quickly.

They were built to move quickly in the heavenly realm. But on the earthly realm, although remaining in a spiritual dimension, they were still bound by the natural rules of the earthly realm. Angels are not omnipresent. They are not in all places at all times, nor can they teleport to a place. When in the earthly realm, they have to move about, adhering to the basic rules of time and space everyone else does. So they moved very quickly, knowing their exposure out in the open left them vulnerable to the many fallens posted as lookouts.

The activity over the last few days coupled with the disappearance of one their own more than likely put them in a heightened state. Fallen eyes were seemingly everywhere. Rusalmeh ruled his region ruthlessly, which made this mission even more dangerous.

They had the horsepower to fight. That they knew. But that wasn't the mission, making this trip even more nerve-wracking for the two seasoned warriors.

"Sam?"

"What?" Sam replied, briefly looking back and to his left toward Petros.

"How much longer?"

Sam checked his coordinates and replied, "About four clicks."

"Okay."

"Any fallen activity?"

"Negative."

"Me neither. Weird."

"Wait."

"What?"

"Down!" Petros whispered hard through his teeth.

They both stopped, collapsed their enormous wings, and dove straight to the earth, both meeting the ground with an impact they both knew would leave a lasting pain impression. They lay motionless for a long moment as they listened intently past the typical sounds of the night around them.

Petros, with his face pressed against the earth, turned slightly toward Sam, lifted his night vision, and simply said, "There."

Sam slowly followed the direction of Petros's eyes as he scanned the horizon. He saw nothing at first, and then there it was. The silhouette of a massive fallen perched on a rock outcropping at the north end of a small grove of trees. His blackness against the night sky revealed itself like a hole in the vast expanse of the universe. "I see him."

"Did he see us?"

"I doubt it. If he did, he would be moving toward us by now."

"One of the lookouts?"

"I've never known any of Rusalmeh's lookouts to be that big."

"Now what?"

"We wait. Let's see if he moves on."

"Okay."

He did. Within a matter of minutes, the massive fallen stepped off the rock and flew into the night.

Sam and Petros gave it five more minutes in case the fallen planned to circle back around for one more look.

Petros stood first, helping Sam and his huge frame to his feet.

"Good eye out there, Pete," Sam said.

"Yup. Just caught that silhouette out of the corner of my vision."

"If you didn't see him, he no doubt would have seen us."

"I have to say I'm not the biggest fan of this 'stay hidden behind enemy lines' thing, Sam."

"Yeah, neither am I. I'm used to sizing up the enemy, planning the attack, and executing. This feels weird," Sam said, taking flight close to the ground again.

"For sure," Petros replied, following closely after.

The rest of the trip was uneventful as they arrived at the homestead according to the coordinates Gabriel had provided. Well, close to the coordinates. They stopped just short, finding a grove of trees from within to hide to properly scope out the area surrounding the home in question. Both the warriors gazed through their night vision, scanning back and forth the horizon and all the surrounding area. No activity, human or otherwise. That would soon change.

"What do you see?" asked Sam.

"Nothing."

"Well, I guess it is the middle of the night. Where did he go?" Sam said, more to himself than anyone.

"Who?" asked Petros.

"That huge fallen we saw two clicks back. I just don't want to get surprised, especially with our family on their way soon."

"Couldn't warn our team anyway. No comms, remember?" Petros said with more than a tinge of disappointment.

"Roger that. Let's find the right spot for us and the team to hunker down, stay hidden while still being able to offer protection as needed," instructed Sam.

Both warriors were peers, but Petros knew Sam's leadership skills far exceeded his, and he was happy to take direction from him.

"Let's check out the grove southwest of our location," suggested Petros. "Looks to have good coverage and good views of most of the house."

They were both just about to ascend when Sam's right arm came hard across Petros's chest plate.

"Wait," Sam whispered. "I heard something."

"Something? Anything in particular?" asked Petros with more than a little sarcasm.

Just then, a huge fallen flew overhead, his massive wingspan cutting the night air every three to four seconds as he worked to stay airborne. The two warriors watched as he circled their position and then landed perched atop the very home they believed their family was to be visiting the next day.

"Perfect," Petros said.

"What are the odds?" A real question from Sam to Petros.

"Slim and none."

"Did they intercept our comms?"

"No way."

"Petros, you answered too quickly. Nothing personal. Could they have intercepted our comms?"

A long silence.

"Negative."

"So this one is just lucky?"

"Win the lottery lucky."

Just then, a moment later, a much smaller fallen arrived. This time from the opposite direction with more of a direct route to the rooftop. The two fallens were communicating with each other, but without any equipment, there was no way of knowing what they were saying.

Normally, Petros would be able to set up equipment that would magnify voices to be heard at great distances. Not this time.

"I've got to get close."

"Close to what?"

"To our friends there," Sam said, pointing to the two fallens clearly disagreeing about something.

"Um. Well. Perhaps you don't remember?"

"Remember?"

"No enemy engagement. I don't even have comms to send for help."

"I won't need any help. Trust me."

"No time for tough-guy talk, Sam."

"Don't worry, Pete. I won't need help because I am not going to engage. I'm just going to get close enough to see what they are talking about. Maybe from that, we can determine our next move."

Petros nodded.

Sam continued, "We still have time to get back to the team and plan a different approach if these two worms decide to hang around."

Moving through the grove of trees, his camouflage still covering his seven-foot frame, Sam moved cautiously. With no way of communicating with the team, no reasonable expectation for backup, and a complete focus on remaining undetected, Sam calculated his every move.

The demons were distracted in their conversation, and even though they appeared to be on lookout duty, they showed no interest in looking out for much of anything.

Drawing even with the structure upon which the demons sat, Sam had a decision to make. His camouflage and the trees gave him all the cover he needed, but he still couldn't hear what they were saying. There was about three hundred yards of open space between the grove he was in and the structure upon which they sat. He would have to move fast and make no noise as the night was still and the moon bright.

Taking a deep breath, he set out fast, hard, and low. His destination was the back side of the structure. He arrived with an abrupt but quiet stop, his back up against the house, his massive frame concealed by camouflage and the darkness the house's shadow cast. Holding his breath, Sam listened intently for any movement or any sound from the fallens up above him. Hearing nothing, he slowly began to make his move along the wall of the house. Every step with extreme intention. He needed to find out why these fallens were here and how long they intended to stay.

As he began to step around the corner, his feet moving first, he turned his head, followed by his massive shoulders, only to be staring face-to-face with the large fallen he and Petros had seen first arrive.

The fallen was massive. Even slightly taller that Sam and just as broad in the shoulders and torso. A pure specimen of a fallen warrior.

Sam stopped cold. The two warriors faced each other. No one spoke.

A moment later, Sam heard the other fallen drop from the roof of the house on the ground he had just vacated a second before. Two against one.

At seven feet tall in human measurement with bright-blond hair, a light complexion, square jaw, and bright-topaz blue eyes, Sam was an angelic warrior designed specifically to take on all those who dared confront him. With a broad, muscular shoulders, arms, and legs designed to stand firm against any enemy, his impressive physique made him uniquely qualified for situations like this. Which was exactly why the first thing Sam did was smile. Sam was always quick to give a smile, bringing comfort and confidence when it was often most needed.

Only this time, the smile brought no comfort to these two demons. In fact, just the opposite. They were doomed, and they knew it. The smile simply acted as final confirmation of their fate should their next move be the wrong one.

"Gentlemen. To what do I owe this unique pleasure?" Sam said with a smile.

"What are you doing here?" The larger demon wheezed, taking the slightest of steps back.

"I asked first." The smile still firmly in place, arms to his side. Relaxed.

"We are on patrol. We lost one of ours, and Rusalmeh wants to know why."

"Maybe we just found out why," hissed the smaller fallen behind Sam who had actually taken a half step closer to the giant warrior.

"I suggest you stick to being this big ugly worm's lackey and leave the thinking part to grown-ups. What do you say?" Sam spoke these words as he turned his head slightly over his right shoulder, ensuring both demons noticed his smile disappear. At the same moment, he caught a glimpse of Petros quietly approaching the scene.

"And I suggest you explain your purpose for showing up uninvited in my territory or—"

"Or what?" Sam interjected. "Oh, please do tell me or what."

"What could you possibly want in this worthless place?"

"Tell you what. I'll continue to not answer your questions because it's none of your business, and you decide to leave quietly as if this little encounter never happened. That way, you get to continue your miserable existence for a little longer, and I continue to carry on."

"No," the small fallen said.

"No? Is he calling the shots, or are you, big boy?" Sam's square jaw set firmly in place and his bright-topaz eyes blazed as he appeared to look right through the giant fallen standing less than three feet in front of him. He knew better to taunt fallens, but it was one of his greatest pleasures. He couldn't avoid it. Not even on a secret mission like they were on.

The giant fallen said nothing.

"Try again. No is not the correct answer," Sam said, his gaze on the fallen in front of him blazing white hot in the chill of the night.

"Two on one is not a fair fight. You sure you want to do this?" the smaller fallen said.

But Sam didn't avert his eyes from the fallen in front of him. But then it quickly dawned on him. The question was not to him. It was directed to the giant fallen.

The giant fallen was considering the question, and silence enveloped the three celestial beings. No one moved.

Of all the evil that seeped into fallens as more and more time passed separated from the Creator, the one evil that seemed to overshadow all others was pride. Sam could see it in both of them. He knew they were going to try to take him down even though they all knew Sam was too much for them. Their pride wouldn't let them, not when they had an opportunity—no matter how remote the possibility—of taking the head of an angelic warrior back to Rusalmeh.

But Sam knew he couldn't engage. The mission was one of secrecy. One that was clandestine above all else. And they already had to annihilate one fallen on their first night of arrival. Two more disappearances of fallens this early in the mission would be catastrophic. He knew that. Petros knew that. That's when Sam decided his next move. Arms still at his side. Relaxed. He smiled and said, "Not tonight, boys."

Before the last syllable left his mouth, he bent his knees, clenched his right fist, and, in one massive movement and with unbelievable force, landed a massive blow as he ascended, in flight smashing the giant fallen's jaw in what Sam suspected was more than a dozen pieces. As the giant fallen slumped to the ground unconscious, the smaller one lunged after Sam. But of course, it was entirely too late, and the fallen knew his mistake the second he made it. He realized immediately he should have taken the loss, but again, pride.

Sam, now about ten feet in the air, quickly turned his entire body to square himself up for where he expected the smaller fallen to be. He was not disappointed. As expected, the fallen's lunge after Sam left him completely exposed from behind, which was exactly where Sam landed his massive right hand to the back of the fallen's head as he landed back on the ground with incredible force. The smaller fallen never saw it coming as he lay in a heap not five feet from his unfortunate partner. Both would likely never be the same after the massive blows they each took from Sam. But they would live. Sam made sure of that.

"Quite a show there, my friend," Petros said, perched on the corner of the house directly above Sam.

"Yeah, thanks for the backup," Sam said sarcastically, not looking up at Petros and thereby not giving him the satisfaction of acknowledging his presence.

"Now what?" asked Petros.

"It's time to go. When these two come to, it won't be long before there will be fallens crawling all over this place."

"Roger that."

"We are going to have to find a way to keep the family from traveling here tomorrow," Sam said, stepping over the fallens as he began to make his way back to the grove of trees.

"Why were they here?" Petros asked as he walked alongside this friend.

"We didn't get that far. They are still smarting over the missing fallen from the night we arrived," Sam replied.

They quickly made it back to the grove of trees, both instinctively checking both horizons for any enemy activity. They completed a final gear check, including their camouflage.

"Let's get out of here," Sam whispered.

"So just a coincidence?" Petros asked as they took flight side by side.

"Nothing is a coincidence, my friend."

No one spoke the rest of the way back.

CHAPTER 18

Frustrated

He was a massive being. Rusalmeh was close to eight feet tall with impossibly wide shoulders and a huge head. It had become his trademark. An imposing figure before he fell. But after millennia separated from the Creator's love, he was dark with pride, lust, envy, hatred, and anger. So after once being a majestic creation of the Creator, he had become one of the most imposing, darkest, and most terrifying creatures in the spiritual realm. And he wore that like a badge of honor. He took pleasure in the fact that even his own fallens were terrified of him. He firmly believed it was his secret to keeping his tight grip on power over his Persian empire.

But tonight was different. As he sat perched on his throne, his shoulders were slumped, his chin in his chest. He appeared defeated.

The two fallens, which Sam had made such quick work of, lay before him prostrate. They had become semiconscious soon after Sam and Petros had fled the scene. They both were in really bad shape. The larger of the two, the one Sam put down first, went by the name Safir. The smaller one, the one who took the absolutely wrong move in a futile attempt to attack Sam, went by the name Tarn.

Safir and Tarn. Useful idiots. It took them both most of the rest of the night to make it back to base. They wondered if they were taking so long to get back after being so resoundingly punished without as much as laying a finger on the angelic warrior because of their wounded pride, their wounded heads, or both. They both knew the answer, even though they never spoke of it. Getting back to base and facing Rusalmeh was worse than any beating handed out by an angel. And they both knew it. And were terrified. They had been summoned quickly to Rusalmeh's chambers and were persuaded by two of his goons to quickly tell Rusalmeh everything they knew.

The news of their encounter and subsequent beating at the hands of the massive angel with the bright-topaz eyes and lightning-fast reflexes did not sit well with the dark prince. He was furious.

"I'll ask you, worms, again. Who was he?" Rusalmeh hissed. His chin not leaving his chest. He couldn't bear to look at his defeated demons that lay before him.

No one spoke.

"Well?"

The massive fallen, Safir, mumbled first, his head buried in the ground, not daring to make eye contact with his evil leader. "I don't know, master. I don't remember him in the previous realm."

"He just kept smiling at us like he knew what was going to happen the whole time," said Tarn who had taken such a massive blow to the back of his head and neck he barely could move it and wondered if it would ever be the same again. He was pretty sure it wouldn't.

"What was he doing there?" Rusalmeh spit the words from his mouth as if the hatred at the mere thought of angelic warriors infiltrating his region was worse than the angels actually being there.

"Sire. Please. He didn't tell us. We tried…" Safir's words trailed off, either out of fear or regret or both.

"Tried? You tried? That's the best you've got? You tried?" The prince came off his perch with a hatred and anger the two failed fallens knew was likely just the beginning of their punishment as a result of their failure. "You two are worthless!" he screamed.

"Two," Safir whispered. His muffled voice weak and trembling.

"Two? Two what?" Rusalmeh screamed.

"There were two of them, master. I saw them flying fast and low as I was arriving at my post." The fallen spoke as if his voice was getting weaker by the second. "They appear to have spotted me a split second after I spotted them as they dove hard to the ground. I went looking for them, but I lost them."

"Lost them?" The prince's voice was still filled with anger, but he was no longer screaming.

"Yes. I'm not sure how I saw them in the first place because they must have been using camouflage or something. As soon as they hit the ground, they were gone."

"And you? What did you see?" Rusalmeh now pointed his disappointment and hatred toward the pitiful Tarn.

"Nothing, sire. I arrived shortly after he did, and he was trying to tell me what he had seen, but I argued with him. I told him he was seeing things."

Rusalmeh said nothing. His rage building by the moment.

"Not long after, I decided to jump down and have a look around the house before checking the last-known location. And that's when I saw him," recalled Safir.

"And?" Rusalmeh shouted impatiently.

"And there he was. We basically ran into each other," the demon responded with dejection, overwhelming his already-trembling voice.

"Describe him," the demon prince hissed.

"Tall. Impossibly tall. As tall as I am. Maybe taller."

Silence.

"His eyes were bright topaz, and he just kept smiling."

"Smiling?"

"Yes. Like he knew something we didn't."

More silence.

Rusalmeh hopped back to his perch, deep in thought. The eerie silence that engulfed the room made everyone in it uncomfortable. Rusalmeh was suddenly somewhere else. Instantly, far from the present moment. Something one of fallens had said had rattled him. It appeared he had lost his lust for revenge and punishment on the two fallens that lay prostrate before him.

Safir and Tarn waited for their punishment. A punishment that never came. Something had rattled the fallen prince, but what? The two fallens waited. And waited. And waited some more.

Safir finally worked up the courage to turn his head up and over enough to catch a glimpse of his master.

The prince of Persia, Rusalmeh, was hunched over, head in his hands, lost in the deepest of thoughts.

"Sire?" Safir asked sheepishly.

"Leave."

The two fallens said nothing and left.

One name kept going through Rusalmeh's mind. Just one name. Over and over. Rusalmeh remembered the massive warrior with bright-topaz eyes and a broad smile. And it frightened him to the core.

Sam.

CHAPTER 19

Change of Plans

Isabella saw them first. They were moving fast as first light was soon approaching. Sam in the lead and Petros just off his right shoulder. Fast. Low. Urgent. "Sir?"

"What?"

"Sam and Petros were supposed to meet us at the family's relatives' place, right?"

"That's right."

"Well, maybe they forgot their favorite pair of shoes or something."

Sebastian said nothing. He just stared at Isabella with a face that wondered why she would say such a thing at that particular moment in time. It was a natural reaction because there was no scenario in which Sebastian thought two of heaven's most fantastic warriors would return without completing a mission.

Sebastian was still processing what would quickly turn out to be inevitable when Sam quickly set foot in the midst of the team with Petros arriving a step behind. No one spoke for more than a moment.

Finally, Isabella broke the silence and asked, "Forget something?"

"Sir, deepest apologies. We encountered the enemy," Sam said. His voice urgent yet steady.

"How?" Sebastian calmly asked. He had recovered from his disbelief from a moment earlier and was already beginning to lay out contingency plans in his head. One of the reasons the Creator wanted him to lead this mission.

"Routine patrol as far as we can tell," Petros said. He continued, "They landed on the very house we were scoping out. What are the odds?"

"Coincidence?" Isabella asked.

"Don't count on it," Sebastian said.

"Agreed, but it really did seem coincidental. They were as stunned to see us as we were to see them."

"Them?" Isabella asked.

"That's right. Two of them," Sam said.

"Did you recognize them?" inquired Sebastian.

"Negative, sir," Petros answered. "Neither of us remember them."

Sam confirmed his agreement with a quick nod. Sam continued, "My guess is they saw us on approach. I'm not sure how, but they did. I went in for a closer look in order to pick up any intelligence I could, and that's when we bumped into each other."

"Bumped," Petros whispered under his breath, chuckling as he said it. "I'm pretty sure both of them wouldn't characterize what happened to them as getting bumped."

"Sam?" Sebastian needed the rest of the information so he could change the plan and prepare for what was next. He wasn't frustrated, just urgent.

"Sir, there were few options. I tried to find out what they were up to but didn't get much. They seemed genuinely surprised to see us, and they did mention they were still on the lookout for the one of theirs that has gone missing."

"And?"

"And knowing we couldn't afford two more missing fallens and a scene in need of cleaning, I neutralized them long enough for us to escape further confrontation," Sam said.

"I'm pretty sure they'll never be the same," Petros offered.

"Sir, they will survive, but they have no idea of our mission or of the family we are here to protect. That was pretty clear."

"And where were you during this chance encounter?" Isabella spoke with a smile, nodding toward Petros who had taken a seat at the base of tree.

"I kept my distance in case Sam needed me, but let's just say Sam took care of business."

"Sir?" Sam asked as he looked at Sebastian. "We can't go. That place is likely crawling with fallens by now. It won't be safe for our family."

Sebastian agreed. It was way too dangerous now that the encounter had taken place.

"Any chance they could have seen you leave?" Isabella asked.

"No chance. They were out," Petros answered.

"Okay. Dawn is coming, and our family will be planning on moving soon. We need to keep them here," Sebastian instructed. "Isabella, did they indicate which animal they were going take on the journey?" Sebastian asked.

Isabella thought for a moment and then answered, "They agreed to take the younger donkey of the two. The male."

"Okay. Sam, take position up in the entrance to the barn. At the right time, make yourself known to both donkeys but especially the one they intend to ride today. Lose the smile and put on the scariest, most aggressive posture you can come up. Those animals are not to leave the barn today."

"Check," Sam confirmed both his understanding and commitment with that one word.

"Isabella?"

"Yes?"

"I anticipate this will be very stressful on our mother. She is very pregnant, planning to have this baby at a relative's house, and we are throwing a significant change at them. I need you to be there with her and bring her comfort."

"Got it," Isabella replied without hesitation.

"You have comforted before, yes?"

"Yes, sir."

"Right before she went toe to toe with Rusalmeh," chimed in Sam with his trademark smile.

"Expect the best, plan for the worst." Isabella smiled.

"Okay. You two. Get together and make a plan. You'll need to be synched and ready to go at any moment," Sebastian directed as he turned his attention to Petros.

"Sir?" asked Petros.

"Need you to establish comms with Gabriel. He needs to know the change."

"On it."

Sebastian stepped away from the team in order to clear his mind and ensure he was making all the right decisions in this moment. It's something he had learned to do in his very first mission as a team lead.

First thing he did was asked the Creator for wisdom for the Creator's plans to be accomplished through him. Next, he sketched out a plan C since he was already on plan B and the beginnings of plan D. He recognized, however, there was no good plan C, let alone plan D, so he had to make this work.

He prayed, whispering aloud, "Creator, for your wisdom, I ask in this moment. Help me to make the right decisions that please you and fulfill your purpose for me."

As he finished his prayer, Petros spoke up, indicating communication had been established.

"Sir?" Sebastian asked.

"Quite an adventure at the moment, eh?"

"I'm sorry, sir. The mission is taking some unexpected turns."

"No need to apologize. Since you are calling, I'm assuming your original plan to prepare the way for the family's journey has changed."

"It has."

"Everyone okay?"

"Affirmative, sir. Everyone is good. Sam and Petros encountered two fallens who happened to be at the very house our family was to be visiting for the baby's birth."

"And?"

"Sam believes it's a coincidence."

Gabriel said nothing.

Sebastian continued, "Sam neutralized the threat long enough for them to escape undetected. They were not followed back here to the family, but we're confident the planned journey is no longer safe."

"The team able to get a positive ID on the two fallens?"

"Negative."

"What's next?"

"I plan to keep the family here for the birth by allowing the team to reveal themselves to the donkeys and paralyzing them in fear. I'll use Isabella to comfort the mother."

"Okay. Be on the lookout for the relatives. I assume when they do not show tomorrow, they will make the journey to our family. And if Rusalmeh is smart at all, he'll send at least a small horde to investigate since they discovered us in the vicinity of the relatives tonight," Gabriel explained.

"What should we do should that happen?"

"No change in mission. Stay concealed but alert. Rusalmeh always sends a fallen to check on every new human birth. So they are going to get a visit once the baby is born anyway."

"Understood."

"And it's too early in the Creator's plan to reveal the importance of this baby. If Rusalmeh catches wind of the four of you all assembled together this early in the mission, it will be impossible to keep this thing on track."

"Nothing is impossible."

"Correct. But I'm counting on you to get this right, Sebastian."

"You ever have a mission go so far sideways so fast?"

"Plenty. It's part of the earthly realm. It's fallen, all of it. Most times, we are the only ones ensuring the Creator's plans are carried out."

"I get it. And it's my honor to do it. But this one seems bigger. Bigger than ever."

"It is, my friend."

"That's comforting," responded Sebastian sarcastically.

"It should be. You were created for this, and your team is counting on your decisive leadership."

"Yes, sir."

"Time to go."

"Thank you, sir."

As he clicked off and began to make his way back to the team, he couldn't shake the feeling that someone had been listening. He shook it off and chalked it up to the frustration he was feeling with so much going wrong on the mission so far.

He was wrong. Someone was listening.

And it could ruin everything.

CHAPTER 20

Suspicion Grows

"What?" the feckless fallen named Safir asked.

"I can't figure it out," said his partner, Tarn.

Both demons were assigned to monitor all communications within a large vicinity of the interaction that took place just a few hours before as punishment by Rusalmeh for taking their angelic beating. An interaction that left two fallens severely wounded, though none of the other fallens in the horde could tell what hurt more—their bodies or their egos.

As soon as the two fallens had reported back to Rusalmeh of their punishment at the hands of an enormous warrior angel with the bright eyes and radiating smile, a portion of the horde had been immediately sent to descend on the area, search for any clues, set up a perimeter to protect against any additional attacks, and monitor communications in the area. As part of the orders, there were to be no fallen communications until further notice.

The fallens knew of the angel warriors' communications technology that masked their speech to emulate fallen speech in order to conceal their communications and plans. That's why the insolent demon and his partner were confused at first.

"I hear it too," Safir said.

"Why are they communicating? The order from the master was clear. Idiots," Tarn hissed with his mouth as black as the sin he celebrated.

"Wait. Do you hear that?" Safir whispered.

"I do. It's gibberish. Nonsense. Which is all the more reason to not be breaking the communications silence protocol," Tarn hissed.

"That's just it. It's nonsense. Sure it sounds like ours, but listen to the words and phrases," Safir explained.

They both listened in silence for a long moment.

"None of it makes sense?" Tarn questioned.

"Exactly."

"Can you tell where it is coming from?" Tarn asked excitedly.

"Not yet, but I'm tracking it now."

Just then, the communication stopped. Silence screamed at them as if they were actors in a play and the joke being played was on them. They both slumped backward, first on their heels and all the way down to the ground where they both just stared at the ground.

"I'm guessing you didn't get a location," Tarn deadpanned, not even looking in Safir's direction. Still staring at the ground as he asked it.

"Don't you think I would have a slightly different demeanor right now if I had?" Safir said, spitting the words back at his partner. He knew Tarn had to ask it, but it didn't mean he couldn't be angry that he did. "What is going on?" Safir asked out loud, but it was really just a question he was asking himself.

So when Tarn tried to answer him, he didn't realize what was happening. "We are getting our asses beat. That's what. First, a fallen goes missing after reporting potential angelic warrior activity, and then two more fallens look like they were pushed off a cliff and hit every rock on the way down. Then we intercept communications designed to sound like us, but we know it's not. All within a radius of just a few miles," Tarn replied, quite happy with his summary of their current situation.

"Are you done?" Safir hissed, not expecting an answer.

He didn't get one. Tarn knew better.

Silence.

*****

"When?" Rusalmeh asked with as much restraint as he could muster.

"Last night," Safir whispered. His head bowed low.

"Of course, it was last night, you insignificant worm." Rusalmeh seethed his breath hot, and his wretched saliva was exploding from his lips. "When last night?"

"Right before first light," Tarn replied.

"Are you sure it wasn't us?" the prince asked.

"We are sure, sire," Safir answered.

"How?"

"Gibberish, sire. At first, I was angry that others would be disobeying your no-comms order. But after listening, I recognized it was gibberish. No conversation was being had," Safir responded.

"Where?"

"I'm sorry, sire. We couldn't get a location. They broke off before we could get a location."

"Of course, they did," Rusalmeh said to himself, but loud enough for the others to hear.

Rusalmeh remained silent. He was perched on his throne, sitting high above his two slaves before him. He was lost in thought as he worked the details of the unusual circumstances recently. Like puzzle pieces, he turned them over and over, his mind trying desperately to begin to see a picture taking shape.

After more than a few minutes had passed, Safir broke the eerie silence, saying, "Sire?"

"Leave," Rusalmeh hissed. "I want you back on station and picking up any unusual communication. If there are enemy warriors in my region, I want to know where, and I want to know why!"

The two fallens before him quickly left without looking back. They were just relieved to escape punishment as Rusalmeh was notorious for doling out punishment based solely on the deliverance of bad news.

Rusalmeh was not interested in frivolous punishments at this point. He was being outmaneuvered, and he felt himself more than a few steps behind. This was his turf. His region.

"What are you up to, Sam?" he hissed. He was alone in his chamber now. He knew no one could hear him, and he wanted to talk it out. "Why are you here? Why now? Who are you protecting?"

To the dark prince, the timing didn't make sense. So many years had passed with limited intervention from the enemy. He couldn't remember the last time enemy warriors entered his region. And Rusalmeh knew the Scriptures. All fallens did. It was required reading. They wanted to be best prepared to attempt to thwart any of the Creator's plans to the degree they could interpret and anticipate.

They couldn't. And Rusalmeh knew they couldn't. It was just one of the many lies he and others like him told the hordes of fallens to keep them focused and attentive.

Deep down, Rusalmeh knew what he would never outwardly show. That is, if the Creator wanted something done, it would be accomplished. But usually, He would come out with it. Send His warriors to swoop in and right the wrongs.

So why the secrecy? What was He really up to? Why now? Who was Sam protecting, and why was it so hard for him to get answers? So many questions.

The answers would come eventually.

And those answers, the fallen prince feared, would frighten him to his core.

CHAPTER 21

Stay

"He's on his way toward you," Isabella whispered, her voice softly crackling into Sam's comms device. Isabella was with the family inside the house and had been since Sebastian made the decision to stay.

The father- and mother-to-be were asleep, although the mother was quite restless, Isabella observed as she arrived to bring comfort well before the sunrise. Isabella sat softly on the mother's bed, softly singing songs of deliverance, peace, and praise. As she sang, almost immediately, the mother's breathing slowed as her restlessness began to subside.

Although she and the other warrior angels were given much latitude in completing their missions, interacting directly with the Creator's special creation was by strict permission only. So Isabella wasn't entirely sure if her singing, designed to bring comfort, actually brought the comfort she intended. She had been sent to comfort the Creator's special creation on more than one mission in her existence, so she figured it mattered. As it turned out, it mattered a lot.

As the mother found reprieve from the restlessness, Isabella began singing specifically over the child in her mother's womb. *Who is this child?* she wondered to herself as she continued to softly sing over the two as they slept. *What does the Creator have planned for this family? For this child?* Isabella knew those questions were unanswerable for now, and only when the Creator deemed the timing perfect to share with the team would they know the answers.

And although the Creator's warriors put the missions He gave them above all else, He still had created them with both curiosity and empathy. Both of which often served them well as they executed countless missions over millennia to ensure the Creator's plans were always fulfilled.

As Isabella continued to sing and pray over the family, the father awoke first and immediately began to conduct the final preparations for their journey. The journey Isabella knew was not going to happen. After checking on his wife and noticing the peaceful sleep she was enjoying, he decided to let her sleep and began to make his way toward the back of the home and out the back entrance of the house toward the barn.

"I see him," Sam replied.

"Want me to join you?" Isabella asked.

"Negative, stay with the mother. I'll make sure the animals have no interest in leaving this barn anytime soon."

"Got it. The mother is still sleeping," Isabella reported, her voice still in a low whisper as if she was afraid of waking the mother. The mother, along with all the other humans, could not hear her. An anecdote Isabella found amusing to herself as she thought about it even while whispering with Sam.

The plan was simple. Sam was to reveal himself to the animals but not to the humans and, in so doing, instill a paralyzing fear in the two mules the family had planned to use for their journey. Sam's huge frame, bright-topaz eyes, square jaw, and broad shoulders was enough to paralyze any living creature on earth, but especially animals. He had discovered this paralyzing fear long ago and had exploited such fear to accomplish more than a few missions during his service to the Creator. For good measure, he decided to remove his magnificent sword that shone like the sun as he unsheathed it from across his back. He knew the sword was overkill in terms of ensuring the donkeys were going nowhere, but he also liked the sound his sword made as it left its sheath and prepared for battle.

The battle, of course, was no battle at all. The donkeys did as expected. The barn was dark, even in the predawn light that began to emerge on the far horizon. So Sam made sure the light from his sword flashed brightly as he stepped out of the shadows in the stall where both donkeys were lying down. Revealing himself suddenly and with the light flash from his sword generated quick movement from the animals. They first jumped to their feet immediately, braying loudly. After a few short moments of absolute terror, they fell back and sideways, their shocked eyes on Sam throughout the entire terrifying experience.

Sam stood firm in the entrance, his head turned slightly to his left as he looked over his shoulder at the single entrance to the barn, anticipating the entrance of the father.

It wasn't long. The man burst into the barn with a look of terror similar to the ones the donkeys were displaying. For a brief moment, Sam panicked, wondering if he inadvertently revealed himself to the human dimension. His panic subsided as swiftly as it arrived as Sam realized the man had heard the commotion the animals were making and had come running.

"He's here," Sam whispered. He himself wondering why he was whispering. He concluded it just felt better for angel warriors to whisper out of respect for the humans in their presence.

"Are the donkeys cooperating?" Isabella asked, knowing the answer before she asked it.

Of course, they were. Every creature in all the Creator's known creation would react the same way. Total terror.

"I may have overdone it slightly," Sam replied, a huge smile emerging as he chuckled the words.

"Yeah?"

"They aren't going anywhere today, and they may be sidelined for the next few days. They are paralyzed with fear."

"You're a natural."

"Is the mother awake?" Sam asked, turning the conversation back to the task at hand.

"Negative. She's still resting peacefully."

"Well, you do have that effect. Maybe you should give up the sword once and for all and become the Creator's go-to comforter for the rest of time," Sam said, only half joking. He knew the Creator had gifted Isabella in many ways, and she was starting to realize the same.

"Very funny. You may need some extra comfort if you keep forcing Sebastian to make changes to the mission," Isabella joked.

"You should wake her now. The father is making no progress with our four-legged friends here, and he looks to be giving up. He'll be coming back to you and the mother soon. You'll want to make sure the mother is ready for the news."

"On it," Isabella replied. "I'll pray comfort over her and wake her gently."

"Excellent. I've done my part. It's up to you now."

"How's his mood?"

"He's less than thrilled, to say the least. I'm not sure if I'd rather be him or the donkeys right now. He has to tell his wife they aren't making the trip, and the donkeys are beyond paralyzed with fear that may last days."

As the father entered the room, his wife was already sitting up, slowly emerging from some of the most restful sleep she could remember since being with child. As they spoke, the father delivered the news, and Isabella prayed and sang. Prayers for peace from the Creator and songs of comfort.

As the mother-to-be absorbed the news, she was surprisingly calm. She even surprised herself. "It's okay," she spoke softly.

"It is?" replied her husband, clearly not expecting that response.

"Yes. I woke with a peace about this day. The Creator's plans aren't always ours, but that's okay. I trust Him."

"Me too."

There was silence for a long bit as Isabella continued to sing softly as she sat among them. The Creator had delivered the comfort she asked for, and a quiet peace filled the entire room.

"Are you ready for our baby?" the mother asked, breaking the long silence as she slowly stood.

"Ready as I'll ever be. Is today the day?" His voice soft and full of love and devotion.

"I have a good feeling about today," she said as she walked past him, her hand brushing his face as she passed.

Isabella smiled. Indeed, today was going to be the best of days.

CHAPTER 22

The Endless Search

"Javva. Come."

Javva's search for the missing fallen and any evidence as to what happened had come up entirely empty. Since two days after the disappearance and Rusalmeh's rage at Javva's perceived insubordination, the fallen creature had been on a nonstop search for clues. He was strictly in survival mode. The only solace he gave himself was the fact that no one else had found any clues either.

But the dark prince didn't blame them. He blamed Javva. And then came the beatdown the two fallens, Safir and Tarn, took seemingly in the middle of nowhere.

Javva had heard of the incident, but it didn't really change anything for him. He was still to blame for the missing fallen, and until he did something significant to right that wrong in Rusalmeh's eyes, he would always be to blame.

So being summoned to Rusalmeh's chamber this particular morning bore no real significance to the demon who knew he was already in line for annihilation. Just a matter of time, he figured.

"I'm here, sire. At your service."

"Don't patronize me, worm," Rusalmeh hissed as he stood from his perch.

"Sire, I—" Javva began to speak, indicating he was, in fact, not patronizing.

But Rusalmeh wasn't having any of it. "Don't waste my time. I have an assignment for you," Rusalmeh said with even more hissing, if that were even possible.

Javva nodded and then dropped his chin to his chest in submission.

"The house where our two demons took a beating last night, there is an older couple that live there. Our intelligence services can't find anything significant about them or their families..." the prince's voice trailed off as he waited for Javva to say something.

He didn't.

Rusalmeh continued, "So I want you to watch them. Day and night. Wherever they go, you go. And I want you to take note of everything they say, everyone they talk to, and everyone they talk about. I want to know everything about them."

"As you wish," Javva replied softly.

"Everything, Javva."

Everything or nothing. None of it mattered to Javva anymore. His existence, he concluded, was meaningless. And the despair he felt crawled over him like a second skin.

"Javva?" whispered Rusalmeh. He had crept close to Javva without a sound and was now less than an inch from his face.

Javva raised his chin from his chest and stared straight into the eyes of the one being he knew had the power to end his miserable existence once and for all. Rusalmeh's eyes burned like fire. Javva couldn't ever remember being this close to his master. Fear stuck Javva like a sword through his neck as he stared down annihilation and wondered if he should just end it all. He figured he could, just by saying something disrespectful to his master. The prince was on edge, and everyone knew it. The slightest offense, perceived or otherwise, would be met with severe punishment, maybe even annihilation from Rusalmeh.

In the end, Javva's self-preservation won out. He answered quietly and humbly, "Everything, sire. As you wish."

Silence again filled the master's chamber.

Rusalmeh's anger burned as he stared at his slave an inch from his face. He finally spoke, "Leave and don't come back empty-handed.

You owe me something, Javva. Take those two useless worms, Tarn and Safir, with you. They are familiar with the area and may be able to help since they were there the night the angel showed up and intercepted enemy communications only hours after the enemy incursion."

"As you wish, sire," the humiliated fallen weakly replied.

Javva turned and left his master's chamber, wondering if he would ever be able to please him or if it would just be better to fail spectacularly in order to receive the sweet release of total annihilation.

Deep down, he knew the answer. And he was terrified.

CHAPTER 23

An Unexcepted Journey

"It's been two days," the woman said nervously.

"Eliza, all is well," the woman's husband gently responded.

"You can't be sure. We need to journey there to be with them," Elizabeth replied.

Her husband looked up from his meal, raising his eyebrows as he made eye contact with his wife.

"I think we should take a physician with us," Elizabeth said without a hint of hesitation. She was committed to it. Something her husband, Zechariah, had come to recognize for what it was. A foregone conclusion. A physician was going to go with them. Period.

"Okay," Zechariah replied.

"Matthan is a physician. He tended to your mother and many of our extended family, including my sister."

"I'll ask him, Elizabeth. But you know it is a lot to ask, right?"

"I do."

"I need you to promise that if he does agree to journey with us, that you will let him do his job as a physician. I can guarantee you he will not need your opinions on how best to care for the new mother and baby."

"I promise," Elizabeth responded with a smile that told Zechariah that she only partially promised.

But that was enough for him.

*****

"I'm sorry, Zeke. We have my grandson with us, and my wife is unable to tend after the child without me." Matthan was a tall man, a full white beard covering his face, and less than half of that same white hair covering his head. He had a slight limp as he walked, but he was a strong man both in mind and in body.

They were sitting inside Matthan's small house not far from where Zechariah and his wife lived in the hill country far from Nazareth, the closest town. After exchanging pleasantries, Matthan had invited Zechariah to join him at the small wooden eating table just inside the home.

"I understand, friend. It's just that you know my sweet Eliza. She has made up in her mind that something has gone wrong with her cousin or the baby or both, and she insists on you joining us. I'll be happy to pay extra—"

"No, you will not pay, nor will you pay extra. Perhaps I can bring my grandson with me on the journey?" Matthan was a caring man and was never able to say no throughout most of his adult life. He genuinely liked to help people. This time, it was no different.

"We would be happy to have him. As you know, it's a little less than a day's journey. We would expect to stay two nights with a return journey on the third day," Zechariah spoke in the best way he knew how to make the journey sound as easy and simple as possible so that, in his mind, he would prove to be as convincing as he could be in that moment. He didn't want to return to Elizabeth empty-handed. He was sure of that.

"He just turned five," Matthan said.

At that moment, the young boy emerged, peeking from behind his grandfather as the two men talked. The small boy had light-brown hair and sharp, clear, brown eyes. He stood at his grandfather's side, expressionless as the men discussed the details of the journey, including when the next morning they planned to leave and when they expected to return. The young boy leaned in close to his grandfather, and it was clear to Zechariah that the two had a special relationship.

With the details set, the two men stood to say their goodbyes, and Matthan asked his young grandson if he would like to join them on an overnight journey.

The boy didn't respond at first as he looked at the guest standing in front of him.

It wasn't until his grandfather scooped him up, looked at the boy eye to eye, and asked, "Well?"

The young boy quickly nodded his head and smiled at the prospect of an adventure with his grandfather.

With his young grandson in his arms, Matthan bid farewell to Zechariah, and as he left the house, the two were once again alone in the house.

Or so they thought. They would never know of the unwanted guest, an invisible evil spirit, lurking in the shadows of the room, capturing every word spoken and every plan made. As instructed, Javva had followed Zechariah to the physician's home and taken note of their plans. Javva decided in that moment that he, Safir, and Tarn would tag along on the journey the next morning.

Little did he know he was about to stumble upon the greatest mission the Creator had ever commissioned.

And just like so many times before, he would miss what was right in front of his eyes.

CHAPTER 24

A Day's Journey

"Papa?"

"Yes, son?" Matthan responded, thinking how much he loved to hear that sweet voice of his grandson.

"Will we see wild animals on our trip?"

Matthan smiled as he replied, "Wild birds? Yes. Wild rodents? For sure. Not much more than that, at least I hope not."

"I hope we see a lion!" The boy squealed as he jumped up and down, excited for the journey.

Matthan thought to himself, *Since I'm no King David, if we see a lion, the journey has gone terribly wrong.*

Just then, Zechariah was rounding the corner of the house with two donkeys. One to carry supplies and gifts for the new arrival, the other to carry Elizabeth on the journey. "I really can't thank you enough for joining us, Matthan. Both as a physician and as a friend," Zechariah said, reaching out his hand to greet the aging physician. Addressing the young boy, he asked, "Are you ready for an adventure, young one?"

"Yes!" the boy screamed. One of the donkeys brayed in disagreement at the sudden loud noise.

A moment later, Elizabeth came out of the house with her hands full of supplies for the journey, including feed for the donkeys, a small basket of bread, and two clay jars of water.

"We aren't taking an army of donkeys, my love," Zechariah said sweetly.

Not having any of it, Elizabeth retorted quickly, "You'll find room, dear. You always do." She continued as she bent down, going eye to eye with the young boy, "And you, little one, we are so glad to have you join us!"

The boy smiled big, throwing his arms around Elizabeth's neck as she stood and hugged him tight. Although not related, they all felt like family.

Zechariah and Elizabeth had been friends with Matthan and his wife and their family for many years. They watched Matthan's sons grow up, get married, and begin to have children of their own, including now this little one with whom they had become very fond as he visited his grandparents often.

The boy's father was a craftsman, skilled in many areas with special skills as a blacksmith. He would often travel weeks at a time as his skills were in high demand across Israel. The young boy's mother ran the household of three children. Since the boy was the oldest, her hands were very full, so she gladly allowed Matthan and his wife to care for the boy whenever they pleased.

It took some persuasion. The boy's grandmother reluctantly agreed to allow the boy to tag along, only after she made Matthan promise on his life that he would bring him back safe and sound.

The sun was rising. It was time to go.

The men completed the final packing of the donkeys, including the one Matthan had brought for the journey. His carried his medical supplies and gifts for the new mother and child, including a spot for his grandson. Zechariah prayed a brief prayer of protection over their journey, and they were off.

It had been three days since Elizabeth's cousin, pregnant with their first and likely only child, along with her husband, were to arrive at their home. They never arrived. So as they set off to join the young family, they were not sure what to expect. They hoped for the best but just could not shake the question of what kept them. Why would they not come? What went wrong?

They would know soon enough, but Elizabeth couldn't stop worrying. She knew it didn't help, but she loved her cousin deeply and knew how long they all had prayed for a child. Would the Creator be so cruel after all these years and all these prayers? Elizabeth pushed these thoughts far from her mind as they set out. She would know soon enough, she told herself.

They all would. All, including the three unwelcome invisible guests joining them. Javva, Safir, and Tarn.

Shortly after the plans between Zechariah and Matthan had been made, Javva made the report to Rusalmeh through his superiors, and the order came back to follow the group on this journey. With no solid leads regarding the missing fallen and two severely beaten, Rusalmeh was desperate. Since the angel warrior attack happened outside of Zechariah and Elizabeth's house, Rusalmeh was going on a hunch, that something about that house brought the angelic warrior there, and perhaps whoever lived in that house would lead them back to the angel.

Javva figured it was beyond a long shot, but he kept his mouth shut and obeyed. At least this way, he could get farther away from his master, who was growing increasingly agitated by the day.

Little did he know he was about to enter the presence of some of the Creator's most majestic and lethal warriors.

And he was ill prepared.

CHAPTER 25

The Baby Arrives

"I'm not sure what to do!" Isabella exclaimed.

"Bring her comfort, Isabella," Sam replied softly.

The area was quiet, at least quiet in terms of fallens. They were not going to let down now, however quiet it might be. Sam, Petros, and Sebastian were strategically positioned to identify any incoming fallen activity that might have plans to descend on the home in which the family was residing.

"We need you to activate your comfort skill right about now, Isabella. Mom will need as much as you can give her," Sebastian encouraged.

"Okay. Whatever is needed, I will do. Still would love to fight."

"Not the mission."

"Just saying."

"The Creator chose each of us specifically for this mission, so we must always trust that."

"I do."

"And don't forget His ways are not ours. His plans for us are beyond our ability to understand," Sebastian said, reminding his entire team, not just Isabella.

No one really enjoyed the lectures from Sebastian, but they did appreciate the reminder.

"Incoming," Sam whispered that one word, and the rest of the team froze.

"Where?" asked Sebastian.

"Northwest. Just above the horizon."

"How many?" Petros asked.

"Three. I see them too," Isabella said.

"Hold your positions," Sebastian commanded.

The three fallens were flying in a formation designed specifically to spot angelic activity in the area. One in front and the other two flanking his right and left. Greasy heads on a swivel. On the hunt.

The warrior team had been able to remain undetected, but existing for an extended period of time in enemy territory without being detected seemed like an impossibility, especially with near-constant fallen activity. The disappearance of one of Rusalmeh's warriors at the hands of Sam the night of their arrival had clearly rattled the demon leader. It's likely what explained the consistent search missions so many fallens seemed to be carrying out since Sebastian and his special forces team arrived.

The three demons flew quick and low, not slowing at all as they flew on past the concealed team of angels watching their every move. As soon as they were spotted, they disappeared again into the darkness.

"Time to go, Isabella," Sebastian said quietly.

"Yes, sir. Don't get into any trouble without me," Isabella implored, only somewhat joking.

"We would never dream of that, Bella," Sam said, his voice crackling through the secure communication protocol Petros had established so they could all communicate with one another.

She could hear the smirk on his face as he said it. She decided not to respond as she made her way quickly from her concealed position just inside the grove of trees that had become their base camp to the house where the new baby was soon to arrive.

It wasn't long before the team heard the beautiful sound of an angel singing praises to the Creator. Songs designed to bring great comfort to mother and child as they worked so closely together to bring the miracle of human life into existence.

The soon-to-be mother had planned to be with her cousin, her cousin's family, and a physician for the arrival of her first child.

Those plans changed after Sam's chance encounter on his and Petros's recon mission to ensure safe passage for the family. Out of an abundance of caution, Sebastian decided to keep them here at their home. It's a home easily defended and the variables more easily controlled.

The change in plans had upset an already-emotional mother-to-be, so when labor pains started later the same day, Sebastian knew Isabella was perfect for the moment. He was right. She was perfect.

As Sebastian listened to Isabella singing so beautifully, he couldn't help but marvel at the Creator's perfect planning. Each of them created by the Creator for a situation just like this. Only He could piece it all together, weaving a masterpiece as unique and unexpected as it is beautiful.

As they heard the first cries of a new human life, no one of the team spoke. Such a miracle designed by the Creator left them without words. Even Isabella stopped singing as she witnessed the birth up close.

As much as they all wanted to witness the miracle of human life, they all instinctively held their positions. This baby was at the heart of their secret mission. The baby was why they were here. To be protected at all costs. So they focused on the task at hand. No one moved. No one spoke.

After a long silence with only the sounds of a crying baby in the distance contrasting an otherwise-quiet night, Isabella spoke three words. Words that would resonate in the spirit of each of the angelic warriors for millennia after they were spoken.

"It's a girl."

CHAPTER 26

A Baby Girl?

"A girl?" Petros asked, not entirely sure why he was surprised.

"She's beautiful," Isabella whispered.

"How's the mother?" Sebastian asked, keeping his full command of the team and the moment.

"Very good, sir. Everyone seems to be doing great," Isabella replied.

"What's her name?" Petros asked.

"Mary," Isabella responded with a smile as she recalled the affection with which her parents referred to her the moment after she was born.

"What is the Creator up to?" Sam said to himself, not realizing his comm was open as he said it.

"Sam?" Sebastian asked.

"Oh, sorry, sir. It's just that I'm wondering what a baby girl means in all of this."

"Well, He doesn't want it to be a big deal. That's for sure," Petros spoke with an authority that surprised everyone.

"How so?" Isabella asked, still marveling at the majesty of the Creator's new life ushered so beautifully into the world.

"Well, here we are, in the middle of nowhere, hunkered down, hiding instead of fighting and waiting for fallens that, outside a few random encounters, seem to not have a clue or even passing interest in any one of the family members we are here to protect. The least of which being this new baby," Petros said, more inquisitive than frustrated but certainly interested in what was next for a seemingly insignificant mission.

"Don't forget what happened to the last baby you were sent to protect," Sebastian reminded him.

"Moses?" Petros asked.

"That's right. He turned out to be the one person the Creator used to free his people from four hundred years of bondage and slavery," Sam chimed in.

"And no one saw him coming either," Isabella added.

"Touché." It's the only thing Petros could think to say in return.

They were right. Petros spent years watching over a young Moses, thinking his mission was insignificant. Until it wasn't. He was part of the Creator's great story of redemption of the Hebrew people.

"But this is not that. How could it be?" Petros said after a long silence.

"Above our pay grade, brother," Sam said with his classic smile.

"We stay on mission," Sebastian said firmly. And everyone knew what that meant. Keep the main thing the main thing. He continued, "Isabella, you good to stay with the family tonight?"

"Yes, sir."

"Petros and Sam, hold your positions tonight and don't miss anything. Just because it's been relatively quiet doesn't mean it won't stay that way. You copy?"

"Copy that, sir," Sam replied for them both.

Not another word was spoken among the team that night. They all stayed alert and ready while listening to the beautiful songs of grace, redemption, and peace that Isabella sang over the new baby girl and her family throughout the rest of the night.

Little did they know the darkness of hell would soon descend, and their mission would be tested like never before.

CHAPTER 27

Visitors

"Do you see them?" Isabella asked from her well-hidden position high in a tree to the northwest of the property they were protecting. It had been a night and day since the baby arrived. The new family was settled in nicely, so Sebastian instructed Isabella to rejoin the team and focus once again on protection.

"I do," Sam replied from his hidden position deep within the northeast end of the tree grove adjacent to the family's property.

"Four humans. Two men, one woman, and a small child," Petros chimed in from his position also deep within a tree grove not far from Sam.

"And three fallens," Sebastian said. His voice firm, resolved. He was likely the most well-hidden as he sat wedged within a rock formation that sat directly north of the family's property, giving him the best view of all incoming activity.

Sebastian knew this mission had been troubling from the start. The need to stay hidden complicated so many things. Confronting fallens and righting wrongs was what these angel warriors were designed to do. Hiding was not in their DNA. But Sebastian's resolve was clear. He knew he was chosen to lead this mission for a reason, and he was not going to fail.

After a moment of silence, Sebastian said, "Hold your positions."

"You think they are coming to our family's house?" Petros asked.

"You can count on it," Sam answered. "My guess is this is the family that owns the house you and I scouted out two nights back."

"When our family didn't show as planned, they decided to make the trip?" Petros asked, piecing it together.

"Copy that," Sebastian said, now with urgency and purpose. "And I'm not surprised."

"Sir?" Isabella asked.

"Not surprised that Rusalmeh would send a scout team after anyone who left that house."

"Yeah, especially after Sam's grand entrance the other night," Petros said with the images of Sam's flawless beating he delivered to the two hapless, unsuspecting fallens still fresh in his mind.

"Do you recognize any of them?" Sebastian asked.

"Javva. The one is Javva," Isabella said without hesitation.

"Javva?" Sam asked. "Last time we saw him was in the palace with—"

"Rusalmeh," Isabella answered, finishing Sam's thought for him.

"He's running a scout mission? Rusalmeh must still be punishing him for his screwup in the palace way back when."

"Looks like it."

"How about the other two?" Sebastian asked.

"Well, they're persistent if they're anything," Sam said with a smile.

"Who's they?"

"Those are the two I turned the lights out on two nights ago. They must be back for more," Sam said.

"Not today."

"Copy that."

"Isabella, I need you in the house. Is there a place you can stay hidden in the house?"

"Negative, sir. Too small, especially with additional visitors."

"What about the small loft above the back entrance? Can you stay hidden in there?"

"I guess so."

"No guessing. Yes or no?"

"Yes. It's small for sure, but I'll go full camouflage and stay completely concealed."

Silence. Everyone was asking themselves the same thing. "How can we stay hidden but still close enough to make moves if we have to? And for how long? We all know we can smoke these fools. Why do we have to keep hiding?"

"Do it. Stay hidden and do not reveal yourself unless the baby herself is in grave danger," Sebastian commanded.

"Is there any other kind of danger for a human baby?" Sam asked, not expecting an answer.

"Go, Isabella," Sebastian whispered as the small caravan drew closer and the fallens no doubt on alert for enemy activity in the area. "We'll be here to support as needed."

"If these fools attempt to harm our baby in any way, trust me, I won't need any help."

Everyone, including Sebastian, had to smile at that. Isabella was a fierce warrior on an any given day, but everyone on the team knew that her instincts to protect innocent human life increased her ferocious tendencies one hundredfold. If the fallens approaching the small farm that night made any kind of aggressive move, for any reason, toward the family they were on mission to protect, it would be their last. Isabella would see to that.

As the leader of this mission, Sebastian knew this. He knew Isabella was itching to fight at any given moment. He also knew the Creator chose her for this mission. A covert mission with its main purpose of staying hidden while watching over a very specific family with a new human life in tow.

As he watched the small human caravan move past his position with three fallens close behind, he wondered why he would have asked Isabella to be the one inside the house. Especially with her bias for action. Her instinct to fight first and ask questions later. He wasn't entirely sure, but he knew it was right. He knew he could trust her to do what was right, especially after he saw the disappointment in her eyes the night they arrived. She knew that she had made a mistake and that her mistake had cost them precious time. And he knew she would not let the team down again.

The baby's father saw them first. He was so excited to see them. He burst out of the house and ran to greet all the visitors as they approached. All of them stopped, greeting one another with hugs and kisses all around.

On a typical mission, one of the angelic warriors would have accompanied the man as he greeted his guests. If for no other reason than to pick up on the conversations being had and capture any meaningful intelligence. This was no ordinary mission. Each warrior stayed hidden. In their positions. Itching to protect and fight but knowing better.

The sight of fallens always aroused a passionate defense of the Creator and His purpose and plans. The fallens had all rejected the Creator, His love, His power, His sovereignty, and His purpose. They had rejected all of it and now existed to do everything they could to influence the Creator's most beloved creation into sin, rejection, pain, and suffering. So the sight of these three goons following close behind the small group of visitors to the family's home aroused these emotions in all the Creator's warriors. They wanted to fight. Every chance to inflict pain on a fallen was another opportunity to right the wrong of rebellion toward the Creator.

"Hold," Sebastian whispered. This one word was spoken for himself as much as the others. Sebastian figured if he needed to tell himself, his team likely needed to hear it as well.

And everyone knew exactly what that one word meant and why. So they held. Righteous anger seething just beneath the surface as they watched the fallens approach. All of them hoping this mission would soon turn into one in which they could fight instead of hide.

"Status?" Isabella asked. She was already in the house in full camouflage, completely hidden in the loft above the back entrance of the family's home.

"Two minutes. Maybe less," Petros said. His was now the best position to view the visitors as they approached. He continued, "The two men are taking the donkeys to the barn, and the woman and small child are heading your way to the house."

Isabella was in a great position to see it all. The women embraced and talked frantically to each other in those kinds of human conversations in which both parties were talking simultaneously while anyone else listening could not understand either of them. But those doing the talking both seemed to understand each other just fine. The new mother frantically explained why they decided not to make the trip while expressing frustration at her inability to let them know. The woman visiting was explaining how worried she had been when they did not arrive and how she prayed the Creator would protect and watch over the birth and the new baby. She explained how she was able to persuade their physician friend to come and how he was here to provide any care that might be needed.

As the frantic, exuberant conversation continued, Isabella kept her eye on the young boy who very quietly had made his way to where the baby girl was sleeping. She was wrapped tightly in a blanket, lying in a small basket in the center of the living space.

Unattended.

CHAPTER 28

What's the Point?

"What are we doing here?" Tarn seethed as he first spotted the small homestead in the distance. His large head, small eyes, and hunched shoulders gave him the look of a fallen past his prime. He wasn't, of course, as spiritual beings don't age like humans do. But he was weary and was always susceptible to bouts with deep depression.

"Shut up," Javva hissed. His patience was effectively gone.

"This is pointless," Safir whined. Safir was tall and thin in a way humans would recognize as severely malnourished, but for Safir, it was his body's response from being separated from the love of the Creator for so long. His gaunt look was enhanced by his large, sunken eyes dark with pain and misery.

"What else do you, worms, have going on?" Javva asked rhetorically.

"The warrior we saw is not here," Safir said confidently. "He was here on a routine scouting mission, and we bounced into each other. To think it was anything more than a coincidence is foolish."

"Is it? And when you say 'bounced into,' does that mean your head 'bouncing into' the ground as you took a beating from an enemy that made a complete fool out of you?"

Safir said nothing. Neither did Tarn. Javva outranked them and was facing annihilation if he was unable to uncover any meaningful intelligence for Rusalmeh soon. They recognized a demon on the edge, and both decided to stay silent.

"We know from the human conversations a baby was expected to be born. They were expecting the father and mother to visit two days ago and stay until the birth of the child," Javva said, his rage slightly subsiding.

"But they never showed," Safir replied.

"That's right," Javva said. "And the night before they were to arrive, you and Tarn got your asses beat."

Silence. Javva's two lackeys were in no position to argue.

"So why was an enemy warrior at the same house the night before visitors were to arrive preparing for a new human birth?" Javva asked, each of them knowing the question was rhetorical. "We have to expect that nothing is coincidental. So we are following this group in the hopes of finding something. Anything."

They stayed silent the rest of the way.

The reunion of the families was happy. Which they hated. A man came running out of a small home, arms waving, yelling as he approached. They stopped for a moment as they greeted one another, and the man spoke of a new baby girl being born just yesterday.

"A girl?" Tarn asked, more to himself than anyone.

No one answered. They moved on toward the house as Javva directed Safir to stay with the men as they moved to the barn. And he told Tarn to stay with him as they followed the man from the house, the woman, and the small boy back toward the small human dwelling.

Javva noticed that it was small and filled with joy and laughter as the women greeted each other heartily. All of which the demons hated. They hated all of it. New human life. The love. The laughter. Hated. All of it.

Isabella watched them as they entered in the small house, following the human guests. Dark and putrid and greasy and hateful. Isabella reminded herself it's what happened after millennia separated from the Creator and His love. She recognized Javva right away. Her up close encounter with him long ago etched his disfigured face into her memory. The kind of memory she didn't want but couldn't escape. The other one with him she did not recognize. He was much taller than Javva but clearly his subordinate. Isabella saw them pause after entering the home as she watched their every move.

As she saw the scene unfold before her, she wondered how the humans would react if they knew two spirits facing eternal damnation were moving among them. What would they do if they suddenly realized there were demons in the same room? The spirit realm is as real as the physical or earthly realm. Just because humans can't see it doesn't mean it doesn't exist. All these questions and thoughts were running through the majestic warrior's mind as she lay in the back corner of the small loft in a small farmhouse in what began to feel like the middle of nowhere in the earthly realm.

And then she saw them both move.

As the women continued to laugh and hug and cry and talk over each other, no one noticed the small boy had made his way over to where the baby girl lay sleeping. How the baby was sleeping during all the recent commotion was surprising, to say the least, to Isabella. Isabella noticed the small boy was carrying something in his hand. A small toy? Perhaps a gift?

The demons noticed it too, and they set across the room to check it out. Just as they were surrounding the boy and the baby's crib, the boy was reaching his hand into the crib, and the baby began to cry.

And it wasn't a small cry either, Isabella observed. The baby was upset.

As soon as her mother and the others heard the baby's cry, they quickly ended their greeting ritual and rushed to the baby's side. Javva and Tarn were mingled among the humans, none of them the wiser of the demented spirits nestled so close to them.

If only they knew how close they were to pure evil, Isabella thought to herself, not daring to make a sound.

The young boy had brought a small gift for the baby. Isabella could tell by the commotion that ensued that he clearly had not told anyone of his plans to give the new baby a gift. There it was. A wooden figurine of some kind. Maybe a sheep or a lion. Isabella wasn't close enough to tell. She didn't pay much attention. She was roiling with different emotions that kept her mind focused on very different things than the small gift from the young boy.

She could hardly contain her anger at the two hapless fallens so close to the one human she and the other warriors had been sent specifically by the Creator to protect. At the same time, she was racked with the fear of making a mistake and accidentally revealing herself at such a critical moment. Such a mistake would be devastating to the mission, would result in three additional annihilated fallens, and would alert the entire region of fallens to this small home and family long before the Creator had planned.

Doing her best to keep her emotions in check, she decided to think of all the ways she could annihilate the fallens in front of her as a way to keep her mind occupied. She was built to annihilate, and her inability to do so on this mission so far had been excruciating for her. But she knew her mistake on that first night cost the mission dearly, and she couldn't do that again. She loved the Creator and Sebastian and the others too much. So she held it together as she watched the two greasy fallens mere inches from the baby she had been sent to protect.

She took solace in the fact that their mission was so secret and the baby and her family so obscure that the fallens who had come that night had no idea what was happening. She smiled, thinking of the moment years from now when these two hapless demons would put together the fact that they had this opportunity to significantly damage the Creator's plans but didn't. Here they were, a front seat to the Creator's grand plan, and they were too stupid to realize it.

It didn't take long for the fallens to lose interest. There was nothing for them here. Just some poor human farmers and their poor friends. It was all just a big waste of time.

Isabella could see the disappointment on their wretched faces and knew their last lead to find their annihilated comrades was a dead end. As they left the home, she made sure to capture their images in her mind's eye. She knew she would see them again.

Only the next time she would see them, she could only hope she would be able to deliver the just punishment they so richly deserved.

CHAPTER 29

The Lion and the Lamb

"We are so glad you are here!" the baby's mother exclaimed excitedly.

"We worried when you all didn't arrive as planned," Elizabeth explained.

"We are so sorry! The donkeys would not move. It was the strangest thing. They just stared at us in terror."

"Terror?" asked Elizabeth.

"Yeah, like they could see something we couldn't, and they were scared to death. One of them even fell over, stiff with fear."

"Oh my. That is strange."

"So without the ability to travel, we decided to stay and hoped you would understand."

"Oh yes, dear. We understand. Just frightened. Is all. It's why we brought Matthan along. Just in case."

"Your physician friend?"

"That's him. And this is his grandson. His name is..." Before she could get the next word out, she noticed him. The young boy had made his way to the small baby bed and appeared to be reaching for the child. "No!" Elizabeth exclaimed.

The two women rushed to the baby's bedside to find the boy was still clutching a small item in his right hand.

"What are you doing, my son?"

"I'm sorry, Ms. Elizabeth. I just brought a gift for the baby and wanted to give it to her."

"Oh, okay, sweetie. I'll take it for her. She is too small for it now, but I'll be sure to give it to her when she is able to play with it. Okay?" the baby's mother said softly as the boy handed her the gift.

The young boy looked innocently up at her and whispered, "Okay."

No one said anything for a moment as they processed the sweet gesture and the sweet moment together.

Then the boy spoke, "My papa said I should make it for the baby."

"That is very sweet of you, my child," Elizabeth said, the baby's mother nodding her head in agreement.

"And very thoughtful too," the baby's mother said.

"What is it, child? What did you make for the baby?"

"It's a lion and a lamb."

"Together?"

"Yes, ma'am."

"Don't lions eat lambs?" Elizabeth said with a smile.

"Not this one. This lion is nice. He's scary, but he's nice to the lamb. The tall man with the bright eyes and smile showed him to me."

"Man?"

"Yeah, the man in my dream. He showed me the lamb and then the lion."

By then, the two women were focused on the baby and didn't hear his answer about the dream.

But the three spirits in the room did hear it. And all three spirits knew the power of dreams. They all knew how the Creator often uses dreams to fulfill His purpose. All three wondered what a young boy's dream could possibly mean.

None of them could even imagine.

CHAPTER 30

Wasted Trip

"Let's go," Javva grumbled, his hand slinking off the side of the baby's bed like a snake recoiling from a flame.

"There's nothing here," Tarn replied as if thinking Javva wanted him to respond.

He didn't.

As they exited the house, they ran into Safir as he followed the men moving from the barn toward the house.

"Nothing?" Safir asked.

No one responded. They just walked past him. A wasted question.

Javva knew his time was running out with Rusalmeh. As they walked about from the small farm home, he knew he would have to go face-to-face again with Rusalmeh. And face whatever he had coming. He figured whatever it was couldn't be worse than the constant fear he had carried around with him since that night. "Just get it over with then," Javva grumbled only to himself.

His two companions heard him but said nothing. They didn't need to.

They all knew. Javva was as good as gone.

CHAPTER 31

Crisis Averted

"Clear?" Isabella asked with the slightest whisper she could muster and still be heard.

"Clear," Petros responded as he watched the three fallens slink away toward the dark horizon.

"Clear," both Sebastian and Sam said at the same time.

At that, Isabella unfolded herself from her cramped position in the loft area above the small living space and just sat for a moment. She was watching one of the men tending to the new human baby girl as if he was checking her over for health problems. "One of the visitors appears to be a physician," Isabella whispered.

"Why are you still whispering?" Sam quipped, his smile coming across loud and clear through the comms.

"Shut up, Sam," Isabella joked.

"What happened in there?" Sebastian asked.

"The young boy brought the new baby a gift." Isabella paused for a moment, recalling the scene. And then she continued, "It was a bit of a surprise."

"Surprise?" asked Sebastian.

"Yes. It drew everyone's attention to the baby's bedside, including the fallens."

"What was the gift?" Petros asked.

"Looks like a lion carved out of wood." Isabella was now standing among the humans at the baby's bedside, getting a closer look. "They were so close," Isabella said to no one in particular.

"They?" Sam asked.

"Yeah, the fallens," she said, her voice trailing off.

No one spoke for a long moment.

Isabella continued, "Her safety is the purpose of our whole mission, and I let them get within inches of her."

"You had no choice," Sebastian quickly responded. He continued, "They don't know of her importance."

"Do we?" Isabella asked, not expecting an answer.

No one responded. They couldn't. Because they didn't know either.

"In the Creator's time, we will know," Petros finally said after the deafening silence.

"Any contact with the enemy at this stage in the mission would have further alerted them to this place, this family, and this baby," Sam reasoned.

"You did what was necessary for the mission, Isabella."

"Which was nothing?" Isabella asked as she still questioned whether her inaction was the right move.

"Yes," Sebastian said, attempting to end the topic of conversation right there. He continued, "Sam, head into the house and spend the night watching over the family."

"Sir?" Isabella questioned.

"It's the best thing right now. I need you to take a break."

She didn't like it, but she knew Sebastian was right. She said nothing as she headed out of the house. As she did, she passed Sam who was wearing his typical wide grin as they passed each other.

"You showed a lot of restraint in there," Sam said, looking over his shoulder as they passed.

"I let them get so close to her," she said, stopping to turn to face her friend.

"You had no choice. You followed orders. You did the right thing."

"The boy had a dream," Isabella said, not looking back at Sam as she said it, knowing that with the comms line still open the entire team heard it.

Sam stopped cold and turned around slowly. Both Sebastian and Petros, in their overwatch positions, leaned in, being sure not to miss what came next.

"The little boy was trying to tell the family about it, but no one heard him. They were too infatuated with the baby." Isabella let the revelation hang in the air a moment longer than she needed to and finally said, "He said a tall man with bright eyes and a bright smile showed him."

"Showed him what?" Sam asked with an intensity that even surprised him.

"A lion."

No one said anything as they processed what they had just heard.

In the silence, Isabella whispered, "And a lamb."

"Together?" Petros asked.

"In perfect peace, together."

Sam spent the rest of the night with the family, enjoying their conversations and praying over them and the new baby human who had so majestically arrived the night before.

Sebastian, Isabella, and Petros kept watch throughout the night, all of them thinking about the boy's dream and what it could mean for their mission. As they contemplated what all of it could mean that night, they made sure to stay completely concealed. Each of them ready for war.

No war came that night. But they all knew they couldn't stay hidden forever.

CHAPTER 32

Shalom

The little boy didn't know what it meant. Maybe it was nothing. Dreams, he thought, could be that way. So many made no sense really. During the dream, of course, they made sense. But once awake, they often offered little continuity or connectivity to any reality.

But this one was different. Almost intentional. The young boy awoke, not fearful as much as he was inquisitive. First, he remembered it perfectly. Every detail. In vivid color. Second, he couldn't stop thinking about it. A lion and a lamb. Together. At peace.

Even though he wasn't even five years old yet, he knew that really didn't make sense. Lions would eat lambs. They would tear them apart. They would feast on them. They wouldn't protect them. They wouldn't lie next to them.

But they were together in his dream. He told his mom about it. She said it was nothing. Dreams didn't mean anything, she told him.

The next day he spent with his grandfather. He planned on staying for the next several days as his parents were traveling as they often did.

His grandfather was a physician by trade but loved being in his workshop whenever he wasn't tending to patients in the surrounding area. And since his grandfather loved woodworking, so did the young boy. He spent a lot of time with his grandfather.

The boy was unusually quiet in the woodshop that day.

"Why so quiet, my son?" his grandfather asked.

"Nothing."

"Sure?"

"I had a dream last night, Papa," the boy said, just coming straight out with it.

His grandfather was quiet for a moment. Then he asked, "What kind of dream?"

"A little scary at first."

"Oh? Tell me."

"There was a man. He was really tall."

"Was he scary to you?

"No. He was nice. His hair was like fire, and his eyes were bright. He smiled big at me."

His grandfather said nothing as he set down the chisel he was using to shape a piece of wood.

The boy continued, "He took my hand, and we started walking."

"Where did you go?"

"To a field. A big green field."

"That doesn't sound so scary."

"I'm not done yet, Papa."

This caused his grandfather to chuckle. The boy was not smiling. His grandfather quickly collected himself and said, "Okay, my son, I'm listening. Go on. Please."

"The man then pointed to a herd of sheep in the field. He asked me what I saw."

"What did you see?"

"Sheep, Papa! I saw sheep!"

"Okay then. You saw sheep. Is that what he wanted you to see?"

"Not really. He asked me to look more." After a long moment, the boy continued, "Then I saw a small one—like a baby one, a pure white one—move away from the rest of the flock."

"What do you mean 'pure white'?" his grandfather asked.

"Like the other ones had brown spots and black spots. They were all dirty, like sheep are. But this one was pure white, Papa."

"The babies are called lambs."

"Okay."

"What happened to it?"

"Nothing at first. It just kept getting farther and farther away from the flock."

"Was there a shepherd?"

"No."

"The shepherd usually goes after the sheep, especially baby ones, that stray from the flock, you know."

"I know, Papa. I didn't see a shepherd." The boy had moved closer to his grandfather and had now climbed on his lap. His grandfather was now giving his full attention to his grandson. The boy continued, "Then I saw him."

"The shepherd?"

"No, the scary one. He ran on all four legs, showed his big teeth, and made a loud, scary noise with his mouth!" the boy exclaimed, his eyes wide and arms open for effect.

His grandfather said nothing, amazed at the level of detail and beginning to wonder if his grandson was making up a story to tell.

Then the boy stopped speaking for a long moment and stared in the empty space of the dark woodshop.

"Was it a lion?" his grandfather whispered into his ear.

"I don't know," the boy whispered back, still staring into the empty space.

"Sounds like a lion."

"It was scary, Papa. He was big and fast and came out of nowhere, running straight toward the small lamb."

"Did the lamb run?"

"No. He just lay down. As soon as he saw the big scary animal, he just lay down."

"Interesting."

"And then the big animal—"

"The lion."

"Okay, the big lion stopped."

"Stopped?"

"Yeah. Just stopped, Papa. And then you know what he did?" the boy whispered, looking up into his grandfather's kind eyes.

"Tell me, son."

"He lay down too."

"He did?"

"He did. Just lay down with that sweet little lamb."

"Then what?"

At this point, both the boy and his grandfather were fully engrossed in the retelling of the dream. They stared at each other for a long moment, both with slight smiles. Both hoping the story wouldn't end.

"The man who took me there asked me what I saw," the boy finally said.

"And?"

"I didn't know what to say, Papa. I didn't know."

"It's okay, my son. It's okay."

"But then he kneeled down next to me, put his arm around me, and whispered a word to me."

It's a word the boy would never forget for the rest of the days he lived on earth. It's a word he would often hear in his family, among his friends, and in his community countless times every day. And every time he heard it for the rest of his life, he would be transported in his mind back to that moment in his dream where the man with the bright eyes and warm smile softly whispered that word.

"Shalom."

CHAPTER 33

Javva Comes Up Empty

"Well?" the dark prince asked as if he already knew the answer.

"It's just a baby. A girl."

"A baby girl?"

"Aye."

"No evidence of enemy activity?"

"None."

"Dammit."

"Are you going to tell him about the dream?" Tarn asked.

If looks could kill, Javva gave Tarn a look that would have sent him to annihilation three times over.

"A dream?" Rusalmeh said, spitting the words in anger. Nothing was to be withheld, and yet Javva was withholding.

"Sire, a small child, a boy, was with the visitors. He told of a dream he had."

Rusalmeh said nothing. Only staring at Javva with a look of hatred and death. It was Javva's not-so-subtle indication to continue.

"He spoke of a man. A tall man with bright eyes and a bright smile. The man showed him a lion and lamb."

"A lion devouring a lamb?"

"No, sire. The lion and the lamb resting together."

"In peace," Rusalmeh growled.

After that, no one spoke. No one had to. The anger in the room was palpable. Everyone in the room at that moment knew something was happening right in front of them. Something massive. But they were out of leads. The trail had gone cold. The enemy was lurking in the shadows, in secret. But why? For what?

Answers to their questions that night would come. Eventually. It would not be until many years later that they would all realize how close they had come to thwarting the Creator's plans. It would be a realization that would haunt all of them for the rest of their existence. Little did they know that such an innocent, inconspicuous, nobody baby girl would be the catalyst to the greatest story of redemption the world has ever known.

They had a front-row seat to it. And missed it all together.

CHAPTER 34

A Thought

"I've been thinking," Rusalmeh spoke, his voice angry.

"Sire?" Javva replied, oblivious to his incompetence.

"You have failed me so miserably I'm not sure why I have kept you in my legion."

"My failure is without excuse, sire."

"Shut up. I've been thinking about the boy."

"The girl you mean?"

"Shut up. The boy who brought the gift. The gift representing the lion and the lamb he saw in a dream."

Javva said nothing, finally getting the hint this was a one-way conversation.

"I think he's connected somehow. He's part of it."

"It?" Javva said weakly.

"I don't know what it is. Not yet at least," Rusalmeh sneered, his voice growing in intensity as he thought about how badly he was being outmaneuvered. He continued, "You are going to follow him."

Javva said nothing. There was nothing to say. This was his fate now. Chasing ghosts. An existence now defined by a fellow demon who vanished, and he was to blame.

Rusalmeh continued, "But this time, you stay hidden. You follow the boy, but you do so without being seen."

"Seen by whom, sire?"

Rusalmeh ignored the question and continued to spit instructions at his slave.

But Javva heard none of them. He simply waited to be told to leave, and then he left. His head low. Longing for the escape of annihilation.

An escape, he feared, would never come.

CHAPTER 35

Things Are Happening

"You are going to see me," Gabriel said, the sound of his voice clear as it crossed dimensions, arriving in Sebastian's comms device.

"When?"

"Soon. I won't stay long."

"Okay."

"And I won't draw attention to you."

"Thanks."

"Stay alert. It will be soon." And he was gone. The conversation was short on purpose.

Rusalmeh was monitoring all communications these days, becoming more and more paranoid as time passed. A demon wouldn't just disappear without a trace unless there was angelic activity. Rusalmeh had finally convinced himself of that and was driving himself crazy, trying to figure it out.

But Sebastian and his warrior team were too good. Too skilled. Too committed. They had all learned to exist in a stealth mode, the likes of which none of them had ever experienced. So with communications monitored constantly, even though Petros scrambled the comms between realms to make their communications sound like fallen communications, they took no chances. Keeping it short meant they could never identify it as something other than their own.

Sebastian wanted more from Gabriel. More information. More mission status details. More of anything. While the team was more committed than ever to keeping their family safe, the length and requirements of the mission were taking their toll on all of them. If they only could see the overall plan. If only they knew the purpose, what it was all for. All the hiding. All the secrecy. If only they knew the end.

As he thought about the brief conversation with Gabriel, the first in a very long time, he wondered what the archangel meant when he said, "It will be soon."

"What was it?" Sebastian whispered to himself as he made his way back to his secure, hidden position. He didn't realize he had kept his comms device open, so everyone else heard him say it.

"Sir?" Isabella asked.

"Oh, sorry, everyone," he said. "I didn't realize comms were still open."

"Sir?" Sam asked, figuring piling on couldn't hurt anything at this point.

"It was Gabriel. It's just something he said. Is all," Sebastian said, his voice trailing off.

No one spoke. Everyone waiting for Sebastian's next words.

"It will be soon," Sebastian finally said after a long bit.

Petros asked, "What did he mean?"

"That's the thing. I don't know. He said he will be here."

"Gabriel?" Isabella asked.

"Here?" Sam asked, following Isabella in rapid succession.

"Yes. We'll see him, but he won't see us."

Silence again. Everyone, including Sebastian, was processing this information. Everyone was trying to figure out what it meant for their mission. Was it coming to an end? What would Gabriel's arrival behind enemy territory mean for their mission? Maybe it meant nothing? All these questions were racing through their minds, and no one wanted to speak. They all just wanted to let the thoughts and scenarios continue to play through their minds a moment longer.

Then Sebastian finally spoke, "Okay, everyone, it's best you don't read into anything here." He continued, "Gabriel is arriving, and it will be soon. He wanted to make sure we were aware so we weren't surprised and inadvertently reveal ourselves to the enemy. Those are the facts as I know them."

"He'll be noticed," Isabella replied.

"Correct. Rusalmeh will know almost immediately," Petros said in confirmation.

"I've never seen Gabriel make an entrance in this realm. I'm pretty sure it will be a show we won't want to miss," Sam said with a smile on his face that couldn't get any bigger.

"Yes. But we'll need to be ready."

"Ready, sir?"

"He will attract a lot of enemy attention, which will put a lot more pressure on us than we are used to."

"Not even Rusalmeh would try to take on an archangel like Gabriel, would he?" asked Petros.

"Not likely, Pete, but he has attempted to take him on before. Plus, we know he is extremely frustrated with a missing fallen from years ago with no resolution."

"Roger that, sir. As I have monitored enemy communications over time, the chatter around the incident has died down, but talk of Rusalmeh's anger over not finding resolution remains very intense."

"That's music to my ears," Isabella said without a hint of sarcasm. She meant it.

"But depending on his business here, he'll likely stir up a lot of enemy activity, and we'll need to be ready," Sebastian concluded.

"To fight?"

"No, Sam. To observe, stay hidden, and stay ready," Sebastian said sternly.

Everyone wanted to fight. The tediousness of the mission began to tear at the very fabric of their existence. Like fish out of water, these warriors were without the ability to fight coupled with the extended period of time separated from the presence of the Creator. And that was taking a serious toll on them.

Sebastian continued, "Nothing we can do about it tonight. Our mission remains. I know what's going through your minds right now because it's going through mine as well. We need to stay in the fight."

"That's just it," Sam replied. "There is no fight."

No one said anything then or the rest of the dark night. Petros kept the comms open just in case. But nothing was said. Nothing else needed to be said. The war was coming. They just had no way of knowing when.

As they kept watch over the girl and her family that night for what seemed, to them, to be the ten thousandth night, they wondered if Gabriel's visit would usher in a new phase of their mission.

The answer would come. Soon.

CHAPTER 36

Mary and Joseph Meet

Mary's childhood was, as far as spiritual activity would go, boring.

Her parents loved their only child as parents of an only child could. With everything they had. But she wasn't spoiled. Her mother made sure of that. Chores every morning and chores every evening, young Mary knew the value of hard work and contribution.

Visits to her relatives in the hill country happened occasionally, and her entourage was always with her on every journey she made. Always there. Secret. In the shadows. Ready for war. But always hidden.

Her angelic special forces protection team didn't spot the fallen hanging around until the third or fourth visit to young Mary's relatives. Mary was, by this time, almost three years old. The physician friend of her relatives came for a visit the evening Mary and her family arrived.

And that's when they saw him. Javva.

The physician had brought along his grandson. The boy looked to be eight years old or so. The young boy greeted young Mary with a sweet hug and a smile as they played in the small courtyard off the back of the house. The air that day was cool but comfortable, so the family decided to spend the afternoon outside as weather permitted. A moment neither of them would remember years from then but one Mary's angelic entourage would reminisce over for millennia. The first meeting of two of the most important people in the Creator's entire story of redemption. Or was it?

"Does anyone recognize the boy?" Isabella asked. She was in full camouflage high in the tree adjacent to the property.

"Negative," Sebastian replied.

"Same here. Don't recognize him," Petros said a split second after Sebastian spoke.

"I do," Sam said. "He was there the night the visitors arrived to greet Mary two days after she was born."

"Bingo," Isabella continued. "He's the little boy who gave her the gift that caused all the commotion."

"Nice kid," Petros said.

"He certainly is. Sweet and gentle with our Mary," Sebastian replied.

They all were watching every interaction every other human had with Mary. Less out of concern over intentional harm but always on the lookout to ensure all accidents were to be avoided.

The presence of a fallen, however, complicated the situation tenfold. Angel warriors would often intervene to avoid mishaps, disasters, and accidents of all kinds that had the potential of befalling the human they were on mission to protect. But with a fallen present, any intervention by a spiritual being would surely be seen by any other spiritual being present.

"Who's the fallen?" Sebastian asked, quickly changing the subject.

"It's definitely Javva," Isabella replied.

"He looks terrible," Sam said with a smile.

"That's what happens after millennia separated from the Creator's love, isn't it?" Petros asked, a statement more than a question.

"Yes, but I agree with Sam. His deterioration seems to be accelerating," Isabella confirmed.

Javva's assignment had begun to take its toll for sure. He was a fallen under constant torment. The torment of restlessness and boredom. A fallen who was once the right-hand spirit of the most powerful demon in the region now relegated to following a child around on a seemingly endless loop of uneventfulness. And it was taking a serious toll on the relegated fallen.

Isabella continued, "He's slumped, vacant."

"Looks like we should put him out of his misery," Petros mused.

"What do you say, boss? Put him out of his misery?" Sam asked, only half joking.

"Stay focused, everyone," Sebastian commanded. "Don't lose your edge. Our job is to stay hidden. This is no different."

"Understood. But I must say, sir, this one is so disinterested we could do cartwheels in front of him and he wouldn't notice," Sam replied, completely joking this time. And everyone knew it.

"Let's put the pieces together here, team," Sebastian suggested with more of a commanding voice. "Why is he here? Who is he shadowing? What does he expect to gain?"

"He's either shadowing the physician or the young boy because this is the third visit here and the first time we have a fallen visitor," Petros said first out of the gate, stating the obvious.

"Agreed," Sam chimed in.

"But why?" asked Sebastian.

"I know this fallen, everyone. He used to be Rusalmeh's apprentice, and now he's in the hill country like an outcast," Isabella said with confidence.

"You've mentioned that before, Isabella," Sebastian said without a hint of malice. No one detected any.

But everyone was quiet for a bit. Thinking. Watching.

Isabella finally spoke, "I bet he is following the boy."

"Why?" asked Petros, not because he doubted her but mostly to keep the conversation going.

"This boy was with Mary. He gave here that gift. Rusalmeh must see some significance there."

"That or he is grasping at straws," Sam chimed in.

"Likely both. My guess is our trail has gone cold, and he's trying to follow anyone he thinks may be connected," Sebastian surmised.

"Good luck with that," Petros said.

"They've got to be real frustrated at this point."

"The last thing we can do is to get overconfident here, everyone," Sebastian said with a hint of confidence of his own.

No one said anything. They knew better.

After a moment of silence, Sebastian spoke again, "Our reality right now is we have a fallen in our midst. That is and will remain our top priority."

The visit lasted most of the day and into the early evening. The physician and his grandson left after dinner as did Javva.

With the fallen no longer a threat, the team was able to relax a bit and enjoy the interactions of young Mary, her parents, and their relatives. Sebastian directed Isabella to join the family inside the home while the others kept watch throughout the night. Isabella enjoyed the time being so close to Mary and the family as she prayed and sang over them as they enjoyed one another's company.

Sebastian wondered that night what would come of Javva. What his real intention was and how his following of the boy would impact their mission. Although he never worried, he did keep Javva in the back of his mind as he had a real suspicion he would be seeing Javva again.

And soon.

CHAPTER 37

Mary Wanders

"Where's Mom?" Sam asked, not yet panicked.

"In the house," Petros replied before Sam finished talking.

Comms were wide-open at this point as enemy activity, with the exception of a lazy flyover from time to time, had become mostly nonexistent.

"Isabella?" Sebastian asked.

"I'm here. What's going on?"

"Mary is out of the house and beginning to wander," Sam described. This time slightly more panicked than before.

"Sam, stay with her but don't reveal yourself to her unless absolutely necessary. Are we clear?" Sebastian commanded. He was famous for statements in the form of a question.

"We are."

"I can see if I can get Mom's attention. Should I try?" Isabella asked.

"Yes, but again do not reveal yourself. The child is in no immediate danger."

"Negative, sir." Sam's word cut like a knife, and no one said a thing. "She is headed for the well."

CHAPTER 38

Intervention

"Isabella, what's the status with Mom?" Sebastian asked, not a hint of panic. He was made for this.

"I'm trying, but she's preoccupied. Deep in thought or something."

"She's at the well now," Sam reported.

"Can you keep her from climbing?"

"Without revealing myself?"

"We need her distracted, Sam, not completely terrified," Petros joked, bringing some levity to the situation. A situation that was rapidly reaching a crescendo.

What the warrior team would discuss later was how surprisingly quickly humans could find themselves in dangerous situations in the earthly realm. This was one of those. Mom distracted. A young three-year-old Mary, curious and adventurous. No one at fault. Just a life coming at you fast.

"Good idea, Pete," Sebastian said, surprising everyone. He continued, "Sam, you are authorized to reveal yourself."

"Sir?" Sam replied, the shock in his voice apparent.

Revealing yourself to a human as an angel warrior would be typically reserved for a select few and only in the direst of situations. Was this one of those?

"Check that. Not a complete reveal. Just enough to distract Mary away from the well."

"A flash or the sunlight reflecting off a wing or something," Petros chimed in.

"Got it."

And that's precisely what Sam did. He moved away from the child but being sure to remain in her line of sight. He used the sunlight to reflect a small edge of his right wing in an attempt to reflect enough light to get Mary's attention. It worked. Curious, Mary spotted the distraction right away and made way toward it. Not finding it, she quickly turned back toward the well. Sam anticipated this and was already in position to make another flashing light distraction, which he did. It worked. But eventually, the young Mary grew bored, and Sam could no longer distract her. Before he knew it, she was beginning to climb the stone wall around the opening of the well.

"Isabella?" Sam asked calmly.

She didn't respond.

Acting as if she did, Sam spoke urgently, "You have to get the mother's attention and now."

Deep in thought, Mary's mother was far away from the current situation.

Isabella knew she needed to do something to snap her out of it. Speaking softly to her spirit was not working. Taking a slightly different approach, Isabella quickly moved to the front of the house. Drawing her sword, she used the massive hilt to make a single loud knock on the front door. As soon as she made the loud noise, she raced to the other side of the room, shouting, "Where is Mary!"

It worked. The sound Isabella's sword made against the heavy wooden door of the home snapped her out of her state of deep thought while at the same time Isabella's question reached her spirit.

Mary's mother sprung from her seated position and started calling for her young daughter. "Mary? Mary?" she cried.

No response.

"Mom is on the move," Isabella said calmly but passionately.

"Good," Sebastian replied.

"I'm getting in the well," Sam stated in a way that no one, including Sebastian, was going to be able to stop him.

Young Mary had climbed up the short stone wall with one leg over the edge of the wall. The other dangling just off the ground on the other side. A stiff breeze could easily knock her off-balance, sending her tumbling into the well.

Except for Sam. Sam had positioned himself inside the well just below the wall. He wasn't entirely sure what he was going to do next, especially if she did fall into the well, but he'd figure it out at just the right time.

Mary's mother was now outside, calling for her child. "Mary! Mary!" Her voice as urgent as she could make it. Isabella right behind her.

As Mary peered over the edge of the well, she looked right into Sam's blazing topaz eyes. He smiled. She didn't see him, but he would never forget the look on her face. One of wonder, happiness, and fearlessness. Completely oblivious to the danger she was in, but even if she had known the danger, Sam wondered whether her demeanor would have changed. She was not afraid.

"Mary!" her mother screamed as she turned the corner of the house and saw her young daughter peering into the darkness of the deep well.

The instinct of a mother in these situations was to shout when they saw their child in danger, but the shout, in this case, distracted Mary.

As she heard the fear and distress in her mother's voice, she swung her head around from peering in to the well to over her shoulder in a split second. The rapid movement of her head sent the rest of her body off-balance, and the earthly realm's gravity did the rest. Mary lost her precarious balance on top of the stone wall as her body turned and began to fall backward into the well. With her back falling first, the leg that was on the inside of the well slipped farther while her leg on the outside of the well had nothing with which to grip. In a fraction of a second, young Mary was falling into the well.

There was nothing her mother could do, except watch in horror as her young daughter rapidly disappeared from her sight.

Except she didn't. Not completely anyway. For it was Sam's decision to jump into the well that day that saved young Mary's precious life. With Mary's back to him, he knew he could reveal himself in the earthly realm without being seen, and that's just what happened. With his massive hand, he gently but firmly stopped Mary's descent into the well and slowly pushed her back up onto the wall.

It happened so quickly it would have been difficult for Mary's mother to recognize the heavenly intervention. From her viewpoint, Mary was falling into the well but was able to catch herself just in time. And like many heavenly interventions in the earthly realm, humans without the perspective of heaven would find ways to explain away supernatural events. Not out of malice or disbelief but simply out of a lack of perspective.

As Sam gently put Mary back up on the wall into a seated position, he heard Sebastian in his ear, urgent but calm, say, "Disappear."

And he did. Just as the mom arrived to scoop Mary into her arms, Sam disappeared from sight in the earthly realm. It was a good thing too, as the first thing the mom did after scooping Mary into her arms was to instinctively peer directly into Sam's eyes as she herself looked into the well.

As Mary and her mother walked back to the house, not one of their angel warriors said anything for a long moment. Their existence on this mission after their arrival and Mary's birth had been, up until this point, well, uneventful. So after such intense few moments, they all stood quietly, each from their own positions.

Finally, after a long moment, Sebastian spoke, "Well done, everyone."

"Thank you, sir," Sam whispered.

"You all worked together and made all the right decisions," Sebastian said.

"It was fun to watch," Petros replied.

"Fun?" Isabella asked with a slight smile.

"Yeah, for about twenty seconds of sheer panic, it was fun to see warrior angels in action," Petros said without a hint of sarcasm because he meant it.

If only he had known how quickly and intensely the action would be coming to them with the redemption of mankind hanging in the balance.

CHAPTER 39

Sick

"Where?" Sebastian asked.

"Trailing behind. Head down," Petros replied.

Two years had passed since the team had seen Javva in the hill country at the home of Mary's relatives. At that time, the team had assessed that he was following the young boy who was related to the physician in some way. They left open the possibility that he was following the physician, but after debating about it for some time, they couldn't find any meaningful reason for Rusalmeh to use a veteran asset like Javva to follow an aging physician. He had to be following the boy. But why? The warriors didn't know the answer, but they knew the answer didn't matter. Javva was downrange and headed their way. So as warriors, they were ready for anything.

As much as they wanted to fight and ultimately annihilate him for the punishment of rebelling against the Creator, they knew it wasn't their place nor their mission.

That, however, didn't stop Isabella from suggesting it literally every time she saw him. "We could make it quick, sir," Isabella whispered.

"For the hundredth time, Isabella—" Sebastian began to say.

"We know. We know," Sam chimed in before he could finish.

"It's not the time. Not the place. Not the mission," Sam, Isabella, and Petros all said, their comms devices echoing in unison.

Even Sebastian had to smile. He *had* said it one hundred times. And his team had his back. They knew what was at stake. They also had all come to terms with their mission and the purpose of it. They had come to adore Mary and her family. They all felt a closeness and a connection that surprised them. From Sebastian's viewpoint as the leader of the mission, it was the added benefit of hiding in the shadows and staying hidden on a such a long mission. The closeness that came both as a team and to the human family their mission was to protect. Sebastian knew he no longer had to admonish or remind his team of the importance of not engaging the enemy or revealing themselves in a careless way. Out of adoration for the family, he knew that no one on this mission would do anything to jeopardize it.

So when young Mary, now five years old, came down with a terrible cough, high fever, and chills, the team was going to do everything they could to ensure both comfort and safety for Mary and her family.

"Do you see the boy?" Sebastian asked.

"Negative, sir" came Sam's response.

"Just the physician, Elizabeth, and Zechariah," Petros reported.

"Hmmm."

Everyone knew what that meant from Sebastian. It meant something in his thinking had changed, and it surprised him.

"We thought he was trailing the boy, didn't we?" Sam asked, more of a statement than a question.

"We did indeed." Sebastian's acknowledgment of Sam's question was delayed. Not out of pride but as the leader of the mission out of a potential strategy adjustment.

The physician was likely going to lay hands on the young Mary and tend to her illness. And unlike his grandson, the physician had the physical strength to potentially harm the child. Not that Sebastian ever thought the man would do such harm to Mary intentionally. But as a warrior angel for millennia, he had seen many humans that had been influenced by their spiritual enemy and had not even known it.

"Sir?" Isabella inquired, breaking the long silence. "What's the plan?"

As the small caravan drew closer, Sebastian needed to ensure he and his team took the right next steps. He didn't want to fall into a trap. He didn't anticipate Javva being anything more than a worn-out enemy slave, but they had come too far to be careless. Plus, he just had a feeling. A suspicion that something wasn't right. So he decided to go on offense. "Isabella, move into the house and stay hidden."

"Got it. I'll be in the loft."

"Perfect." Sebastian continued, "Pete, I have a feeling Javva isn't alone. I'm not sure if I'm right, but I need you to stay focused on the horizon and the shadows."

"On it."

"Any movement of any kind, we all need to know about it."

"Count on it, sir."

"Excellent," Sebastian said, satisfied. He continued, "Sam, as the caravan and Javva pass your position, make your way to the opposite of your current position."

"Sir?"

"I need you to get opposite of Pete's position so you both can keep your eyes peeled for any additional enemy," Sebastian explained.

"Understood."

"I'm going to take Isabella's position high in the tree."

Nothing was said for a long moment.

Then Sebastian gave his final command, saying, "Petros, shut down comms after I'm done here."

"You got it."

"We know what to do. This is likely nothing, but we will take nothing for granted. Protect Mary and stay hidden."

As he took flight, Petros shut down comms.

Sebastian was right. Javva wasn't the only fallen in the area that night.

There was another one, and what he saw might have jeopardized everything.

CHAPTER 40

Tarn Sees Something

"What do you mean something?" Rusalmeh hissed, upset as much at the lack of detail from his slave as he was at being disturbed.

"A flash," Tarn said meekly.

"You disturbed me because you think you saw a flash?" Rusalmeh had descended off his perch and now was spitting the words less than an inch from Tarn's wretched, misshapen face.

It was a tactic the fallen leader used often to separate fact from fiction. Tarn, to his credit, didn't flinch. This told Rusalmeh everything he needed to know. Tarn had seen something, and it could be significant.

It had been years since the missing fallen had disappeared, and although Rusalmeh could care less about the missing demon, he was tortured by the possibility that an enemy mission was happening in his region without his knowledge. Demons wouldn't just disappear. He knew that for sure.

Backing off Tarn, he slowly retreated to his perch and then finally said, "Tell me everything."

"Yes, sire." Tarn paused and then continued, "When you asked me to follow Javva without his consent, I decided to stay well behind and hidden as much from him as perhaps anyone else who might be in the area."

Rusalmeh said nothing as he stared into the distance. Because it meant nothing.

Tarn continued, "Night was descending, but there was still enough light for the humans to see their way to the home in the distance."

"Home?"

"Yes, the same home we followed this same group to years ago."

This caught Rusalmeh's attention, and he brought his distant gaze directly back into Tarn's black lifeless eyes.

"They were visiting the human baby, sir," Tarn explained, quickly picking up from his master that more detail was required.

With a nod of his head, Rusalmeh demanded he continue.

"The home was occupied as I saw firelight coming through the small windows."

"So?"

"And that's when I saw it."

Rusalmeh said nothing. Because it meant nothing. Until it did.

"The flash, sire."

"The flash. The flash. All you mindless slaves ever see is flashes!" Rusalmeh screamed at no one in particular. He continued screaming into the void, "It's like we are chasing the wind!"

Silence filled the boom of the prince's voice as it quickly faded.

The prince continued, "Was it the wind?"

"Sire? I don't…" Tarn caught himself before saying anything more. He realized then Rusalmeh didn't want an answer.

Rusalmeh let Tarn's indiscretion pass. It didn't matter anyway. "Why hasn't Javva brought me this information?" Rusalmeh mused, again to no one in particular.

Tarn didn't answer that question either. It wasn't for him.

For Rusalmeh, he knew the answer. Javva wasn't the fallen he once was, and the prince knew he should take him off this assignment. Perhaps annihilate him altogether. It was just too important, and Javva had failed him too many times. Something big was happening; he could sense it. But down deep, Rusalmeh kept clinging to the potential he saw in Javva, and he couldn't bring himself to pull him off this crucial assignment.

It would be a decision—the decision to keep Javva engaged—he would come to regret for eternity.

CHAPTER 41

Javva before Rusalmeh Again

"Nothing?" the prince asked gently, his mouth less than an inch from the side of his slave's misshapen, slick, featureless head.

"Sire, please. I saw nothing," an exhausted Javva whispered, his voice raspy and weak. His head bowed low.

Javva's arms were stretched above his head, clasped together, and chained to the wall. He had been in this position for what seemed like days while Rusalmeh and two of his goons took turns attempting to extract the truth out of him. What truth, Javva couldn't explain. If he knew the truth they wanted, he would have told them long ago just to make the pain stop.

"You keep saying that, but I don't believe you," Rusalmeh sang as if he were singing the chorus of a song.

It was the ultimate humiliation. How far Javva had fallen. Once the second-in-command to the prince of evil in all of Persia to facing his final moments of existence, being tortured and ridiculed. Javva thought of his inconceivable demise only for a fleeting moment as he turned his attention to what he hoped would be the sweet relief of annihilation.

But it never came. It seemed as if the more he longed for it, the farther it drifted away. No one knew what was on the other side of annihilation, but Javva determined a long time ago that it could not be any worse than the humiliation he now endured as the worthless slave of Rusalmeh. He was a failure. His present circumstance notwithstanding.

As Rusalmeh mercilessly mocked and tortured him for information he didn't have, Javva couldn't help but notice Rusalmeh was unable to follow through with it. Javva wondered why. *Why doesn't he just end it?* he thought.

"I have failed you," Javva whispered, not realizing he was verbalizing the words his warped mind was creating.

"Of course, you have," Rusalmeh said, his back turned away from Javva.

"Then why don't you just do it, sire?" Javva said with a boldness that even surprised him.

"Do what?"

"Send me into annihilation. You have said it, and there is no disputing it. I have failed you."

Rusalmeh said nothing. With a quick nod of his head, he directed the two goons assisting in Javva's interrogation to leave the room. They did without hesitation. Now it was just the prince and Javva. Javva's meaningless existence hanging in the balance.

"No," Rusalmeh said. His voice calm. He paused a long moment and then continued, "Your failure has been so spectacular, so incomprehensible that annihilating you would be doing you a favor. Almost like rewarding you."

Javva said nothing. His head low and his arms restrained impossibly high above him.

Rusalmeh had made up his mind. His punishment for Javva would be a message, a lesson to any other fallens under his command who dared to fail him.

There was a stillness in the room that Javva hadn't noticed before, so he raised his head slightly in an attempt to identify what might be coming for him next. What he saw caused the life to drain from his face. A wretched, swollen face, disfigured both from millennia separated from the Creator's love and from the beatings he had taken during his interrogation, now completely devoid of color at what he saw. In the silence, Rusalmeh had gestured to one of his goons to reenter the room, this time fully equipped with weapons of war.

In that moment, Javva hoped Rusalmeh would use those weapons of war to send him into annihilation, but he knew he was in for something much more painful. As the goon went to work on him, Javva swallowed the pain the best he could before slipping out of consciousness. His torture, disfigurement, and subsequent banishment would be talked about in hushed tones by fallens throughout the earthly realm for ages to come. Javva's failure was to be a message from Rusalmeh to his entire slave army.

But Javva's existence didn't end that night. Rusalmeh's arrogant decision to keep him alive and severely disfigured would come back to haunt him in ways he could have never imagined.

The Creator would see to that.

CHAPTER 42

Javva's Miserable Existence

"Creator, what have I done?" he asked, knowing he would never be answered.

As Javva lay facedown in the cold, swampy mud of a small riverbank, he tried to move but couldn't get his broken body to respond. So he lay there in the blackness.

Because he was originally created by the Creator, no matter how long he had been separated from Him, his default mode always brought him back to the Creator. He hated it. But he also couldn't help it. He hated that too.

"I made a mistake," he said, his voice barely audible. Barely existent. "I can't ever fix it. I can't ever make it right. I chose wrong and failed. And now I have failed the wrong side I chose." His voice growing louder as he began to cry out in a level of anguish he never knew existed.

He was in a nightmare from which he could never escape. As this hopeless reality crept in on him like dense fog, he wept. His weeping was bitter. Angry. Deep. The crushing hopelessness mixed with his fresh wounds allowed him to slip back into unconsciousness.

Hours later, Javva would regain consciousness, curse the Creator for ever creating him, and begin channeling his hatred into assessing his current situation. Barely able to move, he realized quickly the extent of the damage Rusalmeh's goon had inflicted upon him. It appeared Rusalmeh took one of everything or left one of everything, depending on the perspective. Javva was missing his left wing, right leg, left eye, and the most of the right side of his face where his ear used to be. Apparently, the goon got a little sloppy.

The pain was unbearable. As a spirit being in the earthly realm, the rules of earth applied. Fallens, as it turned out, were exposed and vulnerable in the earthly realm to the very pain and suffering they created while on earth. It was part of the curse placed upon them for their rebellion.

As he tried to move, he tried to get his bearings. "Where am I?" he asked to himself.

It didn't take him long to realize the desperate plight of his situation. He had been banished. Cut off. Cut out. No longer a part of the legion of demons under Rusalmeh's command. And unable to ever return.

For Javva, it is the worst-possible scenario in which to find himself. He was disfigured beyond recognition, powerless, cut off from any connection to his fellow demons, and without the ability to do anything except to exist in the void. He knew that even if he wanted to find and torment a human soul, his ability to do so was now gone. When he lost his connection to his source of evil in Rusalmeh, he lost the power to torment. He was a fallen without the ability to torment. A well without a source of water. Utterly useless.

A depth of hopelessness crashed over him in a way he had never experienced. Even the darkest days after the rebellion did not bring the depth of hopefulness he now felt.

He had been longing for annihilation for so long, even desperately asking Rusalmeh for it. But now, with annihilation no longer an option, his warped mind faded in and out between unbridled hatred and inconsolable sadness.

As he lay in the damp muck of a remote riverbank, slipping in and out of consciousness, Javva began the first stages of madness.

The beginning of a long slide toward insanity from which he would never return.

CHAPTER 43

Rusalmeh Replaces Javva

"Javva failed me for the last time," Rusalmeh said matter-of-factly. It was only him and Tarn in the prince's chambers.

Tarn said nothing. He knew better.

"He will never fail me again. I made sure of that."

Tarn still said nothing.

"So you will be taking over his mission."

"Mission, sir?" Tarn asked, speaking for the first time.

"Follow the boy. He's connected somehow."

"Connected?"

Rusalmeh closed his eyes and dropped his head in frustration. He was so tired of the questions. Tired of the inability of his slaves to make even the most basic connections.

After a long moment of silence, he lifted himself from his perch, determined not to let the anger welling up inside him in response to Tarn's ignorance to cloud his judgment. He did that with Javva, and it got him nowhere.

So he decided to take a different approach with Tarn. He decided to bring him in. Give him the details. Get him up to speed. Perhaps armed with the knowledge of the facts on the ground so far, Tarn could more effectively gather the type of intelligence Javva was never able or willing to gather. So he brought Tarn all the way in. He laid out the evidence of angelic warrior activity in the region. The flash in the sky, the night a fallen went missing, the beatings he and

Safir suffered, the intercepted concealed comms, and the flash Tarn saw just the night before.

"It's all connected," the prince concluded. "All of it."

"Yes, sire," Tarn confirmed in agreement.

"There are enemy angels in my region, and I want to know who they are and why they are here," Rusalmeh was whispering now, his face and voice contorting in anger and fear.

Tarn said nothing.

"I've been playing catch-up since they arrived, and I will not be played the fool. You find them, and you do not fail me. Do you understand?" Rusalmeh had made his way to within an inch of Tarn's face. His signature intimidation move.

It worked. Tarn was terrified. He now understood why Javva had lost his way over time. The tremendous pressure mixed with unrelenting fear that Rusalmeh could inflict on his slaves was often well beyond what they could endure.

Tarn held himself together, managing to say the only two words he could form at that precise moment. "I understand."

Nothing could prepare him for the overwhelming force of heaven that was soon to be released on him and his fellow slaves.

And he would have a front-row seat to the carnage.

CHAPTER 44

Who Is That?

"Can you ID?" Sebastian asked in his secure communications device.

"Negative," Sam replied.

"Male. Medium build. Mid-to-late teens."

"A teenager?"

"That's my guess."

"Any fallens tagging along?"

"Negative."

"I'll go check him out," Isabella offered.

"Hold" came the response from her leader. Sebastian followed up with "Let's let him get closer. And everyone, watch the horizon and shadows for fallen activity."

"Check. We've come too far to make a mistake now." Petros had been quiet before saying what everyone had been thinking.

The years had gone by quickly, although no one really got used to hiding. The girl had grown up right before their eyes. They had grown to love her and her parents so deeply. If they were passionate about fulfilling their mission when it first started many years ago, they were all infinitely more passionate now. They would never let any harm come to her or her family. She was the only child, so most of her time was spent with her mother and father rather than any siblings or extended family.

The family would travel from time to time, but not very often. Family and a few friends would visit occasionally. And when they did, her silent, invisible warriors were with her every step of the way.

Sebastian and his team worked well together. They had hunkered down for the long haul, waiting for orders that never came. So they stayed the course. And stayed hidden.

Of course, the mission was not without frustration. Such a long stretch behind enemy territory with the inability to build and execute an offensive strategy was gut-wrenching. They were warriors. All of them. Fierce, stone-cold warriors. The Creator had created all of them to fight and fight with abandon. But here they were. For what seemed like forever. Hiding.

So when the teenager emerged on the horizon, heading toward the home of their precious family, they weren't taking any chances. They would be ready for anything.

Little did they know that the end was just about to begin.

CHAPTER 45

A Gift Revisited

"I can't believe you still have it!" the young man said, genuinely surprised.

"Have what?" Mary responded with the same inquisitive look the man had given her.

"The lion," he said, pointing to the small wooden sculpture he had spotted in her hand. The same hand that she was now playfully hiding behind her back.

"It's a lion?" she asked with a slight smile.

"Hey! I worked hard on that!" the young man replied, a broad smile now spreading across his face.

The two had known each other for years and were childhood friends long before they both knew there was something more. They had learned each other's mannerisms and had grown to love each other in ways most could not imagine. Of course, they didn't know any better; they both just thought their connection was the most natural thing they had ever known. And they loved it. All of it.

"I know. I know. It's the most beautiful lion I have ever seen."

"Now I know you're lying," he said as he gently brushed Mary's hair out of her eyes.

"I still can't believe you made it for me."

He said nothing. He just stared at her as only a man completely smitten with a woman could. "And I can't believe you still have it," he said after a long moment. He continued, "Did you notice something else?"

She looked confused and said nothing. Then she slowly brought her hand that was holding the wooden sculpture from behind her back, cupping it with her other hand and showing it the young man.

He took her hands in his, and she realized in that moment something very special that she would carry with her for the rest of her life. In this moment, the hands that carved this small wooden treasure were the very hands now holding hers.

"There's also a lamb," he finally said softly as they both looked down and stared at it.

She furrowed her brow and looked closely. "Really?"

"Yeah, right there," he said, pointing to a small rounded side of the sculpture.

"Oh, I see it now. I always thought that was part of the lion's leg or something."

Nothing was said for a long moment.

Then the man said, "I saw it."

"It? The lion?"

"And the lamb."

Mary said nothing for a moment and then said, "Where would you have seen a lion together with a lamb?"

Now it was his turn to say nothing for a long moment as he looked into her eyes. He said softly, "In a dream."

CHAPTER 46

Jerusalem

"When?" Sebastian asked from his lookout post hidden from view.

"In two days," Isabella replied.

"To celebrate the Passover," Sam added.

Both Sam and Isabella had overheard conversations throughout the day among the family, and the decision had been made. They were packing for a three-day trip to Jerusalem to celebrate the special day in Hebrew history.

Young Mary was not so young anymore. She was now fourteen years old and quickly becoming a beautiful young woman. Her warrior angels had grown to love her deeply over the years in a way that made their mission less of a mission and more of their purpose for existence.

Long ago, they all had abandoned the notion that this mission would be short-lived. And yet somehow, they knew this was the one mission for which they were ultimately created. So they settled in long ago. Always sharp and focused but growing in care and affection for the family they had been sent to protect.

So when the decision was made to go to Jerusalem, they knew it could be a turning point for their mission. Jerusalem was under Roman rule and, therefore, under Rusalmeh's rule. The Romans had long ago surrendered to the fallen hordes in their midst, and they had the debauchery and sin to show for it.

Mary and her family in Jerusalem created an infinite number of complexities for a warrior team whose mission it was to protect the family in a fallen earthly realm while staying hidden.

"Okay, I'll say it," Petros said, breaking the silence created as all the warriors began processing the idea of attempting to protect the family as they moved around Jerusalem. He continued, "We're going to need permission to stay hidden in plain sight."

"Meaning?" Sebastian asked.

"Meaning, we need to be able to move around freely as if human," Isabella said, finishing Petros's thought.

"Exactly," Petros confirmed.

No one spoke again for a long moment.

Sebastian was a wise leader, so he rarely responded with his first thought. He often took time to quickly process all viable scenarios before answering, especially answering such a daring suggestion as this. "I'll have to get permission," Sebastian finally said. "It's not something I can authorize."

No one responded. There was nothing to say. Everyone knew the implications of such a request. It was a big deal. Really big.

The team spent the rest of the night hidden together deep in the tree grove on the south end of the family's land, planning out what a journey through Jerusalem with the family would look like. They discussed the many different scenarios in which they likely would find themselves and did their best to assess the highest safety risks to the family.

The scenario planning was what gave Sebastian the best look at what they might be facing and gave him enough confidence to make the request. As the night wore on, Sebastian took a moment to recognize how far this team had come. Despite the extreme challenge of staying hidden, unable to unleash the incredible warrior power the Creator had bestowed upon each of them, the team was fully engaged in the mission. And fully connected as a team. As much as they had grown to love Mary and her family, they had grown to love one another as well. A yearslong mission hidden behind enemy lines with only one another on which to depend could create unbreakable bonds. If ever the team was ready for a covert mission to Jerusalem and back, it was now. Sebastian marveled at the Creator's perfect plans and how His timing was always impeccable. He knew his team was not ready for such an important journey until now, and now was the perfect time for it.

"Only the Creator," Sebastian whispered to himself but loud enough for the others to hear.

They all looked up at Sebastian, each with a smile. They knew what he meant, and they all were reminded at that moment of both the Creator's sovereignty and the incredible responsibility they all had been asked to bear. No one knew of the plans the Creator had for Mary and her family, but they had all come to the realization that it was something bigger than any of them could fathom. So they didn't even try. They just smiled and took comfort in the knowledge of the Creator's plans fulfilled no matter what.

After a long moment, Sebastian broke the silence, saying, "Pete, I'll need a secure comm established to Gabriel."

"On it, sir," Petros replied, already up and moving.

"Isabella, the family will be awake soon. Do what you can to get as much detail around their trip."

"On it."

"Sam, stay vigilant and keep on watch for any hostiles. I wouldn't be surprised if our family will be meeting up with other families to make the trip together."

"On it as well, sir," Sam replied, quickly taking flight toward the highest point overlooking the family's land.

Excitement was in the air as the sun rose that day. The team knew their mission to this point would be all for naught should this next phase fail.

Little did they know it would be dangerous beyond their wildest imagination.

CHAPTER 47

Sebastian Seeks Permission

"Here," Gabriel said.

"Thank you, sir," Sebastian replied.

"How can I help?"

"Seeking permission to reveal."

"Approved."

"Well, that was fast."

"Fast is good, right?"

Sebastian hesitated as he was slightly disappointed he wasn't able to present the case he had been working on since the night before.

Gabriel spoke again, "Listen, the Creator knows everything, right?"

"Right."

"He gave me a heads-up and approval to reveal. It's the right thing to do to keep the family safe and allow all of you to remain hidden."

"In plain sight," Sebastian replied.

"Affirmative," Gabriel said with a smile.

Both angels were silent for a moment before Sebastian spoke, "We should go. This comms channel is hot."

"Yes," Gabriel agreed. "One more thing before you go."

"Sir?"

"Tell me about the team."

"Good to go, sir. The team is on mission and in sync. I pity the fallen who accidentally crosses the girl's or her family's path," Sebastian's reported, his spirit lifted as he spoke the words.

"Good to hear, my friend," Gabriel responded. And then he finished the conversation, saying, "Stay alert. It will be soon."

Click. The comms channel was closed.

"There it was again," Sebastian whispered out loud to himself. "Stay alert. It will be soon."

Those words, strung together so precisely by Gabriel and now used both of the last two times they had spoken, ran on a loop through Sebastian's mind as he began to prepare for their biggest challenge yet.

CHAPTER 48

Soldiers

"Dad?" young Mary asked. "Will we be gone long?"

"Why do you ask?"

"No reason. Just curious. Is all."

"Five days. One day to travel there, two days to celebrate the Passover, and two days to travel back."

"Do I get to ride one of the donkeys?" Mary asked expectantly.

"Aye, my dear. You and your mother," her father replied as he worked to prepare the animals and the belongings that they were planning to take on their journey. But before he had finished his sentence, the girl had run out of the barn, heading back toward the house.

It wasn't long before they were on their way, soon after Elizabeth and Zechariah arrived from the hill country to travel to the ancient city together.

Their silent, hidden angelic warriors saw their guests coming long before anyone else did. It was standard protocol to ensure there were no fallens in tow. There was none.

The world had been changing around them, and Mary's father knew of the potential dangers a region ruled by Romans could potentially cause. Their journey to Jerusalem would take nearly two full days with several desolate areas through which they had to travel.

Their first day's travels were largely uneventful as their angelic protectors stayed well hidden. Sebastian's plan was simple. Two warriors, Sam and Petros, ahead of the group and two, Isabella and Sebastian, behind. They had been authorized to reveal themselves in human form as required, so they were prepared to do so.

Their first opportunity to protect the family came on the morning of day 2. Their small caravan of two men, two women, and a young teenager along with three donkeys was no threat to anyone, the least of which Roman soldiers patrolling the region. But the world being unpredictable as it was, especially with the ingredient of human free will laid as the foundation of the earthly realm, their small caravan was stopped by a pair of Roman soldiers with little else to do that morning than to abuse the power they had been given.

Sam saw them first. "Two soldiers," Sam whispered over the open yet scrambled comms among the team. If any fallens intercepted their communication, it would appear to be fallens communicating gibberish.

"Okay," Sebastian replied, keeping communication to a minimum as agreed upon before the journey began.

"They appear to be waving to our family to stop," Sam confirmed.

"I don't like the look of this," Petros replied.

Sebastian asked calmly, "Any signs of fallen activity?"

"Negative," Sam responded.

"Okay. Keep on the lookout. Any fallen presence will alter our next moves here. Isabella?"

"Here."

"I'm going to make a couple of assumption here," Sebastian said matter-of-factly. "Assuming these soldiers intercept our family and assuming we continue to detect no fallen activity in the area, be ready for a reveal."

"Roger that."

"Go now to the back of the caravan and position yourself with our family between you and the soldiers," Sebastian instructed.

Isabella said nothing. She simply began to move.

As she did, Sebastian spoke again, this time to the warrior team ahead of the caravan, "Petros and Sam, status on fallen activity?"

"Negative, sir," Sam replied.

Petros affirmed, "All clear."

Sebastian was team lead for situations just like this. He was calm and precise. Focused and detailed. Confident and infinitely prepared. Even after so many days and nights staying hidden and, for all intents and purposes, dormant, at least by angel warrior standards, Sebastian was sharp, and so was his team. He made sure of that. They were ready, and they all knew it. They would need it.

As the Roman soldiers stopped the small family caravan who happened to be one of the most protected at the time in the earthly realm, they had no way of knowing the incredibly powerful storm they were potentially about to unleash. Angel warriors in defense mode. Not survivable if even the slightest aggressive move was to be made by the soldiers toward the family. The warriors would not hesitate to end their existence in that moment. They had come too far in their mission.

"Halt!" one of the soldiers shouted, putting his hand in the air, palm facing out in the universal gesture to stop.

Everyone stopped. No one said anything for a long moment as the other soldier made his way around the back of the caravan. He unwittingly brushed past a giant angelic warrior standing guard at the rear of the caravan. Isabella was in place. Ready.

"What do you see?" Sebastian asked Isabella.

"I got a good look at the one who just walked past me."

"And?" Sebastian asked.

"I don't like it, sir," she continued. "His eyes tell me he's up to no good."

"Agreed. Be ready to reveal. Your call, okay?" Sebastian asked.

"Okay" came Isabella's reply.

Sam, anticipating Sebastian's next request, said, "Still no fallen activity. These guys are not being followed."

"Thanks," Sebastian replied.

"What is your business?" demanded the soldier who had circled the family and now stood next to the other soldier who had motioned for them to stop.

"We are Jews," Mary's father said. "We are traveling to Jerusalem to celebrate the Passover."

"Never heard of it," said one solider to the next.

"This road requires a tax," the other one said, ignoring the other.

"Sir," Mary's father said, "I mean no disrespect, but I have traveled this road many times without a tax required."

"Well, things change," the soldier barked.

No one spoke for a long moment.

"There is a tax, and we are here to collect it."

Mary's father knew he was in a tough spot. He knew the soldiers could demand any amount, and he would be expected to pay it. There was no recourse. No judge in front of which to plead their case. It was just these soldiers and whatever they demanded.

"How much?" Mary's father asked.

"How much do you have?" came the reply. A question in response to a question. Not good.

"That's none of your business," Mary's father responded as the anger and helplessness of the situation began to well up inside him.

"Why, yes, it is our business," the soldier said.

The other one followed up, "Everything. And I mean everything is our business in this region." The soldier's eyes shifted to look directly at Mary.

Mary's father knew exactly what that meant. If he couldn't pay their tax with money, they would extract payment another way, putting his young daughter at serious risk. Roman soldiers were notorious for abusing their power in many forms, including assaulting women as they saw fit. A consequence of unchecked power driven by hate and greed.

"Sir, I don't like what I am hearing," Isabella whispered.

Sebastian said nothing. He knew Isabella would elaborate.

She did, saying, "They are not so subtly threatening to hurt Mary if their tax is not able to be paid."

"Oh, I'd like to see them try," Sam said with a smile. The kind of smile everyone could hear.

"Agreed," Petros responded.

"Your call, Isabella. We are here to support," Sebastian said reassuringly.

At that moment, Isabella reached with her right hand over her left shoulder, slowly unsheathing her massive sword. She slowly brought the sword strapped across her back, grasping it with her left hand as well. She then slowly raised the sword in an offensive stance, her massive sword extending away from her body, designed for maximum impact should she need to reveal herself. She wanted to make sure her presence left no doubt in the minds of the soldiers of who were in charge in that moment. In the exact position she wanted, she waited. She watched the soldiers. Every movement they made was processed and analyzed by the angel warrior. And then it happened.

Acting on impulse, an impulse that had gone unchecked in a region where subjects were not allowed to say no or deny any soldier's request, one of the soldiers made a move toward Mary. As she sat on her donkey, the shy teenager turned her face away as the soldier drew close. He leaned down, and with his hand, he slowly turned her chin toward him. She was terrified. As was everyone in the family.

Isabella had seen enough. With a flash of light, she instantly revealed herself to the two soldiers, including the one stooping to speak to Mary.

Their reaction to seeing an angel warrior, her weapon drawn and ready for war, was predictable. With the size and power Isabella possessed and her sharp silver eyes cut through them like a razor, the two soldiers froze. Eyes wide. Mouths agape. Frozen in fear.

The natural reaction of everyone was to immediately turn and look for what the soldiers had seen. There was no one there.

Angelic warriors, like Isabella, had been given the ability to be very prescriptive to whom they revealed themselves. This gifting allowed angels throughout millennia in the earthly realm to redirect human actions and reactions to ensure the Creator's plans were effectively carried out. Knowing she only wanted the two soldiers to see her and not the others, Isabella was very intentional with her reveal. And it worked. The soldiers were frozen, literally frozen in fear.

Fortunately, it didn't take Mary's father long at all to assess the situation and recognize this was an opportunity for him and his family to escape what had started to become a very dicey situation. After only a short delay and nothing to explain the current turn of events,

Mary's father directed the donkeys to move, and they did. The caravan maneuvered around the soldiers, themselves standing as if statues, and hurriedly proceeded down the road.

As they drew farther and farther away from the soldiers, everyone in the caravan, including young Mary, would periodically look back to see what would become of the soldiers. Everyone feared at least for a while the soldiers would come to and aggressively pursue them, perhaps making a bad situation even worse. No such event occurred.

As they rounded the bend in the road, the soldiers, still frozen in time, disappeared from view. No one in the caravan spoke further of that particular event. It didn't make sense, but the outcome could have been so much worse that no one wanted to speak of it. So they didn't.

Soon after the caravan was out of sight, Isabella spoke to the team, "You all go ahead. I'll catch up."

Sam spoke quickly with a broad smile spreading across his face, "Bella about to make those two guys wish they never stopped our family."

"Isabella, don't forget the mission," Sebastian reminded her.

"Oh, I won't, sir. Just want to make sure our Roman friends here never get the picture of my face out of their minds."

"Perfect," Sebastian replied. He continued, "Don't be long."

Isabella didn't reply. She was already moving toward the two men.

She came first to the soldier who stopped the caravan initially. She walked around him first to ensure he was able to view her massive frame along with the massive sword she was now carrying at her side. Once again facing the man, she bent over, looking directly into his eyes, and said, "Have you ever seen an angel warrior before?"

The man said nothing. He couldn't. The fear that consumed him was paralyzing. Her sharp silver eyes pierced his, and she kept them there for more than a long moment.

Isabella continued her fun by saying, "If I ever see you harassing any Hebrews again, especially this particular family, you will have wished you had never been born." Her voice was terrifying yet had a gentle sweetness to it. It didn't matter.

The man said nothing as tears began to pool in his eyes and spill down his cheeks. He was a man so terrified that the only emotion he could express were tears as if he were a small child.

Satisfied she had gotten her point across, she now moved to confront the soldier who had touched young Mary's face. If it were up to her, this soldier would no longer be breathing the air of the earthly realm, but it was not up to her. So after circling him once, ensuring maximum terror, she took a knee to produce maximum effect. This man was demonstrably smaller than his partner. So rather than bend down, Isabella decided she needed a more direct approach. "Do you always treat women as tools for your personal pleasure?" Her voice again terrifying.

The man said nothing.

"Oh?" she asked, feigning surprise. "You didn't expect an angel to be, well, someone like me?"

The man said nothing.

"Tell you what, every time you even think about harming a woman, I want you to see my face," she said as her sharp silver eyes blazed into the man like the sun. She slowly brought her sword to the man's face and gently slid the blade across his neck right to left.

The man said nothing. He couldn't say anything. He didn't know what he was seeing. The majesty of an angelic warrior coupled with the terror of seeing her raw power and strength up close and personal. He was paralyzed by a fear he had never known. A fear he would never know again.

In that moment, she was gone. She had accomplished her goal, and it was time to move on. So she did.

But not before she was spotted in the distance by a fallen in flight on patrol. There she was, in all her angelic glory, making sure the Roman soldiers knew their place and, at the same time, completely exposed. And he saw her.

It wasn't a mistake per se, but it would become another clue. A clue the team of angelic warriors could ill afford to give up after such a long time in the shadows.

A clue that could unravel the entire mission.

CHAPTER 49

Another Clue

"Two?' Rusalmeh asked.

"Two soldiers, yes," the demon responded, head low in reverence or submission or both.

It wasn't often an insignificant fallen on lookout patrol was summoned to speak before the high prince. And he was clearly terrified. Just how Rusalmeh liked his hordes. Terrified. Submissive. Angry. Hateful. So he fed all those emotions at every opportunity.

"So two soldiers and one enemy?"

"Yes, sire."

"Tell me more about the enemy."

"It was far away—"

Rusalmeh quickly extended his right hand, gnarled, and mangled as it was as if to stop the demon from continuing. The prince then slowly descended his perch and slowly faced the fallen in front of him. Using his hand, he lifted the fallen's chin and bent down at the same time, both their faces now less than an inch apart. Rusalmeh quietly spoke, "I don't want excuses, nor will I accept failure."

The fallen said nothing.

"Are we clear?"

The slight nod of his head was all the terrified fallen could muster. Collecting his thoughts, he tried again. "The enemy warrior moved different, sire." The fallen's voice squeaking in fear.

"Different?"

"Yes. Not like any other enemy warriors I have ever seen."

Rusalmeh said nothing as his face remained terrifyingly close to his fallen slave's face. "Meaning?" he said to his slave in the most demeaning way possible.

"Me-me-meaning the enemy moved like a woman."

Rusalmeh said nothing as he stared with hate and malice straight into his slave like daggers. Then he finally said, "Like a woman you say?"

His slave nodded slightly, stricken with the fear that came being so close to such hatred and filth.

"What else?" Rusalmeh hissed, his eyes locked into the gaze of his slave, creating maximum control and fear.

His slave continued, "The...the...the enemy drew a sword and showed it to one of the soldiers."

"They could see the enemy?"

"I... I... I think so. The humans weren't moving."

"Like they were frozen?"

"Yes, yes, exactly," the fallen said excitedly as if he was making a connection with his master.

It didn't last long. Rusalmeh saw to that. "Shut up," the prince hissed. He moved away from the slave that stood before him, turned his back on him, and made his was back toward his perch. Deep in thought.

After a long moment, he said quietly, almost introspectively, to himself, "What is Isabella doing here, and what would compel her to reveal herself?"

It would be a question that would torment the prince until the moment his question would be answered in full.

A moment too late.

CHAPTER 50

First Night in Jerusalem

Without further delay or interruptions, the family and their clandestine protective detail arrived in Jerusalem as planned.

They settled in where they would be staying the next few nights and enjoyed a nice evening meal with their host family. As they laughed and connected and enjoyed one another's company, the warriors sent to watch over them were doing just that.

There was an uneasiness everywhere in Jerusalem. The enemy had free reign over the city, ushered in by the unholy alliance established with the pagan Roman Empire. Staying hidden was going to be a real challenge. And they all knew it.

"Check. Check. Confirm comms please," said Petros. As the comms specialist, it was his job to establish comms in every new location.

"Check," Sam said, the first, as usual, to respond.

"Check," Isabella reported.

"Check," Sebastian responded in the affirmative. Sebastian continued, "Okay, everyone, I need a status check. Sam?"

"Fallens pretty much everywhere. I'm well hidden in the grove just east of the family's location with an unobstructed view of the rear windows and entrance."

"Okay. Isabella?"

"All clear. I've got clear line of sight of the front entrance. Fallens everywhere, but none aware of our presence."

"Good. Let's keep it that way. Petros?"

"All good, sir. Scrambled comms established and well hidden in a rock crag just below you."

"Excellent. I'm hidden at the top of the rock outcropping overlooking our house with good views of north and south movements."

No one spoke for a long moment.

Then Sebastian directed the team, "Looks like we made it undetected. Let's keep comms to a minimum tonight and keep your eyes wide."

"Rules of engagement?" Sam asked with a smile.

"Same as always. Getting detected at the farm is one thing. Getting detected here would be disastrous."

"Agreed. But there should be no reason for fallen activity at our family's house tonight," Petros chimed in.

"Aye," Sebastian affirmed. Then he continued, "As a last resort, if any of you need to make a move to protect the family, keep it quiet and make it count."

No one spoke. They all just smiled.

CHAPTER 51

Passover

After an uneventful night, the angel warriors knew the first full day moving around the city would be an important test.

Following Mary and her family undetected through the countryside was one thing, but in a city like Jerusalem during the time of the most important Hebrew holiday, it was something entirely different.

Rusalmeh and his goons were notorious for causing massive disruptions and generating all kinds of fallen activity on this day. Anything the Creator loved and celebrated, they hated and derided. The Passover celebration, commemorating the Creator delivering the Hebrews from bondage and slavery in Egypt, was something Rusalmeh hated the most. For the Creator's people, it represented freedom after four hundred years in Egypt, many of which were spent in slavery and death. For Rusalmeh and his legions, it represented bitter defeat. A lasting reminder of their ultimate fate. A fate never discussed but always known.

The Creator would win, they knew, but how much pain and destruction could they cause before their appointed time came was the question they lived to answer.

And on Passover with the Romans fully in charge, Rusalmeh intended to inflict as much pain and suffering as he could muster.

Little did he know, four of the Creator's most gifted warriors had slipped undetected into his region.

And were ready for a fight.

CHAPTER 52

An Annual Reminder

The day burned in his spirit like fire would consume dry timber. He hated it. It was the day his greatest achievement was dismantled. Hundreds of years of work gone in one night. The Creator's angel of death appeared in Egypt, the last and final plague brought from the Creator and soon after everything changed.

Rusalmeh's enslavement of the Hebrews was over. He had been working ever since to find ways to enslave the Hebrews again, but despite his best efforts, he could never match the brutality and oppression of the Egyptians.

What made it worse for Rusalmeh was that the Hebrews made a holiday out of it. His greatest failure celebrated every year. It was like they were ridiculing him to his face. He hated it. And he hated them.

Under Roman rule, the Hebrews were oppressed, but he and his hordes could not seem to turn the Romans into the consistent brutalizers the Egyptians had become. Of course, they were able to influence one here, maybe ten there, but his efforts to turn the entire Roman Empire against the Jews like he had done with Haman way back when had proven elusive.

But the Passover holiday always presented a unique opportunity. Even though the Romans allowed for religious observances, Rusalmeh knew of the importance of the Passover celebration to the Hebrew people, and he was determined every year to find ways to ruin it for them.

And this year was strange. The sighting of a warrior angel revealed to humans so close to Jerusalem and so close to the Passover was nothing to be ignored. Rusalmeh had been around too long to chalk that up to a coincidence. His suspicions were on high alert. It had been years since a fallen had disappeared without a trace with sightings on and off since then. And then Isabella showed up.

"It had to be her," Rusalmeh said to himself but loud enough for anyone in his chambers to hear.

"Sire?" came the response from one of his commanders waiting in his chambers for further instruction.

"Shut up!" he screamed as he turned violently to face them. Hatred spewing from his eyes like hot volcanic ash spewing mercilessly forth from the earth. "There are enemy warriors among us!" he screamed, his voice still shrieking. "I want them found, and I want them destroyed."

His commanders said nothing. The fury of Rusalmeh was enough to keep anyone quiet. His commanders were no exception.

After a long silence, he concluded, "And I want the humans they are protecting tormented."

With that, the commanders left his chambers quietly. The word would soon go out. Hunt down the angel warriors and remove the threat.

As his commanders left his chambers, Rusalmeh once again turned his attention first to Isabella and then to Sam. He hadn't forgotten about Sam. He hadn't forgotten Sam had delivered a beating to two of his fallens, but then he vanished. Only years later, Isabella appeared. He couldn't shake the realization that both Sam and Isabella were in his region undetected until now. He knew the Creator wouldn't send Isabella for a mission of peace. He knew at some point, if Isabella was involved, it would end up with her wreaking total havoc on his forces. But for what?

The question would haunt him until it was far too late.

CHAPTER 53

Avoiding Detection

"Here we go," Sebastian said.

The family was moving together on their way to the temple to partake in the Passover festivities. The warrior team was ready for such an event. Sebastian had made the decision the night before to kill all comms for the entire day. The unknown of the environment and the complexities represented were too much to risk it. The team agreed. They knew their respective roles to play, and they were ready.

Sam and Petros were up ahead of the family, Sebastian and Isabella behind. They all had the ability to take human form and reveal themselves as needed, but all agreed they wouldn't unless absolutely necessary. The goal was to move with the family and avoid detection while staying close enough to offer protection as needed.

As they moved out that morning, they knew the challenge ahead but were not able to anticipate the sheer number of fallens in and around the city of Jerusalem. It would not be long before their plan to stay undetected would unravel in spectacular form.

The Passover celebrations in a city ruled by the Romans were subdued. The Roman soldiers stationed in Jerusalem were cordial, but the vibe most of them gave off was edgy. They didn't like the Hebrews, and the influx of them into the Jerusalem to celebrate their day didn't help.

The fallens saw to that. They were everywhere. Seething and sneering as they stirred up anger and hatred everywhere they went. It was a free-for-all.

Petros would later recall the scene that day as reminding him of his days in Egypt. Just as in Egypt, the fallens in and around Jerusalem had full reign. It was clear to Sebastian and team that the fallens had been given full permission to wreak as much havoc as possible. This was the holiest day of the Creator's chosen people, so whatever they could do to make it as miserable as possible, they were going to do. For the warrior angels, staying undetected was going to be impossible. Their only advantage was how wild-eyed and preoccupied most of the fallens were. Most were so busy spreading fear, hate, pride, lust, and envy as they whispered in the ears of any Roman citizen and soldier they could find. But Petros noticed them first. They were hard to spot, but they were there. Fallens calm and collected. Moving through the crowds, heads on a swivel. Like they were looking for something. Or someone.

As the family stopped just outside the temple gates, it gave the four warriors a chance to communicate using hand signals and mouthing words.

Sam and Petros each had managed to ascend the building on the east and west of the street. This gave them an advantage but also ran the risk of exposing them to fallens. Especially those fallens clearly on a search-and-destroy mission.

Sebastian and Isabella did their best to stay hidden, being sure never to lose sight of Mary and her family. There were people everywhere, and the chaos of the moment was almost overwhelming. They were constantly losing and then regaining sight of Mary and her family as people and fallens milled about on narrow streets packed in with street vendors, worshippers, and Roman soldiers. As the warrior angels moved from shadow to shadow, they used the chaos of the moment to their advantage. With their full camouflage engaged, they reflected the world around them in beautiful ways. They moved with such grace and purpose, the chaos around them allowed them to easily blend in.

Until everything changed. In an instant, Mary was gone.

CHAPTER 54

A Chance Encounter

"Well, hello, beautiful," the young man said as both his hands cupped Mary's.

"I didn't know you were coming," Mary said, surprised and happy all in one breath.

"Should I go?" the young man asked.

"No! No, Joseph," she said in a hushed voice. "I'm just happily surprised. Is all."

Joseph had spotted Mary in the crowd, and grabbing her hand, he pulled her close. And they moved quickly to an alley for some privacy.

"It's good to see you," Joseph said with a smile.

As Mary looked up at him, she said, "I better get back."

"When can I see you again?" Joseph asked. After a long pause, he said, "It's been too long. I find myself thinking about you all the time."

Mary smiled, and she looked up at him. She said shyly, "Me too."

Just then, a Roman soldier shouted at them from the opposite end of the alley, "You there!"

As the Roman soldier moved quickly and aggressively toward the two, what appeared to be a homeless man lying on a mat, covered in rags, struggled to stand up. Both Joseph and Mary stood there as if frozen in time. Unsure of what to do. As the soldier drew closer to them, it was clear the homeless man intended to confront the soldier. As the man struggled to his feet in front of the soldier, the Roman drew his sword as if he were giving the man a warning to stay clear. The homeless man either didn't see the warning or saw it and didn't care as he stood upright, a bit unsteady on his feet, between the two teenagers and the Roman soldier.

"Anything you have to say to them, you can say to me, soldier," the homeless man said.

"Get out of my way, old man. This is none of your concern!" the Roman soldier shouted mere inches from the homeless man's face.

Calmly and politely, the homeless man said, "I will say this one more time. Anything you—"

Before he could finish, the soldier raised his hand and cracked the back of his left hand across the old man's face. The sheer force of the action and the obvious frailty of the man was sure to result in significant injury. Except it didn't. The man didn't move. The soldier's hand fell to his side as he doubled over in excruciating pain.

The old man, still facing the soldier, turned his head, smiled, and said, "You should run along now."

Mary looked at Joseph, his eyes wide in astonishment. She gently said, "Let's go."

For a split second, he said nothing. Then he looked at Mary, grabbed her hand, and quickly exited the alley back into the anonymity of the crowd.

At the last second, Mary looked back to see what had become of the old man and the soldier. But all she could see was the soldier. He was still doubled up in pain. But there was no homeless man. He was gone. Like he was never there. Mary stopped and strained to get a closer look, but the throng of people on the small crowded street carried her away as she held tightly to Joseph hand.

Joseph felt Mary stop and strain against the crowd, and he gathered her close again. He asked, "What is it?"

"I don't know."

"What do you mean?"

"I looked back to see what became of the homeless man who protected us from that soldier, but he was gone."

"Gone? What do you mean?"

"I mean gone. As in not there."

They said nothing.

They both pondered the moment until they both heard the sound of Mary's mother's voice as she shouted, "Mary!"

"Momma!' Mary yelled above the noise of the crowd. As her mom came toward the sound of her daughter's voice in the crowd, Mary said, "Look who I found!"

"Joseph, my dear. So good to see you!" Mary's mother said as they quickly connected and embraced with crowds all around them.

"Is your family here?" Mary's father asked.

"Yes, sir. We just arrived today. I was happy to find you and Mary, of course," Joseph said, that last part quite shyly. "I should go. I need to catch up with my family."

"When can I see you again?" Mary asked with a whisper.

Joseph shrugged his shoulders and was gone. Lost in the crowd.

Looking for him only briefly, young Mary's thoughts turned to the homeless man. She couldn't help but wonder about him. Where did he come from? Why didn't she see him there before? How did he stand up against the soldier? Where did he go?

As she pondered these questions in her mind, her family moved, with the crowd, closer to the temple.

Everyone oblivious to the evil pulsing all around them.

CHAPTER 55

Petros and the Homeless Man

"A homeless man?" Sam asked as they resumed following the family, dodging in and out of shadows, working hard to stay hidden.

"Yup," Petros replied, quite proud of his efforts.

With a broad smile, Sam said, "Well, I'll give you points for creativity."

"Hey, I had to act fast. When they turned into the alley right below me, I didn't think much of it," Petros responded.

"I saw the Roman long before you did."

"Yeah, I was focused on Mary. By the time I spotted the soldier, I didn't have a lot of time."

"So you went with the homeless motif?"

"Haha. Indeed. Not bad though, right?"

"By the way, did you see how Joseph looked at Mary?"

"Not really. Was scrambling to make an appearance."

"Pretty sure he's got it bad for our Mary. He really loves that girl."

"You think?" Petros wondered.

"Anyway, I'll have to give it you. You got in and got out."

"And the youngsters took the hint and got out of there."

"Do you think they figured it out?" Sam asked, his first genuine question since they resumed their protective detail.

"I don't think Joseph did. He was just focused on Mary."

"And Mary?"

"Yeah, she recognized that something was off."

Sam said nothing. He was trying to replay those fateful seconds in his mind. He knew Sebastian would want all the details, so he wanted to keep them close.

Petros continued, "She looked back after leaving the alley. It was as if she was looking for something out of place."

"And?" Sam asked.

"Don't worry, Sam. I was gone by then. She couldn't see me."

"Sure?"

"Yep. But that soldier's hand will never be the same."

They both laughed. Then Sam said something about the difficulty the soldier was going to have, trying explain what happened to his superior officer.

But Petros didn't hear him. He couldn't. He had just seen a ghost.

CHAPTER 56

Rusalmeh at the Temple

"What?" Sam asked as he noticed that Petros was completely distracted.

Petros said nothing.

"Pete? What is it?"

"He's here," Petros said with a whisper.

"Who?"

Silence.

"Pete, who is here?"

Petros didn't answer because he didn't hear the question. He was too busy firing up comms and ensuring the necessary scramble was in place. "Sir?"

The words crackled in Sebastian's comms device in a way that startled him as much as it annoyed him. "Petros, we agreed no—"

"I know, sir. But he's here. I saw him."

Sebastian said nothing as both Isabella and Sam listened in.

"Okay. I'm sorry. I'm lost. Who is he?" Sam said in a harsh whisper with a bit of a smile on his face.

"Rusalmeh," Sebastian replied.

"Oh. Well, that's not great," Sam said, keeping his smile in place.

"Pete, are you absolutely sure?" Sebastian asked, serious.

"Affirmative. I spent an entire mission face-to-face with him in Egypt. I'll never forget what he looks like. It was him," Petros concluded, equally serious.

"Is he looking for us?" Isabella asked.

After a long silence, Sebastian said, "Probably. The plan doesn't change. We keep hidden and stand ready if needed."

"An all-out war on Passover would be suboptimal but also a cool memory to talk about later," Sam said, trying to be funny. It wasn't.

"We could win it," Isabella responded.

"Indeed, but the consequences of such action would end our mission and put Mary and her family in grave danger," Sebastian replied, a seriousness in his voice the team rarely heard. He continued, "We stay the course, reveal as needed to protect the family. Okay?"

"Okay," said the rest of the team in near unison.

"Petros, kill the comms. And stay safe, everyone," Sebastian commanded. "Oh, and Pete?"

"Sir?"

"A homeless guy?" Sebastian said with a smile.

"Hey, it worked, didn't it?" And with that, he killed the comms.

The team continued to move through the crowded city, evading fallens who seemed to be crawling everywhere. They remained laser focused on the mission. Protect Mary and stay hidden.

But something started to happen. Every shape, every sound, every smell, and every movement seemed to be coming slower now. It was as if the Creator had slowed everything down for them. The urge to fight was palpable, but even though none of them knew the Creator's full plan for their mission, they all instinctively knew this wasn't the end. They knew this wasn't the time to fight. What they didn't know was how soon it would come.

As the family entered the courtyard of the temple, the mass of people gathered made it completely impossible to keep eyes on Mary and her family at every moment. People were dodging in and out, and visual confirmation stuttered in and out like a bad comms connection.

They all saw Rusalmeh. He intended it that way. He sat atop the highest pillar along the wall leading to the temple courtyard. He dared not go any closer. Neither did his minions. Even though it had been centuries since the Creator's temple in Jerusalem had been elevated as a holy place of reverence and worship, Rusalmeh and his hordes of fallen respected what it represented and, it appeared, were not willing to take a chance. The chance being the Creator would, as in centuries past, show up to meet the priest on the annual day of sacrifice. Should that happen, no fallen dripping in evil and hatred anywhere close would survive the absolute consuming fire within which the Creator dwelt. So they hung back. Taking no chances.

Sebastian was right. Rusalmeh was clearly looking for something or someone. Mary's angelic warriors all took hidden positions in full camouflage that reflected their surroundings in the same way a chameleon would adapt his exterior to its surroundings. Each from their own position, they kept a focused eye on Mary and another on Rusalmeh. All remained normal. Rusalmeh on his perch on high alert but no movement. Mary and her family completing their visit to the temple as planned. They slowly made their way back through the courtyard toward the entrance gate. And then it happened.

As if shot out of cannon, Rusalmeh stood straight and threw himself down directly opposite of the gate just as Mary and her family were walking through it. It was clear to each of the angel warriors that one of Rusalmeh's fallens had recognized Mary and alerted him to her presence. But why?

"Sir, the line is open and secure. I figured after seeing what happened, you would want to make a plan," Petros said. The comms device each warrior was carrying came crackling to life with the sound of his voice.

"You figured right."

"Sir, he's guessing," Sam said with confidence.

"I think you are right, but he guessed right."

At this moment, the team kept their distance and continued to stay hidden as they moved with the family through the crowd.

"The prince doesn't travel alone. Can you spot his entourage through the chaos of the rest of the fallens?" asked Sebastian with the steady voice of a commander fully in charge.

"There are at least three," Isabella answered.

"Make that four," Sam said.

"Five," Petros added.

"They are moving with the crowd. Maybe it's not Mary they are after," Sebastian said, knowing it to be wishful thinking as soon as he said it.

"Possible, but not likely, sir. From behind, it's clear to us they are targeting Mary," Petros confirmed.

"Rules of engagement still stand, even with Rusalmeh in the mix," Sebastian reminded as he began to sense the tension rising.

The team was silent. They knew he was right, but none of them liked it.

Especially Isabella. "Understood, sir. But how truly great would it be to send a clear message to the fallens on Passover?" Isabella said with her trademark smile.

"So great," Sam agreed. His smile even bigger.

After a long pause, Sebastian said, "It would be something we would always remember, wouldn't it?"

The team was stunned. It was a rare moment of transparency from their leader, especially during such a tense moment.

Mary and her family were moving easily now through the crowd, laughing and talking as they went, often stopping along the way at various street vendors and shops. Rusalmeh and his five goons kept their distance but kept pace as well.

"You're right, Sam. He's guessing. He's looking for us," Isabella said.

"It's the constant head movement from him and his guys. All of them are constantly looking around," Sam added.

"Looking for us," Sebastian agreed.

"Yup. If he only knew how close he was," Sam replied with a muffled laugh.

Mary and her family, completely oblivious to the spirit world cloak-and-dagger game swirling all around them, made their way back to the home in which they were staying just as dusk settled over Jerusalem.

Rusalmeh and his team followed the family all the way to the home, each taking up a position around the home as if guarding it.

It wasn't long before another fallen showed up. He approached Rusalmeh with extreme deference as if he had been summoned.

None of the angels, securely hidden but close enough to ensure Mary's protection, could make out what was being said between the prince and his slave. One thing was certain, Rusalmeh was not happy. He appeared to berate the fallen unrelentingly.

"That's one of the fallens who was with Javva the night Mary's relatives came to visit her," Isabella said, breaking the silence.

Sebastian had decided to leave comms open and take the risk. The moment was too important. Too consequential. "Have we seen him anywhere else?" Sebastian asked.

"We saw him again following young Joseph when Mary was visiting cousin Elizabeth years ago," Petros answered.

As Petros was speaking, the fallen, head bowed low, slinked his way toward the house, disappearing through an open window.

"Hold," Sebastian commanded sternly but calmly.

A fallen in the presence of Mary and her family was something Sebastian knew would illicit extreme righteous anger in his team, but he also knew it was not enough to unleash their incredible power. At least not yet.

He was right. A few seconds later, the fallen emerged from the house and appeared to confirm with a nod of his slick bald head that the inhabitants of the house were, in fact, who he expected them to be.

"Best I can tell, that fallen was one of the lookouts, and he recognized Mary," Sam suggested.

"Recognized what?" Isabella asked.

"Don't forget, they still have a missing fallen who disappeared not far from Mary's family home," Petros answered.

"I wouldn't be surprised if they picked up some of our comms and maybe even spotted some of our activity in the area," Sebastian added.

"Sir! That hurts. You are going to hurt Pete's feelings," Sam chimed in with a chuckle.

"Haha. He's right," Petros said.

"Our secure comms are secure, but it's not impossible to intercept, especially if we were talking during one of their blackout periods."

"Looks like they are grasping at straws," Isabella said.

Indeed, they were, but Rusalmeh wouldn't know how close he was to thwarting the Creator's plan until it was far too late.

Soon after, Rusalmeh departed with three of his lieutenants, leaving two behind to keep an eye on the house in which Mary and her family were staying.

It would be their last night in the earthly realm before catching a direct flight to oblivion, courtesy of Mary's invisible warriors.

CHAPTER 57

The Wrong Move

Rusalmeh's two goons sat facing away from the house one on each side of the front door. Inert.

"Isabella, do you copy?" asked Sebastian. His voice calm.

"Copy" came the reply. Isabella was inside the home, just in case one or both of the goons decided to make a very bad decision and enter the house where Mary and her family slept. Isabella had entered the house through a rear window out of view of the two fallen guards and found a secure position within which to stand guard.

"The two haven't moved for more than an hour," Sebastian reported.

Sam, Petros, and Sebastian had strategically positioned themselves to ensure both maximum concealment as well as clear visuals of the entirety of the home within which Mary and her family were sleeping.

They were ready. And all of them, for the first time on this infinitely long mission, began to sense an acceleration. A crescendo of sorts.

Something was happening. But without new orders, without an updated mission, they were still completely committed to their original purpose. To stay hidden. Passive. Quiet.

And then he moved.

CHAPTER 58

Two More Missing

"Hey?" a fallen named Grem said to the other equally wretched fallen leaning up against the wall on the opposite side of the door.

"What?" a fallen named Krume replied gruffly, not pleased in being interrupted.

"Why are we just sitting here?"

"What else should we be doing?"

"How about a little tormenting?"

"The prince commanded us to keep watch for enemies in the area."

"We have been here for hours. If there were enemy in the area, we would have seen them."

Krume said nothing.

Grem continued, "Besides, the humans inside this house are all sleeping. Nothing better than a little dream tormenting. Am I right?"

"You're an idiot, Grem," Krume barked. "We are here on direct orders of Rusalmeh. His orders were clear."

"Sure, but it's not like he told us not to torment the humans."

"I guess not, but I've seen what happens to slaves when they don't deliver for the master."

"Meaning?"

"Meaning, dumbass, if we miss enemy activity in the area and it gets back to Rusalmeh that we missed it, we're screwed."

"C'mon. There's nothing here. The prince is losing his mind. Ever since Rafar went missing, he's been chasing ghosts that don't exist."

Krume said nothing.

"Forget it. I'm not going to sit around all night, looking stupid. There's nothing here, and I'm going to have a little fun."

Krume shrugged his shoulders and said nothing as he rested his head back against the wall of the house, and he closed his eyes. As he heard Grem move past him into the house, he wondered if he should lighten up.

It wouldn't be long before his own question would be answered in gruesome detail.

*****

"Bella, you've got company," Sam chirped in his comms device.

"I see him." Isabella was inside the house along the back wall, giving her a complete view of every wall in the small house. Mary and her family were all asleep in a room toward the back of the house. She saw the demon the moment he crossed the threshold and smelled him soon after. The unmistakable stench of a fallen seemed to initiate a primitive violent reaction in Isabella that would require her to contain herself.

The fallen lingered in the front room of the house as if he were investigating. He moved through the middle part of the house where occupants prepared and ate meals. It was there he stopped. The first thing he saw was coincidentally also the last thing he saw.

Isabella, one of the greatest angelic warriors the Creator ever created, drew her sword and swung it through the neck of the fallen with extreme prejudice. The righteous anger she felt of a fallen so close to her precious Mary and her family was overwhelming. Her instincts just took over. See the threat. Eliminate the threat. Ask questions later.

Without skipping a bit, she anticipated the trajectory the severed demon head would travel and snatched it out of the air as the rest of his wretched body slumped lifelessly just a few feet from where

Mary was sleeping. Tucking the head under her left arm, she grabbed the rest of the corpse and started heading back the same way through the house that the fallen had just come a few fateful moments before.

"The threat had to be eliminated," Isabella said calmly into her comms device. She continued, "And I'm heading out the front door with the remains."

"Hold please" came the response from Sebastian.

"Yeah, we'll need to introduce ourselves to our new friend here," Sam chimed in, his signature smile clear to everyone. "So have you ever heard the phrase 'wrong place, wrong time'?"

The voice, in a low whisper, hit the ears of the other fallen keeping watch on the outside of the house. It had only been a brief moment since his fellow fallen had entered the house. He didn't recognize the voice. Had Rusalmeh sent someone else? Was he hearing things?

"What?" the fallen replied, whipsawing his head back and forth, looking for the source of the hushed voice. He saw no one.

"You know," the voice continued, "wrong place, wrong time."

Silence.

"Oh, come on. It happens to you, fallens, all the time," the voice said, this time without the whisper.

It was those two words, "you fallens," that stopped the fallen who heard them cold. As he slowly looked above him, he instantly realized that only an angel would say those two words.

In that moment, that nameless, faceless demon—once a prized creation of the Creator, long forgotten and dying a slow death in the earthly realm—knew the end was at hand.

Coming into view was Sam, his topaz eyes and his massive frame cutting through the darkness like a knife, as he descended off the roof of the house, his sword fully extended just in case. As he landed softly, facing his enemy, Petros and Sebastian emerged from the darkness as all three quickly surrounded the demon who appeared to be frozen in time. Both Petros and Sebastian faced away, their backs to the demon, in order to keep watch. Sam used his eyes as daggers as he stared directly at the fallen mere inches from his face with fierce intensity. No one spoke.

Finally, Sam said, "You didn't answer my question."

"I... I... I..." the fallen stammered.

"Oh, never mind. You wouldn't get the joke anyway. Either Rusalmeh hates you, or you are severely unlucky."

"Probably both," Petros chimed in his back to the conversation.

"Haha!" Sam laughed. A genuine laugh. He stopped laughing instantly and, leaning in as close the fallen's face as he could without touching him, said, "Your friend is dead."

The fallen said nothing. Nothing to say.

Sam continued, "Nothing to say to that?"

Just then, Isabella emerged with the severed head of the fallen she had just annihilated under one arm and dragging his lifeless body with the other. She held it up like a prize in the face of what was now a visibly terrified fallen who knew he was in deep trouble.

The scene was incredible. The middle of the night, four of the Creator's most incredible angelic warriors, hidden together behind enemy lines and now revealing themselves to a single agent of death. A fallen who had no chance and would never be able to speak of what he had seen.

Sam again spoke after a moment of silence long enough to allow the fallen to accept his fate, "So here's what's going to happen. You are going to make a call."

The fallen said nothing.

"That call is going to be to whoever you report to. And with this call, you are going to indicate there is nothing happening here. But you and your headless friend here are going to investigate something you saw." Sam was now leaning in so close to the fallen in front of him he could see every twitch, every pulse in the demon's face. He wanted him to fully recognize his situation.

The demon finally spoke with a hiss, "Why would I do that? You are only going to annihilate me after."

"That's likely," Sam shot back, expecting such an answer. "But your level of cooperation here will determine how fast or how slow your impending annihilation will go."

The fallen said nothing. There was nothing to say.

Surprisingly, Sebastian spoke up, his back still to the fallen, "It doesn't matter what you do really. We'll still win. The Creator always wins."

The fallen's head dropped to his chest, his fate sealed.

"So, worm, what's it going to be?" Sam asked.

With a low growl in his voice, the fallen said, "Go to hell."

"Oh, well, isn't that nice?" Sam responded. "Wrong answer," he said this as he brought his sword out of its sheath and through the fallen in one smooth, swift motion.

The fallen slumped and then fell helplessly to the ground.

"Well, we gave it a shot," Petros said.

"Indeed," Sebastian replied.

Knowing the clock was now ticking, he gave his team his final instructions on how best to dispose and position the bodies according to what they had planned.

And as the team took the lifeless fallen bodies away from the home in which Mary slept, Sebastian wondered how long they could stay hidden. Nothing happened by chance, and he put his trust in the Creator's sovereignty in that moment.

And as he did, he entered the house in which Mary and her family slept to awaken them and lead them out of the city as quickly as possible. The beginning of the end had just begun.

Mary's father woke first. Sebastian gently stirred his spirit in a dream to wake up and take his family home. As he awoke, he audibly asked, "Home? Now?"

This woke his wife, Mary's mother, and she asked, "What?"

He groggily said, "I think we need to leave. Now."

"What?"

"We need to go. Now."

"Why? What are you talking about? It's the middle of the night."

"I can't explain it. But I can't avoid it either."

Mary, hearing her parents talking, woke up, saying, "I've got it too, Mom. We need to go."

At this point, Sebastian was working his way through the room, stirring an urgency to leave. It was working.

After a moment, everyone was awake, packing their things in the dark, preparing to leave. And only a few moments later, they were exiting the house, loading their donkeys, and preparing quickly to depart.

All their invisible warrior angels were back and in position to protect. They had disposed of the fallens they had just annihilated according to Sebastian's instructions and hoped their strategy would confuse Rusalmeh and his minions long enough to get the family home safely and, with any luck, a little bit longer.

CHAPTER 59

Rusalmeh Learns an Important Lesson

"Where?" Rusalmeh screeched.

"Hanging, sire," one of his nameless, faceless slaves said, head down.

"Hanging! Where?" the prince screamed.

"From a pillar along the wall leading to the temple courtyard."

Rusalmeh said nothing for a long moment. "And what of the family they were sent to watch?"

"Gone, sire. It appears they left at first light."

Rusalmeh spoke in a low growl, "They are taunting me."

"Who, sire?"

"Shut up!" Rusalmeh screamed. "Leave me! Now!"

At once, he was alone in his chambers. Since he defied the Creator and followed Lucifer, his loneliness seemed to have reached new depths on a regular basis. But in this moment, he never felt more alone. More isolated. More useless.

As he sat in silence, his wretched mind raced. "Who is annihilating my slaves?" he said to himself out loud. "Why annihilate them and leave their lifeless husks hanging on the same pillar I was on earlier in the day?"

As he stared in the distance overlooking Jerusalem, the darkness descended on his mind like thick smoke from a forest fire. He whispered to himself, "I'm missing something."

Something. Something big. Something big indeed.

CHAPTER 60

Rusalmeh's Offensive

"We did it all wrong."

Safir and Tarn said nothing.

"We made our movements too obvious. Too blatant."

Rusalmeh's slaves knew to say nothing in response. Their leader was riffing, and it was best to just let him go uninterrupted.

"The farm girl and her family are being protected by some of the most badass angel warriors ever to set foot in the earthly realm," Rusalmeh said matter-of-factly. Continuing, he asked rhetorically, "But why?"

Safir and Tarn didn't take the bait.

"It makes no sense. The pieces of evidence don't completely match, and I have no idea how many there are."

After a long moment of silence, Rusalmeh spoke again, "Sam and Isabella are here, or were here. But who else is with them, and why are they hiding?" His mind was racing, alternating between excitement and fear.

"Okay, here's what I want from you two," he said, addressing the two fallens, heads bowed low before their master. "I want you to run a covert operation on the farm girl and her family."

The two nodded in unison, both hoping for more detail. It soon came.

"I believe this girl is important somehow, and I believe there are angel warriors—at least two, maybe more—protecting her."

His slaves said nothing. Another riff had begun.

"For some reason, they are purposely staying hidden from detection but are not afraid to act viciously." He continued, "So I want you to watch the family and every move they make. I want you to find out who is protecting them, and I want to know why."

"What about the boy you asked me to follow?" Tarn asked.

"Forget about him. He's a dead end. It's all about this girl and her family somehow. We have two more dead demons because of them," Rusalmeh responded, spitting the words back at these two slaves standing before him.

"What if we see them?" Tarn asked sheepishly, fearing he was pushing his luck with another question.

"Well, I suggest you don't let them see you, or based on the last few who have seen them, you'll likely reach annihilation soon after."

"In other words, don't get noticed," Safir whispered to his friend.

"Precisely," Rusalmeh responded, his back to his two slaves. "Find out who has been so brazenly in my region, mocking me with impunity. And don't be seen."

As the two slaves left his chambers, Rusalmeh knew he was likely sentencing them to annihilation. But he didn't care. Slaves like Safir and Tarn were replaceable. He needed answers.

What he didn't know was how soon the answers would come and how devastating those answers would be.

CHAPTER 61

The Suitor Is Not to be Denied

"Again?" Sam asked in response to Sebastian's proclamation.

Sebastian said nothing.

Sam continued, "We've only be back less than a day."

"Correct. But being young and in love only happens once," Isabella chimed in as she watched Joseph approach Mary's home to pay her a visit.

"Love is unpredictable and uncontainable," Petros chimed in, trying to join the conversation.

"Yeah, kinda like your hair, Pete," Sam responded, his signature smile heard loud and clear as he spoke.

Petros laughed hard, knowing he walked right into that one.

"Okay, everyone," Sebastian said, changing the subject quickly, "we know Joseph, and he's clear. No need to leave your posts."

"Sir?" Sam asked. "What are you thinking?"

"I'm thinking our hasty little evac a day ago did not go unnoticed."

"And?" Isabella asked.

"And I'm sure Rusalmeh has put two and two together by now."

"Yep, the two goons sent to watch the house Mary was in are stone-cold dead," Sam confirmed.

"Aye. And since we haven't seen any fallen activity around here since then, I have a feeling we are being watched."

"Watched, sir?" Petros asked.

"Affirmative. I just can't quite put my finger on it, but until I can, we need to stay completely hidden and assume we are being watched."

No one spoke for a long moment.

"Understood?" Sebastian asked, finally breaking the uncomfortable silence.

"Understood."

"Petros?"

"Sir?"

"Monitor all communications traffic in the area."

"You got it."

"You're not going to ask why?" Sebastian asked.

"I was taught not to question orders, sir," Petros responded.

"Sam, did you miss that part of the training?" Isabella chimed in.

"Must have" came Sam's response barely a second after Isabella spoke.

"Well, going on a hunch that we are being watched, they may not be using a secure comms channel."

"Roger that. I'll let you know what I hear."

It wouldn't be long.

CHAPTER 62

The Fallens Have Eyes on the Target

"Nothing," Tarn said.

"Keep watching," Safir replied.

The two had stopped well short of the house, finding a small grove of trees within which to hide. If there were enemy warriors guarding the house as Rusalmeh suspected, they wanted to stay as far away as possible and still be able to see what was happening.

Their mission wasn't to fight angel warriors. They both knew they had no chance against one angel warrior, let alone multiple. Their mission was to discover any angel activity in or around the target home.

The two were hunkered down, one at the north end of the tree grove, the other at the south. The two had arrived under the cover of night, and as far as they could tell, no one knew they were there.

As they watched the young man walk past them toward the house in the distance, little did they know they had already made a mistake, for which there was no going back.

CHAPTER 63

Spies Detected

"Sir?"

"What is it, Pete?"

"Your hunch was right," Petros replied.

"Oh yeah?"

"Yeah, I've picked up two fallens."

"Close?"

"I think so. They were talking about Joseph, same as we were."

"Best guess on location?"

"I'd guess one of the tree groves just north of your location, sir."

"Okay, everyone, make sure your reflective camouflage is on. Let's go full-stealth mode until further notice," Sebastian commanded.

No one needed further explanation. They knew the drill. They had been hidden on this mission now for years. An extra level of stealth was no inconvenience. It was expected, especially as things began to move more quickly in recent days.

They watched young Joseph head back the way he came only a few hours earlier, and Petros heard the fallens discuss it, just as they had before.

As the sun began to drop below the horizon that night, Mary's angel warriors knew something was happening. They just didn't know what.

Or when. Or how.

CHAPTER 64

Lucifer Arrives

"Well?" the massive fallen Archangel asked. His voice calm. Steady.

Rusalmeh was on his hands and knees, whimpering. He managed to spit out some terrified words, "Sire, I… I…"

"Yes, my son? Come on with it, won't you?" the great deceiver standing over him asked mockingly.

This was a moment a fallen, like Rusalmeh, never wanted to experience. An unexpected, unannounced visit from the most-feared, most-wicked fallen in the earthly realm. Lucifer.

His visit wasn't all that unexpected the more Rusalmeh thought about it as he crouched closer to the ground, his mind racing. It had been hundreds of years in the earthly realm since anyone had seen anything like it. And Rusalmeh was angry at himself for not recognizing how fast word of such an event would travel.

The day was like any other day. Until it wasn't. Because when Gabriel showed up, everyone knew. Including Lucifer, who wasted no time arriving on the scene to interrogate his slave Rusalmeh inside Rusalmeh's own chambers.

Like a ripple in a pond caused by a stone, except Gabriel arriving in the earthly realm was like a granite mountain causing a tsunami-sized ripple among all spirits in the earthly realm. Like a crack of thunder on a cloudless day. When Gabriel the Archangel arrived in the earthly realm, it's an event.

So as Rusalmeh bowed before his master Lucifer, he dared not tell him of the mounting evidence of angelic warrior activity in his region that had carried on under his nose for years. But he knew it would only be a matter of time before Lucifer would get it out of him. He was, after all, the father of lies. The great deceiver. And you wouldn't get to be that without honing your interrogation and manipulation skills over millennia. Rusalmeh only hoped he could say enough without giving up too much.

"I'm waiting, Rusalmeh," Lucifer said calmly after a long pause.

Rusalmeh collected himself, saying, "Sire, he was in the temple. I have no one there. The temple is—"

"Off-limits. This I know, fool. Don't patronize me. I have no patience for that."

"Forgive me, sire. I only meant to say he made no attempt at concealing himself and arrived and departed all from within the temple."

"I see," Lucifer replied.

No one spoke for a long moment. Rusalmeh hoped the worst was over. It wasn't.

"Why would he conceal himself, Rusalmeh?"

"Sire?"

"You said he didn't conceal himself. Why would you say that?"

"I don't know. Just making the point that he didn't seem concerned with hiding the fact that he was entering the earthly realm," Rusalmeh replied, realizing much too late that he had said too much.

Lucifer was the master at finding the half-truths, the side steps, and exploiting them. He wrote the book on them. Rusalmeh knew this, but he was out of his league. He couldn't stop the inevitable. But he tried.

Lucifer replied, "Gabriel has never concealed his arrival here. In fact, he makes it a point to arrive with such force, such fury that it's as if he is rubbing it in my face."

Rusalmeh said nothing.

So Lucifer asked, "Have you?"

"Sire?"

"Have you ever known Gabe to roll up here 'concealing' himself?"

"No, sire."

"So I'm curious, Rusalmeh, why would you say that." The words dripped with hate and cut like a knife.

Rusalmeh knew the next words he spoke were likely to be the most important he had ever uttered. Should he come out with the truth? Namely that a team of angelic warriors had been taunting him, within his region, concealed for years? Or should he play dumb and hope Lucifer would drop the whole thing? These questions raced through his wretched mind as he sought the precise words to say.

As he lay now prostrate in front of Lucifer, he did the only thing he knew to do. The one thing he was best at. He lied. "I misspoke, sire. That's all."

"I don't believe you, Rusalmeh. But I also don't want to waste another moment of time on a worthless waste of space like you. So I'm going to drop it now," Lucifer said calmly.

Rusalmeh said nothing. There was nothing to say.

Lucifer began to leave Rusalmeh's chambers but stopped, turned around slightly, and said, "Find out why he was here, or I'll find someone who will."

Rusalmeh lay motionless for several long silent moments after the last words of Lucifer had been spoken in his chambers. As he forced himself to sit up, he wondered how he had missed it. All of it. This was so unlike him. He was the ruler of the most significant region in the earthly realm and had been for millennia, but now he was being outmaneuvered by a group of angelic warriors who insisted on staying hidden.

And now, after hundreds of years of silence, Gabriel showed up. Why?

As Rusalmeh pondered the facts of his current situation, he couldn't shake the feeling that all would soon be revealed. And unless he got some answered soon, his very existence would be taken from him.

So right he was.

CHAPTER 65

Gabriel Was Here?

"What do you mean?" Sebastian inquired.

"I mean he couldn't speak," Sam answered. Matter-of-factly.

Gabriel had given Sebastian a heads-up the morning of his arrival, more of a courtesy than anything else. The temple was the only detail he provided. Everyone in the spirit realm would know of Gabriel's arrival, including Sebastian and his team, but Gabriel wanted them to have a heads-up.

Sebastian decided to quickly dispatch Sam and Petros to Jerusalem to keep an eye out. They concealed themselves as Roman soldiers and positioned themselves outside the temple gates. And waited.

Gabriel came and went. Gabriel was so cool. Even for angelic warriors, like Sam and Petros, his arrival was awe-inspiring. As Sebastian had instructed, they hung around the temple gate after watching Gabriel disappear out of the earthly realm, in case there was any intelligence gathering possible.

There was. It turned out one of the priests, Zechariah, could no longer speak. Their interactions with Zechariah over the years had been brief as young Mary would visit him and Elizabeth from time to time. They were family.

So when they reported back to Sebastian that Gabriel had likely visited Zechariah and now the priest could no longer speak, Sebastian and the team discussed the possible meanings and implications for their mission.

"What are the odds?" Isabella asked as they sat together just inside the grove of trees that sat just west of Mary's family home.

"Maybe it's just a coincidence?" Sam suggested.

"A coincidence the husband of Mary's cousin was visited by Gabriel and now cannot speak?" Petros asked. After a moment of silence had by all, Petros spoke again, "No way."

"Agreed," Sebastian said. "There are no coincidences with the Creator."

"Everything is perfectly planned," Sam said matter-of-factly.

After a moment of silence, Isabella added, "And he's never late."

CHAPTER 66

Gabriel Delivers the Message

After Gabriel's first visit, Mary's angelic warrior team settled into a routine of sorts. It was a bit odd knowing a visit from Gabriel was the beginning of something but not knowing exactly what. But they were used to it after all. Spending so much time in the earthly realm on a mission to protect while staying undetected under long stretches of no contact with the heavenly realm had prepared them for this. They were used to not knowing. Almost comfortable in it.

Rusalmeh, on the other hand, was not. The fallen activity in the area had picked up one hundredfold since Gabriel's temple visit, which made keeping concealed a bit of a challenge. Evident to the team very quickly was how lost Rusalmeh was. Sebastian figured he had picked up some clues along the way. The two annihilated fallens in Jerusalem the morning after guarding the house in which Mary was staying was highly suspicious. Add in Sam's early run-in with two of his goons, leaving them both unconscious, along with the still-missing fallen from the first night of their mission and Rusalmeh had some pieces to the puzzle.

That was before Gabriel showed up.

Now Rusalmeh's goons were everywhere but clearly not looking for anything in particular. They still had two of them spying from a distance, but they proved to be unworthy adversaries prone to misdirection and laziness.

Mary was safe. All was well in hand.
Until Gabriel arrived. Unannounced. In her garden.
And in a single moment, the mission changed forever.

CHAPTER 67

Sebastian Leads the Team Through the Chaos

A visit from the archangel Gabriel in the earthly realm was something quite extraordinary.

As an angelic warrior, to see Gabriel arrive unannounced usually meant he was inserting himself into a raging spiritual battle in which his presence was needed to change momentum and deliver a decisive victory.

To have it happen in the heart of a mission whose sole purpose was to stay concealed began a domino effect of events Sebastian knew he needed to manage quickly and effectively. The next few decisions he made would make or break their mission. So while the others were mesmerized by the moment Gabriel entered the earthly realm, Sebastian began charting their next moves. It's the key reason the Creator chose Sebastian for this particular mission. He had the calmness and the fortitude needed to stay on mission regardless of what was going on around him.

So the moment Gabriel arrived with what could only be described as a sonic boom in the spiritual realm, Sebastian immediately communicated with Sam and Petros. "Sam? Petros?" Sebastian said calmly into the comms device.

Silence.

"Guys?"

Silence.

"Guys!" Sebastian shouted. One of the only times anyone on the team had ever heard Sebastian raise his voice.

"We're here, sir. Sorry about that," Petros said for both of them.

"It's okay. There's a lot to take in right now," he said with a small but detectable smile. He continued, "Which is why I need you both to pay a visit to our fallen visitors who have been pretending to spy on us."

"Sir?"

"Well, they are obviously seeing what we are seeing. And since I haven't received any change in our mission, we will still need to stay concealed after Gabe leaves. So—"

"So if they are allowed to report back Gabriel's exact location, our little quiet sanctuary will soon be ground zero for an all-out war," Sam said, finishing Sebastian's thought for him.

"Exactly," Sebastian replied.

"Rules of engagement?" Petros asked.

"Secure them. Don't allow them to communicate. Await my instructions."

"On it," they said in unison, taking flight as they said it.

With two of his warriors now in motion, Sebastian turned his attention to his warrior most in position to hear Gabriel's message. "Isabella?" Sebastian asked quietly. "What is he saying?" Sebastian asked.

"Mary looks terrified," Isabella said. She was in perfect position to observe the entire interaction between Gabriel and sweet Mary.

"I remember when I first met Gabriel. I was terrified, and I'm an angel," Sam said with his trademark smile spreading across his face.

"I think Mary is handling her first encounter with an archangel better than you did, Sam," Sebastian replied. An unusual bit of humor from their leader, especially in this tense moment.

Everyone laughed.

Sam couldn't help but smile. As he and Petros raced toward the horizon to encounter the fallen spies, he recalled feeling so small and weak standing before Gabriel. It was a moment he had never forgotten. Seeing Gabriel stand before Mary brought that memory back.

Isabella continued, "You aren't going to believe this. It's the most incredible thing I have ever heard."

"I can't wait to hear it. Hold your position until Gabriel departs and we'll debrief as a team," Sebastian directed.

"Sir?" Isabella said, her voice soft, urgent.

"Yes."

"Everything has changed."

"I figured our mission would be changing."

"No, sir. I mean everything in the earthly realm has changed," Isabella whispered.

Sebastian said nothing. The words Isabella spoke were heavy. It was as if they demanded silence as they sunk deep.

In the silence, she spoke one word in that moment that each of the angelic warriors would always remember and recall as the moment their very existence, their very reason for being, came into extreme focus.

"Forever."

CHAPTER 68

The Captured Spies

The two fallens were so mesmerized by Gabriel's arrival playing out right in front of their eyes they didn't notice Sam and Petros arriving behind them.

The warrior angels decided to fly quickly past them and then arrive at pace behind the pair, drawing their swords instinctively as they arrived.

"Well, looky there," Sam said, "You guys probably shouldn't include Gabriel's visit in your daily report."

Safir was the first to look behind them. Tarn sat frozen in time. They both were tucked behind a small rock outcropping next to a small grove of trees. Their hiding place gave them surprisingly good cover and a clear view of Mary's home and surrounding area.

Petros followed Sam by saying, "Not too bad, guys. Pretty good hiding spot for a couple of goons like you."

The demons said nothing. There was nothing to say. Gabriel the Archangel was in front of them. And two of the biggest, most powerful warrior angels were behind them, swords drawn. They were completely outmatched under the most perfect circumstances, but now they were totally unprepared, and the surprised showed in their faces.

"Now I'm only going to say this once," Sam said, his demeanor completely focused and practically breathing fire with every word. "Up."

Tarn and Safir did exactly what they were told, practically in unison.

Petros sheathed his sword, stepped close, and stripped the demons of their weapons, communications devices, and any dignity that might remain.

Then Sam leaned as close to the demons as his olfactory senses would allow and said with a smile, "Welcome to the party."

CHAPTER 69

Now What?

"Sir, we have secured the enemy," Petros said matter-of-factly.

"Hold your position for now," Sebastian replied.

"Roger that."

"You boys find anything interesting around here?" Sam asked the two prisoners, not expecting an answer. He didn't receive one. "Well, I wouldn't have much to say either, I guess. Seeing how you probably stumbled into the biggest mission the Creator has ever authorized," Sam said with a wry smile.

"In the earthly realm, that is," Petros chimed in.

"Ah yes, for sure in the earthly realm," Sam agreed. He continued, "The time he threw your boss and you goons out of the heavenly realm probably still ranks as number 1, don't you guys think?"

No answer. There was none to give. They all knew this was all just a delay of the inevitable.

"Wait a minute," Sam said as his memory started to kick in. "Pete, don't we know these guys?"

Petros looked confused.

Sam went on, "Yeah, yeah, these are the two that surprised us when we were on an advance mission a long time back."

After stripping the fallens of their weapons and gear, Petros had tied their hands together along with their feet. The two fallens were completely helpless and their heads hung low. They recognized Sam as the warrior who had single-handedly defeated them that night. Now that Sam recognized them only made their humiliation worse.

"Man, you guys were terrible. Didn't even pretend to put up a fight that night."

Petros finally began to pick up where Sam was going, saying, "Oh, that's right. I remember now. I didn't even get to play along. These two were so worthless I think you knocked them senseless without breaking a sweat."

Sam just smiled and said, "Huh, small world, isn't it, fellas?"

Just then, Sebastian cut in, "Bring the fallens to the high point. We'll meet you there."

"Got it," Petros replied.

CHAPTER 70

What Do You Know?

"Safir and Tarn," Sebastian said in disgust shortly after he and Isabella arrived at the high point, traditionally Sebastian's surveillance post.

Darkness in the earthly realm had set in, further concealing their activity.

"You know these two?" Isabella asked, surprised.

"I do. Never understood why they hooked up with Lucifer."

"Good news. Now you can ask them," Sam chimed in with a smile.

"Nah, no time for that. I want answers," Sebastian said matter-of-factly.

The two fallens were wretchedly submissive, hoping for annihilation to come quickly now.

"First, who sent you?"

At first, neither fallen said anything. But then surprisingly, Safir spoke, "Rusalmeh."

"Why?" Sebastian asked.

Tarn said, his head low, "When the two showed up dead after watching the house, he sent us here."

"Here? Where is here?" Sebastian asked.

The others wanted to ask questions too, but they could all tell this was Sebastian's interrogation, and no one wanted to risk throwing him off.

Tarn continued, "The small farm."

"What have you seen?" Sebastian asked.

"Nothing. Nothing. We haven't seen anything!" Safir shouted in what could only be considered a last gasp attempt to save himself from a doomed situation.

"Why don't any of us believe that?" Sebastian asked sarcastically, not expecting an answer.

He got one as Tarn spoke, "That's not true. We have observed a small family doing what small families do on a small farm."

"Oh yeah. What's that?" Sebastian asked.

"Nothing. Absolutely nothing," Tarn replied.

"And today, what did you see today?"

Silence.

"Of course, you saw him," Sebastian said matter-of-factly.

"Did you relay what you saw back to Rusalmeh?"

More silence.

Sebastian was growing impatient, but he decided to let the silence do its work. The sounds of the night were the only sound being heard for a long moment.

Then Tarn spoke up again, "We didn't. We didn't have time."

Sebastian smiled. He believed him. Even though fallens lied about everything, Sebastian had learned that fallens at risk of being annihilated tended toward telling the truth. It was almost as if when the annihilation they secretly longed for would come into focus, they responded most truthfully. "Petros?"

"Sir?"

"Open a line. We're gonna need Magnis."

CHAPTER 71

Acceleration

"Thanks again," Sebastian said, his back turned.

"No problem, Seb. Anything for you," Magnis replied.

It didn't take long for Magnis to both arrive and clean the scene of the remains of the two fallens who had been quickly dispatched at the end of Isabella's massive sword.

Sebastian ordered their annihilation after thinking through all viable scenarios. There was no way to keep two fallens as prisoners, especially under the current mission of staying concealed. Of course, letting them go would quickly bring the full force of Rusalmeh's hordes upon them. Not good. They could annihilate them and spread their remains just as they did to the two demons the night Mary's home outside of Jerusalem was being monitored. But that would raise even more suspicion since both events occurred so close to each other.

So Sebastian decided on annihilation with removal. His reasoning was simple. By cleaning the scene and removing all fallen remains from the earthly realm, he believed he could buy himself and his team some time. Sure, Rusalmeh would miss them after a while, and he would likely send another crew to investigate. But as long as Gabriel didn't show up in Mary's backyard again anytime soon, he was reasonably confident the team could stay hidden as they had been doing for years.

After a long pause, Sebastian looked at Magnis and said, "I can always count on you."

"You can," Magnis replied. He continued, "Things seem to be getting tense around here."

"Indeed."

"Where's the rest of the crew?" Magnis asked, breaking what felt like an awkward silence. He had forgotten Sebastian wrote the book on awkward silences.

"I sent them back to their positions for the rest of the night."

Magnis nodded, saying nothing. There was nothing to say.

After making his final sweep of the scene, Magnis was preparing to swiftly exit the earthly realm before the next sunrise. As he turned to address Sebastian one last time, he was surprised to receive a strong embrace from his friend.

"I hope to see you again soon, my friend."

"Don't worry. You will. These fools are no match for you and your squad."

"I hope you're right. I have a feeling things are going to get out of control soon."

The two angels embraced quickly again.

But this time, Sebastian held the embrace, saying, "I'm not sure I ever thanked you for saving me way back."

"Way back?" Magnis asked.

"Abel."

"Ah yes, Abel. Of course, I've always regretted not getting there sooner for you."

"Don't. You saved my life."

Magnis said nothing. There was nothing to say.

As the two stepped back to look each other in the eye, Magnis replied, "Just say the word and you know I'll come running."

"You can count on it."

And with that, Magnis was gone.

And with him, one of the last moments of peace Sebastian and his team would remember before the great arrival.

CHAPTER 72

Mary Takes a Trip

"Where is she going?" Sam asked, his voice clear through the comms device.

"To see cousin Elizabeth," Isabella replied matter-of-factly.

"Why?" Sam pressed.

"She isn't saying. Her parents want her to stay," Isabella answered.

"She wants to tell Elizabeth the news," Sebastian said matter-of-factly.

"A new baby for an unmarried woman is a big deal," Isabella concurred.

"Isabella, Sam, and Petros, you will accompany her. I will stay behind."

"Sir?" Sam asked, his question implied.

"Mary is our focus. And she is likely becoming Rusalmeh's as well. I'll stay behind to monitor enemy activity ahead of your return."

"Check" came the simultaneous reply from the three warriors.

"And Pete?"

"Sir?"

"Only open comms between the three of you. No comms back here unless absolutely necessary," Sebastian commanded.

"Understood," Petros replied.

"No need to raise any further suspicions, especially in this part of Rusalmeh's region."

As they departed the next morning, Sebastian couldn't shake the feeling that nothing would be the same again. That Mary would never be the same again. And his team's mission to protect her after so many years was only now just beginning.

*****

Mary was in a hurry.

Her silent warrior team had no trouble keeping up, of course, but took note of her urgency in that moment. Following mission protocol, they worked together to stay hidden in full camouflage and overlapping one another as was their custom to ensure they were hidden from view as much as possible as they traveled. All was quiet as they had seen no evidence of enemy activity.

"Is she afraid?" Sam whispered, breaking the silence.

"No. Not afraid," Isabella answered.

"Then what?" Petros pressed.

"I'm not really sure," Isabella answered.

"Excellent. Thanks," Sam said sarcastically.

"What do you guys want from me?" Isabella replied, fawning frustration.

"Just thought you would be able to tell. Is all. You have a way with the human women," Sam replied, serious with a smile.

"What's that supposed to mean?" Isabella answered, slightly irritated.

"Come now, Bella," Petros chimed in, "Sam didn't mean anything by that."

"No?"

"No, no, it's just that you have a connection with Mary that none of us have," Petros said, saving it a bit.

Isabella said nothing. Comms were silent the rest of the afternoon.

Mary and her protectors arrived at her cousin's house in the hill country just as the sun was giving up its last rays before surrendering to the darkness.

As her cousin Elizabeth greeted her, all three of the warrior angels stood stunned at the scene that unfolded right before their eyes. And it was like nothing they ever expected. And just like that, their mission started to come into focus. The baby they had been sent to protect was herself soon to have a baby.

Soon, they would all realize just how special Mary's new arrival would turn out to be.

For eternity.

CHAPTER 73

Joseph Loses It

"Here he comes," Petros said, first spotting the man from his forward position.

"I see him. Moving fast," Sam said.

"Isabella, Joseph is en route, and he does not look happy."

"I'm here with Mary and Elizabeth. Assuming word got out?"

"Appears that way," Petros said as Joseph brushed by him.

Everyone in the hill country and those even remotely connected to both families were aware that Joseph and Mary were pledged to be married. Everyone was so thrilled as they had watched them grow up together in a lot of ways, and their planned union was destined to be a moment of excitement for everyone involved.

Except when Mary turned up pregnant. Before the big day. The scandal of such a thing was just the beginning. The embarrassment. The shame.

Joseph appeared to be feeling all of it as he approached Zechariah and Elizabeth's home. Elizabeth saw him approach the house and made her way outside to meet him.

"Where is she?" Joseph asked Elizabeth as the two met just outside the front door. Joseph's voice was low, hushed, and angry. Very angry.

"She's here, Joseph," Elizabeth said calmly.

"I want to see her," Joseph said, pushing past her.

Grabbing his arm, Elizabeth said, "I don' think that is a very good idea right now." Elizabeth was about six months pregnant at this time, and while she was a small woman of stature, she was strong and assertive.

Joseph knew this and also greatly respected Elizabeth. So he said softly, "I really need to talk with her."

"You're angry, Joseph, and she is emotional right now. It's not a good combination," Elizabeth reasoned.

Joseph said nothing, taking a step back as Elizabeth released her grip.

After a long moment, Elizabeth spoke, "Let's walk."

Joseph nodded.

As they began to walk, Elizabeth spoke first, "Do you remember the dream you had when you were a boy?"

"Dream?" Joseph asked.

"The one about the lion and the lamb. From it you carved an image of it as a gift for Mary."

Joseph remembered. He had made it for Mary when she was born, and he knew she still had it. Joseph simply said, "Yes."

"Do you know how much Mary treasures that gift from you?"

"She does?"

"You gave it to her when she was only two days old, but she carries it with her wherever she goes."

Joseph said nothing.

"She even brought it here, to visit me, Joseph. It brings her both comfort and joy."

"Why? It's just a toy."

"My son, it's much more than that to her. She treasures it more than you know."

"It won't do me much good in this situation," Joseph mumbled, more to himself than anyone.

"She's scared, Joseph. She needs you more than ever right now," Elizabeth said softly.

"But what am I supposed to say? Sorry you got pregnant? Who's the lucky guy?" Joseph snapped in a way he instantly regretted it.

It wasn't Elizabeth's fault. Elizabeth said nothing.

Joseph continued, “I’m sorry. I shouldn’t be taking out my anger on you.”

“Nor on Mary,” Elizabeth whispered with a smile. After another long silent moment, she continued, “Listen to what she has to say, Joseph. It really is an amazing story.”

“And you believe her?” Joseph asked genuinely. He was looking for something, anything, he could anchor to as his world seemed to be crashing in around him.

“I do,” Elizabeth responded. And then before Joseph could say anything, she smiled, looked directly into his eyes, and whispered, “And so does my baby.”

CHAPTER 74

Rusalmeh Misses the Point

"I don't get it!" he screamed to no one in particular, his eyes and neck bulging with rage.

None of the fallens present in his chamber said anything in response. There was nothing to say. The two fallens, Safir and Tarn, sent to covertly watch the farm house were now missing having missed multiple check-ins. They were officially gone.

Rusalmeh sat stoically on his perch at the far end of his chambers. He stirred with rage at the mere thought of his current position.

At that very moment, he was the commander of Lucifer's most powerfully equipped legions in the most strategically important region in the earthly realm, and he was powerless. Powerless to conduct recognizance without his spies vanishing from the face of the earth. Knowing in his gut angel warriors had been operating in his region for years but powerless to find them and annihilate them. Surrounded by feckless fallens who would rather flee than fight, he was powerless to mount any meaningful offensive, even if he could find the enemy intruders. And if that were not bad enough, Lucifer would be returning soon, looking for answers he didn't have, and he was powerless to get them. Powerless.

As all these thoughts raced through his wretched, warped mind, he slowly came to the realization that something much bigger than a few angel warriors operating undetected in his region was happening.

"Gabriel!" he screamed again to no one in particular. He continued screaming with uncontrollable rage, "Why would that fool disrespect me by showing up in my region twice without my permission!"

None of the demons dared remind him Gabriel needed permission only from the Creator himself. Gabriel moved throughout the earthly realm as he pleased. He needn't permission from anyone. Especially from a fallen. Rusalmeh, of course, knew this.

As he plotted his next move in the darkness of his chambers that night, he decided to change his strategy. No longer would he chase ghosts. He had lost too many demons to that strategy already. Instead, he decided to prepare his legions for war. A war he knew was imminent. A war to defend his region. A war to reestablish his dominance.

A war, deep down he knew, he could never win.

CHAPTER 75

Joseph Confronts Mary

"I guess I don't understand," Joseph said after a long quiet moment.

Mary had just recounted in all the details she remembered from her encounter with the archangel.

To Joseph, it sounded strange. Very strange. He loved Mary deeply, and when she and her family agreed to marriage, it was the happiest, most exciting day of his life. But that was then. That was before she, his soon-to-be wife, showed up pregnant and claiming it was of the Creator.

No one had to explain to Joseph how embarrassing such a thing could be to him and his family, not to mention the scorn, ridicule, and shame it would bring down on Mary. Which was what he didn't understand. If Mary was unfaithful to him in such a personal way, why was she talking of it with such excitement, such reverence?

"What do you mean?" Mary asked softly as she grabbed Joseph's rough, calloused hands.

"I mean, how could this be? And how can you be so happy about it?" Joseph whispered, his head low.

After a long moment of silence, Mary spoke softly, "It's of the Creator. And I need to be ready for whatever He has for me."

"Can you understand my confusion?" Joseph asked genuinely.

"Of course, I can. And I do. I am still trying to wrap my head around what is happening."

"So why did you come here?" Joseph asked.

"The angel told me Elizabeth was with child," Mary answered.

Joseph said nothing, shaking his head slightly in disbelief.

"Don't you see? There would have been no other way I could have known. She has been in seclusion, and Zechariah can't speak," Mary reasoned. She continued, "The angel told me."

"Did this angel have a name?" Joseph asked sarcastically, immediately regretting it. It was not what he intended, but his emotions were all over the place at the moment.

"I think you should leave now," Mary said firmly.

"I'm sorry. It's just that how do you expect me to believe—"

"Please leave," Mary said again.

And with that, Joseph left.

Both he and Mary went to sleep that night with worry on their minds and an ache in their hearts. Their respective worlds had just been completely upended and a once-certain future now the complete opposite.

Observing it all from the corner of the house was Isabella. As a warrior angel assigned to protect Mary, it was clear to her now that Mary's life was inextricably linked to Joseph's. She also knew she should speak up about what she just witnessed but wasn't sure if it was her place.

Her decision in that moment could prove to be the most important of her angelic existence.

CHAPTER 76

Isabella Calls It In

"Pete?" Isabella whispered as she approached Petros's lookout. "Pete!" Isabella whispered, this time rather loudly.

"What? I'm right here," Petros snapped, irritated. He was hidden, camouflage engaged, so well even Isabella couldn't see him. And she knew where he was hiding.

Enemy activity had been minimal since they had been surrounding Zechariah and Elizabeth's home for the last day and half. The sun was completely down now, and Petros had observed Joseph leaving the home of Zechariah. He wondered what had happened, knowing—as all Mary's warrior angels knew—the delicate nature of the current situation. An unmarried woman. Pregnant.

"Sorry. I can't see you," Isabella whispered.

"That's kind of the point, isn't it?" Petros responded, coming down from his irritation.

Isabella ignored the swipe and stayed focused, saying, "I need you to open comms to Sebastian."

"No can do. Strict orders from the boss."

"I know, Pete. But this is big."

"Big?" Petros asked, not moving from his position.

"Really big. Joseph doesn't believe Mary, and she kicked him out," Isabella answered.

"Kicked him out?" Petros asked.

"Well, I'm not entirely familiar with human interactions like these, but I think it qualifies."

"So what's the big deal?" Petros asked, not getting it.

"Well, I don't know exactly. But I get the sense that Joseph is a really important part of the Creator's plans here. You know Joseph has been around since two days after Mary was born."

Petros was quiet for a bit and then responded, "That's true. And I've never known the Creator to work in coincidences."

"Exactly. And without Joseph around, Mary will be alone with her baby."

"So what do you suggest?"

"That's just it. I don't know. It's why I think Sebastian should know."

"Okay. I'll do it, but it's going against a direct order," Petros warned.

"I get it. I'll take the heat," Isabella responded.

As her comms device came to life, she had a feeling the mission would soon change in ways she and her teammates could never imagine.

How right she was.

CHAPTER 77

Isabella Updates Sebastian

"I thought I was clear no comms," Sebastian said before Isabella could speak.

"Not me, sir," Sam said without missing a bit.

Frustrated at her inability to get a word out without being interrupted, she finally spoke, "It's Joseph. He's not taking it very well."

Sebastian said nothing.

She continued, "He and Mary spoke for a while, and she asked him to leave."

"Yeah, he looked angry for sure," Sam chimed in, apparently able to also see Joseph from his vantage point.

"Well, he is angry, and now so is Mary," Isabella added.

"I see," Sebastian said, seeming to wait for Isabella to make her point.

"It just feels like if we can do something, we should. I'm not sure Joseph is going to come back," Isabella concluded.

After a long pause, Sebastian said, "I'll see what I can do."

And with that, Petros shut the comms down to avoid any unwanted listeners. There had been none.

But with a visit from Gabriel, a new baby on the way, and a relationship breaking apart, Mary's team of angel warriors knew their mission would never be the same.

CHAPTER 78

Gabriel Asks for Sebastian's Help

"Go ahead" came the voice from the heavenly realm.

"Thanks for the heads-up on your visit," Sebastian said, a slight smile showing through.

"It was a big one. That's for sure," Gabriel said, returning the smile.

The friendship between the two warriors spanned millennia, and they were always glad to connect during times like these.

"I could use your help."

"What did Sam do this time?"

"Nothing actually. It's Mary."

"Oh?"

"Well, Joseph really. He is really upset, and the team is reporting she's very upset now as well."

"That happens, doesn't it?"

"It does. But I don't think Isabella would have broken comms protocol to report a simple disagreement."

"She thinks it's bigger than that?"

"She does. Much bigger."

"I see. What do you think we should do?"

After a long moment, Sebastian answered, "I think Joseph needs some reassurances."

"Reassurances?"

"Isabella says he's talking of divorcing her. He doesn't believe her. He believes she has been unfaithful," Sebastian recalled.

Now it was Gabriel's turn to be quiet, finally saying, "I think you should talk to him."

"Me?" Sebastian asked, stunned.

"Yes, you, Seb. You know him well. You have seen him grow up, and he's very close to the one you have been sent to protect."

"How?"

"Visit him tonight in his sleep. Let him know all this is from the Creator and to stay with Mary. Encourage him to stay strong and follow through."

Sebastian said nothing.

"He'll listen to you, Sebastian. Even though he has never seen you, he will listen."

"Okay. I will."

"And, Seb," Gabriel said, "war is coming. Make sure your team is ready." And with that, Gabriel ended the call.

That night, Sebastian visited Joseph in his sleep and spoke softly yet confidently to him. He trusted the plan and was confident Joseph would as well.

As he shared his message of hope with young Joseph, he wondered what the future held and of the war of which Gabriel had spoken. Although he knew not the time or place, one thing was for sure. Gabriel had spoken.

War was coming.

CHAPTER 79

Lucifer Wants Answers

"I want to see this place," Lucifer said flatly. He was now on his second visit to see Rusalmeh, each bookmarked by a trip from Gabriel. The archangel. In Rusalmeh's region.

"Of course, sire," Rusalmeh quickly replied.

Lucifer stared at his slave with contempt for a long while. And then he asked, "Aren't you going to ask me why?"

"No, sire, it's not my place to ask—" Rusalmeh began to reply.

"Shut up!" Lucifer screamed. He continued screaming, "I'll tell you why! Because you and your useless slaves have allowed angel activity in your region for who knows how long!"

Rusalmeh said nothing.

Lucifer continued, his screaming somehow growing louder, "And then Gabriel shows up, and you are so unprepared you can offer me no actionable intelligence!"

Lucifer's grip on reality was strong despite his otherworldly ranting. It's what made him so destructive as a spiritual being. His awareness of his inferiority compared to the Creator, in a way, fueled his hatred of the Creator's most prized creation. His firm grip on the reality that he would ultimately lose the war for humanity didn't keep him from temporarily losing his mind when he felt betrayed or otherwise outwitted. This was one of those times. And Rusalmeh was in his path.

Sheepishly, Rusalmeh spoke, "We believe Gabriel visited a farm outside of Nazareth. We had two spies there, and they are missing."

Lucifer didn't respond at first. He just looked at Rusalmeh sideways from where he sat and stared him down. "Which is why I want to go their myself, you fool." Lucifer seethed.

Rusalmeh could only nod in agreement. There was nothing to say.

As darkness fell, Lucifer and Rusalmeh and a small horde of fallens headed for Mary's home.

They wouldn't get far.

CHAPTER 80

Sebastian Confronts Lucifer

"I see them, sir," Sam responded from his hidden position.

It had been a long stretch of eerie quiet since the team had returned with Mary from her visit to the hill country. The baby growing inside of her invoked scandal to be sure, but once her parents and Joseph came to terms with her situation, the baby brought everyone close together. Joseph visited as often as he could, and Isabella noticed how caring and loving he was once Sebastian gave him the special dream-induced encouragement not so long ago.

Mary's angelic warriors had taken up their hidden positions around the clock since Gabriel's visits and Mary's announcement as they anticipated a seismic shift soon to come. Always on high alert, they surrounded the perimeter of Mary's childhood home and had moved back into full-mission mode. Stand hidden. Keep Mary and her baby safe at all costs.

Sebastian saw them first, flying against the last light of the sun hanging on like a receded wave clings to the sand. He asked the team if they saw them too.

Sam confirmed.

"It looks like we've been found," Petros chimed in.

"The mission hasn't changed. Stay hidden until I say so," Sebastian directed. He continued, "Isabella, confirm you have eyes on Mary."

"Confirmed. She is in the house. Her parents are here too," Isabella quickly responded. She continued, "If we do have to fight tonight, let me be the first to send a message."

Sebastian said nothing. He expected it from Isabella. She was created for war, so he didn't blame her eagerness. He would soon learn to embrace it.

As the fallens drew closer, it was clear to Sebastian they were headed for Mary and her home. What he didn't know was how much they knew. His role as commander on this mission was to make split-second calculations and act on them. He soon realized the decisions he made over the next few seconds could easily determine the success of this mission. And that was before he realized just who was leading this particular convoy.

Sam spotted him at the same time. Sebastian's comms device cracked to life with Sam's voice saying, "Sir, is that who I think it is?"

The clouds that night were thick and ominous, and they covered the moon quite completely, leaving the landscape in near-total darkness by the time the convoy of demons arrived close enough to make out who was who.

One particular frame cut against the blackness in a different way than the others. It's like his presence consumed the darkness around him in a way that made him stand out even in near-total darkness. Darker than dark. Dark evil.

The angel team had their night vision fully engaged as they always did as they kept watch, so the figures that approached attracted no light, which told them all they needed to know about this particular visit.

But it was the darkness in the center of the scene that gave them all pause. Only one being could consume such darkness, such gloom, such void. Only one. Lucifer himself.

Sebastian had a decision to make. If they stayed hidden, allowing Lucifer and his goons to descend on Mary's house, they would be exposing Mary and her family to the deepest evil the human world had ever known. However, should they break cover and confront the evil one, surely the mission would change forever and they could easily be overrun.

Sebastian had a decision to make, and he needed to make it quickly. Without hesitation, he commanded his team, "Hold your positions. Isabella, Mary never leaves your sight. Understood?"

"Yes," Isabella responded.

"And protect her with your life if you have to."

This time, Isabella wasn't so quick to respond. But after a moment, she said quietly, "I understand."

Everyone knew Lucifer completely changed the game. His presence alone demanded an entire regiment of angelic warriors to stop his advance. It was clear to everyone in that moment, except for Isabella who could not see the events unfolding, that Lucifer had brought friends. This was about to get wildly out of hand.

"Sir, what are you doing?" Sam asked hastily as his words were finally catching up to what his mind was conceiving.

"I'm doing what leaders do."

"And what is that exactly?" Petros asked bit angrily as he realized the magnitude of what Sebastian was about to do.

"I'm going to make sure our visitors realize the error of their ways," Sebastian said, smiling, "and send them on their way."

"I like to keep things lighthearted, sir, but I'm not entirely sure this is a time for smiles," Sam said, his voice serious.

"Relax, everyone. Not even Lucifer wants an unnecessary fight with the Creator right now."

No one responded.

Sebastian continued, "And we represent the Creator, and He promised to always be with us."

No one said anything. There was nothing to say. The gravity of the moment hung in the air like the densest of fog.

"Watch my back." Those were the last words before he left the secrecy of his lookout and raced headlong into what could be the final battle of his existence.

As the leader of the mission, he knew no other way at this point. The prince of the entire earthly realm was advancing within striking distance of the one human he and his team had been sent to secretly and covertly protect. He had to intervene. There was no other way.

He timed his arrival at the precise moment Lucifer and his horde landed from their low flight. He made sure to arrive, sword drawn, with the kind of force that got everyone's attention. It worked. Everyone in Lucifer's horde, except the deceiver himself, took a step back and drew their swords. Lucifer didn't flinch. Sebastian took note of this. It was as if he had been expecting it.

"Sebastian!" Lucifer cheered as if they were long-lost friends.

Sebastian said nothing. Lucifer grinned deeply with such evil and malice Sebastian had to remind himself to stay calm and focused.

"You see, Rusalmeh, all you have to do is show up and our enemies reveal themselves," Lucifer said, his greasy head and disfigured face remaining focused like a laser locked into Sebastian's eyes as he spoke to his slave who had taken a defensive position behind the head demon.

Rusalmeh said nothing. He knew it was an insult he couldn't avoid and wholly deserved.

"I haven't seen you in millennia!" Lucifer said, his voice inauthentically cheery and sickeningly boastful.

Sebastian said nothing as he continued to assess the situation for his next right move.

"It's great to see you!" the great deceiver said, not breaking character.

Sebastian marveled both at the wretched being he had become separated so long from the Creator and how deceptive he could actually be. In that moment, Sebastian was reminded how so many in the earthly realm could be deceived by his charm. It was incredible.

The last time Sebastian had seen Lucifer was so long ago the memory had begun to fade. Until he saw the evil grin. Then it all came rushing back. The announcement. The rebellion. The expulsion. Sebastian was part of Lucifer's choir in the heavenly realm. Endless worshipping. Incredible memories of love, joy, and euphoria came crashing in. Until the moment he realized he had a choice to make. Rusalmeh chose darkness. Sebastian chose light. And now so many millennia later in the middle of a dark planet, the moment of truth had arrived.

Sebastian finally and simply spoke with authority, "You are not welcome here."

"Oh, come now, Seb. You can't mean that," Lucifer said with a wide evil grin.

"Indeed, I do."

It was at that moment that Lucifer's demeanor changed completely as he dropped the facade and allowed his pure evil to emerge as he said in a guttural, growling voice, "I am welcome everywhere here!" He continued, "Don't you remember this whole realm is mine? I own it all."

Sebastian said nothing.

"In fact, I should be saying the same to you, shouldn't I? What makes you think *you* are welcome here?" Lucifer seethed.

Sebastian stood his ground, sword drawn. Steady.

"I suppose you think you are better than me, and perhaps you are," Lucifer reasoned. "But here you are—alone, in my realm, surrounded by my warriors."

Sebastian said nothing.

"Which makes you worse than me in this particular moment, wouldn't you say?"

"There is nothing for you to see here," Sebastian replied calmly.

"Perhaps only I will make that determination, my friend," Lucifer said, smiling greedily.

"Well, this is as far as you go tonight," Sebastian said firmly.

"Oh, Seb, no need to be so stern. Especially since it's just you."

"I can be quite persuasive if you recall," Sebastian shot back.

"Indeed. I do recall. Quite persuasive indeed, but not *that* persuasive. I've got a lot of firepower behind me, and you're only one—"

Sebastian stopped Lucifer right there, interjecting, "How do you know it's just me?"

Lucifer said nothing.

"You have no idea who is with me tonight, do you?"

Silence.

Sebastian continued, "I've been operating in Rusalmeh's region undetected for longer than you can imagine."

Rusalmeh, feeling the pressure Sebastian wanted him to feel, began to speak, "I've known—"

"Shut up!" Lucifer shouted as he stared directly at Sebastian.

Rusalmeh said nothing more.

It was clear now to Sebastian that Lucifer was on a fact-finding mission on this night and wanted to control the conversation completely. Thus, the reason for shutting down Rusalmeh so quickly. He didn't want anyone else interjecting. He had a plan, and he wanted no deviations.

As Lucifer stared silently and angrily at the massive angelic warrior that stood in front of him, Sebastian knew the demon was calculating his risk in that moment. Reality was, Sebastian surmised, Lucifer really didn't have anything more than bits and pieces of evidence.

Would he be willing to risk a dangerous and potentially costly fight over what could be nothing? Was Sebastian alone? Were there more? These were questions Sebastian assumed Lucifer was asking himself as they both were locked in an epic stare down.

After a long moment, Lucifer smiled, saying, "I don't believe you."

"Believe what you want to believe," Sebastian confidently replied. "But this is as far as you go tonight. There is nothing here for you, and I think you know that."

Lucifer said nothing.

"In fact, I think you are grasping. Your lackey there has been bumbling around for years, sending amateurs and posers to investigate ghosts," Sebastian continued, on a bit of a roll. "And now with nothing to go on but a hunch, here you are, the prince of darkness, hoping you find something."

As his anger boiled over, Lucifer snapped, "I found you, didn't I? Perhaps I'm closer than you intended. Perhaps, dear Sebastian, I found the one thing you didn't intend for me to find."

Lucifer was fishing for any reaction, any clue from Sebastian. The great angelic warrior gave him nothing. Lucifer decided in that moment he had gotten what he had come for. There was, in fact, at least one angelic warrior operating covertly in the earthly realm. His problem was one of number and unknowns.

If Sebastian was alone on some sort of advanced recognizance mission, then perhaps he could send a message to the Creator by annihilating him. Lucifer remembered Rusalmeh reporting his men saw who he believed to be Sam. And Isabella.

It wouldn't be easy, and Sebastian would no doubt inflict mass casualties on the horde he had with them. But what would it accomplish? Plus, if Sam and Isabella were also in the realm, his odds of a battle victory would diminish exponentially.

Lucifer still knew the most important fact he needed remained elusive. And until he knew *why* such a strategic warrior like Sebastian was on the outskirts of Nazareth near a family farm, he decided to stand down.

After a long moment of this contemplation and never breaking his stare with Sebastian, Lucifer simply said, "Let's go." As he and his horde turned to take flight, Lucifer looked back, smiled, and said, "Can't wait to see you again very soon."

Sebastian said nothing. There was nothing to say.

The mission was officially over, and the next phase was soon to begin. A phase that would include all-out war.

Lucifer would be sure to see to that.

CHAPTER 81

A Wedding

It was a small wedding. Really small. Just Mary's parents and her cousin Elizabeth with her new baby and her husband Zechariah along with Joseph's parents and his siblings and their spouses and children. Sebastian counted nineteen in attendance for the ceremony. Most stayed behind for a subdued celebration in which Joseph paid the agreed upon bride price to Mary's father. This Hebrew marriage custom finalized the marriage between Mary and Joseph.

The whole day was hard on Mary. Her warrior team could tell it weighed on her. She knew the Creator's plan for her, but she had stopped trying to convince others. She told Joseph she was at peace with it.

Isabella overheard Mary tell Joseph on several occasions, "They are going to believe what they are going to believe. I can't change it."

Joseph would agree, but it was clearly hard on him as well. Everyone talked. He knew that. His visit from Sebastian in a dream helped him come to terms with it. But he knew, short of a visit from an angel, most wouldn't get it. So he, too, took Mary's approach and let it go.

The warrior team was long past skeptical of Joseph's intentions. They had come to love and trust Joseph just as his love for Mary had started long ago. He would do what was necessary in the earthly realm to protect Mary. Every one of her warrior angels could see that.

The wedding itself went off without a hitch.

Fallen activity in the area had picked up as Lucifer was no doubt pressing hard on Rusalmeh for answers. Rusalmeh, in turn, was putting pressure on his horde for answers.

Despite the increased activity, Sebastian and team were able to stay hidden while protecting Mary. And while fallens were watching the comings and goings at Mary's family farm, there was nothing for them to see.

Sebastian and his warrior team were just better than they were. Superior in every way. So every time a fallen or group of fallens would fly by to look for clues, the angel warrior team saw them coming well before they came close. They weren't going to find anything, and if they decided to harass Mary in any way, they would pay for it with their own annihilation. And it was almost as if they instinctively knew that.

Even though activity picked up after the visit from Lucifer, no one dared get close. The mere mention of Sebastian in the earthly realm was enough to scare most fallens away from doing anything courageous. Add to that the fact that no one could see him, and it only added to the fear. A stealth warrior angel in the earthly realm. Concealed. Dangerous. Unpredictable. Deadly.

Little did they know that Sebastian was supported by some of the most elite warriors the Creator ever created. Had that little secret been known, it's likely no fallens would have gotten even as close as they did.

As night fell on the day of Mary's small wedding, her warriors began to reminisce. Mary had been the warrior team's sole focus for so long in the earthly realm they were surprised at the moments in which they found themselves missing their place in the heavenly realm.

This night was one of those moments. Angels were made to worship. Designed to be in the Creator's presence. Created for His glory and purpose. The Creator's presence was the most powerful force in the universe, and to be without for so long was beginning to take its toll.

It's why the fallens that the angels would encounter in the earthly realm always seemed to shock them. The disfigurement. The distortion. The decay. Millennia away from the presence of the Creator did terrible things to a fallen angel.

And even though they knew the Creator was sustaining them on their seemingly endless mission, they still longed for His presence. They would talk about it often. It helped to talk about it. Especially now that the mission had expanded in ways none of them could have expected. A new baby soon to arrive. A husband.

But Gabriel was still silent. Sebastian had thought of checking in but thought better of it. He knew Gabriel was in full command and would communicate mission changes when the exact time was right. More importantly, they all trusted the Creator, and they knew He would never leave them or forsake them.

So as they watched from their hidden, secure, and battle-ready positions the last few guests depart from the wedding celebration, they couldn't help but wonder what was next.

No one said a word that night. They just watched. And waited. And prayed.

CHAPTER 82

Terrible Timing

"Any one trailing?" Sam asked.

"Negative. Just him," Sebastian replied. Sebastian's most forward and elevated position gave him the cleanest look at those on the road leading past Mary's family home as they left the town of Nazareth.

The warrior team took no chances in these tense days since Lucifer's visit. Lucifer was both a master manipulator and planner, but he was also patient. They knew he wouldn't let too much time pass without responding to a warrior angel concealed in the earthly realm. The only question was whether their mission would change before that response came.

As they watched Joseph return to Mary's family home after only two days away, they watched him closely for any enemy activity that might attempt to follow him. There was none.

"Looks like he's in a hurry," Petros mentioned.

"Indeed, he does," Sam responded.

"Isabella, where is he coming from?" Sebastian asked, changing the subject.

Isabella was the steady source of family information as she spent most of her time in or around Mary's home. It was a great place to stay hidden from any fallens who might be passing by, and it allowed at least one of the warriors to be close at all times.

Sebastian decided this was best, especially since one of Isabella's greatest missions was one of comfort to Queen Esther. Isabella gave the same kind of comfort to Mary and her family, which turned out to be perfect timing since Gabriel had arrived with the news for Mary. Mary trusted the Creator. And Isabella's presence, although invisible to Mary, brought her comfort during these very uncertain and distressing times.

Isabella answered Sebastian's question, "He went into Nazareth, to his family home. Said he has some family business he needed to attend to."

No one spoke for a bit.

Then Petros said, "Well, keep us posted. It looks like he's got some news."

It was long after his arrival that Isabella's voice came through the comms device with an update. "Anyone ever been to Bethlehem?"

CHAPTER 83

The Journey to Change the World

"That's it?" Sam asked.

"That's it," Sebastian responded.

The mood was tense. Sebastian had just talked with Gabriel about the sudden trip to Bethlehem. Gabriel had listened, pondered Sebastian's request to remove the need to stay hidden as part of their mission, and declined it. He explained the importance of the element of surprise, especially at this point in the mission. He also declined his field commander's request for additional warrior resources to be sent.

"You have all the resources you need, Seb. Trust me," Gabriel told Sebastian with a smile.

Sebastian wasn't smiling. As he ended the communication with the heavenly realm, his mind raced with all the preparations and dangers that a trip like this would cause. He wasn't alone.

"I just don't see how we are going to be able to keep them all safe," Petros said what they all were thinking.

"Well, we'll have to think of something because they are leaving in the morning," Isabella said, urgency in her voice.

As the team gathered together outside Mary's childhood home in the darkness to plan how best to protect Mary and stay hidden, they all knew the mission would soon end.

No one knew how, of course, but they just knew.

And they would never be the same.

CHAPTER 84

A New Team Arrives

"Prepare to go silent upon entry. No mistakes," the commander whispered into his comms device.

The three members of his team all affirmed his instructions with a simultaneous "Check" from each of them.

They had just left the heavenly realm and were preparing to enter the most amazing mission of their existence. And they couldn't be more excited. They had followed Sebastian and his team from the heavenly realm for so long. So when Gabriel called them up for this mission, they could hardly contain themselves. Unlike Sebastian and his team, they knew exactly who they were protecting. The Creator Himself in human form. The Creator's plan for human redemption was coming to life in this very moment, and they were going to get a front seat.

The commander and his team were handpicked by the Creator just as He did with Sebastian and his team. The Creator's decisions for every mission and every warrior were ever so perfect. He knew all things across all time and space, so that helped. Things were happening fast now.

So as Gabriel was sending the angelic warrior team off to protect the Creator in human form as a vulnerable newborn human baby, he reminded them to approach Sebastian and his team with caution.

"Why?" the commander asked.

"Because they don't know you are coming."

"Oh."

Gabriel explained, "They need to stay hidden up until the very last moment, and I didn't want to risk a communication being intercepted at this point in the mission."

"So Sebastian and his team do not know we are going to be there?"

"That's right."

No one spoke for a long moment.

Then Gabriel broke the silence, saying, "Isabella is going to be itching for a fight, so just be careful not to surprise her too much."

Gabriel was smiling when he said it and was obviously joking, but the commander knew deep down there was some truth to it. Isabella was the one of the most powerful warriors the Creator had ever created, and everyone in both realms knew it.

"Okay. Here we go. As discussed, as soon as we land, fan out, stay hidden, and be ready to fight," the commander said confidently.

No one spoke. There was nothing to say.

He continued as they all flew silently into the earthly realm to ensure the safety of the greatest gift the Creator had ever given, "Be at your best as we go silent in three, two, and one…"

CHAPTER 85

Arrival in Bethlehem

Full camouflage was in place. Night vision was in place. A full array of weapons at the ready. As the warrior team arrived in the earthly realm, no mistakes were made, and they were completely undetected by the enemy.

The night was dark. Darker than any of the team could remember. They all had been on countless missions in the earthly realm, but none of them could recall such darkness. So very dark.

After they landed in a small grove of trees overlooking the small town of Bethlehem, they all fanned out as planned and waited. They all stood in silence, hiding while looking intently for fallens who they might have alerted.

There was none. They were alone. That was good.

None of them expected them to be alone for much longer. The Creator of the universe was soon to arrive—as a baby, in the earthly realm, entirely exposed to hordes of enemy fallens. And it was going to be up to His small team of warrior angels to keep Him safe until He could defend Himself.

The team's communications specialist activated their comms.

As soon as he did, the team lead spoke first, "I need an all clear from each of you."

"Clear."

"Clear."

"Clear."

"Clear for me as well," the team lead said. "Well done, everyone. Doesn't look like we'll need Magnis tonight."

No one spoke. There was nothing to say.

They had made it safely into the earthly realm. Behind enemy lines. With the biggest anticipated fight they likely had ever experienced ahead of them, each member of the team stayed focused. Ready.

"We'll stay here tonight and chart enemy activity over the next few hours."

"When do we expect Sebastian and team?" a team member asked.

"Sometime tomorrow, we believe," the team leader replied.

CHAPTER 86

A Perilous Journey

The journey from Nazareth to Bethlehem created all kinds of challenges for Mary's invisible warriors.

Of course, Mary had challenges of her own. Her baby was soon to arrive, and although Joseph was doing what he could to make her comfortable, the journey was taking its toll.

The warrior team was spread out. Isabella and Sam in the front. Sebastian and Petros behind. Staying hidden as they traveled created constant near misses, but the team had become experts in staying hidden. Their full camouflage, which reflected the world around them, helped. But a fallen, even paying half attention, would easily notice their movement without the cover that trees, rocks, and structures could offer.

The speed at which angel warriors could move throughout the earthly realm allowed them to easily protect Mary. It was common for them to fall behind during the journey and move ahead one by one based on the landscape and their ability to stay as hidden as possible along the way.

Sebastian and the team were under no illusion; they all knew they were being followed at this point. Lucifer made sure of that after Sebastian made his stand in front of the dark prince.

They didn't worry about the scouts too much. Staying hidden kept conflict to a minimum. Fallens didn't like to be shown up in the earthly realm by warrior angels. That, plus how outmatched they would be should an angelic warrior turn on them, kept the fallen scouts at a distance.

As they made the journey, Mary's warriors were all thinking the same thing. How would this all end?

CHAPTER 87

Confused

As the sun rose over Bethlehem, the newly arrived warrior team prepared for every possible scenario.

They were going to stay hidden, but nothing was a guarantee. They all had reviewed the situation reports that had come out of the earthly realm from Sebastian and his team. They all were under no illusions their plans to stay hidden until the VIP arrived would stay in place. The earthly realm was and always had been the essence of unpredictability.

"How will we know?" one of them asked as their comms devices simultaneously crackled to life.

"We'll know," their leader said with an assurance they all knew made him the perfect leader for this mission.

"There sure isn't much fallen activity in this town," one of them chimed in.

"Just how we like it," another replied.

"At least for now," another said, a wry smile spreading across his face.

The squad of four angelic warriors had prepared for the daylight as they had trained. They were tucked away deep inside a tree grove atop a small rock bluff that overlooked the main entry into Bethlehem. And they waited.

The town was full of human activity as Hebrews came from all over the region, pouring into small towns like Bethlehem.

"Word is Seb and his team have Rusalmeh completely flustered," the team leader spoke, breaking a long silence.

"Is that why we haven't seen a fallen yet?"

"Could be. Chances are Rusalmeh has them spread thin, trying to cover all their bases," the team leader answered.

"Well, they're about to miss the biggest thing that's ever happened in the earthly realm since—"

"Since ever."

"That's right. Since ever," the team leader said. His voice strong. Clear.

As they continued to wait for Mary and Joseph to arrive, they made small talk here and there. But for the most part, they stood in silence, contemplating what lay ahead.

They were not worried, of course. Angels wouldn't worry. They would plan. They would prepare. They would fight. They would achieve.

The last thing they would do was worry.

CHAPTER 88

Rusalmeh Finally Puts It Altogether

"Why can't any of you, fools, tell me anything?" Rusalmeh said through clenched, slimy teeth.

No one answered. They knew the first one to speak would lose, so they said nothing.

Rusalmeh had summoned legion leaders to make sure he was getting the latest updates from the fallens in the field. The pressure Lucifer was putting on him was excruciating. And he couldn't catch a break.

He decided to take a different strategy. His wretched mind replayed the interaction between Lucifer and Sebastian, and he was convinced it was a decoy. So he decided to deploy every available fallen to cover every possible coming and going of humans in his vast region. And he was applying to his legion leaders the same pressure Lucifer was putting on him. He knew deep down something big was happening, and his inability to figure it out was driving him mad.

"If you don't get me answers on what the enemy is up to, we'll all be screwed. And if I go down, you all do."

"There may be something," one of his leaders said, his head low.

Rusalmeh didn't speak for a moment.

The silence prompted the fallen to hastily continue, "One of our slaves reported something unusual earlier today outside of Bethlehem."

"What's in Bethlehem?" Rusalmeh seethed, practically spitting the words from his mouth.

"He claims to have seen something unusual."

"Unusual?"

"Like the sky was moving."

Rusalmeh said nothing as he contemplated what he had just heard.

The demon spoke again, "The two fallens in the area investigated but found nothing."

No one made eye contact with their leader. They knew their very existence hung in the balance.

After a long moment of excruciating silence, Rusalmeh spoke, his voice raging in a low whisper, "Send every available slave to Bethlehem and prepare them to die."

CHAPTER 89

A Long Mission Comes to an End

They all saw them at once. None of them was quite sure how they knew. They just knew. It was like a symphony. A beautiful picture of perfect teamwork and skill.

The number of humans arriving and moving about in the little town had grown tenfold throughout the day, and the team leader began to wonder if they would miss them. One clue that helped was their warrior protectors. Fallens might have a hard time spotting an angel warrior in full camouflage, but it took one to know one, and their movements were something to behold.

As young Mary and Joseph arrived in what could only be described as absolute obscurity, they were surrounded on all sides by one of the Creator's most efficient and deadly warrior teams ever assembled.

"Do you see them?" one of the soon-to-be warrior protectors asked the others.

"Amazing."

"How do they move in such incredible sequence?" another asked.

"A lot of practice," the team leader replied, a smile of satisfaction spreading across his face.

"Who are they protecting?"

"Just watch and see."

Isabella, Sam, Petros, and Sebastian were working together in ways that had become second nature to them. They didn't realize it until long after that their mission had drawn to a close just how incredible their ability to work in complete silence, nearly completely hidden without the benefit of an open communications channel. Few missions like theirs had never been attempted before in the earthly realm and certainly none that had ever lasted so long.

They had been in the earthly realm so long, under cover, hidden. And none of them was quite sure they were ever to leave again. But none of them thought about it much anymore. Their mission was simple, and until it changed, they would serve the Creator in whatever way He wanted. Plus, their love for Mary was incredibly strong. They had known her since the day she was born, and they all agreed they would do anything to protect her. Anything.

As Mary and Joseph entered the town that represented the final destination of their journey, Sebastian remembered his time here. The young boy who had become a king. The town hadn't changed much since then, even though a thousand human years had passed. Sebastian thought it had the same feel. The same smells. The same weight of history. His thoughts preoccupied him as they moved until they didn't.

His voice was steady as he broke his own no-comms directive and spoke, "I think we have company."

CHAPTER 90

The Warriors Unite

"Sir?" Isabella asked.

"I see them too," Sam said calmly.

"What am I missing here?" Petros chimed in, not fully understanding the current situation.

"What else do you see, Sam?" Sebastian asked, ignoring Petros's question altogether.

"Just two. You?"

"Two as well."

No one spoke for a long moment.

"Isabella and Petros, follow Mary and Joseph," Sebastian commanded.

"Sir?"

"Don't worry, Bella. We'll call you if we need you," Sam chimed in.

"Sam and I will check out our reluctant admirers," Sebastian said, this time ignoring Sam's commentary. There was no time for it. Sebastian continued, "Besides, if we see them, then they have seen us. So there's no need for a surprise element here."

"Keep comms open, sir?" Petros asked as he and Isabella formed a front-to-back perimeter around Mary and her husband.

"Yes," Sebastian replied.

As Sebastian and Sam approached the tree grove to make contact with their unknown visitors, they were ready for almost anything. At least they thought they were.

"Sir, could they be one of us?" Sam asked in a whisper.

"I suppose anything is possible," Sebastian answered. He continued, "You'd think if they were hostile, we would have seen them make a move by now."

"Agreed."

"But what would angel warriors be doing here?" Sam asked after a moment of silence.

At that very moment, they reached the edge of the tree grove, and they came face-to-face with what both would later recall as the most exciting and equally terrifying moment of any mission in the earthly realm.

With barely a whisper, Sebastian spoke a name he never expected to utter while on mission in the earthly realm. And as he said it, a thousand questions rushed his mind like rolling thunder.

"Michael."

CHAPTER 91

Michael

"Hey there, Seb," the team leader said. His voice strong, energetic. "And Sam. How are you guys?"

Sebastian and Sam said nothing. They didn't know quite what to say. The revelation that Michael the Archangel was in the earthly realm in that moment shocked them both.

In the silence of that moment, the team leader and his team of three angelic warriors all stood together, revealing their clandestine positions all at once. Sebastian and Sam stared in disbelief.

Michael spoke, "You know this crew. Nathanael on comms, Leo on weapons, and Ariel running logistics and strategy."

They all knew one another, of course. The angel warrior bond was strong. But because it had been so long since Sebastian's team had seen other angelic warriors in the earthly realm and their mission had carried on behind enemy lines for so long, their emotions were mixed, to say the least. They were happy, shocked, uncertain, confused, and a little scared all at once. There they were, standing on the edge of a tree grove outside the entrance of what seemed to be the edge of nowhere, staring into the deep emerald eyes of one of the most powerful angels in the heavenly realm.

Sam spoke first as a broad smile spread across his face, "Wait till old Lucifer hears that Michael has paid a visit to his earthly realm."

It was not a time for jokes, of course, but Sam couldn't help himself, even in the presence of greatness. He began to think invoking the name of Lucifer in a moment as tense as this might have not been the smartest thing to do until he began to see a smile spread quickly across Michael's face. The smile turned quickly into a genuine laugh. The laugh of angels. If only humans could hear. As Michael's laughter contagiously spread to the others, it wasn't long until they all were laughing, smiling, hugging, and greeting one another.

"What is happening right now?" Isabella asked, hearing all the commotion through her comms device.

"Nathanael, can you and Petros sync your frequencies so we can all communicate?" Sebastian requested, tossing his comms device to Michael's comm lead.

Nathanael looked for confirmation from Michael before proceeding. His team leader nodded the affirmative. "You got it, Seb," Nathanael replied, quickly taking Sebastian's device, establishing the frequency, and syncing all of them together.

When Nathanael gave Michael the nod indicating a clean, secure connection, Michael spoke. "Isabella, Petros, this is Michael. How's it going?"

No one spoke for a long moment.

Then Isabella spoke up a bit sheepishly as she asked, "Michael, sir, did we mess up?"

"I thought you would be happier to see me, Isabella?" Michael replied, repressing a smile.

"Oh, I am, I am. Honored for you to be here. It's just—"

"It's cool, Bella. You and the team have done an amazing job. We are here for a transfer of sorts."

"Transfer?" Petros asked.

"Yes. You see, Mary has a gift for all of humankind for all of time that we believe is arriving tonight," Michael said.

"And your mission will transfer to ours," Ariel said, speaking for the first time.

"That's right. A transfer," Michael concurred.

"I don't understand. We've been waiting for Gabriel to give us our next directive."

"This is it."

"This is what?" Sam asked.

"Your next directive," Michael spoke as he motioned for everyone to take a knee and resume a clandestine position. "Word is Lucifer is taking a gamble that this little town of Bethlehem will be ground zero to thwart the Creator's ultimate plan."

"Here?" Sebastian asked, still confused.

"We think so," Nathanael replied, motioning over his shoulder to his communications equipment he was using to monitor enemy communications.

"If it's one thing Lucifer has always had, it's good intuition," Leo said, shaking his head.

"So we'll need you and your team to be ready for battle tonight. Are you game?" Michael asked with a confident smile.

Isabella chimed in without hesitation, her strong voice crackling in everyone's comms device, "We'd thought you'd never ask."

CHAPTER 92

Lucifer Makes His Move

The others noticed the change in Rusalmeh's demeanor, his mood, and even his voice whenever Lucifer was around. He was different. Lesser. Especially now.

There he was, in his own chambers—the place he had ruled with iron hands and excruciating ridicule—now laid low by the presence of his master tormentor.

All fallens were in constant torment. No one spoke of it, of course. They all just lived with it. The consequence of choosing pride instead of humility. Envy instead of love.

Lucifer always made the torment worse. He was the most tormented of them all, and he used his torment as weapon. Not just against those created in the Creator's image but against the evil spirits slavishly following him now for millennia.

As Lucifer paced the ground in Rusalmeh's chambers, the mood was unusually dark and oppressive.

It was now undeniable that a team of at least two, possibly more, warrior angels had been operating in Rusalmeh's region undetected for a significant amount of time. And it was only a matter of time before he and every fallen in his region knew a price was to be paid.

Surprisingly, Lucifer ignored the obvious malfeasance for the moment and appeared to be solely focused on making up for lost time. "Bethlehem." The chief fallen seethed. A statement. Not a question. He continued, "What is the status of my slaves there?" His voice low, vicious.

"Sire, every available fallen in the region is either there or en route before nightfall," Rusalmeh responded as quickly as the words could escape his wretched, greasy mouth. His voice wheezed and trembled as he spoke.

"And what have they seen?" Lucifer hissed, filled with contempt for a slave leader who had failed him so spectacularly.

"Just the report of the 'sky moving' and the humans we have been surveilling arriving in Bethlehem less than an hour ago."

Lucifer said nothing. There was nothing to say. He was placing all his bets on whatever the Creator was planning to happen in a small sleepy town in the middle of mostly nowhere. If his hunch was right, he would have a chance to bend the arch of history and thwart the Creator's plans. If he was wrong, well, he couldn't be wrong. He had to be right.

It had been hundreds of years since the Creator had chosen to speak through a prophet, and much had been gained. The Creator's chosen people were enslaved by a Roman Empire that had proven to be one of the most evil, repressive regimes in human history, except for Egypt. And Lucifer wasn't even close to being ready to give up all that he had gained.

"I will see for myself," Lucifer hissed through clenched teeth as he turned to leave.

No one spoke. There was nothing to say. The only one speaking, unless otherwise spoken to in this moment, was Lucifer. Until it wasn't.

After a long silence, Rusalmeh asked sheepishly, "Shall I accompany you, sire?"

Without looking back and with as much contempt and disrespect as he could muster, he said, "I couldn't care less."

As Lucifer headed to Bethlehem in the moment, little did he know how right and how wrong he was as the sun began to set in the earthly realm. Right in that Bethlehem was the right place. Wrong in his ability to thwart the Creator's plans. He, of all created beings in all the universe, should have known. The Creator's will would be always done.

The rest was always just details.

CHAPTER 93

No Place to Stay

"Sir?"

"Go ahead, Bella," Sebastian replied.

"We have a bit of a problem," Isabella reported.

Sebastian and Michael had agreed to keep their teams hidden in the tree grove while they waited to see where Mary and Joseph would settle for the night. Isabella and Petros were now the only two angel warriors protecting them, and the level of fallen activity in and around Bethlehem was increasing exponentially with every moment that passed.

"I know. We see them too," Sebastian replied.

"It's not that. It appears Mary has no place to stay tonight."

No one spoke.

Isabella continued, "They have checked with all their relatives, and no one has room. Looks like someone has offered them the cattle pen."

Again, no one spoke. There was nothing to say.

After a very long moment of silence, Isabella spoke up again, "Oh, and I'm pretty sure the baby will be arriving soon."

CHAPTER 94

Michael Reveals the Rest of the Story

"We'll need to split up," Michael said matter-of-factly.

"Okay," Sebastian replied.

"I want us to stay hidden for as long as we can, and we all need to set up a secure perimeter around the cattle pen for the night."

"But if all six of us try to get to the barn together, we'll likely be seen," Sam surmised.

"Correct," Michael confirmed.

Leo spoke up, "There are fallens everywhere."

"Keep an eye out for Lucifer," Michael said matter-of-factly into his comms device for all the warriors, including Petros and Isabella, to hear.

No one replied.

He spoke again, "This much activity in one place could only mean Lucifer isn't far behind."

Nathanael said, "He senses something big happening based on the chatter I am picking up from the fallens as they arrive."

The sun was gone, and darkness had long descended on the town.

In that moment, Sebastian looked up from his hidden position into the night sky. What he saw gave him a sobering realization of what was to come. A swarm of fallens so thick and so large it was as if the sky itself were crawling with them.

Eight angelic warriors. Some of the best, most exquisitely crafted angelic protectors the Creator had ever designed against seemingly millions of degenerate fallens. Could they survive? Could they protect Mary? Was this moment their mission all along?

Michael broke the silence when he said, "Before we move, there is something you all must know. Tonight is a very special night. It's a night the Creator had planned before He spoke this earthly realm into existence." He paused and then continued, "All of us were created in part for this moment. And you all are here for a very specific purpose. Chosen by the Creator to be here. Sebastian, Sam, Isabella, and Petros, the baby—now young woman—you were sent to covertly protect will deliver the Creator's redemption to this fallen world."

No one spoke. Everyone hung on the archangel's every word.

He continued, his voice deep, strong, and unwavering, "Tonight, the chosen one arrives."

CHAPTER 95

Wait, What?

Michael's words landed with such force, with such impact, words the warriors would have normally spoken escaped.

Isabella, who had taken a covert position just next to the cattle pen where Mary and Joseph were preparing to rest for the night, spoke first, "I had no idea."

"I think that was the point," Sam replied as he tried to make sense of what he had just heard.

The "chosen one," as Michael referred to him, had always been a part of the Creator's plan for redemption, at least as far as the angels knew.

And every mission in the earthly realm reminded every angelic warrior that only the Creator could fix what the humans, His most prized creation, had ruined.

And for millennia, there had been talk in the heavenly realm of this chosen one. From various angelic warriors came various reports of men through which the Creator spoke, speaking of a chosen one. Men like Isaiah, Daniel, and Jeremiah. The angels knew of the chosen one, but no one had the details.

So to be told in that moment that they had been chosen to be part of such a monumental moment in history rendered them all speechless. For at least a moment.

Sam continued, "All this time in the earthly realm." And then he stopped going deeper into thought.

"Has led to this moment," Michael replied, finishing Sam's thought.

CHAPTER 96

Lucifer Arrives in Bethlehem

"All available slaves are here, sire," Rusalmeh hissed as they approached the town on which Lucifer was placing all his bets.

Rusalmeh had considered not accompanying his master, but only for a moment. He concluded the disrespect Lucifer had shown him was deserved, and there was no other choice than to follow him like the slave he was and always had been. He hated himself for it. But that was nothing new. He had hated himself the moment he decided to rebel against the Creator. His existence had been miserable ever since. The only solace brought to his now-tortured spirit was tormenting the humans and spewing hate at all the fallens under his charge.

"And what of our lovely couple?" the dark prince whispered back.

At that moment, a fallen appeared, her head bowed low, directly in front of Lucifer. She spoke hoarsely, "Master, the human couple we followed has arrived."

"And?" Lucifer replied disrespectfully.

"No signs of the enemy, sire. We followed them all the way here."

"Imbeciles." Lucifer seethed.

The fallen said nothing. There was nothing to say.

After a long moment, Lucifer whispered with great malice, "Where are they now?"

"Sire, they have taken shelter for the night in a cattle pen."

"What?"

"Yes, it appears their relatives have no room for them."

Lucifer pondered this for a long moment as he began to wonder if he had made a massive miscalculation. Nothing was adding up. Everything seemed wrong. Off somehow. He knew trying to anticipate what the Creator was planning was a fool's errand, but he also felt as if he was beginning to better anticipate as well.

In reality, he didn't really know. It hadn't taken him long to realize that part of his punishment for rebelling against the Creator was total insignificance, especially when it came to thwarting the Creator's plans.

In that moment, he thought of enslaving the Hebrews in Egypt, how brilliant his plans were, and how sure he was of his own brilliance. But then, in an instant, all the hatred, greed, malice, and pain he had delivered upon the Hebrews was wiped away. All that work for nothing.

As he stood with his entourage overlooking Bethlehem, he had a sinking feeling that he was getting played once again. Anticipating a great victory, only to be defeated once again.

If this was what he thought it might be, the beginning of the Creator's eternal plan to bring His redemption to this rebellious, sin-filled planet, would it begin in a cattle pen?

As all these thoughts—past, present, and future—passed through his wretched, warped mind, he finally spoke, "Take me to them."

And with that, Lucifer had entered the beginning of a nightmare from which he and his entire horde would never awaken.

CHAPTER 97

The Team Prepares for the Inevitable

Michael the Archangel was not accustomed to hiding. "You've been doing this for how long?" he asked no one in particular as they were all now in position providing full-perimeter protection around the cattle pen which housed the three humans, one yet to arrive.

"A long time, sir," Sam responded with a smile.

No one spoke for a long bit.

The night was dark. It was made darker with the thick cloud of fallens circling above and around them.

"Any idea when we get to fight?" Isabella asked without a hint of sarcasm in her voice. It was a serious question.

"Bella," Sebastian sighed, about to remind her for what felt like the thousandth time to stand down.

But Michael interjected, "Very soon, Isabella. Very soon."

The words had not fully escaped his mouth when Leo spoke with urgency, "Sir, I think Lucifer has just arrived." Leo's voice was urgent but strangely calm. It was almost as if such an arrival was expected by the new warrior team.

Sebastian and his team still felt like they were playing catch-up. After such a long stretch of seemingly nothing of consequence happening, the last few hours had left their minds spinning.

As soon as Leo spoke the words, the earthly realm fell eerily silent. The howls, screeches, streams, and hisses of the fallens swirling above them had ceased.

Even the fallens recognize the power of Lucifer, Sebastian thought as he watched what seemed like millions of fallens fall in behind Lucifer in near unison.

Lucifer was approaching the cattle pen that would soon contain the Creator's most precious gift.

"Are you sure you weren't followed?" Michael asked to no one in particular.

"We were not, but I wouldn't be surprised if they followed Mary and Joseph," Sebastian said matter-of-factly.

"Why is that?"

"I forgot to mention my encounter with Lucifer not long before we left to come here," Sebastian answered calmly.

"And you two had a nice civil conversation, did you?"

"Well, let's just say I convinced him that he shouldn't start something he couldn't finish."

"And that worked?"

"I could tell his intelligence team had failed him because he wasn't sure if it was just me or if I had hundreds of warriors with me, ready to fight."

"So he backed off."

"Indeed, he did."

"Well, he's back, and he's brought just about every fallen in this entire region," Sam chimed in.

Ignoring Sam's comment, Michael simply said, "Hold your positions and wait on my signal."

No one spoke. There was nothing to say.

"Oh, and, Isabella, how much pent-up aggressions have you built on this mission so far?"

"A significant amount, sir."

"Good."

CHAPTER 98

Michael and Lucifer Meet at the Barn

An archangel revealing himself in the earthly realm is an incredible sight. It happens quite often, but rarely does the Creator allow such an event to be seen by human eyes. Those who have seen such events speak of both beauty and terror. Awe and fright. Love and pain.

So when Michael the Archangel stepped out of the shadows to reveal himself to the approaching prince of darkness, the world around him seemed to stop for a moment.

Michael was huge. And terrifying. His bright-silver hair hung at his shoulders. His deep-blue eyes blazed in the darkness. At close to nine feet tall in human measurement, Michael was a living testament to the majesty and creativity of the Creator. His infinitely wide shoulders were eclipsed only by his even broader shimmering white wings that only added to his imposing figure as he cut through the darkness.

A showdown between Michael and Lucifer was going down in what seemed like the middle of nowhere in the shadow of a cattle pen.

"What is happening right now?" Petros asked himself, not realizing he said it out loud for the other angels to hear through their comms.

"I'm not entirely sure," Sam replied through a broad smile, "but it's totally awesome."

The warrior angels held their positions as instructed. But each one of them knew that once Michael stepped out of the shadows and revealed himself, there was no going back. Word of an archangel and Lucifer meeting face-to-face is a cosmic event. An event every angel and fallen instinctively knew would most certainly end in war. They all were about to find out.

To his credit, Lucifer didn't seem to flinch. Or if he did, no one spotted it. Strangely, he acted as if he expected to see one of the most powerful warrior angels in the universe in front of a cattle pen that night.

Lucifer exclaimed, arms extended with a broad, fake, and greasy smile spreading across his contorted face, "Michael!"

CHAPTER 99

The War Begins

"Lucifer," Michael replied flatly, giving nothing away.

"I had a feeling you might be here," the dark prince replied as the fake smile receded.

"By the looks of it, you brought your entire horde of worthless slaves with you," Michael responded, his head tilting up toward the sky crawling with fallens.

"I wouldn't want them to miss out on all the fun," Lucifer responded, his eyes black as the night that surrounded him.

No one spoke for a long moment.

Then Michael spoke, "There is nothing for you here but pain and suffering."

"You forget, my brother, pain and suffering are my business."

Michael simply nodded. Not so much at a loss for words but as a simple acknowledgment that what was going to happen was indeed going to happen.

Lucifer spoke again, "Who is she anyway?"

Michael smiled. "The fact that you don't know makes you and your lackey there even more useless than I had imagined."

The lackey to whom the archangel was speaking was Rusalmeh, who, until that moment, was standing proudly directly behind Lucifer's right shoulder.

After a moment of silence, Michael continued, "Tell you what. You take yourself and your hapless crew and leave and let the real angels ensure the Creator's plans are fulfilled tonight."

This confidence clearly shook Lucifer and made him instantly furious, but he kept his composure somewhat. "How dare you come into my realm and talk to me that way!" Lucifer seethes through clenched, rotting teeth.

"Your realm?" Michael scoffed. "This is the Creator's realm. All of it is His. You own nothing. You are nothing. And if you don't get out of my face this instant, you will learn what it is like to feel nothing for eternity!" Michael's voice escalated with every word. And as he finished, his voice boomed as if it were coming from an army of angels shouting in unison.

It was such a powerful moment that Lucifer and the fallens standing directly behind him all took a simultaneous step back.

Without a word, Lucifer leapt straight up into the night and was instantly out of sight. The others quickly followed until Michael stood alone once again.

After a long moment, Michael spoke to his team of warriors still expertly hidden surrounding the chosen one soon to be delivered into the earthly realm, "The war has begun."

CHAPTER 100

The King Arrives

The cries of the chosen one, the Creator of the universe, as a human baby was like nothing any of the warrior angels had ever heard.

Of course, Sebastian, Sam, Isabella, and Petros had heard the cries of Mary the night she was born. But this was different.

In fact, every one of the warriors that night each had heard hundreds, maybe thousands, of human babies make their first cries as they entered the earthly realm. Thousands of missions over the millennia had given them all such opportunities.

But this cry was different. This cry was the beginning of the most wonderful, most daring, most unexpected, and most ingenious plan the Creator had ever conceived.

The cry of the chosen one held the future of all human existence in His very breath. The cry of the Creator becoming the created. The cry that would change the earthly realm forever rang out into the darkness. And set off a spiritual battle that, to the present day, rages in a war for the soul of the earthly realm.

As the cries of this most precious one rang out, every warrior knew they were created by the Creator long ago for this very moment. And as they all instinctively knelt in reverence in that moment, they could not have been more ready.

CHAPTER 101

The Creator Sends Reinforcements

They first appeared at a severe distance. Like streaks of light. Thousands or perhaps hundreds of thousands. Maybe more.

As the warriors stood watch surrounding the small cattle pen, they grew tense. They now all carried all the responsibility of sheltering the most precious and vulnerable gift the earthly realm would ever know. The Creator's chosen one. Behind enemy lines. On the brink of a spiritual war that would rage for the rest of human time.

Each warrior knew the Creator's plans were perfect. They knew He chose them for this moment.

As they all silently watched the streaks of light in the distance, they each wondered, in their own way, about the next few moments. What would become of them? Were they up to the task at hand? Why did the Creator choose them for such a time as this? All these thoughts and questions faded in an instant.

The countless lights streaking across the night sky instantly became a multitude of angelic warriors. But instead of preparing to fight, they sang.

A song for the chosen one.

CHAPTER 102

The Fight for the Future

The song that night would be joyfully remembered and recorded by human shepherds, but it was the fallens present that night who would remember that night quite differently. For it was the shepherds who were the first to meet the chosen one. It was the fallens who paid a devastating price.

The rest of the story of the "multitude of heavenly hosts" turned out to be critical to the success of the mission to protect the chosen one that night. For it was those same singing angels, who, after disappearing from the sight of human eyes, instantly turned into angelic warriors preparing to fight. From the hallelujah chorus in the physical realm to terrifying war cries, the likes of which the fallens in the area that night had never heard.

The Creator was doing what was necessary to ensure the chosen one's safe passage into the earthly realm that night. The Creator's plans are perfect and His control of every situation total. However, the free will of humans could, at times, insert a level of unpredictability that would require angelic intervention.

On this night, it was the Creator's will to ensure no weapon formed against the chosen one in the earthly realm, be it physical or spiritual, would prosper. And the mission of the singing-turned-warrior angels was clear: seek and destroy any fallen that sought to interfere with the Creator's plan.

Even Michael seemed surprised at the arrival of such an enormous number of angelic warriors that night. As they spread across the sky fanning out in every direction, one of them sought the counsel of Michael.

"Zane!" Michael shouted as the warrior approached his position from above.

The sounds of the hackles and shrieking coming from the fallens had become deafening. In the confusion between the lack of orders and the massive influx of angelic warriors into the realm, the multitude of fallens were losing their collective minds.

"Sir!" Zane shouted as he landed hard, immediately taking a kneel before the archangel.

"Stand, Zane. What brings you here?"

"The Creator, sir."

"All of you?"

"Yes, sir."

"Anything else from the Creator?"

"One thing for you, sir," Zane said as he stood to his feet, removing his massive sword from its sheath. He continued as a smile spread brightly across his angelic face, "Have some fun."

The two angels smiled at each other and embraced for a brief moment.

Before leaping back into the air, Michael grabbed Zane by the shoulders, looked intensely into his eyes, and said, "Can you believe the day has come?"

Zane's bright gray eyes grew wide with excitement as he smiled broadly and replied simply, "Finally!" And with that, Zane was gone. Up into the darkness, prepared to deliver the pain of angelic righteousness for as long as was necessary.

No sooner had Zane departed that Lucifer descended to address Michael once again.

Michael gave the fallen archangel no time to speak as he flatly stated, "It appears the Creator's plan will be completed tonight."

"I wouldn't be so sure about that." Lucifer seethed. His hulking frame heaving with anger and pride.

"You cannot win," Michael replied, his massive shoulders relaxed. His sword visible but not a threat.

"I chose correctly, and my entire horde is here tonight, which gives me more than a fighting chance," the words exited Lucifer as if he were spitting them at Michael.

"Well, why don't you get to it?" Michael asked genuinely.

Lucifer said nothing for a moment.

Michael filled the void with a follow-up question he figured would light the fire he wanted to light, "Fear?"

Lucifer chuckled. Not the response Michael was expecting. "No, not fear, brother. I guess I just want to know what exactly I'm fighting about. Is all."

Michael said nothing.

Lucifer continued, "You see, your Creator wouldn't go to all this trouble and send all of these forces for a standard run-of-the-mill operation."

"Indeed."

"But for what? A baby? In a barn?"

Michael smiled and said nothing.

"I should have never let you set foot in this region." Lucifer seethed.

"Come now," Michael said with a smile, "I can come and go as I please," taunting the dark prince.

Lucifer stared back at Michael. Lucifer used to be slightly taller than Michael, but like every other fallen in the earthly realm, Lucifer was not immune to the effects of millennia spent spirited from the Creator's presence. But he still was a massive fallen, easily dwarfing all fallens around him.

Slightly hunched over, Lucifer and Michael now stood eye to eye. Lucifer was becoming so angry his whole body began convulsing. It was a confluence of anger really. He was angry that his legions, especially Rusalmeh, had not detected what clearly was an ongoing angelic warrior operation for years. His anger, fueled by hatred directed at Michael, was bottomless. He hated Michael for all the reasons anyone would expect. But he hated him most of all because Michael chose the Creator, and he chose rebellion. Ultimately, what made him most furious was that he still didn't know what was really happening. He hated to be surprised.

So there they stood. Good and evil. Angels and demons.

Just beyond both of them, the soft cry of the Creator who had become the created. The fate of the Creator's redemption operation hanging in the balance.

And then it clicked. He hated himself even more in that moment for being so slow to get it. The Creator of the universe had devised a plan to deliver the Savior of all humankind for all time through the most unassuming means possible. And in so doing was able to deceive the one who took so much pride in deceiving others. The great deceiver had become the deceived. The most important moment in all human history was unfolding a few feet from where Lucifer stood, and he had been too deceived to see it. The chosen one, established before the foundations of the world, had arrived to deliver the final defeat of Lucifer and his dominion, and Lucifer had missed it. All of it.

In that moment, Lucifer replayed the words of Isaiah in his mind: "For to us a child is born, to us a son is given. And he will be called Wonderful Counselor, Mighty God, Everlasting Creator, Prince of Peace."

How had he missed it? Laziness, he figured to himself. Laziness and apathy after such a prolonged silence of the Creator in the earthly realm.

But he knew the Scriptures better than anyone in the earthly realm. He made it his business to study the Scriptures and understand their meaning. He had always figured it was both his best offense and defense. Offense because he could use the Creator's words to distort humans and lead them astray. Defense because he could deflect and redirect anyone who used the Scriptures to rebuke him.

But he missed this one. In that one moment, he realized it was all too late. He would fight that night, for sure, but he had no time to build a strategy. He had no time to build networks of humans who he would influence to thwart the Creator's plan. Maybe he couldn't stop it ultimately, but he could ruin lives in the process of trying. But now even that seemed out of the question.

Lucifer was on his back foot in the most important moment of all human history. And as this realization poured over him like a wave crashing hard into his body, he heard them. At first, it sounded distorted but only because he was so deep in thought. Once he focused in on the sound, he heard it clearly. The screams of demons entering their annihilation at the hands of angelic warriors.

The war to protect the Creator's most precious gift had begun. The beginning of Lucifer's end. And he knew it. Maybe he wasn't willing to admit it, but deep in his spirit, he knew it.

And for a moment, he was taken back to the time before his rebellion. He glimpsed the image of himself leading a countless multitude of angels in worship of the Creator. And as soon as the image arrived, it fled. And what replaced it was a fury he had never known. A fury that would fuel his efforts until the end of the human age. A fury that combined his hatred of the Creator, his failure as an angel, his failure in recognizing the sheer magnitude of this moment, and the growing realization that all his efforts to destroy the Creator's creation were being reversed right before his eyes. In this very moment. And up until this moment, he had done nothing to stop it.

And all that hatred and all that fury exploded from deep within him as he screamed one word in a voice never heard.

"War!"

CHAPTER 103

An Unlikely Hero Returns

Javva heard the word but didn't believe his own mind at first. He had been wandering the desert for so long. An outcast spirit. Damned but not annihilated. Rejected. Scorned.

He figured he was just hallucinating. But then he heard it again and again and again as it echoed off the canyon walls that surrounded him. War.

He decided to heed his master's call.

CHAPTER 104

A Spiritual Battle for the Ages

Demons were everywhere. Michael commanded his special forces team to hold their positions surrounding the cattle pen as war raged all around them. The warriors who, a moment ago, were singing with such angelic voices were in the next moment tearing fallens apart with terrifying fury.

But it wasn't enough. What the fallens lacked in power and speed, however, they made up for in sheer number. Angelic warriors were terrifying to any fallen they encountered in the earthly realm, but on this night, the fallens seemed to be gaining confidence in number. Rusalmeh and his commanders were adding to the chaos as they each gathered hordes of fallens and staggered their surprise attacks on unsuspecting angelic warriors.

The effect was devastating. Angelic warriors were falling to the ground at an alarming rate, many with devastating injuries. Taking many out of the fight. Lucifer's plan of attack was stunningly simple yet effective. Overwhelm angelic forces with sheer number, isolate, and attack. One by one, key warriors were taken out of the fight.

Of course, the fallens were being annihilated in even greater number, but the angelic warriors seemed to be losing ground as the battle raged in the skies above the chosen one.

In an instant, Zane dropped from the sky to report to Michael who was still standing guard. Zane spoke urgently, "Sir, we are losing," his voice firm but short.

"Why?" Michael asked calmly.

"It's the number. Lucifer has brought every available fallen."

"Estimate?"

"Millions."

"Millions?"

"Yes. And Rusalmeh and his goons are picking us off one by one with stealth attacks."

Michael pondered the news without emotion.

Zane continued, "We've never seen such a concentrated assembly of them."

"Yes, we have," Michael replied calmly after a long pause.

Zane said nothing.

Michael continued, "He is trying it again."

"Again?"

"Think, Zane," Michael commanded. "Think back to the rebellion."

Zane thought for a moment and then began to smile as his mind made the connection.

"That's right, Lucifer is relitigating his expulsion from heaven. Right here. Tonight," Michael explained.

"And he thinks he can do it this time because we are in his realm and the Creator isn't here," Zane said, more to himself than anyone, finishing Michael's thought.

"Indeed. But the Creator is here," Michael said, smiling.

"He is?" Zane asked genuinely.

With a nod toward the cattle pen, Michael directed Zane's attention to the new family. Zane looked around to see that Mary and Joseph were proudly displaying their new miraculous gift. Zane turned back around, his eyes wide in amazement.

"He's here, Zane," Michael said. "Our victory is already decided."

Zane said nothing as he tried to process what it all meant.

Michael calmly spoke, "Zane, you need to get back in the fight. Command your warriors to stop focusing on annihilating as many fallens as possible and get them focused in teams of four."

Zane said nothing.

Michael continued, "This will work to neutralize the surprise attacks Rusalmeh and his team are conducting."

"Got it."

"And spread out," Michael commanded. "With so many fallens in a concentrated area, command your warriors to spread out and more effectively dilute the superiority their number is currently providing them."

"I understand, sir. Anything else?"

"One more thing," Michael replied. "Have you seen Lucifer?"

"We haven't, sir."

"He's still here for sure. Be sure to keep an eye out and report back if you see him, okay?"

"Okay." And with that, Zane leapt into the darkness.

CHAPTER 105

Lucifer Never Gives Up

He knew it was likely over before it started. He always knew.

But something in him wouldn't let him stop. It had been that way the moment he decided to rebel. He knew the outcome, but he persisted anyway. And now, millennia later, the same desire that damned him to an eternal existence separated from the single source of truth and life existed in his mind in this moment.

He planned to stay out of the fight as long as he could. And his plan to pick off angel warriors one by one turned out to be surprisingly effective until it wasn't. Also something he knew would end poorly. But he had to try. He always had to try.

As he sat perched atop a small rock formation just west of the city, he received the update for which he was desperately waiting.

"There are eight, sire."

Lucifer said nothing as he stroked his chin with his greasy, mangled right hand. After a long moment, he asked with a deep hiss, "Including Michael?"

"Yes, sire" came the response from the reconnaissance leader he had charged with detailing out the enemy positions surrounding the Creator's most treasured gift.

"Where are they?" Lucifer seethed, his gaze locked in a stare beyond the horizon.

"Two layers of perimeter, sire," the worm continued. "In the outer layer are Sebastian, Sam, Petros, and Isabella."

Lucifer said nothing. If those names had an effect on him, he didn't show it.

"And?"

"And Michael, Nathanael, Leo, and Ariel" came the reply, the demon's voice steady, matter-of-fact.

Lucifer did not reply. At least not right away. And then he started muttering to himself as he processed the information he just received. He was the master at finding a weakness and exploring it. And he knew all the angel warriors. He had encountered them each at least once over the span of millennia. He knew Michael the best, of course, as they worshipped the Creator together for what had seemed like eternity. And while the others weren't a mystery to him, he was hard-pressed in that moment to recall weaknesses he could try to exploit.

One thing he was sure of. He didn't have the firepower to overwhelm them all in a traditional spirit battle. That was for sure. His only chance at success that night was a misdirection of some kind. A head fake. A ruse.

And as he sat watching the most epic spirit battle rage all around him in the earthly realm, the idea came to him. A cruel smile spreading across his wretched face.

And in a low growl, he said, "Back to basics."

CHAPTER 106

The Star Beckons

The sounds of weeping, wailing, and gnashing drew closer as he struggled to navigate the terrain. His body was broken in ways he never thought possible, but not so broken that would allow him to slowly slip into annihilation. Rusalmeh made sure of that. Broken but kept alive in tortuous pain. The punishment of repeated failure.

But something drew Javva to the terrifying sounds of hatred and defeat. If his fellow fallens had been winning the battle at some point, it had come and gone. By the sounds of it, an angelic slaughter was taking place, and he was determined to see it for himself.

As he drew closer to the battle, he found a spot from which to peer into the valley below. And that's when he saw it. The most beautiful sight he had ever seen in the earthly realm. His eyes fixated on it, and it became the only thing he could see in that moment.

The sounds of agony and battle at first faded and then disappeared altogether as his wretched mind became singularly focused on something so close he tried to reach out and touch it.

As he forced himself over the edge of the small rock cliff toward his prize, he began to mumble a single word over and over. At first, barely audible, but then it grew louder. One word. Over and over.

"Star."

CHAPTER 107

Lucifer Catches a Break

"Do we own any of them?" Lucifer asked. His voice calm.

"Not exactly, sire."

"I need precision, slave." Lucifer stayed calm but his voice oozed with tension.

"I understand. We own the shepherd's offspring, sire."

"And?"

"And I think we can use the child."

"How old?"

"Fourteen."

"Not much of a child then."

"No, sire. He is strong."

"Excellent."

The shepherds were on their way to see the chosen one just as the angels had instructed.

Lucifer continued, "How long before they reach the cattle pen?"

"Not long, sire. We have sent two slaves to possess the boy."

"Describe your plan."

"The demons are instructed to send the boy to find his dad. They will direct him to the cattle pen."

"And then?"

"We believe he will make it past the angel warriors as he will be known by his father who will already be there on instructions from the enemy."

"Good."

"The demons have been instructed to use the familiarity of the boy to our advantage while eliminating the child."

"Interesting. A fine plan indeed. You'll need a distraction."

"Sire?"

"You'll need some way to draw the attention of Michael and his team away from the child."

Lucifer's slave said nothing. There was nothing to say. He didn't plan for a distraction.

"Don't worry, slave." Lucifer chuckled. "I'll be the distraction."

CHAPTER 108

The Shepherd's Son Possessed

The two fallens found it easier than anticipated to possess the boy. He let them in really. They had found him weeks earlier as he found his introduction to the occult by some pagan traders who were traveling through. He practically invited them in.

So as luck would have it, his shepherd father had been invited to see the chosen one. The demons couldn't believe their luck. So when the two demons returned to tempt his spirit again, he happily agreed.

As they entered and took control of his spirit, Lucifer grinned. The depth of Lucifer's depravity was only matched by the depth of his hatred for the Creator. So anytime one of his slaves possesses a human, Lucifer could sense it. Feel it.

And he felt this one. A crack in the armor. A wrinkle in the Creator's plan.

Maybe this time would be different. Maybe this time he would win.

CHAPTER 109

An Intruder in Their Midst

"Go," the demon whispered into the boy's spirit.

The boy simply asked, "Where?"

The demon smiled and said, "To your father. He needs you."

"Why does my father need me?" the boy asked himself.

"He's found a baby in distress, and he needs your help," the demon lied.

The boy didn't move. He was confused. It was the middle of the night after all.

His tormentor grew instantly impatient as he coiled himself around the boy as he drew near to his face and screamed, "Move!"

The boy obeyed as he threw on his cloak and climbed out the small window of his farmhouse. Out into the night.

To do the devil's bidding.

CHAPTER 110

Lucifer's Distraction

"The boy and his tormentor are on the move," Lucifer's slave reported.

"Good. How long until contact?" Lucifer asked.

"Not long, sire. We should be ready to execute the next phase of your plan without delay."

"Very well," Lucifer said. The sound of his voice trailed off as he pondered these next moments.

He was thinking of anything that he had missed. Any detail that might keep him from changing the arc of history according to the Creator's plan. Was he missing anything?

He had replayed every possible scenario he could think of, but he was at a disadvantage, he knew. As a result of Rusalmeh's disastrous leadership, he was behind. Playing catch-up to the Creator's plan that was no doubt perfect in every way. A fact he hated with every core of his wretched, evil being.

And now, in this moment, in his dominion, the Creator had delivered the chosen one. Almost as if He was flaunting it. He was. The Creator was flaunting His plans directly in front of Lucifer, but Lucifer had made of up for lost time.

The plan for a possessed boy, a son of a shepherd, was going to even the score. It would be so unexpected, so subtle. It just had to work.

As Lucifer gathered his most vicious warriors around him to go over their plan one more time, something told him he was missing something. A gnawing feeling deep in his mind. He couldn't shake it. But he knew he must press ahead regardless.

Time was running out.

CHAPTER 111

Javva Arrives

He couldn't believe what he was seeing and hearing. An epic spiritual war was raging all around him now. The ground was littered with bodies of fallens and angelic warriors alike. The sounds of agony interspersed with the sounds of sword battles and war cries made for a chaotic scene.

Javva could no longer fly, his wings permanently damaged by the beating he had received from Rusalmeh. He didn't need to. Not for what he wanted to do.

He had followed the star in the sky and had finally found its final destination. As he climbed over the lifeless bodies of countless spirits, he kept his gaze fixed on the star. The star gave him a feeling he couldn't explain. A feeling of fear and peace. Of joy and pain. And since the moment he saw it, he couldn't resist it. It pulled him in. As if it were calling to him.

Because it was. The star was his destiny. His existence for being. It was now his singular focus.

And he couldn't not take his eyes off it.

CHAPTER 112

Evil Draws Closer

By the time the boy made it to the field where he expected his father to be, no one was there. The silence, outside the occasional bleat from a sheep, was deafening. No one was there. The sheep without a shepherd. Strange.

Why would he leave the sheep? he asked himself.

"Because it's your destiny" came the reply from the demon coiled tightly around his spirit.

"What?" the boy asked, this time audibly.

"Your destiny, my son." After a moment of silence, the demon continued with a soft whisper, "The star."

As the words entered the boy's mind, he instinctively looked up, searching the blackness that seemed to consume him. He didn't see it at first. There were just so many. Millions. Maybe more. All he could see was the vastness of the universe stretched out from horizon to horizon.

But then he saw it. Low on the horizon. Inconceivably bright. Calling to him.

"That's it," his demon whispered, an evil grin spreading across his deformed face. "That's the one, my son. Go to it."

Without hesitation, the boy began running toward the star.

Soon to be face-to-face with the Creator of all things.

CHAPTER 113

Sam Senses Trouble

"Sir Michael?" Sam asked through the secure comms connection.

There was no need for the secure line now that an all-out war was raging all around them.

"Yes, Sam."

"Sir, don't you think it's weird Lucifer isn't engaging?" Sam asked.

"Meaning?"

"Meaning, he knows now for sure what is going down here tonight, and he's called for war. But he is nowhere to be found," Sam replied.

"Indeed. As long as I have known Lucifer, he has been both thoughtful and cunning," Michael said, his voice still calm and strong. "Both attributes suited him well until his pride overpowered both and sent him into rebellion."

No one spoke.

Michael continued, "And now, after millennia separated from the Creator, his thoughtfulness and cunning have combined with hate and pride to create a master of deception."

"Which means we need to be ready for anything," Sebastian chimed in.

"Indeed, Sebastian, indeed," Michael answered.

No sooner had he spoken those words, Nathanael chimed in urgently, “Okay, everyone, looks like a group of shepherds is heading toward the barn.”

“How many?” Michael asked.

“There are six. They are talking about being sent by singing angels,” Nathanael concluded.

Isabella chimed in, “I see them, and I’m tracking them. No obvious signs of agitation or tension. The threat appears low.”

“Okay. Track them from your position but do not leave your post,” Michael commanded.

“Yes, sir.”

“I see them now, sir,” Leo reported. “Agree with Isabella’s assessment. They appear friendly.”

“Let them pass through but keep eyes on them at all time,” Michael replied. He continued, “I see them now too. These are the first humans to get close to the baby.”

“I really don’t want them to get close, sir,” Ariel said for the first time during the mission so far.

“I don’t either, A, but we need to get used to it. It’s going to be part of the mission,” Michael answered.

As the six strangers entered the small pen, little did they know the eyes of eight of the most powerful, best-equipped angelic warriors were watching their every move.

As the shepherds knelt before the child, Leo’s voice crackled across the secure communications line as he said, “Here’s comes another one…”

“And he’s running.”

CHAPTER 114

Lucifer Makes His Final Move

"The boy is arriving, sire," the demon reported.

"It's time to execute our plan then," Lucifer replied, his voice wretched and evil.

No one in his inner circle said anything in reply. There was nothing to say. They had rehearsed their parts over and over again and knew they would either succeed or be annihilated. None of them cared really. The pride and hate that had built up after so long separated from the Creator created a hollow emptiness they never talked about and could never really explain. They just existed now to do Lucifer's bidding. This was one of those biddings. Little did they know, it could bend the arc of history forever.

Now Lucifer knew Michael was too strong to be defeated, and while he didn't know how many special forces of warrior angels he had brought along, Lucifer wasn't reckless. He knew the battles he could win and the ones he couldn't. And a full-on assault was foolishness. They would be expecting that anyway. He needed to create a diversion and let the depravity of a human do the rest.

As he leapt into the darkness above, he said to no one in particular, "The child is mine."

CHAPTER 115

The Chosen One in Danger

The boy arrived to greet his father without incident.

His father was so surprised to see his son in the middle of the night it took him a moment to respond as he stammered, "What... what are you doing here, son?"

"I came to see you, Father!" the boy responded awkwardly. The cheeriness in his demeanor and his voice was odd, almost out of place.

And Isabella noticed it immediately. "Something is wrong with that kid," Isabella said matter-of-factly.

"Oh?" Sebastian asked.

"Yeah, too cheery. It's weird."

The boy's father, still confused at the sight of his son in such a moment, asked, "How did you find me?"

The boy replied without hesitation, "The star. I just followed the star like he told me."

By this time, the other shepherds were greeting Mary and Joseph and kneeling in reverence and awe before the chosen one who was now wrapped tightly and sleeping soundly.

"Do you have eyes on the boy?" Michael asked to no one in particular.

"I do, sir," Sam replied first.

"As do I," replied Nathanael.

"Okay. Sam and Nathanael, watch the boy's every move," Michael commanded.

"Isabella and Petros?"

"Yes, sir," both responding in unison.

"Keep your eyes focused on the chosen one," Michael instructed. He continued, "Sebastian, Ariel, Leo, and I will stay focused on any incoming enemy activity."

No one spoke for a moment.

Then Sebastian asked, "Anything in particular we need to be on the lookout for, sir?"

The archangel was silent for a bit and then said, "I'm not entirely sure, but it's too quiet."

"Quiet?" Ariel asked.

"Yes. Quiet. By now, Lucifer has put together what is happening here tonight, and yet he is nowhere to be found."

"Sir?"

"Go ahead, Sam."

"The boy is—" Sam said as his voice disappeared as if he had fallen off a cliff.

In effect, he had. The demon that landed on him delivered the perfect blow, taking him completely by surprise. The darkness helped along with the sheer commotion of the battle raging all around. Such commotion had been raging in the sky above him all night and had become effectively white noise as he trained all his attention on the boy who had arrived seemingly out of nowhere. And he was hurt. Bad.

Standing over Sam's lifeless body, the massive demon drew his sword and prepared to fight just as Lucifer had instructed.

The surprise attack instinctively drew every warrior angel's attention as they all heard Sam's voice drop suddenly through their comms devices.

Petros was closest to Sam, so his first instinct was to break from his position and render aid to his friend.

As if on cue, another massive demon fell from the sky with the intention of taking Petros out much the same way Sam had, but the half step Petros had taken saved him. The demon still landed a massive blow, but it was indirect enough to keep Petros in the fight.

He fell to one knee as he simultaneously drew his sword and pivoted back to face his attacker.

The two nearly simultaneous attacks on Sam and Petros had initiated the exact response for which Lucifer was hoping. All warrior angels, except for Michael, responded with swords drawn and distracted looks toward the commotion of their fellow warriors under attack.

Michael knew better as he screamed, "Lucifer! You have already lost!"

But Lucifer gave no reply. It wasn't yet time.

There was more to be done.

CHAPTER 116

The Final Act

With Sam unconscious and Petros ready to engage his attacker, the rest of Lucifer's inner circle arrived.

But with the element of surprise now passed, they emerged from the darkness together, swords drawn, landing hard on the thatched roof of the cattle pen.

The same cattle pen that was currently housing the king of the universe, helpless and exposed as a newborn human child. The chosen one, the alpha and omega, the omniscient Creator of all things past, present, and future born as a helpless human baby in the middle of nowhere, in enemy territory, surrounded by the largest gathering of demonic forces ever assembled.

And now, directly above him, were some of the same fallen angels He himself had cast down from heaven so many millennia ago. And they were out for revenge. All the hatred, all the evil, all the bloodlust, all the anger, all the pride, and all the pain that had accumulated for so long was now rising up inside these fallens as they came so close to the presence of the chosen one. It had been so long since they had experienced the absolute love, truth, and light of being in the Creator's presence that they didn't even sense it. They were completely dead inside. All they wanted now was revenge.

As they dropped off the roof and began to fan out to face their angelic enemies, Michael began to sense what Lucifer had in mind. In that moment, Michael spoke in a hushed tone to his team, "Lucifer knows he can't win a fight like this, so any perceived attempt should be dismissed as a distraction."

"But what is the distraction?" Sebastian asked.

"Nothing has changed," Michael instructed. "Hold your positions. Our top priority remains the safety of the child."

Before the last syllable had left Michael's lips, Nathanael chimed in, "Sir, the boy is advancing toward the baby."

CHAPTER 117

Unlikely Hero

"The baby is your destiny," the demon whispered into the boy's spirit.

The boy's father, still thoroughly confused, had decided to stop questioning his son since it was getting him nowhere. Instead, he had joined the other shepherds in paying reverence to the newborn child.

The teenage boy appeared frozen in time as his two tormentors took turns repeating over and over and over and over, "The baby is your destiny. The baby is your destiny. The baby is your destiny."

As if in a trance, the boy began making his way toward where the baby lay softly sleeping. He had never held a baby, and he said as much as he made his way across the cattle pen.

His demons had an answer, "You won't need to hold him. Just pick him up. Is all." After a long pause, they hauntingly whispered into his spirit, "We'll handle the rest."

As if on cue, as soon as the boy began to move toward the baby, Lucifer descended out of the darkness. His inner circle of demons following his lead. In near unison, they attacked with full force the angelic warriors surrounding the chosen one that night. They were wild-eyed and reckless as if they had nothing to lose. Because they didn't.

Isabella broke from her position first. Never one to back down from a fight with a fallen, she pivoted and swung her sword in a short half circle above her head before plunging her sword into the chest of the advancing demon. She moved with such speed and force the demon anticipated nothing. And in that moment, he achieved annihilation before his wretched corpse hit the dirt.

Chaos immediately ensued mere inches from the sleeping baby. Every angelic warrior on mission to protect the chosen one was thoroughly engaged in battle with Lucifer and his inner circle of demons. Which meant no one was watching.

If they had, they would have noticed the glazed look in the teenage boy's eyes as he took a final half step before kneeling close to the sleeping baby. A stranger, a wild card, an unplanned human visitor mere inches from the Creator of the universe. With demons in his spirit and malice in his heart.

Until an unlikely hero emerged. To make amends.

To reach his final destination.

CHAPTER 118

Destiny

He saw the whole thing. No one saw him. He stopped short, out of instinct more than anything. The star had led him to the cattle pen just like it had led the shepherds. And the shepherd's son.

And then he saw an archangel. In that moment, he knew something was different. Special. And then for a moment, the hate was gone. The evil that had consumed him for millennia dissipated in an instant. He saw Michael the Archangel in that moment, and something broke. He figured it was his will or his passion or his spirit or something. He gave it little thought.

His focus was now solely on finding out what was in the cattle pen. What had captured so much attention from heaven and earth? But he had to pick just the right time to quench his curiosity. Clearly, the archangel and at least four warrior angels, that he could see, were there to protect something or someone special.

And Javva knew his limitations. He was a fallen angel. A demon. And not a particularly special one at that. Add to that his broken body and inability to fly and Javva was no match for any warrior angel, let alone an archangel.

No, he had to pick his spot and hope for the best. Plus, what did he care? He had been cast out of a demon horde, banished to a cursed existence. Alone. So what if he was annihilated that night? Who would know? Who would care? *No one*, he thought.

"And I would care the least of anyone," he whispered to himself as he waited crouched and hidden from view.

He couldn't understand his fascination with the star and the gift it symbolized. He just had to find out. That was all he cared about anymore.

So he waited. And then the demons started showing up. Javva didn't recognize them at first. And then he did. They were Lucifer's warriors. The best of the best. And Rusalmeh.

Rusalmeh. For a brief moment, the hatred with which he had become so accustomed, returned. He had always hated Rusalmeh. All fallens hated one another. It's just how it worked. Separated from the source of all love would do that. Fallens lost all capacity to love the moment they were cast out of heaven. Perhaps the cruelest punishment. But what it meant for fallens was hatred. Hatred for themselves. For one another. For humans. For their very existence. So when hate returned in the moment he saw Rusalmeh, it startled him. He couldn't remember not feeling hate, so when it left and then came back, he was surprised. But then it disappeared again. The hate was gone. Weird.

As soon as he saw the first demon land directly on top of one of the angel warriors, he knew the battle raging above him would pale in comparison to what was about to go down. Lucifer's demon warriors were no joke. They ruled the earthly realm and always did Lucifer's dirty work.

But the presence of an archangel significantly tipped the scales, Javva thought. Plus, he could only count four warrior angels in addition to the archangel. But were there more?

Javva figured an epic battle was about to commence, and that would give him a chance to get close. He would wait. He had nothing but time. He didn't have to wait long.

He recognized Isabella through the darkness and chaos. How could he not? She was unmistakable. So fast. So effortless. The Creator's warrior masterpiece. As soon as she made her first move annihilating one of Lucifer's top lieutenants before he could even think to defend himself, all hell broke loose.

Just as Javva anticipated. So he made his move toward the cattle pen.

It would be one of his last.

CHAPTER 119

Lucifer and Michael: Together Again

Michael had anticipated Isabella's offensive move.

So did Lucifer. His plan was unfolding perfectly. Sucker punch one of Isabella's closest friends and trigger a reaction. It worked. At least he thought it did.

As Lucifer landed hard in front of his sworn enemy, Michael was not there. Lucifer knew if his plan were to work, he needed to engage Michael long enough for the boy to complete his mission. But Michael was gone. As Lucifer frantically looked around, searching, scanning, counting, he didn't think to look up. As a result, he didn't see it coming.

Without a sound, the most devastatingly effective archangel the Creator had ever designed came crashing to earth, landing a direct blow to Lucifer. The massive blow combined with the element of surprise left Lucifer, the great deceiver, semiconscious and momentarily out of the fight.

Michael had anticipated a surprise attack from Lucifer. He just was having a difficult time deciding on exactly when. So as soon as Isabella began to make her first offensive move, Michael made his decision. Without a word to his team, he quietly and quickly ascended into the darkness. As he did, he passed Lucifer in the darkness. Had Lucifer not been so preoccupied watching his plan unfold, he would have seen him. But he didn't. And he paid dearly.

Michael stood his ground, pinning the giant demon to the ground. He knew he couldn't hold him down for long. So he calmly spoke to his team through the comms device embedded in his ear, "Do not lose sight of the baby."

He had no way of knowing if his message was heard. The battle scene was near total chaos. Every angelic warrior surrounding the chosen one that night was heavily engaged with a raging, fanatical enemy.

Sam remained motionless, out of the fight. Isabella, having felled her first opponent, found herself battling fallens from all sides as the hordes of demons fighting in the darkness above descended as if on cue. Petros, Sebastian, Nathanael, Ariel, and Leo were all being pushed farther and farther outside the perimeter they had established around the cattle pen. The sheer number of fallens and the frenzy in which they were attacking was disorienting. It was all they could do to defend themselves from the onslaught.

No one heard Michael's instruction to keep sight of the child. How could they? The screams and screeches from the hordes of fallens surrounding them along with the clash and clamor of swords and armor made hearing anything completely impossible.

So they all did what they were created to do. They let their full instincts take over. And they made war. Raining down massive casualties. Annihilating thousands of fallens in mere seconds. But it wasn't enough. They just kept coming. And they all had lost sight of the child.

Except one.

CHAPTER 120

Only for a Moment

"Hi," the boy said softly.

"Hello," Mary responded as she rested, holding her baby close.

"Get on your knees," the demon whispered in his spirit.

The boy obeyed.

"Now ask to hold the child," the demon instructed.

Before the boy could speak again, his father spoke, "Son, don't get too close now."

"Do you know this boy?" Joseph asked the shepherd warily.

"He's my son. He's fourteen years old," the shepherd replied.

"May I hold the baby?" the boy asked without making eye contact.

"No," both the boy's father and Joseph replied in unison.

There was a long pause. And then Mary asked, "Why do you want to hold him, young man?"

"Tell her the Creator sent you here to worship," the demon instructed.

"The Creator sent me here tonight. To worship," the boy replied, still without eye contact.

"Well, you can worship right here with us," the boy's father responded without hesitation.

Joseph took a step forward between Mary and the young boy kneeling before them. Something didn't feel right.

Mary leaned forward, touched Joseph's waist as if to calm him, and reached for the boy's chin. As she did, she turned his face toward hers to look into his eyes. As she did, she felt sympathy for the boy.

"I only want to hold him for a moment," the boy said, looking into Mary's eyes.

Mary smiled. To her, the boy seemed innocent, lost. Not unlike she had felt since the moment the angel had descended to give her the life-changing news. She couldn't help but feel sorry for him. With her precious baby in her arms, she began to lean forward, beginning to extend her arms toward the boy, when something in his eyes changed. It was subtle, but she detected it right away.

He became distant. Vacant. As if he were gone.

Because he was.

CHAPTER 121

Javva Intervenes

Javva was watching the whole thing. The chaos of the battle raging all around him and of those in the cattle pen was deafening. He could hardly hear himself think.

But that was the thing. He didn't have to think. Nothing mattered anymore. All that mattered to him in this moment was doing something that would somehow make up for the mistake he had made so long ago. Something to right the wrong of the decision he had made to join the rebellion. The decision that had ruined his existence by banishing him from the presence of the Creator and sinking him deeper and deeper into his own sin.

He didn't want to hate anymore. He didn't want to lie anymore. He didn't want to seethe with anger anymore. He just wanted it all to end.

In that moment, as he saw the boy reaching for the baby, he noticed something he hadn't before. Fallens. Clinging to the boy. Wrapped around his head, neck, and torso. Tormenting him.

But why? And what brought them here? Javva knew nothing of the circumstances unfolding around him.

He was a banished fallen. He was nobody. A complete failure. But the star had called him here. And so he followed.

And now the most epic war of demons and angels raged all around him, with the likes of Lucifer and Michael in battle.

Over what? A baby? All these thoughts passed through his wretched mind when in an instant and with all the strength he could muster from his broken body, he screamed, "Demons!"

CHAPTER 122

Michael Makes His Move

Michael heard it first. At least he thought he did. He didn't recognize the voice, but he recognized from where it was coming. The voice had come from within the cattle pen. He was sure of it.

So in that moment, he made his decision. A decision that was not without risk. He would have to leave Lucifer, turning him loose to wreak havoc.

But what else could he do? He had to move. Fallens were in the presence of the chosen one. They had breached their perimeter. The Creator's plan at risk. And so he moved.

With the speed and force of an archangel.

CHAPTER 123

Annihilation

The flash of the archangel's sword was the last thing to pass through his mind. Forever. He had finally reached the annihilation for which he had always longed. In the moment Michael's sword swept across his neck, severing his head from his body, Javva had found peace.

A kind of peace only a fallen angel would know. Not the kind of peace that brought joy or contentment or satisfaction. But a kind of peace that gave closure. Closure to a rebellious decision that separated him from the Creator's love and damned him to an eternal separation.

And with his final act, he hoped, at least in a small way, he was able to right a wrong. He hoped as his spirit embraced the void of annihilation that he, in some way, had once again pleased the Creator with his final act.

He had given his life in a final act of defiance. Defiance to Lucifer. Defiance to Rusalmeh. Defiance to the lies he believed, the pride he amplified, the hatred he embraced.

Javva was gone. His existence forever dissipated into the void.

And he could not have been happier.

CHAPTER 124

Michael Wins

Just as swiftly as Michael dispatched of Javva, he dispatched of the two fallens who had possessed the boy.

Just like Javva, they never saw it coming. They were too preoccupied possessing the boy and executing their plan.

Which made Michael's job that much easier. With his massive sword and expert precision, Michael severed the head of one of the demons whose head was completely exposed as he whispered into the boy's ear. The other one was able to recoil in fear, only long enough to see Michael's massive sword impale him completely.

The boy was now free. And not a moment too soon. His now-deceased demons had possessed him to lunge for the chosen one at the same moment Michael arrived. The sudden movement of the boy toward Mary and the baby and his subsequent collapse, having been freed from his demonic possessors, made for a chaotic scene in the earthly realm.

Joseph responded as any protective husband and father would, jumping in the gap between the boy and Mary and his newborn son. The shepherds all rose in unison to their feet, startled by what had just transpired.

Had any of them been able to glimpse at the war that was raging all around them in the spirit realm, they likely would have been fully overcome with fear.

For them, the moment of worship was over.

The boy's father grabbed him, apologized profusely, and proceeded to give his now-thoroughly confused teenage son a tongue-lashing as he and the rest of the shepherds retreated back to their fields.

The night sky grew quiet. All was calm. All was bright.

CHAPTER 125

The End

With his plan now collapsed in a matter of seconds, Lucifer accepted his defeat that night. He said nothing. He just vanished into the night.

He had lost the battle, but he learned something too. The Creator's plan for redemption was officially underway, and that clarity gave Lucifer a framework. A structure from which he could build his next rebellion.

As disappointed as he was, he didn't dwell on it. He knew his plan to destroy the chosen one that night was a long shot. Thanks to the useless, feckless Rusalmeh, he was one step behind the entire way. He knew there was no way he could outsmart Michael, or any other warrior angel for that matter, being a step behind.

But now he was ready. He had years, in fact. Years before the chosen one would have full command of the universe. Lucifer would be ready. He could still thwart the Creator's plans.

As soon as Michael intervened, he calmly commanded the team to retake their positions.

The warrior angels closed ranks around the cattle pen, ready to repel any follow-on attacks, knowing there would be none. They knew Lucifer's deception was all he had, and once that had deflated, there was nothing left.

Sam had recovered and was no worse for wear. Although his team surely would never let it go.

As the night wore on, the picture of Mary's warrior angels, the chosen one's warrior angels, including Michael the Archangel, was something special to behold.

The spirt world in the earthly realm was officially on notice. There were eight of the fiercest, most devastatingly deadly warrior angels the Creator had ever created in one place at one time. Something big had just happened. Bigger than anything that had ever happened since the dawn of time.

And the world would never be the same.

CHAPTER 126

Home Again

"Would you do it again?" Gabriel asked to no one in particular.

They were back. Basking in the warm glow of love and infinite energy generated by the Creator's presence. Gabriel had called them together to debrief the mission and collect any meaningful intelligence they had gathered. They had been at it now for a long time, and Gabriel could sense their fatigue and restlessness.

Sam answered first, "Indeed. Whatever the Creator needs, I gladly support."

"Really?" Isabella asked.

"You disagree?" Sebastian asked, taking Gabriel's lead.

"I'm not sure," Isabella replied after a long moment. "It was just so long without being able to fight."

"You made up for it on the last night," Petros chimed in. The first time he had spoken in a while.

"Well, someone had to do it since Sam decided to check out for a bit," Isabella joked. Never missing a chance to take a shot at her old friend.

"I deserve that. Can't believe I missed the entire final sequence," Sam said, still bemused over the fact he wasn't available when his team needed him most.

"Every good team needs a decoy," Sebastian chimed in with a smile.

It was unusual for Sebastian to make a joke, especially at a teammate's expense, which made the shot he took at Sam even sweeter for the team.

Including Sam. He had to smile. And laugh. They all did. The laughter of angels.

As the team continued to share their experiences together in that moment, they all instinctively knew they would never be the same. The epic mission the Creator had destined them to fulfill from before time began had been a great success.

They were infinitely better warriors for having completed it. They learned to live for and lean on one another. The mistakes they made were covered by one another. They grew to love Mary with a love they never thought possible. They didn't remember when it happened, but at one point, it stopped being a mission and became an act of love and devotion for a human being they each never thought possible. The mission became more than a mission. The mission had become their destiny. And although they had been separated from the love of the Creator longer than they ever had before, they would do it again. They loved one another, and they loved Mary.

And they helped shape the arc of human history like no other group of warrior angels had before or since. And for that, they would be eternally thankful. The Creator chose them. Each of them. For a mission that would, in time, change the human realm and bring light into the darkness.

And they would never be the same.

ABOUT THE AUTHOR

Paul R. Hevesy is a believer, husband, father, executive coach, speaker and author. He has many accomplishments in a corporate career spanning more than twenty years. But those accomplishments pale in comparison to the sense of pride and fulfillment he enjoys building a life with his wife, Cady, and their four amazing kids in Indiana, USA.

Paul never thought he would write a fiction book. But when three people in his life encouraged him to write a book all within thirty days of one another, he decided this story that God had given him years before needed to be told. A sinner saved by God's grace, Paul hopes for his readers to know the love of God through the story of His redemption.

CPSIA information can be obtained
at www.ICGtesting.com
Printed in the USA
BVHW041431300822
645482BV00001B/1

9 781685 176884